Sacco and Vanzetti
Must Die!

Sacco and Vanzetti

Must Die!

Mark Binelli

DALKEY ARCHIVE PRESS
NORMAL · LONDON

FOR MY PARENTS

Excerpts from *The Letters of Sacco and Vanzetti* by Marion D. Frankfurter and Gardner Jackson, copyright © 1928, renewed copyright © 1955 by The Viking Press, Inc. Used by permission of Viking Penguin, a division of Penguin Group (USA) Inc.

Images on pages 53, 246, and 282 appear courtesy of Photofest, Inc.

First edition, 2006

Library of Congress Cataloging-in-Publication Data available.
ISBN: 1-56478-445-2

Partially funded by grants from the Lannan Foundation and
the Illinois Arts Council, a state agency.

Dalkey Archive Press is a nonprofit organization whose mission is
to promote international cultural understanding and provide a forum
for dialogue for the literary arts.

www.dalkeyarchive.com

Printed on permanent/durable acid-free paper, bound in the United States of America,
and distributed throughout North America and Europe.

CONTENTS

Biographical Notes   5

PART ONE

PART TWO

PART THREE

"There's no story in it. Just a couple of wops in a jam."
—reporter covering the Sacco and Vanzetti trial

"The urge to destroy is also a creative urge."
—Mikhail Bakunin

"So after while I fall sleep, enddid I do not know how long I been
sleep when I was up again with a terrible dream . . . terrible I said yes,
but beauty at same time, and here way it is . . ."
—Nicola Sacco, letter to Mrs. Cerise Jack, March 15, 1924

They emigrated from Italy the same year (1908), both eventually settling in Massachusetts.

A third accomplice, according to witnesses, hiding behind a pile of bricks.

Part of a wave of Southern and Eastern European immigration (1890-1915), and then eventually to Massachusetts—the cradle of the New World! Vanzetti at one point actually living in Plymouth, where he worked at a cordage factory, loading up rope-making machines with enormous bales of hemp. He and Sacco met much later.

The trial stretched over seven years, becoming one of the most notorious of the day, the flimsiness of the prosecution's evidence and a clear judicial bias seen as expressions of anti-immigrant and anti-radical hysteria. (President McKinley , only two decades earlier, having fallen foul of an anarchist's revolver.)

Nicola Sacco (b. April 22, 1891) was the third of seventeen children. He grew up in Torremaggiore, a coastal town in Puglia, in the south of Italy, where he worked on his father's vineyard.

Seven shots. Three PM. (Broad daylight!) Two dead, and just under $16,000 in payroll stolen. The money was never recovered. Two weeks later, Sacco and Vanzetti were picked up while riding a street-car in Bridgewater, Massachusetts. The arresting officer described the pair as "suspicious characters."

Rope-making machines?

Bartolomeo Vanzetti (b. June 11, 1888) held his mother in his arms while she succumbed to cancer, his father unable to bring himself to enter the sick room. This was in the hilly Piedmont region in the north of Italy, in a town called Villafalletto. The main crop of the region was hay. After his mother's death, Vanzetti wandered the woods bordering the nearby Maira River and contemplated suicide. He departed for America two days before his twentieth birthday.

Sacco's nickname for his wife: Rosina. They met at a benefit dance for a paralyzed accordion player.

Their execution (by electrocution, Vanzetti a few minutes after Sacco) took place shortly after midnight on August 23, 1927, all appeals having been exhausted—Sacco and Vanzetti, at this point, having long been embraced as heroes of the left. Over one hundred poems were written about the case in the days just prior and post execution. Often, the poets made note of the time of their poems' composition (e.g., "execution day," "midnight," "after midnight").

Vanzetti: a lifelong bachelor.

Sacco "had a trade," as they say. (Said?) A cobbler, more specifically a shoe edger, which—shoes!—this biographical sketch is covered with their muddy prints, Sacco and Vanzetti's alleged crime being the robbery and murder of a paymaster (Frederick Parmenter) and guard (Alessandro Beradelli) at a South Braintree, Massachusetts, *shoe factory*, and then later the written prison confession (ignored by the court, adding to the view, held by many sympathizers, of the trial as a corrupt and inherently prejudicial) of Celestino F. Medeiros ("I hear by confess to being in the South Braintree shoe company crime and Sacco and Vanzetti was not in said crime"), who, before being picked up for the murder of a bank cashier, had been a member in good standing of the notorious Morelli Gang of Providence, Rhode Island, a gang notorious for *stealing shoes* from freight cars. Also, one witness (a newsboy hiding behind a telegraph pole) testified that he could tell the fleeing gunman was a foreigner by the way he ran.

Vanzetti went from job to job. At the time of his arrest, he was working as an eel monger. He also dug ditches, washed dishes, sold ice cream, poured molten metal in a foundry, installed telephones, broke rocks in a stone quarry, cut wood, sold fruit, worked in a brick factory, gardened, sold candy, and hauled rocks at a reservoir. The historian Paul Avrich describes him as "one of the numerous itinerants of the period . . . who would not or could not adhere to the discipline of the new industrial order."

They were arrested while picking up a friend's car from the garage, police later alleging said car was to be used to dispose of "radical literature"— an anarchist euphemism for explosives. (Though often portrayed as holy innocents caught up in events beyond their control, Sacco and Vanzetti were, in fact, members of an Italian anarchist group devoted to the violent overthrow of all government.)

A brick factory?

They met much later, in 1917, when, on the United States' entry into the war, a group of the anarchist Luigi Galleani's followers fled to Mexico to avoid the draft, and also to await the wave of revolutionary activity that would, inevitably, sweep across Europe from Russia.

The Bridgewater chief of police was not able to question one of the suspects personally because he was rehearsing for a play. The name of the play is not known, though a popular nineteenth-century farce still performed during this period was titled *Too Much Johnson*.

Vanzetti occasionally used the pen name "Il Picconiere" when writing for *Cronaca Sovversiva*, Galleani's Italian-language anarchist newspaper. The pen name roughly translates as "the Pick-Axe Man."

La salute è in voi!, Galleani's forty-six-page bomb manual—translation: *Health is in you!*—sold for twenty-five cents. It was advertised as "an indispensable pamphlet for all comrades who love self-instruction."

The theory being that an accomplice had—to quote Bridgewater police chief Stewart—"skipped with the swag."

Italians planted bombs in churches, at police stations, on Wall Street. A former publisher of *Cronaca Sovversiva* set off a massive explosion outside the home of U.S. attorney general A. Mitchell Palmer, blowing himself to pieces in the process. The Galleanists also made assassination attempts (most involving mail bombs) upon dozens of "enemies of the movement," including John D. Rockefeller, J.P. Morgan, Oliver Wendell Holmes and the Archbishop of Chicago.

Vanzetti never married, or even dated—Avrich quoting him as having no interest in "Epicurean joys"—but he loved to read: Zola, Darwin, Malatesta, Dante, Hugo, Marx, Tolstoy, Carducci. His two favorite books were *The Divine Comedy* (much of which he'd memorized) and Ernest Renan's *The Life of Jesus*.

Again, Avrich: "Like many Italian immigrants of the day, they came as single young men, looking for adventure."

The following is not their story.

Part
One

Chapter One:
Sacco and Vanzetti
Dessert the Cause

A classic comedy team makes its motion-picture debut—cutlery, magic, panoramic painting, and a narrow escape—Hylo Pierce on the role of women in the comedy film—the stars discuss their physiques

After the Pie Fight

(a scene from the 1923 picture Sacco and Vanzetti
Dessert the Cause*)*

So, two guys. One is fat, the other skinny. And then an alley, well-strewn; a series of windows (begrimed); one, finally, popped, shimmied.

So Fatty peers into and then grabs a cardboard box, which is ostensibly in his way, the alley also containing busted pallets, rusting mattress frames, *"Colored Bill" McGreevy, the Trolley Stand Molester, Still at La*— and other crumpled three-day-old headlines, your expected alleyway detritus. Going for a heft, Fatty grunts, releases, tries again, this time succeeding, and then, without the least hint, hurls the box back at Skinny, who instinctively ducks, cowers, and looses a girlish yelp. That would be a yelp of the no-recovery variety—the sound of having just been relieved of one's favorite dolly and/or muff—the box, empty, bouncing off Skinny's forehead and falling to the ground. *Whyyousonofapr* . . . So forth, through gritted teeth. Grappling ensues. Skinny, at one point, attempts to stuff Fatty into the empty box, which is approximately the size of a retirement cake. They stop as soon as the sirens start.

Quickly then: the windows. One, finally: popped, shimmied. You would think Fatty (Nic Sacco) gives Skinny (Bart Vanzetti) a boost, but no. They use an upturned garbage can, Bart holding it steady by the handles, as if something feral wants out very badly.

Inside, the place turned out to be the grinder's.

"Oooga. Man. Well, that's funny, right? At least."

They seemed to be in the back room of a storefront. It was snug and low-ceilinged, with a table running along one of the walls,

13

its width severely reducing the already narrow room's standable floorspace, its length calling to mind a bar in need of tending. An enormous sharpening wheel stood in one corner, a deep sink in the opposite. And stacked upon every available surface, wooden boxes of knives—boxes or else loose, the boxes rising nearly to the ceiling—not just kitchen knives but also saw blades, cleavers, razors, daggers, a sickle, what looked like a pile of fan blades, scalpels, shears. The proverbial works. There was space enough in the room for two, though a mock-swordfight would be ill-advised, and square dancing out of the question. At this point, Bart and Nic had been still long enough to allow for an appreciation of the level of soiled they'd pulled off. Even only half-illuminated by the dim moonlight, the sheer scope of visible blemishment on their ill-fitting tuxedos and exposed skin was truly impressive. Their combined surface areas resembled exotic maps, with unfamiliar shapes and colors stretched across every known territory.

The stain breakdown: 67% beverage and/or liquefied foodstuff (red wine, fruit compost, melted chocolate, fish sauce, punch), 11% solid, tenaciously sticky foodstuff (flecks of pudding and meringue, crème toppings, crushed berry, dangling pie crust, undercooked bacon), 8% soot-ash-gunpowder, 4% raw sewage, 3% motor oil, 3% blue paint, 3% tar-feathering, 1% lipstick (Nic only).

Nic snatched a rag from a shelf, took a sniff and dabbed his face. It didn't help much. Outside, the sirens continued, closer.

"By funny," he continued, "I mean, all the places we might've chosen for hide-outs? And we draw the roomful of knives."

He spotted the sickle, picked it up and gave it an experimental lean, as if testing a new cane.

"This ain't morbid to you, is it? Auspicing bad times? An unwelcome allegorical gift of the creeps? Because I'll stop. I know you're not a superstitious man. But say the word. I will stop."

Bart made no reply.

"I meant funny in the how-time-slips-away sense. Closer to more like tragic. But us having reached that stage in our lives where we can be mature enough to find the humor there as well."

Bart made no reply.

"No? I mean, hey, granted, if that, say, precariously stacked crate of lox knives were to topple onto your head, that'd move us from humor to straight-up tragedy. That would cross a line, for me. But at the moment? The presence of danger, as yet unsheathed? . . . No?

"Okay . . . Okay . . .

"So, I want to preface our argument by saying, that whole scene?

"That whole scene? Come on. Oh. I suppose, now, retroactively, you were into it? Soaking up the culture? Well, then, hey. *Mea culpa* for sandbagging your invasion. Giving succor to your opposition. Puncturing your thermos. Interrupting your deep conversation. What were you guys talking about, anyway?

"I digress. Please except my humblest apologies.

"Most humble.

"You know the presence of a dessert buffet mandates my working it into a mayhem ensues.

"You know flight from angry mob by way of drainage tunnel is the only way to exit a cultural event.

"You know you love me.

"It.

"This.

"The life.

"Shit. Whatever, brother. Harmony's for squares. I thought the idea behind crashing a party was emphasis on the *crash*. But, apparently.

"You's cross as two sticks today, Mistah Barto.

"I could go on."

"Please," Bart said. "Don't."

"What the hell are you doing, anyway?"

15

Bart didn't answer. Though what he was doing was perfectly obvious. While Nic spoke, Bart had stripped off his shirt, tie, and tuxedo jacket. He had hung the jacket neatly from a steak knife handle that protruded from a cubbyhole of knives, leaving his suspenders to dangle at his sides in an especially flaccid manner. He had opened the sink's tap and lathered his face with a bar of gray hand soap. And then he had begun shaving, slowly and methodically, using a thin-bladed, six-inch beef-deboner, selected from the box closest to the sink. The scraping of the day-old stubble from his cheeks, which had been displaying a propensity to jowl since his eighteenth birthday, sounded like old paper burning. A burnt smell also lingered, the odor of the thousands of hours of grinding the room contained, atomized particles of heated steel and moist stone weighing—*misting*, practically—the air. He held a meat cleaver in his other hand, as a mirror.

"That sting at all? It looks painful, I gotta say. Specifically, them like rivulets of blood. Maybe you should let me—? No. Okay. Rather cut your own throat. I understand, completely."

"I need to be clean. This beard has been bothering me all day."

"Right. Clean. You realize, beyond the beard, you're covered in seven types of pie? Just saying."

Nic brushed off his jacket, then wandered over to the wheel and, absently, attempted a spin. It didn't budge. He glanced back and watched Bart shave, noting, in particular, his partner's dimples, which, at the moment, had flared. They always tended to flare in conjunction with Bart pursing his lips in what appeared to be tight displeasure, as if he were using his mouth to pinch off a tube delivering oxygen to someone he despised. Were dimples still technically dimples, Nic wondered, when they were associated not with mirth but spite?

"Heavy mother. You ever grind? I did, let's see now, summer I turned fifteen? Maybe sixteen. Back of a truck operation. We'd drive around from dawn till dusk. Restaurants, fishmongers, butcher shops. We had three guys: the driver, the sharpener and yours truly. I honed." Nic picked up a curved steak knife and demonstrated his honing technique on a rectangular whetstone at the far end of the table. "See, it's all in the wrist. You kind of arc it, down and out. Gotta be careful not to stab yourself in the lower stomach or groin. You're not looking. That's okay. So speaking of stabbing, one afternoon this broad walks by, swell, I do not deny, but the fellow at the big wheel, I can't even remember his name, but this off-the-boat Luigi motherfucker, as he's eyeballing this dame, slides a butcher's knife he's grinding right off the wheel and gouges me in the leg. Right here." The expected pants-dropping occurs, revealing a white, wobbly grimace of a scar, almost two inches across. "You believe that? It's like having a tattoo of somebody *else's* girlfriend's name. You know what I'm saying?"

When Bart failed to respond, Nic buckled his pants, cleared a space on the table and boosted himself up, listening for a moment at the window. Then he plucked a hair from his head and, squinting with one eye, attempted to split it with the steak knife.

"See, my thing with the cleanliness is, I got no problem with clean, but once I'm dirty, I figure why not just settle in, you know? I forgot about your proclivity for dandyism. So, going back to the party, I'm sorry if I interrupted your deep conversation. You two discussing that painting?"

Bart had finished shaving and begun drying his face. "It *was* an unveiling," he said. "The fellow brought up Turner." Nic stared blankly. "English landscape painter," Bart continued. "Which in turn made me think of one of his famous works. *Regulus*. I don't know if you're familiar—"

"Hey, no, but are you familiar with my production of *Too Much Johnson*?" Nic asked, grabbing his crotch.

Bart coughed. "One of our countrymen. Regulus. A Roman general. He spent his career defending Sicily from the Carthaginians. He was eventually defeated and taken prisoner, and the Carthaginians sent him back to Rome to negotiate a peace settlement. He was released on parole, an honor-system parole in which he agreed to return after the negotiations. When Regulus reached Rome, he advised the Senate to reject the Carthaginian offering and then, in spite of the protests of his wife, children and fellow Romans, stayed true to his word and returned to the enemy camp, where he was promptly tortured to death. Some accounts depict him as having been placed in a barrel, with spikes being driven into the barrel and the barrel being rolled down a hill. Another account involves death via sleep-deprivation. In the third, most violent version, his eyelids are sliced off and he is forced to stare at the sun until he goes blind."

To illustrate this final torture, Bart pulled down one of his own eyelids and traced the air surrounding the upper ridge with the point of his shaving knife.

"Ouch. Would that kill you, though? Option number three? I guess they probably let him wander around blind for a while and then maybe some drawing, a little quartering, huh? Something along those lines. So, barrel of spikes or eyelid removal? I think I'd almost go with the eyelids. I'd have to see the spikes first before I could make an informed decision, but yeah. I'll take eyelids."

"Turner's painting is from Regulus' point of view, at the moment he has been pushed outside and begun to be blinded by the sun. He wanted to illustrate the effect staring directly at the sun would have on one's eyes, and he used the Regulus story to that end."

"Okay, so, someone nails your dick to a tree and hands you a knife. Do you cut it off or kill yourself?"

Bart cocked his head and assumed a faraway look. The sirens had stopped.

"So?"

"What's that, now?"

"So's that it? You're not gonna tell me what this spectacular painting looks like?"

"In words? I couldn't begin to do it justice."

"Give it a go, how's about?"

"It's a cityscape."

"I'll need more than that."

"It's a cityscape as painted from the point of view of a man going sunblind."

"Still ain't doing it for me."

Long pause. "You could say light was the dominant tonal theme."

Nic sighed. "That story sucked."

"To create the light-effect, he would smear his paint with chunks of bread."

Nic considered this statement, then shook his head no.

"Not," he said, "enough."

Bart slipped on his tuxedo jacket, smoothing out the lapels, and nodded. "Breakfast, then? I could eat."

TRANSCRIPT

*(from a series of interviews with Nic Sacco and Bart Vanzetti
for* Motion Picture Monthly, *conducted the week of July 14,
1963, at the Beverly Hills Hotel)*

Our first decision, really, was, "Who will be the Fat One?"
　　The key, right there.
　　Because there is always a Fat One.
　　Well, you know. I can think of a couple exceptions.
　　We wanted a Fat One.
　　None of the Marxes was all tha—
　　We wanted a Fat One.
　　Agreed.
　　But yes, if you look back at some of our earliest publicity stills—
　　Those singing-cowboy shorts I did for Wilner, before I met this
guy?
　　You were never exactly svelte.
　　I'm not saying—
　　But we were roughly the same build.
　　We were *young*, is what we was.
　　Pliant. Though you had the more natural propensity . . .
　　Also, better name.
　　For fat.
　　Sacco.
　　Obvious choice.
　　Had the perfect sound, for our purposes.
　　Fat Sacco Shit. That sort of thing.
　　I was thinking mor—
　　It rolls off the tongue. Steaming Sacco Manure.
　　We seem to be getting off-track.
　　Unequivocally Tragic Sacco Drowned Puppies.

We seem to be getting off-track.

In other words, a name too perfect to pass on. It's difficult to explain if you're not in the business. But certain words are simply *funny*, independent of their meaning.

Almost a kind of physical property, we're talking.

Not that we were especially verbal comics.

Sure. Though, I mean, we *did* have that element. Me, moreso. It wasn't like we was a couple of clowns, rehashing old bits from the silents.

I didn't say that.

Any rate. Fatty and Skinny.

A classic comedic scenario.

Could say I'm the manic one.

The verbose one.

Always spouting off.

The team id, if you will. Whereas I'm the sullen, intelligent one. The dour—

I wouldn't say I was necessarily *un*intelligent.

I didn't say that.

Describing yourself as the intelligent one implies—

Not the intended implication. The studio, incidentally, initially pressured us to speak in an ethnic dialect.

Some kind of Chico Marx shit. 'Atsa good, Doc!'

Which, frankly, I found offensive. Still do.

Ditto here. 'Mama mia!'

Not to get overly—This is going to bore you. I was just going to mention that we worked in a classical tradition. The *commedia*. Speed plus incongruity equals funny. It's especially compelling for us, as Italians, because we're working in a tradition that can be traced back to the Ren—

I'm sorry, we're running out of time. One last question: Your favorite type of pie would be . . . ?

(Laughter)

To eat? Cherry. To take in the face, I'd have to go with shaving cream. We tried whipped, but it spoils quick under them lights and can get pretty unpleasant. But cream pies create the most spectacular effect for the viewer. So Jonesy, our prop man, would make up these mixtures of shaving cream, aerating it, somehow. Never understood exactly how he did that.

I hate pie.

(Pierce, Hylo. A Funny Thing Happened on the Way to
Mr. Mayer's Office . . . Revisiting the Golden Age of Film
Comedy. *New York: Little, Brown, 1988.)*

One of the few comedy teams able to make a successful transition
from vaudeville stage to Hollywood screen, Nic Sacco and Bart
Vanzetti have been rediscovered in recent years by a new generation
of film scholars. Certain of these critics have a tendency to group
the work of Sacco and Vanzetti with that of the more asexual film
comics, e.g. the overtly cartoonish Three Stooges, boys in men's
bodies who treat women and marriage as deeply problematic neces-
sities, at best. (For a classic of the genre, see the 1937 Stooges short
The Women Haters.) But if examined more carefully, the Sacco and
Vanzetti films fall in a gray area, closer to Buster Keaton than the
venerable firm of Howard, Howard, and Fine.

In the case of Keaton, fans might recall the fact that nearly all
of his pictures end in marriage. The classic example—and, not
incidentally, a favorite film of Bart Vanzetti's—would be the 1924
feature *Seven Chances*, in which lovelorn lawyer James Shannon
(Keaton), unable to work up the nerve to propose to his longtime
beau (Ruth Dwyer), discovers that he must marry by seven p.m. on
his twenty-seventh birthday or he will forfeit a seven million dollar
inheritance. Naturally, he makes this discovery *on the morning of his
twenty-seventh birthday.* When the beau refuses, Keaton's partner (T.
Roy Barnes) takes out an ad in the paper explaining the plight, and
two-hundred frenzied, would-be brides, sporting various degrees of
wedding attire and resembling a mob of militant suffragettes, arrive
at the church where a lone Keaton has been waiting. A virtuoso chase
sequence—incorporating rockslides, barbed-wire, bee stings, an
angry bull and gratuitous pants-dropping—ensues, before Keaton

and Dwyer, his true love, finally unite in matrimony, thus ensuring his patrimony. This outcome is never in doubt. Yet it remains difficult to forget the image—one worthy of the gloomy Swede Ingmar Bergman—of Keaton sitting alone in a cavernous church, awaiting his fate. The clown is made up like a cadaver, his face, as ever, an inscrutable Noh-mask, void of any human expression. He could be a mourner at his own funeral.

It would be forty years before Keaton would appear in the playwright Samuel Beckett's largely silent *Film*—Beckett biographer Anthony Cronin, on the pair's first meeting: "Every now and then Beckett, almost like someone meeting Samuel Beckett for the first time, would venture a few words, to which Keaton would respond at best in monosyllables"—and yet, as early as *Seven Chances*, Keaton managed to convey, no matter how superficially happy the ending, a sort of existential loneliness that could not be slipped with a pratfall, could not be cured with a poke in the eye or a bop on the noggin, could not, in short, be Seltzered away.

Returning to Sacco and Vanzetti, it's true that women are scant in their earliest shorts. And numerous critics have pointed out the homosexual subtext running throughout their work—most evidently the 1924 short *You're Shvitzing Me*, in which the boys hide out from a gang of bootleggers in a bathhouse on New York's Lower East Side; the following year's *Jacks in the Box*, a truly bizarre short which, aside from a brief set-up and coda, takes place entirely in a wooden crate, in which S&V are trapped for the duration of a five-day sea voyage, along with a book of matches, a flask of rye, a collection of Shakespeare's sonnets, half a salami and an organ-grinder's monkey (wearing a vest, boots and a fez and, unfortunately, trained to steal meat) aptly named Sir Filch-a-lot; and, most explicitly, the never-released "lost" 1943 feature *Take It Like a Man!!*, set on Devil's Island and co-starring a young Bing Crosby, with its infamous laundry-room gang-rape sequence (thwarted only when

Sacco oversuds a load of linens) and der Bingle's talent-show-winning number "Dames (Who Needs 'Em?)" Still, I'm hesitant to read much into these themes, beyond a desire to buck convention and a willingness to go for a broad laugh, considering the rather vigorous and well-documented heterosexuality of Sacco, in particular, who was married four times.

In fact, it is much more interesting to examine the role of women, however peripheral, when they *do* appear as love interests in the S&V filmic oeuvre. Of course, these trysts, as with every other plot convention, are played for laughs, as in the 1943 feature *Caesar! Thou Art Mitey Yet*, in which the boys play managers of a midget-wrestling tag team. In the film's second act, Vanzetti begins romancing Miss Estelle (Gwen Evers), the girlfriend (also a little person) of one of the members of the team, Bug Bernstein (real-life midget wrestler "Half-Pint" Nelson.) This leads to rich comic material, including a romantic rivalry between Nelson and Vanzetti (who is eventually jumped by a gang of masked midget wrestlers in a hilarious gymnasium sequence involving a medicine ball coated with itching powder) and the equally broad courting scenes with Miss Estelle. The most notable of the latter scenes remains, of course, the date at the soda shop: a bumped head while adjusting her stool; several minutes of straw-jockeying over the shared malted; and that immortalized near-kiss, only interrupted by Vanzetti's slow realization that his burger has been spiked with alum. Is there not, despite the shtick, a universal being approached here?

Sensitive Dependence on Initial Conditions

(a scene from the 1923 picture Sacco and Vanzetti Dessert
the Cause*)*

"Mrs. Enid, or, may I? *darling*," Nic began.

This was much earlier, at the unveiling of the painting, Nic, absently, fingering the tablecloth's corniced hem. In hindsight, he could pinpoint the notion's debut with unusual precision, *exactement* to this arrival at the coast of the buffet. A mustachioed pastry chef, his shirt-back Rorschached with sweat, fussed over the desserts. Nic shot him a sympathetic glance, having realized the evening's clear inevitability, though a chefly preoccupation with the proper stacking of Napoleons kept the fellow from returning notice. One of those mustaches that, if detached, could be used to apply varnish. The table went on for miles. Nic closed his eyes, cloth still betwixt fingers, attempting to divine a thread count. "Well over two," he murmured, meaning of course two-hundred, though the entire time savoring, more than the feel of expensive fabric, the yawning, almost electric sensation of power that comes from standing with your back to a party. Was that overwrought? Nic could not help but marvel, though, at how simple taking command of an entire room could be. You only had to reject the general for the hyper-specific. The party's presence, meanwhile, continued to swell behind him, impossible to wholly ignore, but present in a standing-in-the-surf, facing-beach-ward (as opposed to oceanward) sort of way, the chatter having become rhythmic and incidental. The higher the thread count (threads per square inch), the finer the cloth. Though not always. The length of the cotton must also be taken into account. Nic had had too much to drink. Somewhere behind and to the left of him, a small clarinet ensemble played lower-key dance numbers, though none of the partygoers actually danced, milling being the consensus move. Nic's eyes remained closed. The chandelier lighting pulsed mildly on the far side of his lids, the effect being that of faded stars painted on the dome of a planetarium. He tried to inhale all of the smells wafting from the table at once, to reduce himself to a single sense. Ironically, the sliced tongue dominated, along with some woman's exotic perfume, coming from a southwesterly direction. He could pinpoint the exact moment he realized he'd had too much to drink. He'd been enjoying the plenitude of exposed bosom a low-cut, high-society gathering of this sort happily supplies. Then, feeling a sudden panic coming on, he'd been forced to turn away. There had been too many (bosoms), and they all seemed to be quaking with rage, at first he thought, at something he'd done, though he soon decided it was a rage at their own captivity (the bosoms'), which, really, Nic already considered pretty lax by reasonable standards, a bondage approaching out-on-parole. This was not the moment Nic realized he'd had too much to drink. The room seemed designed to maximize the party noise, to essentially combine hundreds of disparate conversations into the sound of a crowd cheering some violent spectacle. Only for each person in the room, basic narcissism combined with the flush of festive occasion to make the surrounding cheer, on a subconscious level, feel personally directed, feel *all for you*. Themes of female dress tending to vary from one social event to the next. This party's theme centered on cleavage. Last party they'd crashed it'd been stoles, most still headed. Adding to the indignity, the little fox-mouths had been fashioned into clasps. True, a practical, even elegant solution to the how-to-clasp-it dilemma. Other hand, a bit unnecessarily gruesome, no? Verging on gloating. Though no tribe lacks costume. He remembered another job, that museum gig with Bart, back in New York. Night watchmen. His favorite room held primitive art from the Pacific Islands. He'd spent hours staring at the full-body basket masks, supposedly invented by a starving orphan child as a means of frightening off adults and stealing their food, now suspended behind glass. The straw torsos had been woven as tight as shirts of mail, with grass skirts hanging beneath and tortured, gape-mouthed helmets offering, like skulls in a still life, drafty glimpses of inner-void. Opposite, a forty-foot bark canoe, merely impressive by day, looked eerily barren, all that remained of some mysterious massacre. The moon shone through the skylight and flickered the display base in such a way as to evoke dark waters that hadn't quite settled, the bodies still sinking into the murk. A row of totems loomed nearby, arranged like teams of acrobats, man-shapes straddling the shoulders of other man-shapes, leering, squatting, thrusting their outsize pricks. Even the ones that didn't have much in the way of length could be used to stopper a wide-mouthed jug. Some of the other guards said that savages always had an enormous penis, that you had to watch out for that. Nic couldn't say, never having had the pleasure. Bart insisted he'd seen plenty, that they were nothing you'd put on a postcard. The moment Nic realized he'd had too much to drink was when he began to imagine the ladies' bosoms as frontally papoosed infants who had somehow managed to flip themselves over to flash their buttocks at him. Nic gave the tablecloth a gentle tug. The crystal tinkled. That being, obviously, the point. The more valuable the object, the more easily it could shatter, exactly the point of sipping from something so easily destroyed, so opposite the utilitarian and vulgar, something that you couldn't drop or bump or jostle but would handle like a pale woman who bruises easily, or certain types of fruit. Those totems, though. You could see how rumors got started. It seemed like a nice tradition to Nic. Leave the men be men. Or, rather, leave the men reduced to symbols of manhood. Why not? The women got these what they called slit-gongs, which, how subtle, right? The slit-gongs were towering hollow statues that actually doubled as musical instruments, with a head on top and then stretching below a huge vertical slit that one rubbed to create a noise. How subtle. They'd worked on a blues. The first line was *Baby won't you rub my slit-gong*. They'd stalled over the second line's end-rhyme . . . *can't be wrong? . . . all night long? . . . my neighbor's pug-dog Wong?* A reductive view, certainly. But wasn't there something nice about knowing exactly what you brought to the table? A precise delineation of duties. A yardstick, so to speak, to measure one's worth, and even if one inevitably fell short at least one would know by how far. No, but really, the party was fine. He couldn't say as to the exact point his mood had shifted from mild amusement with his surroundings to more like a state of nervous agitation, but, at a certain point, shift it had, and unfortunately for those who do not appreciate a good pie fight, this point had dovetailed with his fingering of the tablecloth. Voices occasionally broke through the celebratory din. They said, "Did you try the little chocolates shaped like rare coins? No, you can *eat* them!" And, "The moral power of world public opinion. That's what." Nic, perennially, had trouble stopping himself from pulling the old short-roped-tie gag, the old "Oh, this is *your* wig?!" routine, the arguably funnier, "Oh, this is your *wig*?!" variant, or in-general misbehaving. Is there (Nic often wondered) anything better than tricking someone into repeating a word that, said aloud, quickly, will make them blush? Of course a respectable gentleman did not walk into a party—an art-opening—*an unveiling*—with the objective of setting off a pie fight by intentionally screwing up the old tablecloth trick, intentionally screwing up the old tablecloth trick being one of the oldest means of starting a pie fight, as in a single swoop it not only quite literally sets things in motion but tends to make partygo-ers quite *agitato*. Nic's problem, or gift, depending on your perspec-tive, was his realization that everyone possesses *some* potential for mutiny, however buried. He wanted nothing more than to draw that potential out. So a pie fight could in part be described as a hostile act, true, but it could also be described as an act of love. An out-reach. People almost never responded in the way one hoped. But one must continue to hope. As if on cue, Nic spotted Bart across the room, out on the "deck," talking with a new friend. Eye-contact ensued. Bart appeared annoyed. His eyes were saying, "Don't you fucking dare." Nic smiled. He knew what his friend really wanted, on some root-cellar level of consciousness, perhaps, but still there. Bart having now broken off his conversation and begun storming this way, his eyes saying, "Do not Marrakech me, pallie. You will survive to regret this." Nic pulled a big droopy sad-clown's face, then smiled again and winked. Knowing, deep down, somewhere, that his friend understood.

"Mrs. Enid, or, may I? *darling*," Nic said loudly, turning to the matron standing directly behind him. "I hear you're a great lover of art, and wine, and song, all good stuff, yes yes yes. But, right now? How about a little magic?"

The tablecloth trick, as generally practiced, works on the basis of Newton's First Law (inertia, velocity, torsion, bodies at rest will remain, etc.), the "trick" being speed and steadiness. It is especially key to yank the cloth parallel to the table, not at an incline. The classic pie fight, on the other hand, could be considered an application of chaos theory, which was discovered by a meteorologist, Edward Lorenz, in the early 1960s. Lorenz was using a computer program to study weather patterns when he discovered the prime concept of chaos theory, which he called "sensitive dependence on initial conditions," and which is more popularly understood as "the butterfly effect," i.e., the causation of a tidal wave in Indonesia by a butterfly flapping its wings in Houston.

There is also a painting of Turner actually painting *Regulus*, called *Turner on Vanishing Day*. (Turner having sold his first painting by the age of thirteen, exhibited in the window of his father's London barbershop. He loved to paint Venice, sunrises, the sea, the sky, "the dramatic possibility of natural phenomena." Rainbows.) Every year, the Royal Academy set aside three or four so-called "Vanishing Days" for artists to retouch their submitted works. Turner famously submitted relatively monochromatic paintings, after which, on Vanishing Day, he would splash on his notoriously vivid colors, to dramatic—some said melodramatic—effect. (Storms. Shipwrecks.) The painter John Constable said of Turner's work on Vanishing Day, "He has been here and fired a gun."

The Dramatic Possibility of Natural Phenomena
(a scene from the 1923 picture Sacco and Vanzetti Dessert
the Cause*)*

Ten minutes earlier, Bart had leaned against the room's starboard
rail, gazing out at the squall as it crept past in the near distance.
With his head thrust out far enough towards the canvas, he could
hear the *clikclikclik* of the waves as they spooled out of sight. It all
struck him as lifelike—the strained faces of the sailors aboard the
passing vessel as they muscled various ropes and winches into or
out of place, struggling for balance on the rain-slicked deck; the
men overboard, swimming for the splintered planks that bobbed in
perpetuity, offering a distinctly spiny salvation; and everything else
arcing in every possible direction, the fish and the waves and the
foam and the sail. An outstretched hand.

Unfortunately, the hand reminded Bart of the evening's likely inevitability (a pie fight), and he became sullen. Well: *more* sullen. It's
not like, minus inevitable pie fight, he'd be back inside, in the thick
of things, mingling with the dates and their gentlemen. Strangers
tended to offer depressingly predictable posits regarding his willful
apartness, and the psychopathological origins thereof. He'd been
pegged as self-loathing, misanthropic, aloof, shy to the point of
catatonia, a dullard, or just plain dull. More likely a combination,
though Bart, whenever he bothered with a self-exam, rare enough,
merely felt vacant. Scooped out with a pronged spoon. The vital
parts, at any rate. He couldn't tell you why. His powers of self-
exam were limited, an impotence that could be chalked up to either
grace—a divine gift of sweet ignorance—or disuse.

Bart stared down the creeping seascape and considered how the
difference between the hand of a drowning sailor and the hand of

a pie-tossing *galasaboteur* was merely one of degrees, *literal* degrees. (Of the wrist, the pie-tosser's tending to closer to a right angle, post-launch.) He wondered at what to read into this fact, its possible symbolic resonance. Pie fight as desperate wave to passing ships? Drowning as hostile, nihilistic act? Still, there was no denying: he'd been involved in far too many pie fights. He could show you scars. Well. Tell you stories. You think it's all flaky butter crusts. You think the snooty *maitre d'* with the double chin always ends up encased with the stickiest custard. Not true, both counts. Not that Bart would allow himself to be caricatured as some prudish anti-pie-fight reactionary. Hadn't he, after all, coined the phrase *coup d'eclair*, which Nic had proceeded to run into the ground? And he'd always found something oddly relaxing about a roomwide loss of control, about reducing your body of choices to a mere two, in the case of a pie fight those being the go-with-the-pie-fight option or the hide-under-a-wine-cart option. Which, the latter, incidentally? Never works.

And yet one can also not deny the part of the equation known as diminishing returns, wherein the tenth direct-hit (on the president of local railroad monopoly; the bejeweled sulfur-mine heiress; the cuckolded butcher-shop owner, still in his stained butcher's smock) produces far less *frisson* than the first. Unless you are Nic Sacco, whose eyes, the moment they emerged from the "lower decks," alit upon the long, lavish dessert table, laid out ballroom-center. Bart caught the observation and immediately started in with a plea for restraint. But Nic was already off, a half-hearted "Come again, Jackson?" tossed over his shoulder like keys to a valet. Bart knew, then, at least an *attempted* pie fight would be coming. They'd been coupled for that long, enough to smooth out the variables of any given situation, to make for decent odds. Bart had, in fact, taken to thinking of their partnership as The Act, and furthermore taken to thinking of the centerpiece of The Act as The Two-Sided Coin

Trick, in which he was the head and Nic— Well. Sometimes the most obvious joke also happens to be the most appropriate. Though, really, to be fair, Nic was closer to guts than rear. The trick of The Two-Sided Coin Trick being, however you flipped it, you wound up with both sides. Get it? It took some puzzling. Nic: *Like one of them Buddhist riddles.*

At any rate: that's how Bart found himself on the deck, alone, admiring the painting up close. A panorama. It'd been ages since he— Well, since anybody. Years back, the form had more or less died, the domed, once-grand exhibition halls converted into skating rinks, circuses, riding schools, the audience for three-hundred-sixty-degree photo-realist landscape painting having all but evaporated in the face of the motion picture. In Europe, during the panorama's reign, the driving principle of the form had been less aesthetic than escapist, transportive, i.e., Why travel to Algiers, which, after all, does involve travel, along with multiple varieties of unfamiliar (food, beds, bodily odors), when one could take an identical view of the Casbah in downtown London? Verisimilitude being the key. Bart remembered, on a boyhood trip to a panorama in Rome, the terror-wonder sensation, clutching his mother's hand as they made their way past the ticket booth, down the dim and narrow hallway, up the creaking stairwell and finally emerging onto the circular observation deck—crafted to look like a mountaintop *rifugio*—emerging to find themselves surrounded by a rotunda-spanning painting, wall to wall and floor to ceiling. Its title was *The Montgolfiers*, the canvas (its top edge concealed by an umbrella-like canopy, its bottom by *faux* bushes, rocks and other three-dimensional props) depicting a skyful of hot-air balloons, in a race. There were dozens, all around them, with an Alpine scene in the background, and swooping hawks, and crowds of women far below waving white kerchiefs, and a cloud shaped like a cheetah, looking ready to pounce, and one of the pilots, his scarves billowing back like a pair of stripped wings, tilting up his oversize goggles ever so slightly as he calmly examined the guttering flame that kept him aloft. That was about all Bart had time to digest before his mother began to complain of vertigo and they'd stumbled back down the steps, emerging from this bubble of another world into the crowded, cobbled square, suddenly once again blinking in the true sunlight and trying to remember to dodge puddles and horse droppings. (Though, as recompense for the aborted entry, he did receive a sweet ice of his choice from a visored, purring street vendor who called him *dottore*.)

Bart saw no other panoramas until he emigrated to America. By this time, the panorama as art form had already taken its rapid turn towards extinction. And Americans, in any event, made far different demands on their transportive entertainments. When it came to the panorama, what they demanded was velocity and square footage. And so the observation decks of the American panoramas simulated steamboats (this was in Chicago), or trains (Detroit), with the paintings now miles long (or so shilled the banners out front) and attached to twin spools, the depicted scenes of the past (*Life Along the Mississippi*, say, or *A Journey Westward*) actually *scrolling past*, if not quite as fluid as life itself then at least proceeding in that general direction.

This particular panorama was the most lavish Bart had ever seen. The building was designed to replicate a luxury trans-Atlantic steamer. One entered through lower-level cabins and emerged into a grand ballroom, with windows on two sides and doors leading out to the deck, which was where the painting flowed—a different painting running along either length of the room, was the novelty here. The sheer excessiveness felt, somehow, appropriate, as the panorama, at this late date, was, for Bart and everyone else at this grand unveiling, an exercise in nostalgia, akin to riding a horse and buggy through a park—not a last gasp, but the gasp that followed, as performed by a ventriloquist, something to spook the crowd as the coffin was

36

lowered into the ground. Still, being on the deck reminded Bart of his voyage to America, on a similar vessel, in oft-stormy weather, and he found something both soothing and ironic about the dual nostalgia. He'd sailed third-class, and so never experienced anything this grand, though nightly, he would steal out to the deck, his insomnia always raging. Now, gazing out at a near-identical scene—the boats having all passed, by this point—he felt comforted by its evident falsehood.

The party din grew louder, then muted again, as, somewhere behind him, the door to the ballroom momentarily opened.

A stranger had wandered onto the deck. Though he could have chosen any spot along the rail, he planted himself directly beside Bart, their shoulders nearly brushing. He wore a short beard, trimmed in so fastidious a manner it seemed to suggest any number of character traits—the ability to draw a straight line without the aid of a ruler occurred to Bart right off—and colored, by nature, a blazing red.

"You know," the stranger began, "they originally considered spraying the deck with water and flickering the lights, but then they worried it might drive too many people indoors."

He paused and gave the air a vigorous sniff, as if to salt his constitution with a lungful of sea breeze. His voice matched his demeanor, flat and unaffected.

"I'm here with a friend," he continued. "Colleague. But he's inside, working young Miss Dureen. Have you had the pleasure? She's no great shakes. She's barely average shakes, to be frank. Talk about picking off the wounded gazelle at the rear of the pack. That's his move, though. And yours would be? Contemplating nature, obv—"

"Are you," Bart said.

The stranger held up a finger and assumed a stern look, as if searching out something in the distance that had promised, and failed, to appear. Then, abruptly, he leaned over the rail and began to retch. Bart looked away, though not before glimpsing the man's contorted visage, his eyes squeezed tight in the manner of a mentalist attempting to move an object with his mind. Eventually, his spasms subsided. After hanging limply for a moment, he wiped his mouth with his sleeve and straightened himself, nodding.

"They have water inside," Bart said.

Waving his hand no, the stranger loosed a mild, odoriferous belch. "Glad we're not courting," he muttered, then barked out a short, high-pitched laugh. His face, despite the beard, became extremely boyish, though the look disappeared as soon as the laughter stopped, and he immediately reverted back to a cold, blank glare.

"My wife left me," he continued. "That's the other big news. There is nobody else. We did not bicker. I earn a living. There was no compelling reason for her departure. She simply couldn't stand my presence any longer."

He remained silent for so long that Bart felt obligated to respond in some manner. "Well," he finally said. "That's incredible. You're quite a catch." He thought for a moment, then added, "There probably *is* another man, though, if that's any consolation."

The stranger smashed his fist on the railing, then caught himself and released another of his unsettling giggles. "No, you see, I've been following her. Actually, this is an amusing story. I'd been convinced she'd been having an affair with her ballet instructor. Are you familiar with the Russian position? I don't care to describe it to another man. It involves testicles. Not the way all sex involves testicles. I mean they actively come into play. I will leave it at that. Her ballet instructor is Russian. I pictured them, together, assuming various Russian positions, him communicating at her with grunts that she would have learned to understand, by that point. Yes. I pictured myself viewing this from the fire escape across the alleyway, through a pair of opera glasses, camouflaged by suspended undergarments. But when I found myself out there, here is the truth: she wasn't up to anything. It was like going to the theater expecting to see high treachery, bestial adulterous rutting, a violent and tragic denouement, and instead wandering into a placid slice-of-life in which the main character serenely reheats yesterday's stew, flips through her favorite pulp magazines, and lounges with her feet on a sofa. In other words, the same banalities once performed in your presence, only performed with a new serenity, with a tangible air of contentedness." The stranger lowered his voice to a whisper. "See. There's the shit of it. You watch her sticking her feet out of the bottom of the blanket, the way she always did, because her feet for some reason have this tendency to heat up even though the rest of her body gets cold, which doesn't make sense because the feet are the extremest of the extremities, but there you have it. Or she lights a cigarette and runs a bath in the old claw foot tub, and you remember how, back in earliest days of the marriage, you always interpreted this move as an invitation for romance. 'I'm taking a bath,' she would say, and you would say, 'An e-ro-tic bath?' and she would roll her eyes, in a way you assumed to be a teasing extension of the seduction. But, really, you now realize, she was just rolling her eyes. She was just taking a bath. The baths will go on, with or without you, and in fact, the whole bathing process seems to be proceeding as much more smooth and even pleasant an operation in the without column." The stranger looked wistful. "Around this point, the neighbor and his two teenage sons caught me on their fire escape, dragged me inside and beat me with broom handles. They were apparently professional sweeps of some sort."

Bart could do nothing for a moment but nod in agreement. He felt pressured to dispense some form of advice. "Women are, or, rather, can be," he began, then cleared his throat. "Well. I'm no expert. I'm more the rambling type. Never really stick around long enough type." He tried to grope back in his mind for a suitable anecdote involving a woman. Or even the last time he'd *been* with a woman. Must have been that barn dance in Burlington. Furtive, out behind the parking lot, choosing a spot near a tree in a nod to propriety. Forget about a name—he couldn't, for the life of him, come up with a face. There were the soft hairs coating the back of her neck, which he'd reached forward and stroked, with one finger, close to the finish. He'd actually hesitated before attempting that level of intimacy. But she hadn't seemed to notice. She'd told him to hurry up. He could still remember the feel of hiked wool skirt on exposed waistline, creating a distracting alternate friction. That, and the buckling of the knees, to make it all work out, which always felt foolish and unnatural, as if squatting to lift a large stone. His most vivid memory of the evening was the accordion player, Martello, an old friend of Nic's who'd been paralyzed in an accident involving a safe and pulley. He still wore his accordion, even though he could no longer move anything below his chin. They had wheeled him onstage to sing. All of the other musicians moved back, lowering their instruments. His singing voice, formerly a booming baritone, had changed after the accident, becoming a high, frail keening. Now everyone had to keep quiet to hear. A strangled sound, verging on the unpleasant. Not knowing the back-story, you would assume it was a novelty act, somehow incorporating gargling. But still affecting, in its own way. Or at least memorable. It was an old festival dance from Calabria, a tarantella, here slowed to the speed of a dirge. He sang:

La la la la la
Lalla lalla la lilla lalla la
La la la la la
Lalla lalla lera lalla lalla la

La la la la la
Si non ballu eu

Non balla nuru cchiu
La la la la la
Lalla lalla lera lalla lalla la

Bart realized that he'd been humming the song for several moments, but not speaking. He glanced over at the stranger, who had begun to weep. The man had bowed his head and clamped his eyes shut. It was then that Bart noticed the storm had passed. They now looked out upon a placid, moonlit sea. A lone gull hovered in an angular glide. Further out, in silhouette, a cluster of archipelagos beckoned—or not—still and mysterious. "Ho," he said. "Look."

The man snorted. "I don't have to," he said. "I spent the past year working on this." He covered his face with his hands and moaned, "I'm such a miserable hack."

Bart frowned. "So this is—?"

"My work wasn't selling. I needed the money. They hired a whole team of us, about forty men. Huge walls of canvas were stretched out, with painters four-high on scaffolding, while our foreman barked out orders from a crow's nest, keeping an eye on the big picture." The stranger snorted and laughed ruefully. "You wouldn't believe the way they cut costs. Back in the heyday of the panorama, they paid an enormous amount of attention to detail. Now it's all shoddy work. Just slapped up."

Bart nodded. "And what's your own work like?"

The artist dismissed the question with an angry wave. "Irrelevant," he said. "They didn't hire me because I paint a pretty landscape like Turner, that's for damned sure." His voice rose, broaching the hysterical. "I admire the work of the Futurists. But do you think people care about my personal vision? They want reality." He cleared his throat of a bit of bile, hocking it over the rail. "They hired us for this job based on specialties. Architecture. Landscape. The human form."

"What did—"

"Birds," the artist sniffled, stabbing himself in the chest. "Cloud formations. The occasional fish." He paused. "I'd almost rather not be certain, you know? I'd almost rather imagine her with the Russian than just know it was a rejection of me." He glanced at Bart. "Pardon me, sir. I realize I can be a bit high-strung."

Bart shrugged. "We all have our problems. I've been called low-strung, myself." He stared, again, at the canvas, the artist's mention of Turner having made him think of Turner's own seascapes, the froth and light and color, Turner's vision of reality being *so* real it verged on the abstract. Did people want *that*? Did they want Regulus? *Regale us.* People had no desire to stare at the sun with their eyelids cut off, to be startled by a gunshot of color on Vanishing Day. He was eager to make this argument, but at precisely that moment, he happened to glance into the ballroom and make eye contact with Nic, standing on the other side of the long table.

All he ended up saying was, "So, reality. Though, on the other hand, why look directly at the Bay of Naples, when you might catch a draft?"

The artist made an impressed little nod at the reference. He was about to say something else, but Bart excused himself, saying he had to check on a friend.

"I'm more the rambling type.'" (p. 39)

"By little of school and very much experiences (well and rightly understood) I became a cosmopolite perambulating phylosopher of the main road—crushing, burning a world within me and creating a new—better one."

—Bartolomeo Vanzetti, letter from prison.

". . . *Lalla lalla lera lalla lalla la*" (p. 40)

If I don't dance
No one will dance anymore
Lalla lalla lera, lalla lalla la

"The artist made an impressed little nod at the reference."
(p. 42)

Sir William Hamilton is often crediting with "inventing" the panorama painting after he placed a pair of conjoined mirrors in the corner of his bedroom so guests could see the Bay of Naples without turning to look out the window. (A guest went on to paint a panorama version of the mirrored scene.)

Chapter Two:
Sacco and Vanzetti
Meet the Heavyweight
Champion, Primo Carnera

The boys take on "the Venetian Giant"—the old mirror gag, mobsters, a fixed fight, an accidental drugging, Benito Mussolini's private screening room and a surprisingly vicious kangaroo—film historian Hylo Pierce on the use of the cameo and inauspicious debuts—an excerpt from the private journals of Bart Vanzetti—the stars discuss their humble origins

*(from the transcript of an interview conducted with film
historian Hylo Pierce on* Arts and Minds, *a weekly National
Public Radio program, originally broadcast from WDET-
FM Detroit on January 11, 1995)*

*We're back, discussing film debuts with critic and writer Hylo Pierce,
whose biography of Leo McCarey has just been released in paperback.
Now, before the news, we were discussing another comedy team, Laurel
and Hardy, who made their first onscreen appearance together in a film
called . . .* The Lucky Dog?

Correct. The action hinges on Ollie, or Babe, as he was still called
at the time. He plays a supporting role, a robber, accidentally stuffing
a wad of stolen bills into Stan's pocket.

Stan being a hapless bystander.

Stan being a hapless bystander.

*Now, this film is not considered a classic of any kind, is it? I for one
have never heard of it.*

No. It is, in fact, astoundingly mediocre. There's debate among
historians as to whether *The Lucky Dog* was even released in this
country. But the scene I've just described is literally Stan Laurel and
Babe Hardy's first time on the screen together, and so certainly of
interest.

*Any glimpse of the rapport they'd eventually develop, this early
on?*

I would say no. Babe Hardy, as the "bad guy," for lack of a
better phrase, menaces Stanley with gun, and later with dynamite.
Interesting bit of Red Scare trivia, by the way: when he initially produces the stick of dynamite, Babe's title reads, "I love this Bolsheviki
candy!"

*Now, if you could, Hylo Pierce, contrast this first Laurel and Hardy
meeting—which was more or less accidental, correct?*

49

Correct, yes. Stanley and Oliver were not yet a comedy team at the time of *The Lucky Dog*. In fact, they would not officially become a team for another eight years.

So as a contrast, take Sacco and Vanzetti. Who had worked together on vaudeville.

Correct.

They actually made a film about their vaudeville years, if I'm not mistaken.

Ventriloquism and Its Discontents. Although we should stress for the sake of historical veracity that the film is almost entirely fictional.

Such a terrific film, though, isn't it?

Not among my favorites.

Well, let's talk about their first short, then, which centered around a pie fight.

Which was not a new thing. Mack Sennett, in a number of the Keystone Kops pictures, had staged quite elaborate pie fights prior to Sacco and Vanzetti's onscreen debut.

Which was Sacco and Vanzetti Dessert the Cause.

Yes. A derivative film, on one hand. And of course, what Sacco and Vanzetti ended up doing later in their careers is, on a filmic level, much more sophisticated and interesting.

Until you reach the very end of their careers.

Well, yes, there's the Hercules picture, which I cringe at the mere mention of. But even discounting those final embarrassments, I wouldn't simplify their careers to the extent of early-bad, later-good. Some, for instance, consider the Carnera film, one of their first talkies, a huge step, but I wonder if it's not dated, in a sense.

Dated how? I have to admit, I adore the Carnera film.

Dated in the specificity of its references to the popular culture of the time, for one. This may be a personal bias, but from my standpoint, there's always a certain desperation implied on the part of the artist in trotting out a prominent cultural figure, whether this occurs in a film or a novel or an epic mural. If a film has any staying power, such hyper-specificity—the use of a cameo, in effect—will, long-term, act antithetically, dating the picture, filling it not with rich period detail but the cheapest of headlines. It is a lining made of newsprint. Which, as we all know, yellows in rather unpleasant fashion.

Int—

Also, Sacco and Vanzetti overused the device. Certain of their films remind me of bad historical novels, they are so crowded with "significant"—and I say that in quotes—figures of the day. "Oh, look, it's Mussolini! And here comes Carnera, the heavyweight boxing champion. And there's Italo Balbo."

The Italian Lindbergh! Love that picture.

Though I could also argue the other side—namely, that all of these historic "cameos" highlight one of the more interesting aspects of Sacco and Vanzetti's career, which was that they never shied away from their ethnicity. Sacco and Vanzetti, one could argue, made quite canny use of these "cameos" as a means of expressing a sort of Italian pride.

That's a very interesting point. I'd like to shift our focus back, though, to the topic at hand, which is the early years of some of our most cherished film comics. So to that end, tell me about the dynamic between Sacco and Vanzetti, particularly in these first films. Was it in place?

In a word: yes. And it's a fascinating dynamic, by all accounts one that existed in their offscreen, interpersonal dealings as well.

On a very basic level, Vanzetti was the straight man and Sacco was, well, whatever the opposite of the straight man would be.

The clown. Though to my mind, that appellation ends up simplifying things drastically. What's important to note is, neither Sacco nor Vanzetti fulfilled these roles in a traditional way. Unlike other comedy-team straight men—Bud Abbott, for example, or even Babe Hardy—Bart Vanzetti doesn't really seem to object to the antics of his counterpart. Nor is he merely a mean to be dipped above or below. He's ultimately less a straight man than a non-presence, an observing specter. And yet, at the same time, he possesses a mechanism wherein he can also signal to the audience that he is, on some level, actually affecting, perhaps even steering, the actions of the clown. It's enthralling to watch him, and the subtlety he brought to the role.

And Nic Sacco?

Nic Sacco, by the same token, Leonard, is not your typical clown. He's no innocent bumbler, in the vein of a Stan Laurel or a Lou Costello. Nor is he quite the borderline-malicious prankster, *a la* Harpo Marx, or the genially havoc-wreaking man-child, like Curly Howard. Sacco has no interest in or desire to control himself. He is a willfully destructive force. He actively wants to tear things down. But to return to Bart Vanzetti, that was a guy who could really take a hit.

What's a hit?

I'm sorry. A pie hit. This is going back to *Sacco and Vanzetti Dessert the Cause*. He was wonderful at underplaying slapstick moments. As you know, the first instinct of a comedian is to go for a broad sort of over-reaction—in the case of a pie hit, for instance, one's first impulse might be to allow one's mouth to hang open in a sort of gasp, as if coming up for air after a near-drowning. The other obvious choice would be to underplay the hit, for instance, by allowing the pie to drop from one's face like a scab, while remaining stock-still and doing a deadpan take, very casually wiping off some of the filling and tasting it. That would be the typical Babe Hardy reaction. Slightly annoyed, but more along the lines of a deep sigh, as if someone had just sat on his hat. Now, in *Sacco and Vanzetti Dessert the Cause*, there's a great moment where Vanzetti ducks a pie by crouching into a squat. Once he's assumed this position, the camera cuts to his point of view and you realize he's now facing a little boy, a Little Lord Fauntleroy type. Of course, the child is holding a pie.

That's excellent. So how exactly does he take the hit?

Oh, he doesn't. That would've been the expected thing, yes? Instead, when the child goes to hit him, Vanzetti grabs the edge of the pie at the last second and they move into a quite funny and overdramatic bit of grappling, in the manner of the hero and villain of a gladiator picture wrestling over a dagger. Really a clever turn-around, I must say.

Right, right. And then—

Eventually Vanzetti takes hold of the pie and grinds it into the boy's face until the boy cries.

Ha ha. Pies. And you haven't ever been hit in the face with a pie, have you, Professor?

Ha ha.

We'll be right back.

THE PRE-FIX MEAL

(a scene from the 1934 picture Sacco and Vanzetti Meet the Heavyweight Champion, Primo Carnera*)*

The old mirror gag. The glass, unbeknownst to Skinny, having been smashed. (And just before his daily shave!) Fatty, the secret smasher, poses on the opposite side of the empty frame, ready to dupe every move.

Skinny lathers his right cheek, Fatty his left. Skinny lifts his straight edge. Fatty lifts his straight edge, in tandem.

The precision of reflected Fatty's mimicry. (Identical movements, outfits.) The grotesque disparity in their physiques.

Bart is the first to speak. Though the gag has been interrupted, they continue to shave.

"We have a plan, correct?"

"This is starting to remind me of, remember that time?"

"No one is bandying about the word 'flawless,' note."

"Florida Everglades."

"But a plan it is. Empirically. Which is more than we can claim to have had, say, a half-hour ago?"

" 'Nic, how hard could it be? I mean, gator wrasslin'? Come on. You think it actually requires the skills of an actual wrestler?' "

"Now . . ."

" 'It's like palming hearts. Weights and birthdays.' "

"I really . . ."

" 'Kid's stuff. Magic from a box.' "

"Still, not exactly end times, in hindsight."

"It ended with one of us being bitten in the head by an alligator."

"Yet you survived. A miracle, some said. If we're speaking about boxing, though, I can't help but think of chicken fights."

"Those tooth-scars running along the base of my neck look like a dotted line."

"Have you ever been to a chicken fight? It's an interesting phenomenon."

"Permanent gator-tooth dotted-lining."

"Some call it barbaric, but in fact, it's quite natural. Put a pair of roosters together and they *will* attack one another. Unlike dogs, which must be tortured from birth to transform them into creatures willing to fight to the death. Which is why, for me, dog fighting crosses the line into the unnecessarily cruel."

"But you can rally behind a good chicken fight."

"Humans, in this regard, seem closer to chickens than dogs. Which is why boxing earns my unequivocal nod."

"And so, coming back around to this plan we been discussing, if we're discussing a boxing match that involves—"

"Multiple species? Entirely dependent on the species involved."

"So, does it got a name?"

"A name?"

"A name. My opponent. The kangaroo."

"Does it matter?"

"I like to know the name of what I'm fighting."

"I believe it's Chupacabra."

"Chupacabra?"

"Ring name, I should stress. Outside the ring, it may respond to an entirely different name."

"I'm fighting a Mexican kangaroo . . ."

"Don't be absurd. There are no kangaroos in Mexico."

"Named after . . ."

"It was trained by Mexicans. In the Bronx."

". . . a blood-sucking vampire thingy?"

"Could be meant ironically. You know, in the manner of a big fellow named Tiny."

"Where's that flyer?"

"I've always wondered how one trains a kangaroo to fight."

"Give it here."

"I would guess pull its tail. Put gunpowder in its mash. Hook up electrodes to its pouch. Aim for the pouch, by the way. It's supposedly quite sensitive. Housing the teats and all."

"*'The last man who dared step into the ring with the fearsome Chupacabra was carried away on a stretcher.'*"

"They have to hype these things up. Remember how you bulldogged that alligator?"

"It bit my head."

"But before that? You straddled it and held the jaws together as if they were an unwieldy hoagie. Then you flipped it over and it passed out and you grabbed a paw and made it wave to the crowd."

"Then it bit me in the head!"

"They have incredibly small brains."

"Relax. I'm in."

"That's why they pass out when flipped."

"Just one question."

"The crowd always loved that part of the act."

"Where do we plant the dynamite?"

Bart does the shaving equivalent of a spit-take. (Spasmodic wristjerk, flecking Nic's face with blood, foam.)

Nic, frozen, holds his razor perfectly still, having yet to mimic this move.

Putting on the Fix

Lit from above, the ring conjured, for some viewers, the lamposted corner of Fourth and Broad, where, after dusk, the boys squint and lean, holding up their trousers via thumb-loop, a maneuver that the expert can manage so as to discreetly flare the crotch. The boxers, here in the ring, peacocked beneath the floodlights in a similar manner. Though to Carlo F., gazing down from the second tier of seatage, it evoked more along the lines of a police line-up: the fighter standing frozen in the honeyed light, blinking out at the surrounding coliseum as if hoping to glimpse a snitch. Carlo F. swiveled his neck towards his partner, *junior*-partner, Mike Ellero, thinking to share this observation, but the kid was working something black and viscous out from under a nail, using a pocketknife. Carlo F. sighed, then tilted his head back on its immense axis, his lower jaw dropping open to receive approximately one-third of a bag of popped corn. Ellero not so busy with the nail to glance up and think how you could practically hear the hydraulics.

Carlo F. breathed heavily through his nose while he scanned the crowd for trouble. Of late, his wife had been mandating his sleeping on the couch, on account of his snoring, beyond the mere volume of which (and "mere" apparently was not an appropriate modifier of volume, according to Mrs. Carlo F., who insisted the closest noise-equivalent to her husband's snores would involve dragging a shovel up and down a cement driveway) also involved frequent moments of not breathing. These moments (according to Mrs. Carlo F.) lasted a few seconds and were followed by a jolt and a frantic gasp for air, as if the hand holding Carlo F.'s head below the surface of the bath had suddenly been removed. Carlo F. wondered if these nightly moments of not-breath damaged his brain in small, incremental ways, like flakes of gum from the spine of an old book, which always began as harmless dandruff and wound up with entire pages jack-knifing off in the first summer breeze. He tried to count backwards from Z to A. Accidentally went Z-W. Cursed his brain damage, his wife's lack of vigilance. Began worrying about that night when the not-breath would be a permanent one. The eternal inhale. He tried to stop thinking morbid, melodramatic thoughts, which had plagued him since the age of thirteen, after the death of a favorite uncle. (A stroke, while yanking nails from an old board.) He tried to focus on the gig at hand, the Chupacabra match. Simple orders: if it looks, at any point, as if the kangaroo is about to win, take the fucking thing out, whatever means necessary. Still, Carlo F. could not help himself from dwelling. More than anything else, Carlo F. did not want to die.

The kid, Ellero, started talking, only intermittently looking up from that nail.

"Hey, hey, I tell you I'm making it with the round-card girl?"

"You are, huh?"

"Oh, yeah. She's good. She is good. Her hands are strong, from hefting those cards every night, if you know what I'm saying."

I'm not sure what strong hands—"

"You obviously never been with a round-card girl. *Show us your tits you dirty slut!* Good crowd, huh? Nice and feisty."

"Jesus Christ, kid, could you maybe—"

"How about that Carnera? That off-the-boat tub of spoiled olive oil. Did you catch the Sharkey fight? I was there, my friend."

"So it's fixed. What do you want?"

"Hey, hey, you hear about the Italian flat tire?"

"I don't like your jokes, kid."

"Dago wop wop wop wop wop wop wop."

"Don't assume I'm laughing inside."

"Garçon! Garçon! Another couple dogs, and refills on these beers!"

In his powder-blue monkey's suit, the ring announcer *did* look like mid-rank waitstaff. He shot an angry glare in the direction of Ellero. Then a vine-mike, dramatically lowered and eventually clutched by the announcer, silenced the crowd. The announcer stared out, relishing the moment, its fleetness.

Then: "Is Jersey in the house tonight?"

A bifurcated eruption of yay-nay catcalls exploded throughout the coliseum. He nodded, then held up his hand again.

"Ladies and gentlemen, before we begin with our initial contest, we would like to take a moment of seriousness, and pay our respects to the memory of Anthony Buckley, known to his friends as 'Irish Tony,' who passed away last month after an unsuccessful shot at the middleweight title. As is customary, please bow your heads and remain silent as we ring the bell ten times, in honor of our late friend and colleague."

The geriatric bellman, nicknamed 'Modo by the announcer and other officials (he didn't get the reference, but in fact was beginning to develop a bit of an old-man's hunch) gave the oily string its first yank. The bell sounded. 'Modo waited for the echoes of the first ring to settle down before pulling the string again, which made for a strange effect on the crowd, his playing the bell like an instrument rather than firing off rapid, utilitarian bursts of *achtung*.

Guy somewhere in tier two cleared his throat.

Meanwhile, almost directly below the ring, in the dank cinder-block bowels of the coliseum, Nic, Bart and a drugged kangaroo, putting on the fix.

"Do you have the tail?"

"Well this ain't me trying to seduce her from behind."

"I'm just making sure you're ready to drag. Once we hide this fellow, we'll locate coffee and get you prepared for the fight. How do you feel?"

"Tranquil."

"We'll get you some coffee."

"Ized."

"Posthaste."

The plot, thus far: Nic and Bart decide to enter a kangaroo boxing match to win the prize money. Complications arise when Nic, in qualifying for the bout (through a series of mishaps at the elimination tournament, most of which involve ether), accidentally displaces the ringer planted by a low-level mobster, who had planned to bet against odds-on favorite Chupacabra. The mobster threatens Nic and Bart into service, forcing the pair to kidnap a second, presumably less fierce kangaroo from the zoo (where mayhem ensues), sneak the kangaroo into the coliseum (in an enormous perambulator, disguised as a horrifically burned infant; mayhem ensues) and distract Chupacabra's trainer (an excitable, hirsute Mexican) while Chupacabra is shot with a tranquilizer dart and kangaroos are swapped. (Accidental tranquilization of Nic ensues, plus confusion as to whether or not the correct kangaroo was shot, as they all look alike, creating obvious tension: will tranquilized Nic be stepping into the ring with a relatively tame zoo-napped kangaroo or with the deadly Chupacabra? Plus the more immediate tension of having this drugged kangaroo to hide.)

They end up ducking into an empty dressing room. Inside, a long table is set with food for six, utensils for one. Bart hides the kangaroo under the table. Nic chugs coffee straight from a pot, burning his mouth and performing an especially nuclear spit-take.

Above, the coliseum has grown eerily quiet. The bell begins to toll. Bart mentions how splitting might be a good idea at this point. Suddenly, the hallway door opens, revealing that the dressing room belongs to one half of the evening's main event, none other than—

"Say," Nic said, still holding the coffee pot, still dewed with tell-tale coffee-spittle, literally shadowed by the massive presence filling the doorway, "aren't you the former heavyweight champion, Primo Carnera?"

A little-known fact: Primo Carnera enjoyed playing the violin.
Carnera defeated Jack Sharkey on June 26, 1933, at Madison Square
Garden, becoming the first Italian heavyweight boxing champion.
At 260 pounds and over six-foot-five-inches tall, he remains the
heaviest heavyweight boxing champion in the history of the sport;
he was reportedly twenty-two pounds at birth. Nicknames: the
Ambling Alp, the Gorgonzola Tower, *Il Pugile Tanto Gigantesco.*
Carnera left home at eighteen to work for an uncle in France, but
found carpentry did not suit his temperament, and so joined the
circus as a strongman, wrestling all-comers as "Juan the Terrible."
He once claimed, to a biographer, to possess a "telepathic ability"
to predict punches. Though perhaps technically not the most ac-
complished *pugile.* He was also an inspiration for Thirties accordion
virtuoso Harry Bigood, an Englishman who performed as "Primo
Scala," the surname borrowed from Emilio Scala, a contemporary
winner of the Irish Sweepstakes. Actually a dreadful fighter. But
huge, enough so to capture the imagination of the day. Reporter:
What do you think of Hollywood? Carnera: *I'll knock him out in second
round.* Dubiously undefeated. (At the time, accordion-based big
bands were quite popular, the more traditional rhythm sections replaced with multiple accordions. Bigood apparently thought a more
ethnic-sounding name would go well with his instrument.) Don
Shena, writing in the New York *Herald-Tribune*: "Close students of
fistic matters advance the theory that the gondola-booted Venetian
Giant's astute board of managers would not be likely to toss what
they logically call a one million dollar property into the Golden

Ring unless they felt practically certain that their ponderous protégé would emerge victorious in spectacular fashion." Carnera received his initial title shot after defeating Ernie Schaaf, who had been seriously brain-damaged during an earlier fight; in the thirteenth round of the Carnera fight, Schaaf collapsed and subsequently died. Press reports at the time placing Carnera's "gondola boots" as size eighteens. In France, Carnera was discovered and subsequently managed by boxing promoter Leon See, who had ties to American mob figure Owney Madden, an Irishman who'd grown up in Hell's Kitchen. Mussolini claimed Carnera's win over heavyweight champion Jack Sharkey as a "victory for the Italian race" and had an extra-large black shirt specially tailored for Carnera, who was photographed with Il Duce giving the Fascist salute. One year later, he was defeated by Max Baer. Carnera expressed deep remorse after Schaaf's death, but the publicity didn't hurt. After the fight, the New York State boxing commissioner declared that Carnera was too dangerous to fight normal-sized boxers, that he should only fight a special class of "superdreadnaughts." His "wins" included Eliziar Rioux (KO in 47 seconds, Rioux failing to throw a single punch), Ace Clark (another KO, Clark decisively taking rounds one through five, dropping thirty seconds into six, later claiming he'd been flashed a pistol by one of Carnera's handlers between five and six) and Leon "Bombo" Chevalier (who claimed he was told to drop but refused, and that his own seconds rubbed Vaseline in his eyes and nose and eventually threw in the towel after he continued to whip Carnera while blinded.) After the Baer defeat, Carnera's comeback was to be delivered via a much-publicized fight with an up-and-coming Negro fighter, to be held at Yankee Stadium. (Italy at the time making moves in the direction of Ethiopia; Carnera at the time an Italian military reservist.) Punditry types warned of race riots in Harlem if Joe Louis went down. (Press reports afterward depicting Louis as something dangerously Other ["Something sly and sinister and perhaps not quite human came out of the African jungle last night to strike down and utterly demolish the huge hulk that had been Primo Carnera, the giant"], echoing, faintly, the reactionary fantasy writer H. P. Lovecraft's description of anarchists in his short story "The Street" ["for the swart, sinister men were skilled in subtlety and concealment . . ."])

Louis's cornerman: "A tree like this here you need to chop down."

FACCIA A FACCIAO COL NEMICO

(a scene from the 1934 picture Sacco and Vanzetti Meet the Heavyweight Champion, Primo Carnera*)*

In the press photograph, Carnera stands on a beach, or else a studio tricked up as one. The sheer abundance of stuffed swimsuit crowding the frame prevents much in the way of backdrop scrutiny. The sand definitely looked real, though. Carnera had planted his boots, black-and-golden and laced nearly up to the knees, a good seal's-length apart, his legs' shadows trailing back like grounded smoke signals. Other than the boots, Carnera wore only a leopard skin, draped over a single shoulder and bottoming in a neat loincloth.

Seven girls. "One for each day of the week," Carnera bragged, though in reality he'd always felt even more outsized and awkward in the presence of ladies than with men. The top one rode his shoulders, straddling his neck from behind, her legs scarving a pucker shape around his chest. (Whenever he took the time to flip through his old publicity album, he remembered, still, that pulse of humidity emanating from her bikini's apex and traveling from the base of his neck all the way down his spine, like telegraphy.) His flexed biceps acted as perches, with two more girls standing straight up on either. They flanked the central-shoulder girl, holding onto her shoulders for balance. (The one in the bathing cap stands as rigid as if it's a two-volume dictionary balanced on her head, while the capless horsy one leans forward, looking eager to chomp.) The fourth and fifth double-belted his waist, again in an opposing duplexity, their legs clamped in scissor holds, their hands clutching at whatever piece of his arm was left to grip. The last two girls hung off these two like ornaments, earrings, pretty little baubles, their knees flexed off the ground, so they too were held aloft by the Giant's strength alone.

Carnera's signature, perfected after months of practice on diner napkins, defaced the just-as-perfect girl-tree pose in diagonal bisecting ascent.

Carnera = the trunk. "A tree like this here you need to chop down."

Nic took in the details above in the two-second gap that occurred as Carnera extended the autographed glossy, requested by Nic, in a moment of quick-thinking that'd earned an admiring illicit wink from Bart, when the champ had caught the duo in his very own dressing room, at that point not having spotted the drugged kangaroo's tail-tip, protruding from beneath the buffet table's floor-length cloth like an orphaned loafer. When Carnera lifted his arm, Nic violently snapped his head back, as if having just received a savage and expertly delivered uppercut. The head-snap jerked his body backwards into a wild somersault, the total maneuver a single, fluid elision that ended in a splintered chair, a broken mirror, Nic slowly sitting up and hand-testing his jaw to a roomful of involuntary winces. The speed-bag, directly above, performed a lonely metronome.

"Damn, champ," he finally said. "I heard about them punches of yours, how they was so quick you couldn't even see 'em connect a guy. But merciful lilies of the field I—"

One of Carnera's handlers balled his fists and started a brisk advance, but Carnera chuckled and held up a hand.

"*Calabrese?*" he asked.

Nic pinched a fold of his robe and shook his wrist, ringing loose the shards of mirror bejeweling the fabric. "No," he said, clicking his tongue. Then: "*Torremaggiore. Puglia.*"

Carnera nodded, looking immensely satisfied by the answer, as if Nic, in confirming his suspicions, had put Carnera's status as genius and seer beyond question. "You go now," he mumbled at his entourage, accentuating the order with a smoke-clearing wave.

As the last of the muscle backed out of the room, Carnera opened his mouth to speak, until his glance lit upon the buffet. His grin broadened.

"You fellows launch a raid on this spread here, yet?" he asked, removing a silver dome from the central edifice. Craggy, oversized dumplings mined an oily yellow broth. Nic could not recall having laid eyes upon a meaner-looking soup or stew. Carnera greedily ladled several of the bready tumors into a large bowl. "*Canederli!*" he boomed, passing it to Nic with a flourish. Carnera seemed the sort of big man whose gigantism was yoked to some form of hearing loss and thus had difficulty modulating his own voice. Nic held the bowl with both hands. At close range, he could make out bits of parsley and onion and pinkish meat protruding from the wrinkles, just as hair and teeth would from a true malignancy. Carnera handed him a spoon. Like the bowl, it was slightly larger than standard-issue.

"You're *un poco giù* for knowing *canederli*, huh?" Carnera said. "Without the red sauce, you *pugliese* won't touch." He glanced down at Bart, who had stooped to better hide the kangaroo tail, while ostensibly retying one of Nic's boots. "But your friend, he is from the north, huh? I can see from his color. He knows how to eat. How you would describe this delicacy to your buddy, huh, *cugino?*"

Bart cleared his throat and yanked distractedly at the boot's bodice. "It's a bit comparable to that matzo ball soup, Nicky. Only made with Italian bread. And ham." The tail felt more like a cable, its fur barely covering the solid mass of tendon beneath.

Carnera handed down a second bowl to Bart and, after ladling himself a generous third, crossed the room and lowered himself into an overstuffed settee. "Eat, eat, anything you like," he said, immediately digging into his soup. He wielded his own spoon like a spade, as if working around some fiercely embedded rock.

"The answer to the question," he said, hoisting both spoon and bowl then wiggling his lower half to include the settee. "The question my friends, my family, they all want to know, it is simply the why. You know? You got to prove nothing, Carnera, they say. Everybody know you tough, just to look at you. So, why? And I always tell them, hey, now, what about my spoons? When you are Champ, they make your spoons the right size for your hand. The world never fit me until I had enough Champ on me to *make* it fit, you know? For me, I mean, hey, it might not sound much to you, but for me? That's a pretty good one. Reason. Better than others."

Carnera's voice, besides the lack of modulation, remained on the edge of mirth, even his most innocuous sentences bearing the taint of a near-chuckle. Bart found that he could not gauge what level of sincerity was being offered up, so he merely nodded in a vague fashion and poured himself a glass of red wine, marveling, still, at the sheer size of Carnera's head, which, if detached and catapulted, would cause serious damage to a home or body.

Nic, the tranquillizer having kicked in, had fallen asleep standing in the center of the room. Carnera remained too intent on soup and speech to notice.

Carnera: So why'd you giving me the knee shot, huh? Why you want to do Carnera like that? Try and take him down like a sissy. When all he's doing is trying to uplift the race?

Bart (*Covertly splashing glass of wine in Nic's face.*): No hate from this end of the room, my friend.

Nic (*Blinking, sputtering, bobbling soup bowl.*): Mama?

Carnera (*Chewing methodically; staring down into soup bowl as if methodical chewing required full concentration; speaking with filled mouth.*): You can hate me. Carnera don't care no more. Why care about these things? Too short. You see picture of me with Il Duce? Man is very bald. More bald than he look in the pictures. You lean close enough, you see reflection. Otherwise. Who know? They talk about the *kareezma*. But I see no *kareezma*. I wait for him to tell me a joke, or excitement story. Some kind of thing with his famous *kareezma*. But he like every other. You met him before, if you met anybody.

Bart (*Using a loose Nelson drag in an attempt to maneuver lolling Nic from behind, in the direction of an industrial-size can of smelling salts; failing to notice that the kangaroo has woozily risen from behind the buffet table.*): Well, gee, sir. I have to tell you, not personally having met the man, but only going by what I read in the papers and, I grant you, my own political biases, still, I would be forced to merely comment that what you're saying smacks of a moral relativism bordering on the nihilisti—

Carnera (*A half-loaf of Italian bread is also involved.*): He screened for me a picture. You know he love the comedy pictures?

Bart (*Finally taking note of kangaroo, unceremoniously dropping Nic face down into the tiramisu, vaulting over table to grapple with kangaroo, which bites him; stifling scream; slamming kangaroo's head repeatedly into cement floor; all of the following, obviously, spoken through panted breath.*) Yeah. I'd. Heard. That.

(Carnera goes on to detail the experience of watching a film with Mussolini. He could not recall the name of the film, nor of its performers—because of the size of the average theater seat, Carnera rarely went to the pictures—though he remembered it involved a pair of bumbling piano movers. Not accustomed to sitting still for any duration, Carnera was easily distracted. He wanted to spring out of his seat and pace about the room, but unable to do so, he began to watch Mussolini watching the picture. The Duce, who normally cut such a fearsome figure, appeared imbecilic in profile. The light from the projector had palled his skin a queasy gray, while his undersized fish's mouth hung its width, frozen in an open-ended gasp. When he laughed, his mouth did not participate, instead remaining immobile as a cave's, the laughter echoing like the cries of a search party gone astray. Only his eyes added life to the pudding, darting and thrusting at the images on the screen in a manner so desperate it almost became touching.

(Still, the moment the lights rose, Mussolini reanimated with startling vigor and attempted to engage Carnera in a probing critical discussion. On realizing his dismissal would not be imminent, and furthermore that he'd be required to bluff his way through a bizarre over-analysis of what he saw as essentially a barely strung-together series of sophomoric comedy bits, the giant panicked. Mussolini, though, remained largely content to monologue, pointing out subtleties in the actions of the comedy team that Carnera had found crude and obvious. But an insistent Mussolini went on about their gymnastic ability, and the timing and agility required. To Carnera, the film had quickly grown tedious. The pair would do things like push a piano up a hill, only to have it roll back down, likewise in a narrow stairwell, likewise up to a second-story window with an elaborate system of pulleys. He did not understand the humor in the continued Sisyphean misery of this pair of morons, but he kept his thoughts to himself. The only tense moment in their "discussion" came when the Duce brought up the film's comic centerpiece, which involved the morons hanging onto a runaway piano as it rolled down a hill, merged with rush-hour traffic, cabooseed onto the back-end of a streetcar, somehow caught fire, scattered an outdoor wedding and finally plunged into a river, Mussolini positing the scene as a brilliant synthesis of all film comedy to date. Carnera, without thinking, pointed out how irritating he'd found the scene's impetus, which had the morons hoisting the piano up yet another steep hill, one pushing and the other pulling, the pulling moron eventually growing frustrated, spitting into his hands, performing a belly-flop *atop* the piano and yanking on it by the downhill end. The pushing moron [the skinny one, of course] notices the added weight and begins a redoubled, running-in-place shoe-slide before glancing up and spotting his partner. At which point he promptly lets go of the piano to smack his partner with his hat. At which point the piano begins rolling downhill, nearly running down the pusher, who becomes entangled in a rope and finds himself dragged along by the plummeting piano, the puller, too, hanging on for dear life. The problem, Carnera insisted, boiled down to the simple fact that nobody is that stupid. This would never happen in life. It was an annoying premise that pulled any reasonably discerning viewer from the movie. Mussolini reddened. "That is the point of the clowns," he hissed. "Clowns are stupid." But, Carnera pointed out, it defies the logic of the picture. "What logic?" Mussolini snapped. There has to be some logic, Carnera began. Mussolini quickly interrupted, "They roll down a hill on a piano!" That could happen, Carnera pointed out, but what could not happen is a man actually believing he could pull the piano backwards by jumping on top of it. "How can you be such a misunderstander of comedy? This is wasted on you! The beauty of the moment is that it is nonsensical. Of course they could never do that. How could you take such a willfully obtuse position regarding a masterpiece? Would you criticize Dante for believing in the concept of eternal damnation? Gloucester, for not recognizing his own son's voice, or 'the brink of a cliff" for level ground? That's the thickest argument I've ever heard. Beyond which," Mussolini added, "we all know people really are that stupid." Spittle flew from his mouth as he spoke. The other ministers in the room exchanged meaningful glances. Carnera, at this point sensing his own foolishness, held up his hands and grinned, saying, "*Ma, allora, mio Duce*, maybe we should wrestle?"

(Mussolini burst out laughing and the tension of the moment was immediately broken. He signaled to an assistant to wheel out the Victrola, on which he played Cole Porter's "You're the Top," gesturing with delight at the line, "You're the tops, you're Mussolini!" Carnera had omitted this portion of his audience with Mussolini from subsequent retellings, as he'd found it impossible to convey without making the Duce sound rather vain and boorish, when, in fact, at the moment, it was quite charming.

(The talk of wrestling eventually shifted conversation to Carnera's time in France. Mussolini was insatiably curious about circus life, particularly backstage details. He wanted to know if Carnera ever wrestled ringers from the audience. [On occasion, Carnera said, but only if no real audience members were willing to volunteer. Mussolini nodded approvingly. In fact, there were never real audience-member volunteers.] He also demanded prurient sex-gossip. [Carnera considered telling him how everyone had taken turns with the Fat Lady, but at the last moment spun a more salacious lie involving the Siamese contortionists.])

Carnera: We also talk about the girls.

Bart (*Extracting hand from mouth of unconscious, possibly dead, kangaroo.*): We've been in the circus. We're familiar with all of those stories.

Carnera: Your friend get tired with my talking?

Bart (*Standing; trying nonchalantly to brush kangaroo hairs from vest while simultaneously shoving kangaroo body under table with foot.*): No, we really should go. Funnily enough, he's actually fighting tonight, so I really need to—

Carnera: Too tired to wrestle? Come on now, let's go. All this talk about the wrestle make me miss—

Bart: Oh we really—

Carnera (*Grinning, boxing Vanzetti's ear.*): Come on.

Bart (*Holding sore ear.*): Oh we really—

Nic (*Pulled from tiramisu by Vanzetti, his face entirely coated with tiramisu; speaking in yawn.*): Well, yeah, but that's really a specious argument because—

Bart: Sadly, we have an appointment and so really must be heading . . .

Carnera: Oh, hey, no worry, *cugino*. First thing first, though, we need to wrestle.

Bart: You seem to be blocking the only—

Carnera: I want to wrestle.

Bart: We all of course—

Nic: I'll wrestle this motherfucker.

Carnera: Two-one. Come on. You leave. But you get through me, first. Let's go!

Bart: Mmm, though a compelling offer, the thing is—

Nic (*Simultaneously drops head forward and loses control of bowels.*)

Carnera (*Charging.*): Aaaarrrrggh!!!

Bart (*Remarkably calm; we notice he's still holding the broken wine bottle.*): Okay. Plan B, then.

(*Also, the kangaroo is not quite dead.*)

"[Mussolini] . . . also discarded his bowler hat when he noticed that in American comedy films (for which he had a passion and installed a projector at home) they were no longer worn except by his favourite stars, Laurel and Hardy."

—Dennis Mack Smith, *Mussolini*

"Well, yes, there's the Hercules picture, which I cringe at the mere mention of." (p. 50)

Featuring beefy strongmen in loincloths doing battle with mythical beasts and gladiator-types, the cheap, popular Ercole (Hercules) pictures were made in Italy in the Fifties and Sixties. Titles included *Le Fatiche di Ercole, Gli Amore di Ercole, Ulisse Contro Ercole, La Vendetta di Ercole, La Furia di Ercole, Il Trionfo di Ercole, Ercole Sfida Sansone, Ercole Al Centro Della Terra* and *Ercole e La Regina di Lidia*, the latter released in 1959 and starring American muscleman Steve Reeves as Ercole and former boxing champion Primo Carnera as one of Ercole's nemeses, an unnamed "giant." By this point in his career, Carnera had turned to professional wrestling, having been swindled out of his boxing earnings by crooked handlers and having long-since fallen out of favor with the Italian government. (In 1935, Mussolini banned Italian newspapers from printing any photographs of Carnera lying at the feet of the Negro Louis.) He would be dead in four years (cancer), never making another Ercole movie, but appearing in a number of other B-pictures, including the *King Kong* spin-off *Mighty Joe Young* (in which Carnera and a team of wrestlers lose a tug-of-war match with the titular gorilla) and the Bob Hope vehicle *Casanova's Big Night*, which featured a dream sequence involving a group of midgets. Film footage also exists of Carnera boxing in an exhibition match with a kangaroo.

May 12, 1965

Arrived this morning in Milan. Drive into the valley, Val Rendena, circuitous, mildly terrifying, approximately five hours. Dolomites spectacular, though basking difficult from the backseat of a Fiat traveling at approximately 80 KPH on a narrow mountain road. Overpowering scent of diesel fuel adds to the general nausea. Nic and I had requested separate transport, but at the airport were greeted by a single chauffer (Federico) bearing a single sign ("La Fiat di Ercole.") Latest Contribution to World Cinema operating under certain budgetary constraints. Nic groused ceaselessly re. said constraints, our underappreciation, their double-crosses, "their" referring to, at various moments of approximately five-hour grouse, the producers of this film, producers in general, studio bosses, gossip columnists, "the fans," Nic's ex-wives, Nic's ex-girlfriends, Nic's current girlfriends, Nic's arch-nemesis Lou Costello. Demanded to know, repeatedly, why current producers have not booked us at a hotel in the fashionable resort town (Madonna di Campiglio) which overlooks the valley and where moneyed of Europe travel to change their air, but rather have lodged us in the bowels of the valley, in an unfashionable village he'd never heard of (Pinzolo, Federico's hometown), a rhetorical question, generally coupled with the rueful statement, "I could smell the garlic on this one a mile away." "This one" referring to our current project. "The garlic" referring to the participation of too many Italians. "Too many" referring to a sum greater than two. Still, when we finally arrived in Pinzolo, I found it fine (enough)—cobbled village streets, ancient stone houses, church steeple the only structure taller than two stories, "the majesty of the Italian Alps." That sort of thing. Nic asked if Pinzolo was reminiscent of my place of birth, also in the north. Offered his condolences before I could reply. Actually not much in common with Villafalletto. Federico explained that Pinzolo's rocky soil never allowed for much in the way of farming. Nic asked what locals got into besides the stray lost sheep. Federico chuckled at Nic's joke, then, when he realized we honestly had no idea, said, "You really don't know? We sharpen knives here." Nic and I exchanged meaningful glances.

Apparently, Pinzolo is known, far and wide, for its *moleta*; after the war, many emigrated to the States. According to Federico, town legend has the grinders starting off as lumberjacks, until one especially harsh winter, when they decided to earn some extra money by going door to door and sharpening the villagers' knives. (As woodcutters, they had been skilled at sharpening their axes with a simple file.) Eventually, with the advent of the easily mobile push-wheel, they began to travel each winter, first to neighboring villages, next as far as Milan, and eventually to neighboring countries like France, Austria, and Switzerland. The local dialect remained a patois of foreign words and phrases brought home by the grinders and Italianized—which, in fact, I noticed the moment we climbed into the car, when Federico told us to "*bodgia da la banda*," the non-standard "*bodgia*" apparently meaning scoot over, deriving from "budge."

In all, an interesting development. Rather shocking that Gianni or one of the other producers never bothered to share this bit of rather pertinent news about our destination. Federico also told us a joke: One winter, a young man leaves the valley to make his living sharpening knives, traveling far and wide. When he returns, his father demands the money earned. The son says, "Well, half, *el mangia 'fo*." To which the father replies, "Well, give me the other half, then." To which the son replies, "*Mangia sensa bivro?*"

77

May 14, 1965

Filming began today. Simple gag involving Nic, wearing only red woolen flap-bottomed pajamas, attempting to mollify an angry bull. Your humble *scrittore*'s role consisting primarily of shouting the epithet "*Zia Buona!*" whenever the bull, which remained unmollified, came too close to partner Nic. Also met our Ercole, a big Greek from Coney Island. Seemed fine (enough), though reminded me of Carnera. Hands like steak dinners. Brinking panic in the eyes. (The eyes of a dull boy just sharp enough to know he's not *quite* following the plot, and so always scanning his peripheries for hints, secret signals.)

Director a pup. Probably harmless, but still too early to say. He's not reverent enough for Nic. Though to be fair, a humpbacked manservant would likely fall short in that department.

Sole (shabby) victory thus far: a successful lobby to have the title changed from the truly awful *Sacco and Vanzetti, Meet Hercules!* to the still quite bad *Labor Pains*. Though neither in the vicinity of the badness of the planned Italian domestic title, *Ercole Al Casa di Merda*, over which we have no control.

Ah, yes. The script. Haven't mentioned it yet. To be honest, not quite up to that particular labor at the moment. Let's just leave it at there have been worse. *Inamoratos Inna Mexican Jail*: unquestionably, hands-down worse.

Nothing else comes to mind at the moment.

Though would also like to point out, for posterity's sake, that the script really did hold a promise of sorts, early on. (And later, seemed plausibly reparable.)

The third time a barnyard fence Nic was intended to clamber ended up collapsing under his weight, he looked my way, shook his head and muttered, "Just hang on to the gallows and hope it floats." No one else caught the allusion.

(To Stan and Oliver's final picture, *Utopia*. Also shot in Europe after everyone in Hollywood said no, Stan near-death by that point,

Ollie bloated almost beyond recognition. Specifically, a reference to the point in the picture where Stan and Ollie's utopian island paradise sinks into the sea—luckily enough, just at the moment they're about to be hanged. So off they float. We should be so lucky.)

May 17, 1965

Shooting stopped early after Nic, drunk before noon, burned himself —*mildly singed* himself—with a branding iron left too long in the coals, which had heated the entire shaft. Nothing serious, but Nic insisted on emergency-room treatment. The nearest hospital, in Tione, was an hour's drive.

Had anticipated more nostalgia, perhaps even ennui, being in such close vicinity to one's own boyhood. But thus far (knock-knock), I remain as free of discernible affect as ever. Perhaps like a ballerina's sole, my own (soul) has callused after years of unnatural contortion, exposure to hard flat surfaces, support of entire body weight at odd angles for prolonged periods. Reader may continue to overextend metaphor as he sees fit.

Nic dated a dancer once. He used to stick needles into the bottoms of her feet. I remember her as quite beautiful, but her foot-flesh was a lizard's, as white and thick as the frosting on a wedding cake. Nic claimed he once used her foot as a representation of the state of Tennessee, tacking out the major points of interest along their planned route to the Carolinas. She made (he swore) not a peep. He dragged me into his hotel room one night, insisting I stub out a cigar just below her big toe, eventually doing it himself in the face of my repeated refusals. The whole time she lolled near-nude, reading Henry Miller, occasionally groaning and sharing the too-awful-to-keep-to-oneself description of tumescent cock with the room, but otherwise giving no mind to our antics. He wanted to write a like scene into whatever picture we had underway at the time, but the censors, predictably, balked.

This film had to be an Ercole picture. The only stipulation of our Italian investors. Our Hollywood backers having long-since moved along. Our American audience having long-since discovered new comedy for tumultuous times. The Italians insisting we can do for the Ercole genre what Bud and Lou did for Frankenstein, the Mummy et al. They had Nic at Bud, Nic a Lou-hater from way back, Lou having (Nic insists to this day) fed Nic's dog a poisoned cutlet when the two were neighbors in Palm Springs in the early days. Ask Nic why in the world Lou would poison his dog and he will—to this day—give the same response: *Exactly*.

The Italians said the specifics of the script remained our call, as long as Ercole factored in reasonably large, beyond which anything we liked, a deference to our status as "legends," that kind of smoke. Nic and I met at my old place in Malibu (right before the sale) to brainstorm. While relieving himself in my pool, Nic came up with the Augean stables. Never been done, he pointed out. We would play the lazy stable hands who haven't cleaned the place in thirty years. Give Ercole a love interest—the King's daughter, say. Stretch out the time of the labor from a day to a week, Ercole not quite focused on the labor at hand because of said love interest. It sounded good at the time. We were truly excited, getting back some of the old creative spark. Barnyard animal gags, I said. Muscle-man gags, I said. Horseshit jokes, Nic added. I stipulated no. Nic tried to argue me down. I insisted no. He finally said fine fine fine, Mister Highbrow, Mister Auteur, Mister *Fellini*, no horseshit jokes. I said fine, then, it's settled. More later.

May 23, 1965

Day off. Rode cage-lift up to the *rifugio*. Quite literally a cage. One stands upright and is conveyed via cable in herky-jerk fashion, the faded azure bars the only grippable physicality between you and the humbling spectaculars of the natural world. Honestly, though, a very nice view.

Informed yesterday of scrapping of original ending, which to my mind had brilliantly solved the major problem of the myth-as-written, namely Ercole's completion of his labor by flushing out the stables with a diverted river. The problem being his diversion of the river is by hand, i.e., he *lifts* the river like so much fancy carpet. All of which plays fine on papyrus, but in a modern picture, even one involving thunderbolt-tossing gods, it flaunts too much internal logic. And so, our brilliant solution, a last-act scenario in which, time running out, Ercole dashes up a mountainside and hurtles an enormous boulder into the river, damming it completely, causing a spectacular flood, washing the stables clean, washing us away, allowing Ercole to rescue his girl as we float, bicker. So forth. Roll end credits.

Now, money trouble having ensued, a new ending has also ensued. Ercole will complete his labor and win his girl by competing in a Western-style bull-riding contest, using crudely patched-in footage from an American "rodeo."

Occurred to me, while sipping an espresso at the *rifugio*, that Freud wrote *On Transience* while staying in the Dolomites. I remembered, as a boy, the shift of clouds behind a mountain creating the illusion of movement of the mountain itself. I was thirteen, on my back, calm as the matted grass; the mountain above me seeming to lunge and sway. My stillness taught me a false sense of power from which I have yet to recover.

May 24, 1965

Nic continues to lobby for horseshit jokes. Has taken to quoting farting gags from Chaucer. I pointed out the script's lack of similarity to Chaucer. *Exactly*, he said.

May 26, 1965

En media the "eavesdropping scene"—Nic and I asquat in the hay whilst Ercole and his love interest secretly tryst in the next stall over—Nic attempts to force a horseshit gag by "accidentally" tripodding his fingers in an easily avoidable foothill of goat dropping (deposited by a supporting player after several takes involving the eating of Nic's hat), which, of course, elicits a big laugh from the director and the entire crew, after which Nic "casually" deadpans, "Hey, this is just a thought, but wouldn't that have been funnier as horseshit?" Nods all around. As per Nic's design, my veto comes off like the snob's, his horseshit gag like the people's. Later overheard him joking with the director: "The deal with Bart is he's never had to change a diaper, so he gets a little squeamish."

May 27, 1965

The recurrence of "fame" has been an odd adjustment. Had grown to enjoy fading back into anonymity over the last decade or so in America. I felt a bit like a double-agent, disguised, wandering about markets and bookstores unrecognized. With impunity. Gathering information on the civilian populace. *If they only knew.*

Here, though, they know.

Nic, of course, has been delighted at the reclaimed attention.

In line this evening at the local cinema (last year's Steve McQueen picture, dubbed), I was besieged by autograph-seekers. A woman with a cane (though barely thirty if a day) asked if I knew Victor Mature. I said we'd been introduced once at a party. Evidently, the Maturi family—she made a point to spell it—hailed from Pinzolo, though they'd already resettled in St. Louis by the time of the future leading man's auspicious birth. The woman spoke of Mature disdainfully: for changing his name, for secluding himself atop the Hollywood hills, for never visiting Pinzolo. By this point we had nearly reached the ticket window. The woman smiled and said she'd been lined here the night the theater opened, now twenty years past—it was the first, and remained the only, movie-house in town—and that in fact they'd played a Victor Mature film. When she'd returned home from the cinema that evening, her grandmother was still awake, so she told her about the opening, how she'd just seen Victor Mature in *Sfida Infernale*. (The Italian title, I later figured out, of *My Darling Clementine*, Mature's best role, playing the drunken Doc Holliday to Henry Fonda's Wyatt Earp.) "Oh, that's nice," her grandmother, who had never seen a moving picture, replied. "He must have been happy so many people from Pinzolo were in the audience."

May 29, 1965

Is my distaste for jokes involving bodily functions actually a childish recoiling from the bodily, a greater denial of the body's ultimate failing (death) disguised as a sophisticate's polite decision to not speak of the leaks and odors that plague the animal world?

Nic said if I pulled the stick out of my ass there probably wouldn't be shit on it, it would likely be a clean and sweet-smelling new stick, but still, that shouldn't stop me from allowing others to appreciate a good horseshit gag. We'd been arguing at length about whether jokes involving the stench of the stables constitute horseshit gags. I argued yes, pointing out that such a gag exists roughly on the level of passing gas in a crowded elevator. Nic rebutted by loudly passing gas, eliciting big laughs from cast and crew. "I rest my—" Nic continued, before interrupting himself (and punctuating his concluding words) with a second arpeggio of flatulence that (a trick of the ears but nonetheless) seemed to actually sing a drawn-out *caaaaaaaase.*

May 31, 1965

Dream last night: Nic and I, adrift on a gallows. No ships or land visible. Nic nonetheless ties the noose around his waist, and attempts a swim-tug in the direction (north) he's sure is the busiest naval route. The sturdiness of the gallows is a comfort. "They are built to withstand shock, as well as weight," Nic points out, rapping on the crossbeam as he treads water. I fall back into a crucified recline. I close my eyes and try to conjure a gag appropriate to our current situation. Sharks, pirates, desert isles—all too obvious. Likewise, the enormous kettle, surrounded by dancing flames and leering cannibals. Contrived! When I open my eyes to ask Nic's input, he has disappeared. The noose floats behind the gallows like a dog's leash abandoned on a city street. Suddenly, I have my gag-solution: a hungry Nic twirling the noose like a cowboy, vainly attempting to lasso passing gulls, accidentally lassoing himself, accidentally lassoing me, eventually snagging a puny bird but then not quite sure how to kill or for that matter cook the thing. (Strangulation? Suffocation? Drowning? And how exactly does one start a fire on a floating gallows? A: *Verrrry* carefully.)

I awoke, upset—not *by* but *at* Nic, for leaving me, in his apparent dream-death, with no one to share my gag.

June 7, 1965

The final week of filming. Despite repeated gentle reminders of the anachronistic nature of Nic and I as "rodeo clowns" distracting bulls during climactic riding contest, the final sequence proceeds as reconceived. Anagnostaras (the big Greek, our Ercole), showing off for his leading lady, upon whom he has developed an off-screen crush (despite her having from day one spent all of her free time with the producer's playboy son), literally grabs a bull by the horns, and is badly gored. The remainder of his scenes can be shot, the director determines, with a stunt double (his face either shadowed or blurred from a distance), artfully blended with existing footage of Anagnostaras, in close-up, reacting to various threatening or appealing situations. (Though the giant only possesses a single facial expression.) The larger (in both senses of the word) problem remains finding a stunt double sizable enough to plausibly double for the Greek.

It was my first day off in weeks, so I decided, finally, to properly explore the town. The woman at our *albergo* recommended walking to the town graveyard. I chuckled mordantly at her suggestion, as I'd been feeling increasingly depressed all week. She explained the graveyard's chapel had a famous fresco painting of the *Danza Macabre*, which was well worth seeing, even though it had recently been defaced by vandals—locals, everyone had inferred, upset by the town's recent decision to disinter and relocate a number of the graves in order to better shape the graveyard's overall expansion. The vandals had splashed the fresco with acid. Art experts from Florence had flown to Pinzolo to see if the painting could be restored, but after several weeks of gentle scraping and intent sample studies, they determined that nothing could be done.

The graveyard was more or less as I'd expected—garish, Italian, a crowded skyline of towering statues of the Madonna, enormous headstones adorned with glass windows opening onto yellowing photographs of the deceased, a weeping Christ staring up at the heavens, arms outstretched, as if asking His Father, "*Why?*" Even in—perhaps *especially* in—the smallest towns, Italian graveyards do not disappoint.

The *Danza Macabre* itself reminded me of damaged film stock, wherein the image is devoured, frame-by-frame, by blotches of varying shapes and sizes. The procession of skeletons, which appeared to represent an assortment of professions—I could make out a balladeer toting his mandolin, a peddler pushing his barrel of goods and the disembodied, hatchet-wielding hand of either a grinder or a woodsman—all had been bespotted in a similarly haphazard non-pattern, as if by nature. Death defeated by nature! I left the graveyard in high spirits, the most cheerful I'd felt in weeks.

For the next hour, I wandered the town's narrow streets. I passed the old church in the town square. From Madonna di Campiglio, looking down into the valley, one could pick out the steeples of

Pinzolo, of Bocenago, of Strempo, on down, the respective towns seemingly grown around these focal points, which surely when connected form a grand and mysterious pattern. I wandered into the grocer's to buy some fruit and bread, then into the shoe store just to smell the overpowering leathery musk inexplicably absent from its American counterparts, eventually arriving in front of Bagatto's bar, at the very edge of town. I was about to enter when I spotted a statue of a *moleta* in a square a few hundred yards away, where a man was making a photograph of his two boys, one perhaps eight, the other half that age. The younger boy had clambered into the arms of the slightly larger-than-life-sized grinder. One of the statue-grinder's hands worked the knife's handle, the other guided the blade along the wheel, forming a kind of U-shaped cradle. The elder boy had scaled the grinder's cocked hip and hung himself from his neck. This boy spotted me and excitedly pointed, shouting "Daddy! Daddy!" in English. The father lowered his camera and turned about, his face immediately breaking into an enormous grin. Nearly running over, he pumped my hand and began to speak to me in thickly accented English, eventually lapsing back and forth into Italian when he realized I understood both languages. He expressed delight to meet me, explaining that he'd grown up in Pinzolo and left home in his twenties to grind knives for his uncle in Detroit, eventually taking over the uncle's business. He and his wife and sons had returned to visit his parents and sister. He said he was a fan of our films—particularly, of course, of the pictures in which we portrayed knife-grinders: In fact, he went on, he and Marco (the eldest boy) had made a ritual of watching the old films, which reran on a local Detroit station Sunday mornings. They had watched some of the Ercole filming one afternoon, and during a break had gotten Nic's autograph. I had apparently not been feeling well that day and had left the set early, according to an assistant.

He insisted I accompany him to his sister's house for supper. I would normally refuse such offers, but the man was so friendly I relented. The sister was similarly effusive, as was his wife, who had been born in Campiglio, but emigrated when she was two and so had no trace of an accent. The couple had met in the émigré community in Detroit. It turned out to be their last day in Pinzolo, so the brother-in-law was making polenta, cooking it the old-fashioned manner, in a copper kettle over an open flame in a specially built stone fireplace in the yard. He spent a half-hour stirring the corn-meal mix by hand, with a long wooden *trisa*, which he also used to sporadically threaten the children with a spanking. Eventually they served up the polenta in the center of the table, a rude yellow blob the size of a large hatbox. The brother-in-law slid a long piece of string beneath the polenta and then sliced upwards, garroting off huge, bricklike slabs, which were then covered with generous heapings of beef and mushroom stew. They spoke in the thick local dialect, though quickly remembered to switch back to "proper" Italian whenever I appeared confused. They asked for stories about Hollywood, but not as many as most. The eldest cousin wanted to know if I'd met Elvis Presley. (I had not.) The middle girl asked after Mickey Rooney. (I didn't mention his "watch trick.") Marco was shy. Reminded me a bit of myself. We talked about grinding lore. Apparently, an American relative, trying to recreate a trick from one of our films, had lost a thumb. I apologized, which they all found quite funny. The father imitated the uncle's later attempts to cut steak with a knife and fork, tucking his thumb behind his palm for effect. When we had finished eating, the old *nonno* (only seven years my elder—Lord, I don't feel *that* old; though I'm closer now to what will probably be my final decade than to sixty) passed his plate around and everyone placed any fat left over from the stew meat onto his plate—a family tradition, they explained. He ate it down greedily.

In all, an extremely pleasant night.

(from a series of interviews with Nic Sacco and Bart Vanzetti for Motion Picture Monthly, *conducted the week of July 14, 1963, at the Beverly Hills Hotel)*

Not meat, meet.

That's what I said, meat. See what I gotta put up with, with this guy?

Meet.

Am I squinting intently at your lips or having problems with speech-volume or doing anything else that might indicate I'm a deaf man? I said I heard the question, and I said I don't have a favorite meat.

Meet.

I mean, if we're talking desert-island meats? I'd have to go with pig meat. Cook it right, that's quite a tasty beast. Though again, you know, I have to repeat, "favorite's" such a—

All right, I will begin. I was selling eels at the time.

Oh, "meet." As in, "How did we?" Gotcha. Right-o. Yeah. Well, of course, in those days, this guy was a lowly eel-monger.

I prefer "humble" to—

Selling eels out a barrel, on a street-corner. Can you conceive of the lowliness?

Perhaps we should mention what you were doing?

I'd stand there next to him. Try to feed him lines, you know, help him sell himself a little bit. "Physician, eel thyself." That sorta thing. Cause you're not just selling eels out there, you're selling a little piece of *you*, was my point. "What an eel-advised ingredient for your stew, madam." 'Long those lines. I mean, but better. It's been a long time. I'm giving you rough approximations, not primary-source quotations.

What you were doing for money, is closer to my meaning.

Surviving by my wits, as ever.

I seem to remember an illegal dice game on the F train.

Ah, days I had.

As I recall, it was a few days before Christmas, the day we met.

Late nights. Rearmost car. Gamblers jumping off and on, their convenience. We called it a "floating game." Get it? By the end, I had three tables, a cigarette girl, street urchin running a little bar. You know, just beer and snacks, but still. Classy.

I remember the date because Christmas is traditionally the busiest time of year for an eel-man. Italians consider the eating of an eel on Christmas Day good luck.

Never liked the stuff, myself. Slimy. Too much like a snake.

Considered a rare delicacy, at the time.

Rare the way you rarely find yourself chewing meat off a spine. And delicate like a girl from Lago di Garda's—

Okay.

A *carina* from Castelbuono's . . .

All right.

A *donna* from Cremona's . . .

Might we—

Never brought me no luck, all I'm saying.

You met me, didn't you?

Ladies and gentlemen, this guy doles out the straight lines like fake Madisons.

So, how exactly did we meet? Well, one evening, after a long day's work, I boarded the F train

Ho! That one, again? That crumb-cake's a little stale, innit, sir?

Our recollections of our first meeting differ, slightly. Nic, as I recall, seems to believe we met on the street.

He's fishing eels out of this giant tub. Barrel, I guess you'd call it. Pathetic, gotta say. So I stroll over . . .

What I've told Nic repeatedly, though he doesn't seem capable of grasping the concept, is that, in fact, his version of our meeting was a version we concocted for *our characters*, for an unfilmed—

Bart likes to make out these differences between us and "our characters." While, you know, call me a simpleminded wop, but I don't believe a guy can truly escape his character. I think character's destiny. A little corny, I know, but—

Nic likes to pretend there is an actual semiotic connection between "character," meaning a role played by an actor, and "character," meaning gut-deep immutable inner-self, which, give me a fuc—

All I'm saying is maybe there *is* a connection? And while we're at it, let's go over all the differences between our "characters" and our "selves." I could stand to lose a few pounds. So could "Nic Sacco," star of stage and screen. I'm funny . . . Hey, so is "Nic"! Bart's a real sour bastard with a problematic attitude; likewise, "Bart." I could go on.

So by your definition, that display of logic would be considered genuine idiocy, whereas by mine, we could give you the benefit of the doubt and say you were in character as "Nic Sacco."

Funny. Though I have to object and point out that "Nic Sacco" the character is not an idiot. He's just excitable.

Let's stay with the topic of your working-class backgrounds. You both worked a wide range of day jobs before getting into show business. How do you feel those experiences shaped your on-screen personas?

Oh, immensely. You can see it in all of our pictures.

Yup. A certain sensibility.

It's cultivated. It cannot be faked.

You work and you struggle and, you know—here we are, back to the character thing again, but—it builds character.

Resentment.

Drive.

Hatred of the ruling system that has oppressed you, your family, your people, for generations, and that's designed to—

I made shoes. Edge-trimmer, actually, was my technical position. I dug ditches. Sold candy. I could regale you with a long list of menial jobs.

Course, we both ground some knives in our time.

Funny you should mention that, because of course in later years that became a point of controversy.

What didn't?

A *point* of controversy. Nice. This guy's okay, Bart, huh?

What doesn't, when you reach a certain level of fame, is what I more specifically meant.

I am of course referring to the lawsuit by one Clemente Bonapace, a knife sharpener who claimed that he was a neighbor of yours during your vaudeville days, and that you stole your act from—

Another point of controversy was that explosion at the end of the Carnera picture. I mean, we got plenty of controversies for you, if you want 'em.

To have a career worth having, you create controversies.

People say we blew twelve kangaroos to bits at the end of that Carnera picture.

A filthy mendacity.

Only four of them kangaroos actually *died*.

Ha. Nic jokes.

Okay, I got a joke. We're comedians, right? And relax, because it also involves violence towards defenseless animals, so I'm staying on-topic. Anyway. Guy's out hunting bear. Takes a shot, misses, bear runs off. Second later, he feels a tap on his shoulder, turns around, it's the bear. He says, "Please, don't kill me!" The bear says, "Okay, I'll let you go, but you have to give me a blowjob." Guy gives the bear a blowjob, and true to his word, bear lets him go. Guy drives home, pissed, gets a *machine gun*, goes back to the woods, finds the bear again, and just starts blasting. Birds, squirrels, raccoons, all falling from trees. But somehow, he misses the bear. Sure enough, second later, tap on his shoulder. This time, the hunter gets down on his knees and begs, says his wife'll be widowed, twins orphaned, all that. Bear says, "Mother*fucker*! I let you go once, and you come back to kill me again? But okay. Give me another blowjob and I'll let you go." Guy gives the bear another blowjob, drives home, even more pissed, second blowjob was much nastier, he's got a bad taste in his mouth, the bear has to die. So he gets a *bazooka*, goes back to the woods, finds the bear, blam! Blows up half the forest. Smoke clears. All that's left is a crater. Guy climbs in, looking for the carcass. Tap on his shoulder. Turns around. Bear says, "You're not really coming out here to hunt, are you?"

We never stole that guinea's knife shtick.

So tell us about your start in vaudeville.

Chapter Three:
Ventriloquism
and Its Discontents

The boys are discovered—a barbershop, impressive voice-work, a cast of characters from the Golden Age of vaude-ville (including Helen Keller), and the debut of Sacco and Vanzetti's famous knife routine—Hylo Pierce dissects "dangerous" comedy

(a scene from the 1937 picture Ventriloquism and Its Discontents*)*

The barber, Scrotti, greeted the clowns—the fat one toting a battered salesman's valise, the other pushing a ramshackle grinding wheel—with an irked glare. Waving his soap-streaked razor, he conducted them to a row of chairs along the wall, then returned, with a pointed brusqueness, to his task at hand. The face of the dummy remained approximately two-thirds creamed.

Even so, this particular dummy would be recognizable to any fan of the vaudeville stage as Bill, the goggle-eyed, short-tempered half of the once-famous team of Professore Scrotti and Bill. Scrotti's own title referred both to the school for ventriloquists he had run for years out of the back room of this very barbershop and to his stage persona, that of a pompous art history professor constantly attempting to seduce his young female students. A dedicated few might even be able to hum the pair's minor hit recording, the jaunty ukulele-driven duet "Absolutely, Professore? Mosta-Surely, Dottore!"

Though Scrotti's gags could be hackneyed and inconsistent, anyone who'd caught his act would have to agree that, on the level of sheer technical skill, he was easily the greatest ventriloquist of his generation. Yet, oddly, the more recognition and acclaim Scrotti received, the less inclined he became to throw his increasingly famous voice in public. He found performance to be impure, and his perfectionism had reached a level that made his own routine a perpetual disappointment. And so, though he continued to direct a vaudeville revue at a small theater in Chinatown, Scrotti found himself, for the most part, retreating into the realm of theory.

In-the-know types wishing to see a performance by the master would surreptitiously enroll in his workshops, during which he rarely used his lips while speaking, his lectures delivered by dummy, dog's mouth, or the garishly painted nutcracker hussar standing at attention in the corner of his desk. A favorite trick involved pointing a book at the class and flipping the pages with his thumb while making it "speak" a passage from its pages. This was generally Keats. While reciting the poem, Scrotti stuttered in syncopation with the rustling pages. He once delivered a two-hour talk on the short-lived genre of ventriloquist literature (thrillers usually revolving around a ventriloquist who employs his powers for sinister purposes) *entirely from a button* on the dress of a girl in the back row.

Women also attested to more private performances from Scrotti, who, in the bedroom, was known to make their genitalia speak (by all accounts, banal plaintives along the lines of, "Please. Please. *Please*") and, on occasion, his own (most memorably, it once sang an entire verse of the old chestnut "Pucker Up, Baby (And Kiss Me Until Them Lips Give Out)"), which provoked giggles, moans of pleasure (Scrotti's more carnal whispers shall not be recorded here) and, at times, sneers of disgust (at which point, Scrotti would quickly switch back to speaking with his own mouth, his dedication to his craft having its limits).

Few considered Scrotti a handsome man. His neck bulged in an unpleasantly tumescent fashion, due to the disproportionate exercise it had received over the years, the voice-thrower (a little-known fact) drawing primarily upon these muscles. Like Houdini, with his propensity to show off his feats of stomach-strength, Scrotti, proud of his bull's neck, liked to place it on the slab, so to speak, and issue challenges to all-comers. This typically involved exhortations to "choke me, go-head, throttle the life out of me," which ended with a winded taker asking Scrotti to go easy on his sore fingers when they shook hands and took their gentleman's leave, his neck having flexed into a bridge cable. Once, backstage at the theater, an actor who had trained in Oriental judo and other "martial arts," and who had just demonstrated his skill by splitting a spare beam from the set, broke his pinkie and ring fingers when attempting a repeat performance on Scrotti's neck.

Scrotti's favorite trick was dubbed "The Oxbow Incident" by friends. It involved a chair slowly dragged to the center of the room and a noose slowly tied around a beam, at this point the crowd noise having died down to nervous whisperings as Scrotti mounted the former and donned the latter. There would be a few anxious titters during the brief yet interminable pause when Scrotti stood on the chair, still as a statue, no one wanting to seem uptight enough to object to whatever was about to happen. Then a confederate, at a nod from Scrotti, would deliver a savage and lightning kick to the chair. Audible gasps. Scrotti, his neck muscle tightened, the rope straining against his weight, would bob himself, once, twice, three times, at which point the rope would finally snap and the trickster would land on his feet to deliver a flushed bow. As a final touch, he would slowly turn the noose around his neck so that the snapped end of the rope hung down his front like a tie, which he would proceed to wear for the remainder of the evening.

TRANSCRIPT

*(from a series of interviews with Nic Sacco and Bart Vanzetti
for* Motion Picture Monthly, *conducted the week of July 14,
1963, at the Beverly Hills Hotel)*

There was no barbershop.

Writer came up with that one.

No "Scrotti," for that matter.

Guy's real name was Pete. Radio ventriloquist.

A craft as difficult as it sounds.

What Bart means is, "not very."

And yet, oddly enough, the art of radio ventriloquy experienced a brief renaissance. You're probably too young to recall, but . . .

Anyway, some point, Pete's rich daddy kicks, and he inherits a pile of bread. So he decides to put together this vaudeville revue.

That much is true. We did "cut our chops," as they say, on the vaudeville stage. A handful of jokes. A little singing and dancing. Though music was never exactly our—

Your—

. . . forte. *Our.*

I had a voice for it.

A polite silence settles over the antechamber.

We ought to play my version of "The Blighted Farmer's Yodel."

That would give us something to discuss.

And you were so terrific.

It's large of you to say so, especially after my own cruel yet honest assessment of your work.

Our manager, Danny, always thought we should make a musical.

Of course, in the old days, you had to be able to do it all.

He ain't lying.

Hoof.

Croon.

Shuffle.

Chirrup.

Pick.

Pluck.

Twinkle.

Bugger.

Scat.

Blow.

Bugger?

Hey, he's listening. Dosey-do.

Drop dead.

Open up the eye-faucets.

Take a punch.

Master trapeze or foil, unicycle or fiddle-saw.

Hammer a nail straight up a nostril. Eat glass. Stilt-walk. Soliloquize. Mime. Juggle buzzsaw blades.

We could go on.

We never did coon shouts.

Despite his irrational hatred of the darkies.

He jests.

His boxer shorts, to give junior more space to mambo.

In short, to succeed as a performer, back when we started in the business, one was required to possess a full arsenal of showman's skills.

Knife bit was something we came up with to set ourselves apart.

There were so many other comedy teams. Bud and Lou, of course. But many others long-since forgotten. Clark and McCullough.

Always hated the way they tried to copy our knife bit, there at the end.

I would like to completely dissociate myself from the preceding joke.

Aww, come on. You love a tasteless joke.
I don't und—
You're too young, kid.
Next question.

Modern Warfare Is by No Means Limited to the Use of Explosives
(a scene from the 1937 picture Ventriloquism and Its
Discontents*)*

Nic seized upon the embarrassment of dummies the moment they walked through the barbershop door. They (the dummies) were surprisingly long (over three feet, extended), hanging, as many did, from the coat-and-hat hooks that ran the length of the wall. All wore suit coats (in a variety of styles and colors), and most had hats as well. Nic had no idea why the barber was shaving one. He assumed the barber had his reasons. One must keep one's shaving wrist limber. One tends to cultivate one's own especially refined fetishes. One may enact elaborate cleansing rituals just before certain acts, or else just after. Nic approached one of the dummies hanging on the wall, slowly extending a finger towards the center of its eyeball. It did not blink. Nic touched the eyeball. The marble felt cool on his fingertip, slightly damp. The ravaged arc of his fingernail covered much of the dummy's pupil. He moved his fingertip so that more of the pupil peeked from the side. He rolled the eyeball to the left, then to the right, up, down, massaging the orb in its socket. The manikins all had green eyes. Nic wondered if this was an aesthetic choice or a color of fake-eyeball bought in bulk. Were dummies called dumb because they couldn't speak without covert assistance? Nic had once seen the blind and deaf prodigy Helen Keller on stage with her teacher as part of a vaudeville program. He remembered Helen Keller had threaded her fingers through the fingers of her teacher's hands. That had been their manner of speaking. Then Helen Keller had spoken aloud, in an surprisingly clear, if erratically modulated, voice. Helen Keller had said, "I am so happy to be here." Nic wondered, in hindsight, if the teacher had not, perhaps, been an incredibly talented ventriloquist capable of throwing her voice. Perhaps the teacher had quickly discovered that the Keller girl was an imbecile with no hope of conventional learning, and so had decided that no harm would come from exploiting the girl's underutilized corporeal self. They would both become wealthy and famed, and who could, in the end, really lodge complaint? During the show, Helen Keller had taken questions from the audience, the show being a variation on the performances of mentalists, in which feats of the mind (performances of incredibly complex mathematical calculations or recitations of long passages of literature from memory) would be enacted for an audience. Keller's teacher would take a question from an audience member, nod, pass it on, tactilely, to Keller—it was almost as if the question were a *physical thing* being passed, the way they grasped hands—Keller would cock her head to one side for a moment, then she would screech her answer. Nic had complained to his neighbor that he found her delivery somewhat braying. The neighbor, irritated, had explained that the girl was blind and deaf. "Ohhhh!" Nic exclaimed, ill-timed, as, just at that moment, a hush had fallen over the crowd, the teacher having clasped Keller's hands for another intimate fricative whisper. Dozens of hostile shoosh-winds gusted in Nic's direction. Nic scoosied himself, riveting his gaze back at the stage. Eventually the audience became bored, began to call out for the sea lion act, or Barbette the she-male trapeze artist. There was hissing and catcalling. The teacher became visibly flustered, while Helen Keller sat in her stool, smiling moronically. The questions became increasingly rude, e.g., "How does she wipe her bottom?" The questioners laughed bawdily enough to make other men seated nearby chuckle, and the teacher blush. Nic, meanwhile, had discovered a sensual pleasure in the physical manipulation of the manikin from the outside. It was a physical manipulation that felt almost improper. He pulled down the dummy's jaw, inserting his finger and tempting a bite. "The control rod is pushed through a hole in the wooden head and hooked into an eye on the torso," Nic said, quoting a book on puppet-making from memory. He chucked the dummy affectionately under the chin. Its head popped off and fell to the floor with a sharp crack. The barber's cat, which had been curled on a ledge alongside various tools of the trade, jumped and hissed. The head rolled into the corner, coming to a stop against a burlap sack filled with hair sweepings. The hair-sack disgusted Nic. It looked like a living, heaving thing. He felt an odd compulsion to stick his hand inside. "Back in the old country?" he said. "My grand-dad would tie up bags of hair and stash them around his garden, to keep away the deers and the birds and the other animals. They smell human smells, they get scared." Nic's grandfather had once made a scarecrow stuffed with human hair, in fact. Nic and his sisters cut openings in targeted portions of the scarecrow's anatomy, causing it to sprout black tufts of secondary sex characteristics: under the arms, on the face. They got a bit too excited while operating on the groin and wound up making an overly large hole, so that most of the hair stuffing the torso spilled out from between its legs, less like a tail than a diarrheic expulsion. Nic imagined shitting hair. It would probably feel nice, but Jesus. What an ugly sight. "Hey, look, Bart," Nic exclaimed, fingering the unsightliest dummy. "Funny we'd run into *your* pops here." Bart shook his head and lit another cigarette. The obvious response being, "Better here than a public toilet frequented by sailors. Say, how *is* your Nonna doing?" Bart, in this case, not making for the obvious.

"... the fat one toting a battered salesman's valise, the other pushing a ramshakle grinding wheel ..." (p. 95)

The sharpener pushes the grinding wheel, known, in northern Italian dialect, as a *mola*. It is spun by foot-pedal, its frame attached to a pair of wheelbarrow handles and a single wheel, allowing the cutlers to roll the contraption door-to-door, directly to prospective customers. A metal stalk, also attached to the frame, curves over the grindstone, budding in a cone that dribbles water from a tiny hole during the sharpening process, keeping the stone cool and moist. Knives are passed over the spinning stone in perpendicular swoops—right, left, repeat, repeat, inspect blade with thumb and eye, wipe clean, proceed to next knife—the grinder's leg all the while pumping with the exactitude of a mechanical part.

The second cutler, meanwhile, hauls the sample-case, which generally contains chef's knives, boning knives, fish knives, fruit knives, paring knives, curved butcher's knives (known in the trade as "scimitars"), all razor sharp. The second cutler's spiel consisting of lines like *Sharped knifes for all the occasion!* (Tomming up the accent helped sell the service, any spieler could tell you, the customers appreciating the old-world charm, believing it a seal of authenticity.)

Feel-her that cutter. Go-head! Be care you no open your finger. See how sharped we do?

A blade, extended: unhostile. An offering.

If the customer requires further scrutiny, the spieler peels back a sleeve—sometimes the customer's, more often his own—then, gently, shaves off a few strands of arm hair, the customer squinting for a moment at the fresh-mown birthmark before, invariably, loosing a nod of assent.

(a scene from the 1937 picture Ventriloquism and Its
Discontents*)*

Scrotti, while not, in point of fact, deaf, spent the bulk of his days
with wads of cloth stuffed deep in his ears, operating under the
mulish belief that insulation from exterior noise better developed
one's interior sound-producing abilities—a plainly ludicrous notion,
but who dared question the methodology of the greatest ventriloquist of his generation?

This self-imposed deafness explaining his continued shaving of
the dummy and otherwise wholesale ignoring of Bart and Nic, who,
eventually, tired of being disregarded, were prompted to turn to the
sample case, visual aides seeming (to Bart, initial grabber of case)
like an obvious final recourse.

There followed: a sample case, tussled over; a latch, caught in
a sleeve; a perhaps unwise amount of yanking; a latch, suddenly
sprung.

And then: knives, everywhere!—

(soaring, plummeting, spinning, narrowly missing)

—eventually resulting in:

an eyebrow, partially shaven;

a necktie, completely severed;

a shoe, staked to the floor;

the shoulders of a coat, pinned to a barber's chair, its sleeves torn
free only seconds before a knife pierces the phantom groin-area of
the chair's just-liberated resident;

an eleven-inch butcher's knife, caught upon Bart's suspender strap;

Bart's suspender strap, caught upon Nic's wrist, and stretched
back like a sling;

the eleven-inch blade of the butcher's knife, facing Bart when the strap is inadvertently released;

this last bit looking pretty bad;

and yet, midway through the snap-back, the knife, somehow, flips, with the handle bopping Bart in the sternum and the blade slicing his suspenders, leaving Bart with approximately two seconds to stare at the knife, agog, before his pants drop.

Also, the shaved dummy is decapitated.

No one else is injured.

Afterwards, Scrotti, who had taken cover behind the second barber's chair, rises and pulls the wads of cloth from his ears. This takes some time. The cloth-wads are lengthy, and gilded with wax. Finally, when he has finished, he says—*speaks*—his lips visibly moving: "You boys think you could do that again?"

(Pierce, Hylo. A Funny Thing Happened on the Way to
Mr. Mayer's Office . . . Revisiting the Golden Age of Film
Comedy. New York: Little, Brown, 1988.)

After another feeble showing with the 1931 stinker *Counter-Revolutionaries*, which finds the boys playing soda jerks and stooping to gags involving loose waitresses and Limburger cheese, Sacco and Vanzetti were truly adrift, their studio backing tenuous and their longtime manager, Danny "Fritz" Lapidus, publicly expressing concern as to their ability to ever recapture a mass audience. But soon after the *Counter-Revolutionaries* debacle, Bart and Nic began work on a feature that would change everything.

It was called *A Couple of Sharpies*, and with it, the boys, essentially, created a sub-genre all their own—the "knife-grinder" comedy. The plots of these pictures, all remarkably similar, hinged on at least one member of the duo (but generally both) portraying a knife grinder, which allowed for increasingly intricate slapstick scenarios involving no stunt doubles and extremely sharp blades. The genre was perfected over the course of twelve knife-grinder pictures, the best-known of which include *The Daily Grind* (1934), *Whichever Way You Slice It* (1936), *A Couple of Wops in a Jam* (1944), *A Couple of Cut-Ups* (1946) and *Sacco and Vanzetti Take One More Stab* (1949).

A Couple of Sharpies set the template with the classic "All Thumbs" routine, a deceptively simple bit that has been widely imitated but never truly repeated. (Though often described as Abbott and Costello's 'Who's on First?' replayed with knives, it's worth noting that "All Thumbs" debuted nearly a decade earlier.) The sequence begins with Sacco attempting to hand Vanzetti a knife, blade-forward. Vanzetti, who is nearly cut, angrily tells Sacco to pass the knife *handle*-forward. Sacco assumes this means *he* must hold the knife by the blade, and so begins to flip the knife around, at which point Vanzetti shouts "No!" and Sacco, startled, whips the blade back in Vanzetti's direction, slicing off the tip of his cigar. This continues for some time, and remains, on the level of velocity and rhythm alone, a marvel to behold, even to eyes jaded by today's computer-generated effects. After several near-geldings and -guttings, wrists are grabbed, ties commingle and Sacco and Vanzetti find themselves face to face, the knife, now between them, pointing at the sky. Whose hands are whose has become, by this point, quite unclear. Eventually, a three-count is agreed upon. On three—after several requisite false-starts—they jerk apart, and the knife, unfurled from hands and ties, shoots straight up in spinning-dart fashion, embedding itself in the ceiling. (The gag continues for several more minutes, involving a shaky attempted-boost, with its attendant crushed fingers and crotch-in-the-face, the blade meanwhile having poked through the floor of the room upstairs, a dance studio, in which the oily instructor, attempting to seduce a student during a lesson, must fox-trot around it, to a particularly speedy Duke Ellington number, as the bumblers below yank and rethrust.)

The riskiness of the knife sequences increased precipitously from picture to picture. As the routines became more complex, S&V rose to the occasion with a vigor unseen in their previous work, and arguably unrivalled in the work of their peers. By balancing their comedy on a *literal* razor's edge of tragedy, many of these bits remain enthralling to this day, worthy of mention, on a level of sheer kinetics, alongside greats like Keaton and Astaire. (Other comics attempted to imitate the Sacco and Vanzetti knife technique, with generally middling to disastrous results. Most famously, Harold Lloyd severed an Achilles tendon while attempting to back-kick a cheese knife into a bin while blindfolded. Bootleg footage of Lloyd, shrieking and bleeding as he collapses into a fetal position, the laughing extras taking several moments to realize the boss isn't clowning, reputedly circled Hollywood for years, though this writer has never seen it himself, nor does he especially wish to.)

The knives also lent themselves ably to the assertively high-concept scenario—for instance, in the 1946 feature *Sacco and Vanzetti Meet the New Gymnosophy*, the plot of which hinges upon S&V, as a pair of grinders, delivering knives to a secret Adamites' colony, where, as per the rules of the colony, they must shed their clothes. The combination of elaborate knife-gags and an entirely nude cast—never, of course, revealing inappropriate body parts—makes for a virtuosic level of choreography. Due to the complexity and cost involved in setting up such elaborate scenes, many of the film's shots were *single takes*. To this day, *The New Gymnosophy* is endlessly dissected by film scholars and merely marveled at by the average lay viewer. (A personal favorite scene would be the kitchen "swordfight" between Vanzetti and the head chef, the latter employing a pair of ten-inch butcher's knives, the former armed only with a sharpening steel.)

As the knife-stunt scenes grew increasingly (forgive the pun) edgy, it almost seemed as if the pair were pushing themselves to a manic degree, as if the level of danger would never be enough, as if each new triumph had immediately dissolved into an even more severe disappointment. In *Never a Dull Moment*, we find Vanzetti behind the wheel of a knife van—the old-fashioned sort, with a grinding wheel right in back—his face scarved by a ridiculously large road map, while Sacco, behind him, continues sharpening. The Vanzetti-piloted van jumps a sidewalk curb, narrowly missing a group of jaywalking children and a blind man, and barrels the wrong way down a one-way street, while in back, knives fly like porcupine quills, all narrowly dodged by a somersaulting Sacco, who also, repeatedly, grinds his own nose and chin on the wheel. For the gag's punchline, the van careens through the safety railing of a winding mountain road, rolls down the side of a steep incline and crashes to a halt against a jagged rock formation. Vanzetti crawls from the wreckage, wails and has already begun the rending of garments when the back door of the van falls open and Sacco, his outfit cut into high-fashion frills, his hair hacked into a sort of prototypical mohawk, the edges of his mustache now pointing *up*—but otherwise unbloodied!—staggers forth to deliver the film's final line, which could, of course, be nothing other than, "We there yet?" (It should go without noting that the crash sequence was one of the few *not* actually enacted by Sacco and Vanzetti.)

Children, always a large part of the S&V fan base, were beginning to find this stuff scary, and so, toward the end of their careers—when the slapstick comedy team was, in any event, becoming a lost art—they returned to more generalized shtick, leaving their best work behind them. Oddly enough, though, a demonstrable tension remains when one watches the best of those old scenes, even today, *today*, when Sacco and Vanzetti, when their cinematographer, when their directors and lighting-technicians and sound-crew, all are long dead. This tension should no longer exist. There is no reason to be afraid for the men we are watching. And yet, we are. (This viewer is, at any rate.)

These scenes also open themselves to a wide variety of interpretation. A number of critics have called the knives stand-ins for death, arguing that the clowning antics of S&V are a victory, of sorts, against our own fragility and mortality. They see the constant dodging of these knives as a sort of transcendence, a celebration, reading onto these scenes a joyous quality that, in the end, becomes life-*affirming*. (Most famously, *Cahiers du Cinema* editor André Bazin described a sequence in *A Couple of Cut-Ups* as "a kinetic form of gospel music, church-as-dance.")

Others have put forward a darker view, watching these same scenes and detecting less triumph than hysteria. Yes, death, in any of these scenarios, is dodged, once again. And yet, the perils remain. They will return. They always do. The world of Sacco and Vanzetti, after all, is filled with such dangers. While Buster Keaton famously insisted his stunts had to be possible in real life, the hyper-calamitous films of Sacco and Vanzetti make no such promise, as if rather insisting *anything* can happen . . . so watch out!

One final note: it would take several chapters to adequately detail the controversy that dogged S&V for the latter half of their careers. I'm referring, of course, to the Bonapace lawsuit, ultimately settled out of court after a protracted legal struggle and preliminary trial, but remaining a source of contention to this day. In brief, Sacco and Vanzetti partisans will argue that Bonapace made his claims *years* after Sacco and Vanzetti had incorporated grinding into their act; those sympathetic to Bonapace would counter that the poor immigrant knife-sharpener had few recourses to legal aide early on, and that he had patiently awaited a good-faith promise by Sacco and Vanzetti of recompense and ultimate crediting of his act. Further muddying the case is the fact that both sides were able to produce witnesses from the old neighborhood claiming to have seen both plaintiff and defendants performing an early version of the knife act well before the other side's claimed 'invention' of said act. So much speculative ink has been bled on this topic, I hesitate to take any further space doing so myself, particularly in a book meant to celebrate, not expose peccadilloes. (Though it is worth pointing out that both men vehemently denied all charges, with Sacco, in particular, never expressing anything less than contempt for Bonapace "the gold-digging wop.")

ALL JIVE ASIDE

Later that week, Bart and Nic made their vaudeville debut at the Paladin Theater in Chinatown, Scrotti himself, after witnessing the impromptu cutlery slapstick routine, having offered the pair a headlining slot. (For the normally unpleasable Professore, a first.)

"All jive aside," he'd said that afternoon in his shop. "And I do not say that lightly."

Scrotti's voice, out of practice when it came to conventional speech, no longer quite synchronized itself with the movement of his lips. Listeners often found this effect disconcerting.

Later, Bart wondered if they should have been so unreflecting in their acceptance.

"I'm open," Nic insisted, "to a wide variety of reflection."

"Well, for one," Bart began, "our acceptance of the gig will necessitate our recreating the stunt."

"So what's your point?"

"It was a fluke. An accident. We'd never done anything like that before. We're not jugglers. We're not knife-throwers. We have no training. We really have no business appearing on this program."

"Can you get to the objections, already?"

"A strong likelihood of severe maiming."

"You gonna tease this out much longer?"

"A not unlikely possibility of bleeding to death in front of a paying audience."

"Beats pushing that wheel."

This was, perhaps, true.

All of this was back at their flat. Bart had slipped into the lower bunk, the lip of his nightcap pulled over his eyes. He could hear Nic having at the clawfoot tub, a few feet away. It was weekly-bath night. A sustained battle would be forthcoming, Bart knew. Nic's speech had been punctuated by splashes, garglings and percussive porcelain echoes.

"Here's a thought," Bart said. "We put together a set of special performance knives."

"You suggesting we take the edges off?"

(Grinders can undo their work as easy as a surgeon or cobbler.)

"Thus," Bart continued, "minimizing risk, but not the perception thereof."

"You suggesting *we cheat our fans?*"

Bart opened his eyes. His lashes tingled as they brushed the nightcap, sending a static charge through his cheeks.

"We have no fans!" he shouted.

The ceiling's bare bulb, seen through the cap's pale gray cloth, looked like a moon obscured by smoke. Bart closed his eyes again.

Nic said, "Is there any wonder, with you as a partner?"

The following afternoon, they met Scrotti at the Paladin an hour before showtime. Nic had insisted upon wearing an ill-fitting yellow tuxedo, which he revealed with a showman's pizzazz, snapping off his overcoat *voila!*-style, the coat the white cloth, himself the candlelit dinner for two. Without swiveling his head on his barrel-neck, Scrotti allowed his gaze to float from Bart's workaday grays to Nic's just-about parody of *hoit*, with its gratuitous frills and vestigial collars, white kerchiefs protruding from every unclaimed slot.

Bart coughed, then mumbled, "Here we are."

"Right," Scrotti said. "I like it." Nic, beaming, gave the Professor a command performance, a tossed-off soft-shoe routine that ended in a splay-armed squat.

"What I can appreciate is, it's a look, a definite look," Scrotti continued. "People need to be able to tell you two apart. Discernment is elemental to comedy. If you confuse, if you force *thinking*, you're standing in the way of the laugh. Worrying which of you is which should never be high in the audience's concerns. Not that, with you two—" Here, Scrotti paused, giving Nic's gut a deferential nod. "But, still. A professional never begrudges an extra cue."

Eventually, they were introduced to the rest of the bill. There was Borrah Minevitch and his Harmonica Rascals, a musical act, and the Chinese magician, Ching Ling Soo, and Barbette, the world-famous French cross-dresser and trapeze artist, and El Brendel, the Swedish dialect comic, and Aunt Jemima, a blackface singer, along with a juggler, a yodeler, a vamp, a sea lion act, a comic drunk, a bickering husband-and-wife song-and-dance team, an Irish crooner, a fast-change artist, and a young kid by the name of Durante with a nose like a battered fist and only a handful of jokes to distract from it.

"I realize," Scrotti began, "a certain level of resentment might be engendered by my eleventh-hour filling of the coveted headlining slot with a heretofore unknown comic duo."

Nic, on cue, flicked a wing of his bowtie, hoping (Bart assumed) for a spiffy windmill effect. Instead, the tie (wrong one, a clip-on) sprung from its neck-berth and pecked Ching Ling Soo in the eye, causing the Chinaman to emit a pained squeal, followed by a stream of indecipherable curses. Scrotti waited patiently for Ching Ling Soo to calm himself before proceeding.

"As our new colleague has just illustrated, there is a fine line between the comic and the extremely sore. To that end, if—"

Scrotti paused and attempted to knock on El Brendel's forehead. Brendel, apparently used to this gag, dodged the rap and flashed an inane grin.

"If an accident occurs," Scrotti continued, "none of you will be forced to follow a severed thumb."

Also, Scrotti pointed out, audiences will stick around for a defiance of Death, as long as they sense a possibility of Death beating the house odds and triumphing over the would-be defier. Death, though, had to have a shot. And so, naturally, one withholds, for as long as possible, deliverance of whatever happens to be keeping people in their seats.

"And Barbette, though I realize you float above such petty concerns and would certainly never stoop to pointing this out, I want to be on record as saying that, of course, you defy Death every day. Twice if there's a matinee performance. But it must also be acknowledged that your act forefronts beauty and motion over Death-defiance, and thus remains more akin to aerial ballet than mere stuntwork."

Despite Barbette's carefully crafted public persona of queenly indolence, unmussable even when executing a flying Inverted Crucifix from fifty feet—a maneuver which Barbette could, indeed, perform as if she were an androgynous angel, floating from swing to swing as if the trapezes were neighboring clouds—Bart detected a visible melt in the heat of such expertly delivered flattery.

"He's good," Nic whispered.

After Scrotti ticked through a list of minor technicalities, the assembled cast and crew dispersed themselves throughout the hive and a certain showtime-approacheth bustle began to kick in, humidifying the air. Bart, for his part, felt a familiar, opposing sense, one of impending disarray.

"Hate to nag," he told Nic, "but I really think winging this one is not, perhaps, the best—"

"You sweating it, pal?" Nic asked. "You shouldn't sweat it. No good for you."

"I'm just suggesting now—"

"Me? Skipping stairs on the way up generates more sweat."

"—might be the perfect opportunity for—"

"Let me tell you: sweating it will have about as much an impact, in the end, as closing your eyes and making a wish."

"—slipping outside and working out of some sort of routine?"

"Why didn't you say so?" Nic asked. "That *does* seem like a clever plan. Wise, wise, wise. Let me just meet you right back here in approximately two to seven minutes." He gave his belly a gentle bongo slap. "I need to seek out the commissary. If no such place exists, a nearby chop-suey joint. But I will be back."

Bart had tuned out at seems, knowing better than to expect a return, knowing, too, that even if Nic managed to take care of lunch in a timely fashion and subsequently agreed to iron out the routine, any prep-work would merely be incorporated into the ensuant disarray.

With that in mind, he settled in to watch the show. Borrah Minevich and his Harmonica Rascals opened, Minevich mugging shamelessly while his Rascals jigged and blew. Bart, decidedly underwhelmed, could not help but feel the concept of an all-harmonica orchestra lacked a certain subtlety.

Borrah himself alternated between working the crowd and mock-conducting the Rascals. At one point in the performance, he even broke into song, though his delivery hewed closer to recitation, with a certain hiccupy bounce. For "The Curse of the Aching Heart," he donned a turban and squinted his eyes in what was apparently meant to pass for Near East fashion. "Der's a Boat Dat's Leavin' for New York" was treated with more of a coon-shout and shuffle. Throughout, no matter what foolishness he happened to be perpetrating with the rest of his body, Borrah's own face retained a moony, simpleton's cock—as if certain a revelation of great import not only impended, but would be spoken quickly, and in *sotto voce*, and he did not wish to miss a single word. Which was not (Bart thought) a quality befitting a star, who, after all, should be the one being eavesdropped upon, the one being espied. Though some aspect of Borrah's utter scrutability obviously appealed to a crowd.

It was a tight set, give him that, Borrah clearly understanding the advantage the Rascals possessed over an outfit like, say, Prima Scala's accordion-based orchestra—namely, mobility. The overall choreography worked as a sort of manic anti-choreography, keeping the audience convinced a spectacular collision was imminent, with the Rascals zigging and zagging the length and breadth of the stage. Throughout the chaos, the midget Rascal—who, naturally, wielded the heftiest mouth organ—took every opportunity to slide, with a flourish, between Borrah's legs. This last maneuver may have been performed twice too often, but no matter. The crowd ate it up.

"Yumping yiminy, that's some kind of teaming, huh?" noted El Brendel, who had sidled over to Bart's corner of the stage.

Bart nodded. "So I take it," Brendel continued, dropping the sing-song delivery, as well as any traces of Scandanavia, "you'd be the straight man of the team?"

Bart tasted the lower bristles of his mustache and took a quick survey of the faux-Swede. El Brendel wore a ludicrously tailored plaid suit, of the variety that could go either way—costume or not— but that, if sincere, would certainly match his civilian accent, that of a corn-fed Midwestern huckleberry. His orbular face reminded Bart, for some reason, of a molded cheese, perhaps because it was almost entirely hairless, a slight accretion of skin at eyes' edges the only betrayers of age.

"Straight," Bart said, "seems my lot."

"Lamentably," Barbette trilled, floating past within a nimbus of feather and sequins. Gazing over her shoulder at Brendel, she added, "As for *your* lot, you'll need to stuff a few more socks in those trousers to pass for Swiss, let alone Swedish."

Brendel fired off a barrage of rude kissing noises at Barbette's retreating plumage. Turning back to Bart, he grinned, "She's a funny faggot, ain't she? But anyway. Straight-manning. That's always struck me as the heaviest lifting of a team, not to mention most underrated. What do you say, boss?"

Bart shrugged, but before he could answer, Brendel went on: "Interesting dynamic, there, got to say. I never partnered up, myself. But yeah. Bad marriages. Historically funny. Classic-funny. Right? Less you're in one."

On stage, the Rascals froze, the harmonicas lodged—no hands!—between their lips like grotesque, grafted-on Sambo grins. The crowd hooted approvingly.

Brendel continued, "Conventional wisdom's got the straight man, yourself, acting as a moderating force on his counterpart. Is that true, though? 'Cause it seems to me, if you're standing there, time and again, watching while your partner snips ties or chunks pies or gives coppers the old hot-foot, you can flatten your hat 'til your chin starts to sag, but you're still part of the problem, tacit-like, as they say. Ain't you?"

Bart shrugged and began, "Well, it's funny, I—" Just then, the Rascals, having taken their final bow, shuffled past Bart and Brendel in a musky line. As the applause worked towards a crescendo, Minevich sopped his brow with a rag, scowled at his boys, and finally nodded at the stage, whereupon the Rascals hustled back into the glare.

Bart watched for a moment. "I've considered," he said, "the fact that I may have latched myself to the likes of Nic to live out a vicarious anarchy, and perhaps goad it along as well." He paused. He had, in fact, given a fair amount of thought to what going through life as Nic might mean. The appeal being the absence of bounds, of course, an utter lack of beholdeness to any convention, the ability to stroll right up to whoever you wished and say howdy-doo or *va fungoo*. To disrupt a masked ball. Sic moths on a haberdasher's. Spin yourself dizzy in a revolving doorway, in the process eluding an irate bellhop. The ability to enter a crowded pie-shop and see *nothing but possibility.*

The disappeal, then, being the realization that going through life so boundlessly would drive nearly anyone nuts. There's a reason people square themselves. One must limit one's options. One chooses a wife, a job, a certain number of children. One makes a trip to the store and takes the same route, proceeding in a fashion that's been tested and deemed most efficient, most reasonable. Perhaps people go farther than necessary. Bart wasn't sure. He'd considered the fact that he may have always wanted something else, and simply not had the guts, and so found Nic instead.

"I've considered this," Bart finally went on, then cleared his throat. "So, how did you work up your act?"

Brendel sighed. "Granddad on my mom's side was off-the-boat Swedish. Always thought he talked funny." He snorted and mimed a masturbatory act. "My act's bullshit. Yours is the bee's knees, we all been told. Where you guys been hiding yourselves?"

"Here and there. We . . . did some shows out West. Chicago's been good to us."

"Yeah. Huh. Well, what I was starting to say—"

The Rascals began making their way offstage for the second time, grinning and pumping their hats, though the moment they passed beyond the audience's line of sight, the grins dropped away and their eyes went dead. The first pair of Rascals grabbed Bart, each taking an arm.

"Pardo—" Bart began, not prepared for the fist in his stomach, courtesy of the third Rascal, the big brute of a tenor. Bart made a noise. He sounded like someone trying to inflate a sack by humming. Doubled over, Bart willed himself not to vomit, concentrating instead on his feet as he felt himself being dragged in the direction of the stage door. Hazily, he watched the floor recede through the slow-panning V formed by his tattered shoes, their soles flapping loose like meat from a bone left too long in stew. Where was Scrotti?

They tossed him outside. The stage door swung too far open, in broken-spine fashion, banging against the outer wall of the alley to produce a tympanic echo. As the last Rascal kicked the door shut, the first two propelled Bart over a trash bin, then propped him up as the others massed in a tight phalanx.

Oddly, Bart did not feel afraid, but more like inappropriately exhilarated. Maybe there was something to what had, frankly, seemed like a rather superficial interpretation of his personality. Maybe he thrived on disruptions from the norm, but lacked the genetic capability to be the direct agent of said disruption. Maybe something inside him thrived on being *acted upon*.

Back in the theater, he could hear gasps and applause. Ching Ling Soo was making something disappear.

His vision flickered in the direction of the mouth of the alley, which, glimpsed between the hostile faces, seemed a faraway, flipped-telescope perspective. He thought he could make out passing Chinamen on the twilit street beyond, and vaguely considered a cry for help. He remembered strolling through the neighborhood one evening and coming across a crowd of Chinamen thronged around a man selling some unknown wares from a cardboard box. It turned out to be live pigeons. With a practiced move, the entrepreneur would pluck a bird from the box, yank up its wings and twist them together, once, and then again, tight as the bottom end of a paper funnel, before stuffing the crippled thing into a bag and passing it to the next customer.

The faces parted, and Borrah and Brendel squeezed into the breach. Brendel had assumed a blank, almost curious stare, as if he'd stumbled across some unfamiliar breed of dog. Borrah, meanwhile, had completely battened his bay-window gaze, his eyes, now a sentry's peering through the slat in the door, unwelcoming and certainly not impressed.

"We have not officially met," Borrah said.

"He ain't the friendliest," Brendel said. "I tried friendly."

"The other struck me as friendlier," Borrah said.

"Yeah, where is Fatty, by the way?" Brendel asked. "We never got around to that."

Bart managed a single-shouldered shrug. To make sure the gesture was not misinterpreted as dismissive, Bart added, as an afterthought, a crooked half-grin, which he hoped would have a softening effect. Borrah slapped his face.

"Do you know I once beat a man to death with a harmonica? This was right before a show. Then I went on and played that very harmonica. A red mist floated out with every note I blew. People later told me it looked like I was trying to conjure a devil."

"He never played better," Brendel said.

"I played like shit," Borrah snapped. "I'd just killed a man! You think I'm concentrating on playing a fucking harmonica?"

"I was just trying to improve the story," Brendel said.

"Yeah, well maybe retell it in a Swedish accent, you stupid fucking Polack," Borrah said.

"I'm actually more Polish than Swede," Brendel explained to Bart.

"Look," Borrah said, "we are all professional people here. We follow an informal yet time-honored guideline known in the business as professional courtesy. All that's happening right now is curiosity. We are wondering how a couple of guineas can show up from nowhere and take over our gig. You got some kind of guinea-thing over Scrotti? That your story?"

When Bart failed to respond, he heard one of the Rascals stage-whisper, "You want me to squeeze his nuts, boss?"

Borrah shook his head. "If his nuts need squeezing, I will handle that personally." He leaned closer to Bart.

A breeze from the far end of the alley passed over the back of Bart's neck, cooling a trickle of sweat. Bart still felt inappropriately calm. His absence of fear, in fact, reminded him of one of Nic's pet theories—namely, if one was willing to ignore the world's stated laws, one could get away with far more than one would imagine. By "laws" Nic did not simply mean the man-made variety, but also, for instance, the law of gravity, which was why, he insisted, their knife-stunt had worked. One passes through life (Nic's argument, here) accepting in a rock-hard ground, an up-sky, a sun that melts all ice. In this way, the world seems immutable. But if—Nic, again, insisting—you are willing to ignore these laws, they might well ignore you.

As a rule, Bart tuned out Nic's more willfully fatuous pronouncements, designed, or so they seemed, primarily to bait him. But in this case, he'd come around to the idea of a pliancy in the world. Or, rather: how the mere belief in such pliancy might allow one to slip around patently existent laws far more easily than if one acknowledges their presence and operates under the assumption that ignoring them will result in the dire. Perhaps it was a question of confidence, similar to the budding-thief's epiphany that stealing often comes down to choice more than skill, that the world is chockfull of objects easily taken, thus shifting the question to the size of one's sack, and what to leave behind.

"So what's this knife bit?" Borrah asked. "I know members of your tribe excel at the quick-change acts. I once saw a dago in Philly perform all of *Rigoletto* in seven minutes. Whereas your act, from the way it has been described, is sounding to me closer in spirit to a knockabout act, which is traditionally the purview of the Irishman. Sounds to me like you two smack each other around like a couple of Micks, only with knives. Take the whole thing one step further."

"Well, to be honest, we're not profess—" Bart began.

"I been thinking about Scrotti's little speech, before the show," Borrah continued. "Defying Death, and all that business. So here's a question for you, along those lines. How cut up do you have to get before it stops being funny? For instance, can you actually draw blood, or does that cross the line? Let me give you another example. Let's consider an alternate comic situation involving danger. Let's say you've got your comedian, your clown, in an office building. His hat blows out the window. He climbs onto the ledge to fetch it. And go-figure, who'd-a thunk, *he slips!* And he falls. And he finds himself hanging from the minute hand of the giant clock-face on the side of this building, thirty stories up."

"I think I seen this one," one of the Rascals interjected.

"Quiet," Borrah snapped. "Now, so far this is funny, right? I mean, I am a musician. I'm no comedian. I'm asking you. But I think I can safely predict your answer, which would be yes, despite the mortal danger in which our clown finds himself, there's something humorous about this situation. So let's keep going. Let's pull in tighter, for a close-up on his hands, clutching this clock-hand for dear life, white-knuckled and sweaty and sloooowly slipping. Still funny, though, right? I would say yes. Cut to his feet, a-dangling there, pumping wild like he's trying to pedal the air. That is always funny. Cut to the hat. Can't forget the hat. Reason he's in this whole mess. Cut to the hat, which gets caught by a gust of wind and blows off the ledge. The clown makes a grab for it, he clamps the thing on his head and then we get a brief pause where both clown and audience realize, concurrent-like, that he's used *both hands*, and now he is hanging in space. We get an *uh-oh* face. And then he begins to plummet. Hysterical! Tell me it's not. Okay. Next we get a close-up of his mouth, him screaming as he's falling. We shoot so far down his throat we catch his tonsils quivering like a tuning fork. Still a gas. Cut to a longer shot of him going down, a shot from above, his arms and legs working like a pinned bug's. This is all terrific stuff. Now. Here is my question. My real question. Why does it stop being funny if he hits the concrete? Let's say he does. Smack!" Borrah slapped his hands for emphasis. "An explosion of fallen clown. Passers-by get splattered with fallen-clown-guts. We could make the passers-by millionaires. Which makes the joke funnier, right? I mean, we would laugh if they got spattered with mud. But no one is laughing. And so my question is, is this a flaw in the joke, its execution, or does it have to do with us as people, who cannot fully appreciate a joke when it reaches its logical conclusion? What's the problem? But here I am yapping away, and you're the comic talent, and I'm just a shticky band leader. Really, though: what's the problem with my joke?"

Bart coughed nervously, seemed ready to speak, paused. Then, finally: "I'd make it worse."

"What's that?"

"Worse. Than what you said. A direct splat is not funny. But maybe he lands in a grid of live electrical wire, which happens to be just below. Or a passing nail-truck. A tank of piranhas, being wheeled to an aquarium."

There was a silence.

"Or, I don't know," Bart continued. "What if he bounced?"

Borrah chuckled. "Bounced?" he said.

"And then he lands on a kitten," Bart added.

An even longer silence followed. Then they all started laughing, Borrah first, then Brendel, soon every last Rascal. Tears welled in every eye. Faces contorted. Even Bart—and as straight-man, one cannot commit a more cardinal sin—even Bart laughed until his lungs began to dully ache. Until, at a certain point, he noticed—still unable to stop laughing, which was funny in itself—he noticed Borrah nod at one of the Rascals, who pulled a bottle from his coat pocket, doused a handkerchief and pressed it to Bart's face. Bart's laughter was now muffled and incorporating some rather intense fumes. The last thing Bart heard was Borrah choke-laughing out the words:

"Shame

"you
"gon'
"miss
"curtain."

In his dream, Bart stood on the grounds of a vast estate. Its sprawling lawns extended in every direction. The grass, however, had fallen parched. Just a few dozen yards away, Bart spotted a garden hose connected to a spigot. Glancing down at his own rough dress, he realized, immediately, that he was the groundskeeper. Bart picked up the hose and went to work. He watched, with immense satisfaction, as the water made a brilliant arc in the clear summer light. As he adjusted its flow with his thumb, he reflected on how rewarding certain tasks—so simple, yet possible to complete with a degree of absolute perfection—could be. At that moment, abruptly, the flow of water ceased. The once-solid stream froze, mid-arc, plummeting rudely to earth in the form of thousands of individual droplets. As a final trickle leaked over the tip of Bart's thumb, he felt himself become surprisingly enraged. Winding the end of the hose around his wrist, he peered, one-eyed, into the nozzle, thinking he might squint out some obvious, removable blockage. At this point, without warning, the water began to flow again, now with the force of a geyser, pummeling his face, momentarily blinding him, and giving his shirt a rather thorough dousing. As he hurled the hose to the ground, Bart heard a giggle. Whirling about, he spotted a little boy clutching the far end of the hose. Holding it aloft for display, the boy bent the hose and once again stanched the water's flow. Laughing all the while, he bent and unbent the hose several times, as if Bart were a dull audience member who needed the joke carefully and repeatedly explained. Snarling, Bart charged the boy, intending to give him a tanning to remember. But after his first steps, his legs became entangled in the hose, and he tumbled down a hill, which he had either not noticed or which had magically appeared. As he rolled through the spiny grass, the hose wrapped him in a python's grip, water spraying him at irregular intervals, the boy's cackle echoing at some level of distance. He opened his mouth to scream.

He awoke on a pallet, in the rear of a dimly lit basement. A Chinaman sat at a desk against an adjacent wall, copying Oriental script from a scroll to a book. Dozens of birdcages hung from the ceiling, the majority populated with multicolored Chinese songbirds, all serenading one another. Bart threw the blanket from his lower extremities and righted himself. The Chinaman glanced back at the sound of the pallet's creak, Bart unsure how he'd been detected over the incessant chirruping. As if reading his thoughts, the Chinaman grinned and gestured at the cages.

"For Chinese, this radio," he said.

Bart nodded and stood. Now that the man faced him, Bart could tell that he was in fact a white man who had disguised himself as a Chinese. He wore a long satin robe and a Mandarin beard and mustache that appeared pasted-on. Crudely applied black make-up exaggerated the sharpness at the corners of his eyes. The "Chinaman" stood with Bart and performed an approximation of an Oriental bow.

"Doctor Yee," he said.

Bart pushed past him to a staircase leading up.

"Why aren't you Chinese?" he asked. "Where am I?"

The birds' singing increased in cacophony and volume. Doctor Yee said, "I solve-y crime. I top-one detective."

As Bart bounded up the stairs, he heard Doctor Yee calling out after him, "I solve-y *you* crime, cheap-cheap. Like bird! I like bird. Cheap-cheap."

Outside, Bart found himself in the heart of Chinatown. It had become quite dark. Bart, sure he had missed his curtain call, began a frantic dash in the direction of the theater. Chinatown was no easy racecourse. The streets remained crowded, even at dusk. Bart jostled his way past strolling families, hunched ancients, a man selling eels from a barrel. As Bart approached, the eel-monger dropped one of his eels and it began to slither down the sidewalk.

A little girl walking in the opposite direction pointed and howled, "Look, mommy, a snake!"

As he chased his eel, the monger paused and scolded, "Not snake! Eel!"

Bart had no time to reflect upon this scene. More than anything, he did not want to be late. His concern, he knew, made little sense; it felt, in fact, like an extension of his dream, like nonsensical but futile-to-resist dream-logic.

In the alley beside the theater, Barbette leaned against a wall, pulling on a cigarette through a holder and crumbling her pet bulldog Dozer bits of an orange-colored scone.

"A professional daredevil never takes risks when it comes to curtain time, monsieur," Barbette noted.

Ignoring her, Bart burst through the stage door, shoving his way past young Durante, the crooner O'Leary and a startled cluster of Rascals. Scrotti prowled the edge of the stage, looking frantic. The moment he spotted Bart, he pounced, grasping him by the lapels.

"Where have you two been?" he hissed. "I had to send Ching Ling Soo back out there. He's been stalling for ten minutes now. The kid's about to start pulling flowers out of his assho—"

"Long," Bart gasped. "Story." After his wheezing subsided, he continued, "Where's Nic?"

"He's not with you?" Scrotti cried.

"Present and accountable!" Nic called out, emerging from a dressing room. His tuxedo looked more disheveled than before, and now sported an assortment of stains, all inclining toward an unpleasant shade of brown.

"Our luck," one of the Rascals muttered. "*Doofus ex machina.*"

"What the hell happened to you?" Scrotti asked. "Never mind. Just get out there."

"Aunt Jemima," Nic whispered to Bart. "You know she's Italian? Real name's Teresina."

"Shoe polish on your tongue," Bart said.

"Yeah," Nic said.

There was no time to discuss the act. The curtain dropped. They rushed past a scowling, winded Ching Ling Soo. The curtain rose. As the audience whistled, Bart glanced at Nic, realizing, at once, that Nic did not have the sample case of knives. Nic grinned, shrugged. Flashed the crowd his brown tongue. He was met with silence, followed by a smattering of Bronx cheers.

Bart heard a whistle, stage-right. Turning, he saw Aunt Jemima holding the sample case. She shook the case above her head, then slid it across the stage. The moment Bart lifted the case, though, he knew something was amiss. It felt too light. Beyond that, something inside seemed to be moving.

The crowd stared at him expectantly. Clearing his throat, he said, "Well, at least we have this sample case of knives, here, now. Sure hope we don't cut ourselves!"

There was another minor eruption of boos. He tried to conceive of a smooth way to slip backstage and determine the problem.

Nic, sensing his hesitation, said, "Hey, how's about we just open that right now?" As he spoke, he made a grab for the case.

Bart kept his grip, tight. "Sure, pal. But first, let me duck backstage a minute, okay?"

"Just open it."

"Backstage a-sec."

"Why you wanna be such a little bitch?"

"I think—"

"Too much."

"I really think—"

"Now!"

The latch popped. The case dropped. They both tumbled backwards as it burst open and a half-dozen pigeons, their wings broken, fell to the stage. Certain elements in the crowd chuckled. Others hissed. As the birds staggered to and fro, Bart sat up, groggily. Nic attempted, in vain, to grab a bird. He let another peck him in the face. No laughs.

"Where are your knives, you stupid wops?" someone yelled.

Catcalls followed. In the wings, Bart could see Scrotti making some sort of crazed hand gesture, though not being a theatrical professional, he had no idea what the gesture signified.

Another member of the crowd tossed something onto the stage. It struck the wood with a loud crack and slid between a trio of pigeons, who squawked in fright. Bart instinctively flinched.

It was a pocketknife.

"There's your knife!" the thrower shouted. "Now do us a goddamn trick already!"

The crowd roared its approval. Bart stared at Nic. They both looked at the knife. Nic dropped the pigeon he'd been mock-throttling. Bart sighed. Nic nodded. Bart flipped from a backsided hand-lean to a frontal sprinter's stance. Nic raised an eyebrow and gave an impressed little nod. They dived, simultaneously.

The sound of their heads, colliding, resounded with stunning acoustic force. The audience collectively winced. Scrotti, from the wings, averted his eyes. After the sympathetic groans died, a pregnant silence fell over the house. Bart, fleetingly, found himself back on the dream-lawn, only now the grass had become thick and verdant. And the hose worked just fine. Bart took a break from his watering to enjoy a long, cool sip. Out of the corner of his eye, he spotted the mischievous little boy, unconscious and bound with thick cable to a tree.

The silence was finally punctured by a single, protracted laugh.

Soon, a second audience member joined in, then another. Bart and Nic, still unconscious, lay center-stage. The knife remained unopened. A handful of hobbled pigeons writhed around the scene's perimeter. Scrotti, who had begun to motion for someone to lower the curtain, picked up on the growing momentum of laughter and lifted a hand. The Rascals looked at each other and nodded with grudging admiration. "Not a bad gag," one muttered. Borrah stared at Brendel, shrugged, gave a weak smile. Eventually, Scrotti whispered something to the yodeler and the sea lion trainer, who jogged onstage and grabbed the clowns by their legs, slowly dragging each into an opposite wing.

As he was being pulled along the wooden floor, Bart could vaguely make out the laughter. He felt like he was floating on his back, on water. When he attempted to crack an eye, a blur of colors and lights blinded him. He shut his eye again.

If he had been able to focus, he would have witnessed Sacco and Vanzetti's first-ever standing ovation.

"I know members of your tribe excel at the quick-change acts."
(p. 122)

Leopoldo Fregoli (1867-1936) was the most famous of the so-called "quick-change artists." According to *Who's Who of Victorian Cinema*, Fregoli's acts included *Maestri di Musica*, in which he performed a whirlwind series of impersonations of composers such as Verdi, Wagner and Rossini. He could also enact an entire trial, changing costumes in under thirty seconds in order to portray judge, jury, lawyers, and accused. Georges Méliès made a short film of Fregoli (*L'Homme-Protée*, 1899) in which he played twenty-eight characters. A favorite of the Italian Futurists, Fregoli also has a schizophrenic condition named after him—Fregoli Syndrome, in which the afflicted believes a persecutor has the ability to take on a variety of appearances.

"Sounds to me like you two smack each other around like a couple of Micks, only with knives." (p. 122)

The Three Keatons were the best-known of the so-called "Irish knockabout acts" popular on the vaudeville circuit at the turn of the century. From a 1905 ad: "Maybe you think you were handled roughly as a kid. Watch the way they handle Buster!" The act revolved around Joe Keaton, the father, comically slapping about his four-year-old son, supposedly nicknamed "Buster" by an early vaudeville co-star, Harry Houdini, for his ability to take a fall. Father and son wore identical flesh-colored "bald" wigs and Amish-style beards, young Buster on occasion passed off as a midget to concerned child-welfare authorities. Buster was also thrown (allegedly once at a heckler), punched and kicked. He began to sustain more serious injuries as Joe's drinking worsened and his timing eroded. Later, Buster recalled the development of his famous dead-pan with his father, who would cry, *"Face! Face!,"* which meant, Buster explained, "freeze the puss." Joe Keaton famously refused to allow the act to be filmed, insisting, "Nobody's gonna put the Keatons on a bedsheet at ten cents a thrill."

Buster, again: "I found the more seriously I took life, the bigger laughs I'd get."

". . . the Chinese magician, Ching Ling Soo, and Barbette,
the world-famous French cross-dresser and trapeze artist . . .
and Aunt Jemima, a blackface singer . . ." (p. 114)

Ching Ling Soo was killed while performing the famous trick in which the magician appears to catch a bullet between his teeth. (He was shot in the head.)

He was not really Chinese.

Born Vander Clyde, in Round Rock, Texas, Barbette, as a teenager, responded to an ad placed by the Alfaretta Sisters, "World Famous Aerial Queens," a trapeze act. One of the sisters had died, and the surviving Alfarettas convinced Vander (so goes the legend) that crowds would respond with far more favoritism to a daring young *lady* on a flying trapeze. Barbette's act always concluded with a dramatic removal of his wig, an extremely butch wrestler's pose, wild applause.

He was described by Jean Cocteau, a friend and admirer, as "an angel, a bird, a flower . . ."

Aunt Jemima's real name was Tess Gardella. Though she performed in blackface, Gardella did not "croon or coon shout," the latter musical style a popular genre in the early part of the century, with hit titles including "Every Race Has a Flag But the Coon!," "I Never Liked a Nigger with a Beard" and "Coon! Coon! Coon!"

133

"If he had been able to focus, he would have witnessed Sacco and Vanzetti's first-ever standing ovation." (p. 130)

This climax was reminiscent of the classic "Dead and Alive" routine, made famous by the vaudeville team of Secchi and Alfano. The routine begins with the clowns engaging in a head-standing contest. Secchi is caught cheating. The pair come to blows. Alfano is apparently killed. A panicked Secchi attempts to drag the body offstage, but each time he stoops to grab a limb, Alfano twitches, sending Secchi recoiling back in horror. After several repetitions of the gag, Secchi leaves the stage, returns with a wheel, clamps Alfano's hands to the wheel's axel and—hoisting his legs like the handles of a wheelbarrow—rolls him offstage, to sustained laughter and applause.

Chapter Four:
Sacco and Vanzetti
Pay Their Respects

The boys attend a funeral—the sole documented case of forensic hairdressing?

Sacco and Vanzetti Meet "The Sheik"

(a true account of the 1926 funeral of Rudolph Valentino)

The funeral had entered its fourth week. The peasants, it seemed, could not get enough. (Women dressed in mourning, their men jealous of a corpse.) Rumors had the real body on ice in a secret back room. The Valentino on display in the window of the parlor, they said, had to be a wax dummy ordered up by the studio for this, his final publicity blitz. "These flowers fake, too?" Sacco wondered, flicking open the miniature sympathy card of a particularly garish bouquet of posies with his thumb. The card read: "From a real fan, to a real Gentle Man." "They smell real enough," Fairbanks said. "Of course, I'm not the most sober botanist, I will admit." Langdon snorted. "Between Doug and the Sheik, be hard-pressed to say who's more full of formaldehyde." "I'm meaning," Sacco said, "they're not really from Mussolini." Vanzetti, who had been sitting quietly in a stiff, velvet-backed love seat, was trying to work out a comedy routine in his head, which, without pad and pencil, was proving a trick. In the bit, he and Nic would play pallbearers. So far, he had the coffin sliding down a muddy hill, with them straddling the thing like a toboggan sleigh, slaloming between headstones. Would audiences find this sacrilegious? Naturally, they had to coast over a newly opened grave, forcing the Negro digger to duck and then reemerge for a pop-eyed doubletake. Though, come to think of it, he and Nic as gravediggers might be funnier, and would then allow a play on *Hamlet*. Pearls before swine, considering the capacity of the average cinemagoer to grasp literary references beyond the scope of the latest comic strip adventure of Boob McNutt. But Vanzetti firmly believed that a desire to amuse himself, first and foremost, had been key to his success. Regardless, the real problem remained—where does the runaway coffin end up? You had two options with this sort of gag, known in the comedy business as a "runaway." You could go with the spectacular crash (into lake, septic ditch, glass-blowers' stall) or, alternately, with a "surprise" coast to a gentle stop, this latter take ending with the clowns gaping at each other, stunned yet wholly unharmed, and surrounded by the destruction which they have wreaked. (Audiences tended to respond favorably to either scenario, making the choice one more of aesthetics than science. "You'd think," Nic had once said, "they'd either wanna see us beat up or else see us trash the place and get away scot-free. But they don't seem to really care." To which Bart responded, "It is the trashing, not whom or what is trashed.") "I believe the boy is trying to come up with a gag," Chaplin said. "Look at the level of concentration on his face." "That, or a bowel movement," Langdon said. "Not to be crude. Hey, kid, you eat somethin' funny?" Sacco and Vanzetti were the junior members of the assembly. "Only times Bart gets that thoughtful," Sacco said. "To that, I'll attest." "Okay, okay, I got one," Langdon said. "This one's not for me. I could see Buster. Maybe Lloyd. Set-up's this: a guy and his girl looking for a place to get into a little trouble. Right? She still lives with her folks. Pop's got guns, and is the protective sort, always snooping. So they try the old back-seat-of-the-jalopy routine, but get rousted by a cop. Then they try the old last-row-of-the-movie-theater routine, but, I don't know, something else winds up spoiling their mood." Chaplin: "Perhaps one of your pictures is playing." Sacco: "Title-card: 'Shit, honey, I can't go through with this right now, I think I'm gonna be sick.'" Langdon: "Har-de-har. Can a colleague finish his set-up, please? Okay, so eventually, where do they end up?" Chaplin: "A funeral home." Langdon: "Prick." Chaplin: "It only seems obvious because we're here. Please, go on." "What," Langdon said, "you want I should write every gag for you bums? I'm handing you the set-up. Morgue gags is kids' stuff. The accidental coffining. The unintended urn-spillage. One of the lovers holding a hand they think's a living hand, but the audience knows better." Sacco: "Title card: 'Jesus Christ, honey, you better warm up these fingers before you go sticking them up my—'" "See," Langdon said, "you love it. A rigor mortis gag. Something with flowers." Sacco grabbed a rose, en garded Fairbanks, who was adjusting his tie in a mirror. "You're looking awful pretty yourself, Zorro," Sacco said. "Knock it off, kid," Fairbanks said. He turned to the group. "Okay, I'm no comedian," he began, pausing for the chorus of *wellll*s and *sez he*s and *does intentionality count*s to die down, before continuing: "But I got one. Famous leading man dies an untimely young death. Exotic wop-type. This would be a good plot for you two," he asided, nodding at Sacco and Vanzetti. "Pay attention. People shell out big dough for ideas this rich. So, listen, the fans are so crazy for this fellow, they're lining up for weeks to get a gander. And the studio comes up with this idea to fake up the body, stick a wax dummy in the window of the funeral home and meanwhile keep the real thing on ice. Well, these two clowns who work in the parlor keep accidentally melting the fake body. Perhaps the lights are hot. Perhaps one of them smokes, and tends to be clumsy with his matches. Maybe they break off a hand, or the head comes loose. The joke is—" Fairbanks gestured at Valentino: "He's so goddamned beautiful, you know? A perfect specimen. And these guys keep messing him up, and desperately attempt to fix him, and it doesn't work. They're just making it worse." Sacco reached a finger towards Valentino's cheek, peeking out at the uniformed *fascisti* who'd arrived to "guard" the corpse, through a crack in the window-shade. "I think that one on the right was an extra in our last picture," Sacco said. His finger stopped just before touching the corpse. Langdon said, "What, you think even them guards is fake?" Vanzetti, still chaired, said, "I hate to publicly agree with my partner, but if they *are* real, how did she get in here?" All heads swiveled with Vanzetti's nod, which directed the collective gaze to a strange woman—black-clad, wild-eyed, crouching and clutching her purse—who had suddenly appeared beside the room's grandest floral bouquet, a cluster of gardenias arranged to resemble an enormous, disembodied turban. The woman was nearly as pale as the petals, aside from the black smudges underlining her eye sockets—pale enough, Vanzetti thought, to pass for on-screen, her face looking powdered by professionals. Paler than the damn Sheik, and he had four weeks on her. No one in the room moved or breathed. Finally, Langdon began, "How you doin', honey? Before you answer that, let me point out, you didn't really know the guy, okay? And we're all here to tell you, he was no great shakes. Or Sheik, for that matter. Ha." In response, the woman released an unholy wail, hurling herself across the room and prompting the men to recoil. As she landed atop Valentino and began to weep and keen hysterically, Vanzetti thought, *How movie-like.* Sacco, the closest to the coffin, had grabbed the woman by the shoulders and managed to tear her from the body. "Could somebody maybe gimme," he began, before groaning and crumpling to the ground in concordance with her heel making a fairly impressive backthrust-connect with his groin. Wrestling herself away, the woman made a break for the exit, where, suddenly, she took to the air and crashed in a violent sprawl—Chaplin, as she passed, having calmly extended his cane. Before she could rise, he pinned her to the ground with his foot, which he placed firmly in the center of her back, his cane raised to strike. "Um, Chuck," Langdon said. Chaplin glanced back. "I mean to subdue her," he said. "Clubbing her insensible seems, to me, the safest and most practical route." "Maybe just let her go," Fairbanks suggested. Chaplin shrugged and lifted his foot, allowing the woman to scamper off like a crab. When she reached the exit, she stood, turning around briefly to address Valentino alone. "We never met in life," she cried. "But God willing, in the world to come." As the door slammed behind her, Langdon muttered, "Like I said, sister, you didn't know the guy, and I don't think you wants to be headed for the place where he's definitely at." "Man, though," Sacco said, "what a mess that broad left." He was staring at Valentino. The Sheik's cheeks, smudged with lipstick, now appeared bruised, while his hair had been mussed to a wild inappropriateness, the hair of a sleeping child. Sacco pulled a handkerchief from his coat pocket, spat into it, muttered, "I won't tell him if you guys don't," and began to clean the lipstick from Valentino's cheeks, also smoothing out, as best he could, the layer of foundation that'd been painted on by the studio make-up artists. (The hacks from the funeral home had been sent home for this job.) After he finished, he replaced the handkerchief, pulled out a comb and went to work on the hair. "He's a real stiff, incidentally," Sacco reported, giving Valentino's forehead a gentle tap with his forefinger. "Fake as this whole funeral's been? He's no special effect." As if cued, Chaney entered. "Who was the doll?" he asked. "And what did you do to her, Langdon, you baby-faced pervert?" Langdon snorted, gave an aw-shucks shrug. "Anyway, they're ready in the chapel," Chaney reported. "Boys ready to do some heavy lifting?" "Be thankful it ain't Arbuckle in there," Langdon said. "Though," Chaplin said, "the hysterics out there would be considerably younger, and so perhaps easier to subdue." "Shouldn't we say a few words before," Sacco began, his voice interrupted by Chaney slamming down the coffin lid. "Oh, right," Chaney said. He started to reopen the thing, but after fumbling with the latch for a moment he just waved his hands and said, "Ahh, fuckit. I mean, there'll be words out there, right? That's what we have writers for." True, true, all agreed. And so they took their positions. "Uh, you two should probably," Fairbanks pointed out. And the swashbuckler swapped places with Vanzetti, so he could be opposite Sacco, for symmetry, and the sake of the fans.

"A former publisher of Cronaca Sovversiva *set off a massive explosion outside the home of U.S. attorney general A. Mitchell Palmer, blowing himself to pieces in the process."* (p. 8)

Investigators, according to Avrich, took the scalp "to a French hairdresser." This was in D.C. "Show me the man's hair, and I will tell you his nationality." The detectives nodded, Art thanking the Frenchman and telling him relax, evidence'll be arriving momentarily. An interrogation room. Bleak, as per design. Art asked the Frenchman if he needed a coffee. The Frenchman lifted a fussy little manicured hand. Art glanced down at his own nails, which, when mustered in a half-fisted reveille, looked crooked and yellow enough to make him feel like a hillbilly with bad teeth. Like, *Better vise up that smile, boy.* Like, *Them hands's fit fo' two thangs, breakin' heads 'n scratchin' balls.* "So why me," the Frenchman asked. "Why not just take the man's fingerprints, my wife wonders." *Wife*, Art snorted, to himself, aloud saying, "You're familiar with the phrase blew himself to bits? Well let's just say this wop was a very literal-minded wop." Gannon, Art's assistant, said, "We found what we thought was a thumb but it turned out to be a toe." The Frenchman made a face. "Alleged wop," Art added, "meaning you combine the natural propensity of members of the Italian race to engage in blackhanded acts of murder, and then you put that alongside the physical evidence of an Italian-to-English dictionary discovered at the scene of the crime, and you naturally arrive at these allegations." Gannon said, "We found a piece of spine in the Norwegian ambassador's residence." The Frenchman rounded his lips into a tube of concern and touched the base of his back. "Shot right through his kid's bedroom window," Gannon said. "Kid cried when we took it. Tried to get his dad to call Oslo, get the King on the horn. Little shit."

Art interrupted, "What sort of hair you dress?" The Frenchman gave him one of those non-looks, the sort normally seen on faces of certain coloreds, the ones who'd developed the ability to maintain a perfectly respectful conversational tone while an incorporeal self snickered from above, this self so expertly removed from the scene you were left with only the vaguest traces of mockery in the air, never anything solid enough to act on. Still Art liked this guy, couldn't precisely say why. His uncowedness, he supposed, at least partwise. Also Art being a quarter Frog himself, on his mother's side, he'd inherited a natural affinity. Though his granddad had technically been French-Canuck, which, totally different animal. A distinct absence of couth in that particular breed of French, all loggers and sheep-fuckers up there, not sipping their little coffees while painting naked women in a way that somehow managed to look fruity. "*Vanitas vanitatum,*" the hairdresser was saying. "The expensive kind of hair." Just then Timperly from Evidence entered with a salutatory doorframe rap, dangling a plastic evidence bag. "'Ya go," he said, handing it over. Art nodded, turning to the Frenchman. "So how'd you like to do this?" The Frenchman said, "One moment, please," and began riffling through a voluminous satchel, eventually removing and setting upon the table a squat, roughly neck-widthed block of wood. "Please," he said, gesturing at the wood. Gannon and Timperly shot Art looks. Art held up a finger, meaning, "Watch it," but also by pointing to the ceiling meaning, "You know this goddamn idea came from on-high and not me so cut out that looking." Art removed the scalp from the evidence bag with a pair of tweezers and draped it atop the wooden block. "No, no, place it this way, please," the Frenchman whinged, before he'd even finished. Art said, "You put these on, you can fix it any way you like." The Frenchman nodded, tugged on a pair of forensic gloves and began to adjust and readjust the scalp, just so. It was dark and bushy, not as blood-flecked as you'd imagine, though no wig, either—too mangled in the back for that, like a stray dog'd got at it—any flash of the raw underside especially dewigging, its undertexture that of an orange peel, if oranges were meat. The Frenchman had removed and laid out a series of instruments from his satchel, which he'd now begun using to poke at and arrange the scalp, including a couple of combs worked in tandem and a mirror. "Hey now, don't get carried away and trim nothin'—that's evidence," Timperly said with a grin. The Frenchman shot him a withering look. "I'm just gassin' you," Timperly said. Gannon snickered. Art gave him a jab. "So you found no fingers or thumbs but did find this scalp," the Frenchman said as he worked. "That's right," Art said. "Found it on a rooftop, actually, several blocks from the Attorney General's residence." "Morris effed up," Timperly said. Art glared. "Belvedere should've double-checked his fuse's all I'm saying," Timperly said. "So the idea was to plant a bomb at Attorney General Palmer's home, but the bomb detonated prematurely, killing the bomber, is the current police theory," the Frenchman said. He'd slipped into barber mode, Art noticed. Hairdresser mode, whatever. The mode wherein you squinted down your thumb and cocked your head and lifted seemingly haphazard strands for closer examination, all the while small-talking, but never looking up. "He painting a still life or somethin'?" Timperly mumbled. The Frenchman had combed and uncombed a central parting, then switched to a forward comb-over, then started more like poufing out the whole thing. "That is a fair summation of our theory, to date," Art said. "The A.G.'s been cracking down pretty hard of late on the Reds and other radi-cal elements, so they hate him. He's definitely on their target list." Gannon asked Timperly, "Art tell you when we got there Roosevelt was standing outside?" "The secretary of the Navy?" Timperly asked. "Yup," Gannon said, "Assistant. Lives next door to Palmer. He told us Palmer was raised a Quaker, and that he was so shook by the bombing he fell back into talking Quaker-talk from when he was a kid, all theeing and thouing everybody who'd listen. 'Thank thee, Franklin!' kinda shit."

Moier burst in. "This the Frenchie?" he asked. Looking at the scalp, he said, "Hey, damn, it's the world's worst ventriloquist's dummy." Art said, "Moier, cut it." Moier loud-whispered to Timperly, "Imagine taking your kids to see this guy. He comes onstage with a bloody scalp on a piece of wood." Timperly hawed. Moier said, "'Ello, Scalpee." Then changing his voice to a high-pitched puppet's answered, "'Allo, Monsieur." Timperly and Gannon both hawing now. "So, Scalpee, tell me about zees eetching problem?" Hawing all around, except for the Frenchman and Art, who said, "I said cut it, Moier. Not to mention your mouth was moving." Gannon said, "Not to mention it's wop hair so the accent should be a wop one." The Frenchman looked up and said, "So, yes, I have an answer." Art said, "Tell us." The Frenchman said, "Italian, between the ages of twenty-six and twenty-eight." Timperly said, "Hot-damn."

The Frenchman said, "He wore his hair six inches long in the front." Moier said, "Okay, so how about this. 'Ayyy-a, Scalpo, watcha out—you drink alla dat *vino*, itsa gonna go to you-a head!'" Art rebagged the evidence, shaking his head, the Frenchman meanwhile also packing up, at the same time softly whistling a song—

vive le son
vive le son
de l'explosion

—from his youth. Art told Moier, "You'll need to brush up that act."

Chapter Five:
The Trial (I)

TRANSCRIPT

*(from the record of Commonwealth of Massachusetts vs.
Nicola Sacco & Bartolomeo Vanzetti, 1920-1927)*

Moustache, or no moustache?

I worked in the sole room.

At present, an attendant for an invalid.

They looked to be foreigners to me.
Could you tell what nationality?
Well, Italians, I think.
You have worked with Italians, have you, in your work?
At this time I did, in that cellar.

In the rear tonneau.
In the rear seat?
Yes, sir.

"dark complected"

"the demurrer"

Do you mean—
(*The defendant Sacco stands up in the cage and says: "Take a good
look. I am myself."*)
Then you mean the man who just stood up and made the
remark?
Yes, sir.

The man they call Sacco?
Yes.

(*Though other accounts quote the defendant as saying, "I am the man? Do you mean me? Take a good look."*)

I told Officer Vaughn to fish Vanzetti.

I was driving a baker wagon.

Did you say anything about either one being a regular 'wop'?
I may have said he looked like a wop.

Because Italians sometimes look like that, dark complexion, and rough-looking like that.

That he was a wop by his clothes.

"gentlemen of the jury"

What is your occupation?
Piling stone.

License. Oh, you have a license to dig clams?
Yes, sir.

"short, low-sized men"

Stout.
What do you mean by stout?
Well, I would say thick-chested.
What?

Full-chested, that is all I know.

In what capacity was he employed?
When he first went to work for us, he was employed as an edge trimmer. That is a part of shoe making they call edge trimming. Then he worked as taking care of the boiler nights.
What was he doing in April 1920?
Trimming edges.
Edge trimmer at that time?
Yes, sir.

How long would it take you to sell 488 pounds of fish?

I go away for not to be a soldier.

Yes, in a shanty, you know, the little house where the Italian work and live like a beast, the Italian working man in this country.
The 'beast' part of it locates it, does it?
Yes.

After I sold them clams, I went to Boston.

Well, you think I have only one shirt? I am a poor man, but I like to go clean.

Because it is a winter shirt.

Because I was asked if I am a socialist, if I am I.W.W., if I am a Communist, if I am a radical, if I am Blackhand.

It was a little hole there. (*indicating*) Soft . . . a little hole . . . from usage.

What say?

Get out of the way, you son of a B.
Using the English language?
Fully.

I can sell 150.
What?
I can sell 150, 200 pounds in a day.

After the eighth of April, I peddled just one week.

Sacco brought to me that his mother was dead.

How come she to give them to you?

How come you to get them?

He is a businessman of olive oil.

Mr. Moor, we cannot hear this witness.
Speak up, Mr. Sacco.

Mr. Sacco, how long have you known Mr. Vanzetti?
Because no personality but I know the name about four years,
pretty near.
Personally, you mean?
Yes.

F-r-a-z-e-t-t-i

Is that your cap?

(*witness examines cap*)

I never wear black much. Always a gray cap, always wear gray cap. Always I like gray cap.

That is not an answer to my question

(*witness puts cap on head*)

The way I look. Could not go in. My size is 7 ⅛.

We went in the woods, that day, me, him, and his wife, playing and shooting in the wood. Mostly destroyed moths.

Those women's shoes, I never trimmed on women's shoes before. It was very hard for me to trim them, the heel was too high, so I couldn't make no more.

Then two dollars a day. I decided to leave the job and go pick and shovel be better.

what you call a nickname

another fish peddler

I should say I

I can tell you all the way, all the time of my life I take a ride in an automobile.

How many times? Well, nevermind. That is all.

Did you love this country in the month of May 1917?

I did not say—I don't want to say I did not love this country.

Do you understand that question?

Yes.

Then will you please answer it?

I can't answer in one word.

You can't say whether you loved the United States of America one week before you enlisted for the first draft?

I can't say in one word, Sir Katzmann.

You can't tell this jury whether you loved the country or not?

I object to that.

I could explain that, yes, if I loved—

What?

I could explain that, yes, if I loved, if you give me the chance.

And is that your idea of showing your love for America?

(*witness hesitates*)

I did not run away.

You mean you walked away?

Yes.

You don't understand me when I say ran away, do you?

That is vulgar.

That is vulgar?

You can say a little intelligent, Mr. Katzmann.

Don't you think going away from your country is a vulgar thing to do when she needs you?

I don't believe in her.

Do you think it is a cowardly thing to do what you did?

No, sir.

Do you think it is a brave thing to do what you did?

Yes, sir.

Oh, different food that we did not like.

And you had Italian food there, didn't you?

Yes, made by ourselves.

Couldn't you send to Boston to get Italian food sent to Monterrey, Mexico?

If I was D. Rockefeller I will.

So the first reason love of America is founded on pleasing your stomach?

I will not say yes.

Did you notice 22 extra cartridges in your pockets?

No.

We will stop here for lunch.

Did you shave this morning?

Yes, sir.

Have you shaved every day since this trial opened?

Yes, sir.

That is all, sir.

Part
Two

Chapter Six:
Sacco and Vanzetti
Take a Night Off

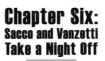

The boys stay in—mayhem at the Cardinal's banquet

Fatty in the top bunk's automatically funnier, was the reason Bart always got stuck below. Basic rule of comedy. Fatty could brain himself on the ceiling, buckle the ladder, collapse the bunk entirely, sandwiching Skinny twixt the tenement bedding. But flip it? Not so funny. Arguably free of yuks, in fact. Why's for theoreticians. You know: why why *why*'s stuttering a perennial gas? Why's a rubber chicken rather than rubber never an elaborately woven yarn? Why does "free of yuks" (arguably) work, while yuk-less (first choice, rejected, despite the tempting pun on luckless) on some level grate?

It's more than just taste.

"I guess, reversed," Nic offered, "that is, you on me, it's more along the lines of a broke fall."

"And what, pray tell, is amusing about that?" Bart murmured from below, frowning distractedly at his worn edition of the *Commedia*.

"Nada. Nada. Nada damn thing. It's a rescue picture, at that point. Heroics."

"Send in Rin Tin Tin."

"Exactly! Now you're talking sensible."

"If I'd wanted trampolines, I would have hired some children and bought a home movie camera."

"Say it."

"I said it."

"Wait—so, would I be the trampoline, in that configuration?"

"Look, I think we've just about exhausted this topic, so if you prefer the bottom bunk, just come out and say—"

"Am I actually putting on weight?"

"Do you want the bottom bunk?"

"So the sight of me disgusts you and the rest of slender humanity? Say it. For once, give your cruelty a utilitarian purpose. Be cruelly honest!"

"Take the bottom if you want it."

"Haven't you been listening to a word of our conversation? Me on bottom isn't funny. *I can never be bottom!*"

"We're alone. There's nobody else here. You don't have to worry about funny every second of every day. In fact, it's counterproductive."

Bart underlined a random line of Dante with an especial precision, then glanced up at his bunk's mattress-ceiling, taking note of the sudden silence. He quizzically butterchurned his jaw. The line was:

non furon leonine, ma di volpe.

By "random" he meant quite literally, as in, "Any card." He liked the idea of sliding splinters beneath the microscope—the notion that, through sheer diligence of observation, one might glean poetry from the dried starfish at the edge of a painted seascape, from the wizened creases of a second ballerina's arched toe-shoe, from any number of seemingly forgettable details that accrue into a greater sublime. Of course, he also knew the *Commedia* back-and-forth enough to make him feel that, on some subconscious level, the selections were not random at all.

To that end: the lion and the fox, eh? He came close to audibly snorting at the obviousness of his mind's workings, then realized he didn't really know how the fox-lion thing fit their odd little dynamic. Clearly Nic, with his utter absence of subtlety, could never be fox. But he didn't exactly possess the regal comportment *del leone*, either. As for his own totemic counterpart, Bart felt more comfortable wearing the tail than the mane, though the fox implied a certain predator's cunning that he surely lacked. He tried to come up with an animal more given to cowardice and lurking. Rejected vulture, serpent. Wondered if a species of monkey that tended to hang back and instigate existed in some far-off jungle. Probably had extincted itself. Regardless. *That* would be him. Or, at the very least, his closest representation in nature.

Above, Nic shifted. The mattress clenched, dipped. Bart heard a stagy *fuckit* and glimpsed a blur of red thermal as Nic dropped from the end of the bed. The downstairs neighbor, Xufei, pronounced "SHOO-fay," a Chinaman, probably toiling diligently on a new routine of his own, began, in near-instant retaliation to the seismics of the landing, a furious attack on the ceiling—having first conscripted (or so it sounded to Bart) an upright battering ram and a pair of circus strongmen.

As a rebuttal, Nic flung himself to the floor and launched into a contrapuntal series of head butts, underlaid with a staccato and rhetorically unremarkable monologue ("Knock. Knock. Who's. There? *Fuck. You. Mother. Fucker*"), the latter's delivery through clenched teeth and violent grunts of pain easily doubling the overall listener irritation.

"Nic," Bart said.

Plus the whole thing's much funnier if you put him in a helmet—Kaiser-style, say, or barring that, your classic head-in-bucket. Minus protection, though, you risked the time-again proven unfunniness of blood and/or closed head trauma.

"Nicky," Bart said.

Eventually, Nic rolled onto his back.

"That," he mumbled woozily, "was probably a bad idea."

Below, the thumping continued for several more beats—at first actually increasing to such a degree that Bart wondered if Xufei's endgame might actually be full penetration—before abruptly ceasing. Nic sat up.

"Shit," he said. "Sorry. I'm in a funky mood tonight. Can't even remember why I got out of bed, now."

He winced and shook out his head as though it were a limb that had fallen asleep.

"So. Hey, remember that time we were dogcatchers, and that lady walked by with the perambulator, and the baby she was strolling had a creepy grown man's face, like a Renaissance painting of Christ, and I netted them both with our giant dogcatcher's net, by accident?"

Bart sighed. "That was this afternoon."

"Right," Nic said. "So you remember, then? Here's my real question: How would you rate today's bedlam, overall? The quality of the manufactured commotion that went down?

"We're still talking work?" Bart went silent, eventually clearing his throat. "It all depends upon the scale."

"One to ten. One being a historical exception. Ten being a vanguard of the postcolonial struggle."

"I could be persuaded to go as high as two-point-five."

"Really? This is including the netting of the lady and the man-faced child, *plus* the locking of our boss in the Doberman's kennel, *plus* the accidental euthenizing of the mayor's wife's prizewinning Schnauzer? Not to mention my driving." He paused. Bart stared at his book. "Wow. You're tough on us." Nic scratched his head. "Oh, wait, I got it! Women. Reason I got out of bed, is what I mean. I'd been thinking I'd step out, land me some. One'd do."

"Are you expecting me to object?"

"Frankly? Yeah. You tend to be an objectionable sort."

"No, go-head. Have fun."

"I thought we could maybe go together."

"Nah. I'm in for the night." Bart waggled his book.

Nic stared at him. "All right. I might just fly a solo mission, then."

"Sure. Go-head. We spend enough time together. I won't be lonely."

Nic stared. "Come on. *Bart.* I'm going crazy in here. Night after night. I'm losing it. Shit."

"So go out then."

"I should."

"We're in agreement."

"Maybe I will."

"There's the door. We're only four flights up."

Nic sighed and kneaded his eyeballs. A few moments later, he rose, wordlessly, and wandered over to the window. Bart stole a glance. Nic was either studying something on the fire escape or trying to pull a specific detail from his own diluted reflection. Bart *sympathized*, there was no question of that. The lives they'd chosen lacked the basic comforts desired by most, and had become a paradoxical merging of tedium and instability. The moves from city to city. The same-seeming rooms where they found themselves cooped together, nightly. Days spent at the latest shit job. The ever-present fuse, connected to the inevitable gag.

And yet. The alternative was acquiescence. Comfort equals collaboration.

Like numerous itinerants of the period, they would not or could not adhere to the discipline of the new industrial order.

Specific mayhems were never planned out, exactly. They just tended to ensue. Though Bart and Nic certainly helped them along, certainly accelerated a given situation's entropy.

They had dug ditches, washed dishes, sold ice cream, poured molten metal in a foundry, installed telephones, broke rocks in a stone quarry, cut wood, sold fruit, worked in a brick factory, gardened, sold candy, hauled rocks at a reservoir.

It always ended badly.

Mongered eels. Sharpened knives.

Inevitably badly.

"Remember our last downstairs neighbor? Time-before-last, maybe," Nic asked.

"Sure," Bart said. "Saddest Girl." A nickname. In real-life something like Meg.

"That one," Nic said.

"What about her?"

Nic shrugged. "Just remembering."

Bart fanned himself with his thumb and the pages of the *Commedia*, reconjuring he and Nic, on the floor, horizontal, profiled, *faccia a faccia*, opposing ears cupping hardwood, hands flat, elbows winged, muscles bracing, as if . . . What, exactly? Pushing back might suddenly become desirable? The position demanded balance? A maximization of tactile surfacing might increase the overall sensual sensitivity, and thus help them hear better?

Saddest Girl, below, sobbed herself to sleep nightly. They never figured out why. Her sobs were possibly the only close-to-literal *boo-hoos* Bart had ever been privy to. Though, to be wholly accurate, they sounded more like *baaaaaaa-HA!!-haaaaaaaaa.*

Nic mouthing, sideways: "This. A. Put. On?"

Bart head-wobbling a *think-not.*

Their faces were inches apart. They listened for hours. A symphonic misery.

"Weird chick," Nic said, now. "Wonder what she was crying about. Had to be some guy, right?" Beat. "Why didn't we. I don't know. Help her."

"Not our place to meddle."

"Right. Although if she'd told us to fuck off, we could've, fairly immediately. Fucked off, that is."

"She would've been embarrassed. Nobody wants to be caught like that."

"What?"

"What?"

"Caught like what, exactly?"

"Crying. Vulnerable. Broken."

"Hmm. Yeah. Well, you don't. Not sure I'd everybody it. Guess it just boiled down to *pleasant*, in a weird way, having that company. You know? However through-the-floorboards. However miserable *she* was. At least it got me out of this room. That room, rather. Not me, but my head. You know what I mean. Jesus. I need to get out of here."

Bart had moved on. His new line

sì che s'ausi un poco in prima il senso

made him smile, the line reminding him of Everest, only reversed, in that when scaling mountains, one paused, periodically, to adjust to the drop in oxygen.

"That was when we lived near the slaughterhouse," Nic said.

"What's that, now?"

"Saddest Girl-era Sacco and Vanzetti."

"Oh. Right."

"Funny we never worked there. Strikes me, in retrospect, as our kind of shit job. Something we could've. I don't know. Done something with."

"You can't make chicken-killing funny." Bart thought about this for a moment. "*Trying* to kill chickens and ultimately failing could, in theory, be funny. But you approach the line with that sort of gag."

Walking home, they'd often spotted strays that had escaped, beakless, or half-plucked, dragging a crushed foot or disjointed wing, peering skittishly from alleys and abandoned storefronts. Bart recalled how one chicken made its way up the stairs to their old flat (nearly identical to the current flat, its amenities including one (1) sink, one (1) hot plate, one (1) crate-table, one (1) bare bulb, one

(1) bunk, the air saturated with peeling and overuse), scratched at the door and somehow managed to squawk past Nic, fluttering low across the floor and only coming to a halt when it smacked into the side of the clawfoot tub.

"Oh, wow," Nic said, at the time. "I think it's blind. Hey. Chick-chickchickiechick."

The chicken ignored him. When it got tangled in a lamp cord, Nic grabbed the bird and threw it in the tub.

"Should we stew him?" Nic asked.

Bart shrugged. "You were just chicking the thing five minutes ago."

"He doesn't like me."

"If you cut off the head, it'll run around."

"We could suffocate it in this bag."

"That's not a bag."

"It's not?"

"That's my good shirt."

"Oh." Beat. "You *own* a good shirt?"

This had gone on. Cut to: *Same time, following evening. A crude assemblage of chicken wire has been erected around the tub.* Nic, standing on the crate-table, crumbles day-old Italian bread through slats of wire.

Nic (to chicken): "Chickchickchickiechick."

Nic (to Bart): "The fattening process can take a bit of time."

Bart (now) glanced up from his book. "Remember the bit where the poet is warned by his guide to pause before descending further, so as to allow his body to acclimate to Hell's increasingly foul smells?"

Instantly realizing what he just invited, Bart grabbed the bunk's frame and braced himself for a thunderclap. But nothing came. He craned a look in the direction of the silence.

"Nic?" he said.

Nic hadn't moved from the window. There was no view, just an alley.

"Some life we worked out for ourselves, huh?"

"My, you *are* in a melancholy way tonight," Bart said. Nic did not respond. "I'm supposed to be the melancholy one, remember?" Distant barking. Car horns. Bart cleared his throat awkwardly, then, finally, offered, "*Comes da revolution, we'll all be eatin' strawberries.*" He gave the line half a sing.

"Think we'll actually live to see it?"

Bart considered the question for a moment, then said, "Our kids, if not present company per se."

"Kids, huh? Now that'd be the math. *Considering we get no tail. Per se.*" Nic slowly turned away from his ill-reflected self. He held a letter. "Hey, look what I found," he said. Then, reading: "'Cara Mama, Circumstances find me little different. The days remain lengthy, stultifying, obvious. I find it far too bright in the sun.'"

Bart snapped his book shut. "Give it here."

"'Nights,'" Nic continued, "'are just us, back in the flat.'"

As quickly as Bart launched himself across the room, Nic's swiftness proved untoppable. (His agility, off-the-clock, all the more impressive when viewed relative to his on-the-clock ineptitude.) By Bart's arrival he'd already gained the fire escape and secured the window (his feet propped against the window's outer lip, his back braced against the fire escape's upper rail), leaving the latter to attempt a tug, then impotently fist the pane.

He read: "'Of course, we chose the life. Or our personalities chose it for us. No matter. We have only each other, now, as we are forever divided from the vaster Them. Cast out by our knowledge. And then it's the rest of your life, trying to make the others see what you see. The world as it is. On to the next disruption!' Wow, you write like you talk, preacher. 'The specificity of the gigs change with a fair amount of regularity. Some involve shovels. Others, pails, or scaffolding, or the corpses of animals. Knives more and more frequently come into play.'"

Bart moaned and gave the window a violent yank. It didn't budge. His breath steamed the glass.

Nic, tilting the letter toward the light of the flat, speedily scanned the rest of the page, his lips moving in silence. "So, your *mom*, huh?" he finally said, looking back up and grinning. "I'd really always believed you were writing some secret girlie, somewhere, all these letters, night after night. But Mama. Huh. That's not some dirty nickname for your child-bride, I'm assuming? No. Not your style." He skimmed again. "Plus, you'd always told me your mother died before you came over. Why would you lie about something like that? That's just not right, man. I thought we was buddies."

Bart relaxed his arms and propped his head against the window. "She is dead," he murmured. "It's a sort of journal. I just use the conceit of writing to my mother to prevent me from becoming horribly self-indulgent."

"Wowza," Nic said. He stared at the letter again, as if desiring a written proof. "That's kind of weird, pal, got to say." He paused. "Plus, isn't self-indulgence the point of keeping a journal?"

Bart looked up at Nic, then suddenly bore down—or, more accurately, *up*—on the window, displaying a renewed fury. Nic, though, had not shifted himself, and so the window remained locked down. After a final, futile grunt, Bart collapsed once again.

"Possibly," he gasped. "But I wanted to force a certain degree of rigor onto my thoughts."

Nic nodded. "So, okay, I'd like to map out the parameters of your insanity. In these letters, do you find yourself censoring what you write, so's not to offend maternal eyes?"

Bart made eye contact with his own distended visage, floating on the surface of the glass, Nic's pale moonface hovering just above and beyond the reflection.

"I suppose," he admitted, "I do tend, in the letters, to accentuate certain elements of the narrative, while at the same time tamping others."

Why, he couldn't say, let alone to Nic. But it was true: in the letters, he more or less restricted himself to complaints about the drudgery of their calling, never questioning its essential worthiness. Which was odd. Because while Nic truly believed an ideal existed out there, somewhere, waiting to be had—that what they did, everything they pulled, could ultimately lead to some preferable other—Bart shared none of these utopianist impulses, so clearly a by-product of their upbringing in the Roman faith. (However much Nic might bristle at this suggestion.) Bart, if anything, considered himself a nihilist, more or less assuming things would remain mired at a comparable level of bad until the sun exploded, at which point they would be slightly worse.

"Hey, I understand," Nic said. "'Mother's' feelings. Make 'her' believe a kernel of hope exists, deep in your black heart."

"Are you suggesting that, via the letters, I'm tricking myself into emending the record?" Bart asked.

"You? Tamper with the evidence?"

There was a rap at the door.

"You're standing," Nic said.

Bart nodded and shuffled to the door. It was Xufei, the Chinaman who lived downstairs. He was wearing a beard of bees.

"*Neigh*-bor," Xufei pronounced slowly. The care which Xufei took in moving his lips seemed to be helping his English.

"Oh," Bart said. "Hello."

"*Yes*," Xufei said. His teeth remained visible and clenched, the fringes of his mouth twitching imperceptibly, forming as much of a grin as he could muster. Even that small movement provoked a momentary but startling swelling of beard.

Bart backed away. From behind him, he could hear Nic, who had slipped back inside, exclaim, "Xufei! You're up here about all the racket, huh? I've gotta apologize, my friend. I was just telling my boy, 'Bart, you need to stop pounding on the floor like that. Them floors is thin, and there's people trying to live their lives below us.' But you know how it is. What can you do? He's a rude beast with barnyard manners. I try to teach, but he's grown. He'll die a dirty, selfish sonofabitch. Some people just end up that way. So how are you? I see you've got a beard of bees coming along there, huh? What's your story?"

"There's really no need for elaboration," Bart quickly cut in. "It's clearly difficult for you to speak at the moment, we can tell."

"Funnily enough Bart and I was just talking work talk," Nic said, pointedly ignoring Bart while gesturing for Xufei to take the apartment's sole chair. "I'm assuming the bee-beard is a work-type thing, huh? So tell us some trade secrets. How exactly do you get them buggers to stay put?"

Xufei continued to grin in a manner that made him look like a simpleton—though, to be fair, the bee-beard forced an unflattering rictus.

"It. Ve. *Ry*. Comp. *Li*. Ca."

Bart coughed loudly. "Don't let Nic bother you with trifling questions, friend," he said. Turning to Nic, he hissed, "What is your problem? Clearly, he wrangles them. He does not want to *talk* about it."

"See what I gotta put up with?" Nic said to Xufei, then, to Bart, continued: "Funny, though, how he's willing to work during his off-hours." As Nic spoke, he pushed his palm in the direction of the beard, in the manner of a conductor moving a gentle string section. The beard swayed as if caught by a breeze, puffing to the right, then collapsing back into place.

Xufei's eyes widened, it was unclear whether with alarm or delight.

Bart, to Nic (hissing, still): "Leave the beard alone, would you, please?"

Nic, to Bart: "Guess not everybody can just 'leave their work at the office.' Turn it right off at five. Ignore the revolution and proceed with things thusly." To Xufei: "So, you got a routine worked out for it yet, or are you just perfecting? Cause I got one for you. This is on the house, by the way. Okay. Guy walks into a barbershop, asks for a shave. Rub is, he's wearing a beard of bees. Barber double-takes. Mr. Beard-of-bees sits down, deadpanning it. Barber, a consummate professional, attempts a variety of means of shaving this beard. He grabs a straight edge, approaches. The beard flares up. He retreats, nervously mops his brow with a rag. He grabs an enormous pair of clippers. Repeat. He starts trimming little hairs from the base of the customer's neck. Beard-of-bees, who's been dozing, notices, gets hot, points agitated-like at his beard. The barber apologizes. So forth. This goes on."

A pregnant pause.

Finally, Bart sighed, admitting defeat. "So?"

"So what?"

"I refuse to beg for it. How does the gag end?"

Nic grinned. "He pulls a feather out of his pocket. Tickles the customer under his nose."

Bart half-smiled, in spite of himself. "A close-up on the sleeping customer's face. Nose twitching."

Nic: "*Ahh. Ahhhhh.*"

Bart paused. "But so, how would the climax work out, exactly? Obviously, the beard explodes. There are bees everywhere. But has the barber run outside his own shop, to watch through the plate glass window? Or has, say, a police officer with a ridiculous mustache, who threatened the barber at the beginning of the first reel, opened the door at the exact moment of the sneeze, prompting a hairy, pulsating bee-cloud to chase him into the street?"

"I," Nic said, "kinda lean to the idea of cutting to a shot of the barber's from the outside, maybe across the street. Some guy's sitting on a bench, reading the paper, or chatting with a girl, and over their shoulders—they're not even looking—over their shoulders you see in the plate glass window the beard exploding and suddenly the window goes like black. Bee-black. You can't see nothing. It's almost like the glass is shaking. And finally the door gets knocked open and the bees go flying out—you know, harmlessly. Into the sky. And then we cut back inside to the barber, who is horribly stung. All swolled-up."

Bart: "Now, is the customer stung, or is he merely rubbing his nose, recovering from the sneeze?"

"I'm thinking latter. So he opens his eyes, sees his clean-shaven self in the mirror, rubs his cheeks happily. The barber's exaggeratedly stung. His clothes are torn. His hair's a fright. The shop's trashed. Looks like a bomb went off. But the beard guy notices nothing. Tips the guy a nickel and walks out."

"Or perhaps he's a bit short for a tip and so says, 'Sorry, pal, I'll get you next time.'"

"Barber faints dead away. Final shot."

Bart gazed into the distance for a moment, contentedly. Finally, he said, "Yes. I like that. It could work."

Xufei, who actually understood very little English, had been humming softly to his bees throughout the entire conversation. He trained his bees by humming, in the manner of a lullaby, often songs his mother had once hummed to him, songs which she, in turn, had learned from Chinese songbirds they'd kept, back in Guangzhou. People would take the birds to parks, or restaurants, and neighboring birds would sing to each other. He knew, of course, that the bees were not "hearing" the songs the way he did, that they were simply responding to vibrations of the air, to a cool wind on their thorax. Still, he reasoned, he may as well hum something pleasing to his own ears. Today, it was the American National Anthem. They seemed to like that.

> *"The Galleanists also made assassination attempts (most involving mail bombs) upon dozens of 'enemies of the movement,' including . . . the Archbishop of Chicago." (p. 8)*

A debutante's hiccup. (Gloved hand to mouth. Troubled, uncharacteristically reflective gaze. The pinkest of blushes. Like a small, downy creature, startled by predators.)

"Bun? Bun? What is it, dear?"

Start here.

(A purse, awkwardly mustered into service. Later: soup tureens, planters, ornamental vases, men's hats; in one extremely ill-advised case a wife's dress-train, yanked out like safety netting.)

Across the main banquet hall of the University Club, Cardinal Mundelein, the new Archbishop of Chicago, noticed nothing, his Eminence at the moment wholly absorbed by the generalized glow of his celebratory dinner and, more specifically, by the conversation of the mayor's plumply *charmant* wife. She was speaking about Delhi, a city she had recently visited for the first time. The trip, she explained, had caused her to revise her overall theory of the Hindoo race, which she believed, prior to her trip to India, innately duplicitous, if not outright sinister. She'd based this belief wholly on past visits to Turkey. With the Indians, a certain level of Eastern inscrutability remained, of course, but she'd come to realize the people of the vast country were essentially *like us*. The Cardinal listened to these idiotic statements with a genuine interest, as he'd long ago genuinely convinced himself that all of God's creatures were as fascinatingly varied as—well.

Insects! Snowflakes! Clouds at dusk!

Still, it was his honest belief. He felt no shame. He loved this fat, spoiled, sheltered heiress with her laughable theories and her plucked eyebrows reshaped into bizarre peaks that poked through the clouds up into the thinning air. Because he believed, if given the chance, and the means, and the ideal circumstances, she would change for the better. He could see it, inside her.

Also, he wanted to hear about the food in Delhi. He'd heard the Indians ate lamb much differently from the English-style, and he wondered how, exactly, it was prepared.

Just at this moment, he happened to glance down at the piece of beef on the end of his fork, which seemed to wiggle and squirm. He felt his soup course coming up. Absurdly, he clamped his mouth shut. The mayor's wife was saying, "The odor of the Hindoo is also peculiar, I will grant the critics *that*." As the Cardinal felt his mouth filling and his cheeks distending, he wondered if he had any hope of excusing himself with nothing but hand gestures. He waved vaguely in the direction of the washroom and began to stand.

Strasz, the Cardinal's birdlike assistant (the back of his Roman collar, as always, speckled with dandruff), glanced over and noticed his superior's distended cheeks. He thought immediately of a cousin from his childhood who, whenever drinking, would fill his mouth with the beverage in question—generally root beer—would fill it *completely*, to the point of extreme cheek-distension, after which, he would set the glass down for a moment and methodically gulp this enormous mouthful, his cheeks and throat pulsing like a bladder. It had always struck Strasz as an especially greedy way to drink, and he was adding this newly discovered trait to a mental list of things he disliked about the Cardinal when, suddenly, the Cardinal stood up, so brusquely he almost knocked over his chair, abrupt enough so that he did, in fact, topple his beverage glass. Everyone around him looked up as if the Cardinal were about to give a speech, but Strasz noticed the sweat, as well as a terror in his eyes, a confusion.

"Your Excellency," Strasz began, touching the hem of his robe, when the Cardinal pitched forward, vomiting across the round table, neatly tracing a diameter down its center—a violent and gristly diameter, really, so "neatly" not the best choice of adverbs, but nonetheless, there it went, spattering the mayor and his wife and a handful of the wealthiest church donors invited to sit at the Cardinal's table, coating the duck with a fresh glaze, refilling several wine glasses, garnishing the vegetable course and snuffing both candles. As Strasz stood to grasp the Cardinal's shoulder, he had time to think of the rotting priest in *The Brothers Karamazov*, and wonder if the Cardinal's rude outburst might shake the faiths of the wealthy much as the odor of a holy man's corpse did so in Dostoyevsky. But he only had time to savor this for a moment before realizing that, around the ballroom, similar episodes were erupting with what, in a contemporary painting, would undoubtedly have been criticized as a Flemish overkill.

None of this was as funny as it might sound. The crowd scrambling, glancing about, panicked, slipping. The waiters backing off, forgetting years of training. One tablecloth's edge grabbed, yanked, bringing down the careful architecture of the settings. So much concentrated heaving sounding more like screams. The stench made Strasz think of a radiator filled with bile. It burned to inhale.

Neither the Cardinal nor any of the two hundred guests were seriously harmed. The poisoner, Nestor Dondoglio, a professional chef who was also follower of the radical anarchist Luigi Galleani, had used too much arsenic in the soup. He slipped out during the vomiting and was never captured.

"'The urge to destroy is also a creative urge.'
—Mikhail Bakunin" (epigraph)

"Passion," in some translations, substituted for "urge."

Chapter Seven:
Sacco and Vanzetti
Meet the Fascist
Aviator, Italo Balbo

The boys plot a kidnapping—heroic flight, the wonders of science, reproductive mysteries of the eel and the 1933 Chicago World's Fair

BIOELECTRIC FORCES EXIST WITHIN LIVING TISSUE

(a scene from the 1943 picture Sacco and Vanzetti Meet the
Fascist Aviator, Italo Balbo*)*

From the roof of the tenement, the sky over Lake Michigan vista'd,
unobstructed. A crowd, squinting at a naked sky, milled, its mood
on the anxious side of festive, its necks haphazardly canted, and
not even a cloud shaped like an angel to justify all the saluting
palms, and identical crowds clustering on every rooftop in view and
beyond, waiting, in Nic's phrase, which he not only coined but also
disseminated, loudly, repeatedly and most often without solicitation,
"for a flock of guinea-birds."

Alternately: ". . . dago pigeons."

Alternately: ". . . Italian dodos."

Once: ". . . the pere*guine*ation to reach its . . . its . . . uh . . ."

Mrs. Beltrami, the brick-maker's wife, shook her head, her eyes
(vaguely sympathetic) belied by her dimples (stern) and a sigh more
appropriate for the war dead.

"Not at all, huh?" Nic asked.

His answer came in the form of a second sigh, this one deflat-
ing into a *Niconiconico*, delivered in the mumbled, barely audible
manner of an old spell that's never worked.

"Right," he said. "Well, you know. Can't always. Fellow who
risks not. All that."

Mrs. Beltrami, opened her mouth to say something, then recon-
sidered, her gaze dilating into a blankness that read as too weary to
bother with contempt.

"You think," Nic asked, as the old woman wandered off, "she took
offense?" Bart glanced around the rooftop. Nearby, the butcher's fat
teenage daughter sold balloons from a dwindling bouquet. A quartet

of boys crouched in summit, the tabled question concerning the division of labor in the spectacular reception being planned—too-clever Donatello trying, gamely, to convince his skeptical coconspirators that the holding of the firework could actually be the more rewarding task than the lighting of the same, and that furthermore (this being the point most decisive to his wholesale loss of the group's until-then hearty support) the fact that he'd expressed a preference for lighting should be looked upon as an act of pure altruism. Closer to the edge, Signora Pucci roasted pigeons on a trashcan spit, while her son's twin daughters ladled *limonata*.

"I'd say the subtlety of your efforts to seize control of certain slurs may be lost on the crowd," Bart said.

"Stupid fucking wops."

"It's an interesting dilemma, much like the colored man's playful, at times even affectionate use of the word 'nigger' amongst his own kind. In a similar fashion, you are attempting a rather bold theft of what may be the oppressor's most prized weapon, his language."

"Most prized? Shit, man. That be the case, I can think of plenty other weapons I'd just as soon take off the Man's hands. Start with pistols."

"And . . ."

"Ropes. Cattle prods."

"yet . . ."

"Pitchforks. Axe-handles."

"we . . ."

"Acupuncture needles. Those baseball bats with the nails sticking out the top. What are those called, anyway? Is there a word for those types of bats?"

"Might we not read a basic insult in your use of wop, an insult that says there's something inherently woppish about the Italian race, that you really *believe this*, but that it is okay for you to say so as a bona fide member of the tribe?"

Scarcelli, the tunnel worker from two doors down, sidled over. "Hey, you two got my knives?" he asked. "I need them knives. Also, I got some scissors to be sharped."

Every third word, Scarcelli sucked the powdered sugar from one of his fingers. Nic watched Scarcelli as if he were eating candied nuts from an overstuffed bag and rudely not offering to share.

"Been getting into some *zeppole*, huh?" Nic murmured.

"Huh? Yeah, yeah," Scarcelli said. "So, hey, Bart, nice day for it, huh? Clear enough." On "it," Scarcelli made a poke in the direction of the sky, his left index finger (unlicked) arcing dangerously close to Nic's mouth (still agape), Nic at this point adopting an alarmingly feral expression.

Bart took this opportunity to preemptively intervene, slapping Nic full across the face.

"That," Bart said, "was entirely called for."

Nic ran his fingers along his cheek. "You think?"

"Violence as a last resort does not always best serve the cause." He turned back to Scarcelli. "Rain," he offered, "would have been worse."

Scarcelli nodded and began a reply, but a radio report, wafting up from the open window of an apartment, drowned his voice.

"Balbo, the Fascist Minister of Aviation, and his formation of twenty-four Savoia-Marchetti SM.55X flying boats are due to arrive in Chicago on the hour, having made a historic flight from Rome, across the Atlantic Ocean. The Italian hero is scheduled to make an appearance at the World's Fair, being held on the shores of Lake Michigan. In fact, the flying boats will, we are told, be landing *on* the lake."

A couple of kids, tagging at each other, darted around Bart, treating him like another chimney pipe. A mother scolded the boys for skirting so close to the edge. "There's nothing down there to see," she snapped. "You look *up*, not over. You live down there."

Bart tilted himself enough to peer over the ledge. The narrow alley, from above, looked like a cross section from an anatomy book, the cluttered clotheslines hanging like strands of diseased gut.

"When it comes to the field of aviation, the Italian people have always excelled at flights in formation," the radio voice continued. "Mussolini has reportedly sent a bowl of fresh figs along with Balbo, as a gift to President Roosevelt. The President has said he looks forward to meeting with the Italian hero at some point in the coming week."

"Funny," Scarcelli was saying to someone else, "how we can fly so good in formation, but try to form us on the ground and you get nothing but yelling and dick-grabbing."

Nic meanwhile had waved over a boy with a basket of pears around his neck. "Hmm, let's see," he muttered, scanning the fruit. Suddenly his gaze shifted to the distant sky. "Hallo. That—?"

The boy whipped his head around, at which point Nic palmed a pear and retreated closer to the ledge, calling over his shoulder, "Sorry. Must've been bats."

Lowering his voice, he turned to Bart and said, "Hey. I have an idea. Let's go over the plan again."

"Perhaps," Bart said, "not on a crowded rooftop."

Nic considered this point, shrugged, then, holding out pear as prop, announced, "Revolutionary expropriation." He paused, seemed ready to sink his teeth into the fruit, then went on: "Say, while we're grabbing him? We might as well try and snatch them figs. Maybe, hey, why not a plane? Sorry. 'Flying boat.'" He finally took a bite, the size of which verged on the gratuitous, consuming, as it did, nearly half of the pear. Cheeks ballooning, he concluded, "While we're at it."

Bart marveled at the fact that someone had hauled an accordion and its paralyzed player up to the roof. He tilted his head to listen, but the tune's name evaded him. The lyrics used birds as a metaphor for the inconstancy of the heart. As he listened for the chorus, Nic made some approximation of speech, though mostly just exhaled masticated pear-bits, flecking Bart's face and neck.

Bart took him roughly by the arm and yanked him with a certain brusqueness to the alleymost ledge.

"Dance?" Nic said. "Why of cour—Heyyy, eas—"

They stepped off the side of the roof and dropped six feet, spooking a sleeping tom. The warped metal slats of the fire escape vibrated with the force of their landing. Nic tottered momentarily, sea-leggedly, his face contorting into a grimace equal parts startled and furious.

"Why," he finally panted, "would you do that?"

Bart removed his hat, straightening the brim. "I felt like discussing the plan on a crowded rooftop was a bad idea."

"You might have said something."

"Ahem."

"Do you have to sweat everything?"

"Would you like to hear my assessment of the situation?"

"Very much so."

"More specifically, it is an assessment of your character."

"Don't hold back."

"Once upon a time, there was a chubby little boy. He was teased and tormented and poked with sticks. You've heard this story before. The point is, young Fatty, one day, on his way to school, trips on a loose shoelace, and to make matters worse, he does so right in front of a pack of the cruelest of his tormentors, who are milling in back of the school with cigarettes. And at this very moment, he makes a split-second decision that will, in large part, determine the trajectory of the rest of his life. As he stumbles forward, rather than collapse lamely to the street, he decides to launch himself into a spectacular pratfall. An enormous bellyflop. Perhaps he topples an applecart. Perhaps he lands upon the tail of a small dog, or splatters a passing alderman with mud. Regardless, the scene is bathed in hilarity, and more importantly, it is a hilarity controlled by Fatty. The tormentors laugh, of course, but for the first time, the laughter is tinged with a degree of affection. That is how it begins. That is how Fatty discovers clowning equals love. Which, it's elementary psychology at this point, right? But eventually, somewhere along the course of a life, a line is crossed. And on the other side of the line, Fatty, unbeknownst to himself, becomes the sort of person who used to torment his young, prelapsarian self, in that he is no longer just trying to win over his oppressors with his clownish behavior but he is actually *bullying the bullies* with the sheer size of his personality, by not only falling, but falling with aggression, falling like a bomb falls, falling in a manner that—quite literally—brings down the house. Of course, when I say 'falling' I am speaking more broadly of any manner of antic. And now, nothing in the pottery shop is safe, no matter how innocent or beautifully crafted. Any scene, if depicted in stained glass, will end in shards. The feast will be floored. You have, in short, become a spiteful clown, the worst kind of clown. The laughter has become nervous."

"You through?"

"That more or less covers it."

"Here's me on you. Once upon a time there was a guy liked to watch. That was his thing, to hang back, deadpan, taking everything in. A scold. Real brooder. I could go on. But you've heard this story before, right? Thing is, poor bastard's convinced himself it's a conscious refusal. That he has chosen to withdraw. When, in fact, come on. We all know he'd happily join the club, if membership were proffered. If he weren't too frightened, or broken, to interface with the world. First in fucking line, this guy. And yet, in his mind, it's a bold stance, this absenting himself, this not fitting in—a sign of genius. *Of radical thinking!* When everybody but him knows the truth. It's a defect, my friend. Not a gift."

"You through?"

"Reckon, yeah."

A long silence, interrupted, finally, by a crowd noise from above, the sort of cheer that erupts like a scalding.

They stared up at the narrow swatch of sky visible between the building-tops, at the neck of the alley.

"What do they expect to see, anyways?"

"Twenty-four planes, flying in formation."

"So why are wops so good at formations?"

"It seems odd, especially since our formations on the ground tend to end in yelling."

"Dick-grabbing."

"*Putana vaca!*"

"*Porco dio!*"

"*Ostia!*"

"Right. Think it'll be exciting, then?"

"In theory."

"Think there'll be tricks?"

"I think the idea is more of a spectacular show of strength. Plus the distance traveled."

"All the way from Italy!"

"Exactly."

"Really, though, how do we know?"

"What's that, now?"

"That they're telling the truth? Like, who watched them fly over the ocean? What if that was all a bunch of noise, and they just flew down from, like, Canada? Or *Detroit?*"

"Well, I suppose one never knows."

"See?"

Bart responded, but his voice was drowned by a roar overhead. His mouth moved. They looked up again. The patch of sky visible between the aperture of the rooftops remained cloudless and vacant.

Silently, they waited.

Redemption Springs from Audacious Revolt

(a scene from the 1943 picture Sacco and Vanzetti Meet the Fascist Aviator, Italo Balbo*)*

They'd chosen Balbo for the obvious reason—namely, his possession of an inestimable symbolic value. The cloud-tousled hair. The roguish mustache. The scarf whipping back from the neck of his wind-blasted leather jacket, as rakish as a cad's loosened tie. The precarious cant of his cigarettes. That way he had of fixing the camera with an ironic, penetrating stare, always on the verge of (but never quite) mocking. Balbo had become not merely Mussolini's heir apparent, but the pinnacle—not only a figurative but a *literal pinnacle*—of Fascist Man, even well pre-Duce the concept of the aeronaut having been exalted by Marinetti and the Futurists as an embodiment of their manifesto, of flight and speed, a defiance of gravity, a penetration of the stratosphere.

Snatching all *that.*

In honor of Balbo's flight, the Italian Exhibition Hall at the World's Fair had been constructed in the shape of an aeroplane, complete with "wings," smaller "tails" and a long central "body." The entrance, a tower formed after the Fascist insignia, did not quite match the aeronautic theme, but added necessary grandeur. Before arriving, Bart had mentally prepared for organ grinders and gondola rides. But he found himself pleasantly surprised. The exhibit was primarily devoted to a history of Italian science, from the Romans to Galileo to the present-day experiments of a young physicist named Errico Fermi, who was doing work on atomic energy. A Verdi aria piped warmly throughout the halls.

"The Italian exhibits," explained a sign, "tell the story of achievements in engineering, physics, medicine, geography, astronomy, agriculture, shipping, and aviation."

After a quick surveil, Bart positioned himself near the entrance, keeping an eye out for Balbo's arrival. A small crowd stood, rapt, in front of a man in a white laboratory coat, who in turn stood behind a long table arrayed with various electrical devices.

"One of the first men to experiment with the effect of electricity on animals was a Bolognese anatomist, Luigi Galvani," explained the demonstrator, whose oratorical skill suggested a professional link to the theater rather than the laboratory. As he spoke, he removed a flayed, severed frog's leg from a jar of fluid and held it aloft for the crowd to see, eventually resting it in the stirruped arm of a display pedestal.

"Galvani's experiments in electrophysiology reached a critical point in 1786, when he managed to stimulate muscular contraction in the legs of skinned frogs," the lecturer continued, "once by touching a nerve with a pair of scissors during an electrical storm, and subsequently with the use of a spark-generating electrostatic device, which we have reproduced here." He paused to gesture at an unadorned mesh of wire and glass tubing. "Galvani was also able to produce leg twitches by inserting brass hooks into the frogs' spinal cords," he said. "These twitches took place whether there was a storm or, as Galvani wrote, the sky was 'quiet and serene.'"

With the studied dispassion of a magician performing a card trick, the lecturer inserted a metal pin into the dangling leg. A wire ran from the pin to the electrostatic device. The lecturer activated the device with the flick of a lever, and a low, crackling noise erupted from the tubes, sounding like clumps of dried grass tossed into a fire. The frog's leg began to feebly kick at the air directly in front and to the left of the lecturer's right hand, in which he held a stub of chalk.

On the easel behind him, he'd written: BIOELECTRIC FORCES EXIST WITHIN LIVING TISSUE.

"In 1791," he went on, "Galvani made public his findings in an essay titled '*De Viribus Electricitatis in Motu Musculari Commentarius*,' which translates as 'Commentary on the Effect of Electricity on Muscular Motion.' Galvani attributed the contractions to something he called 'animal electricity'—an innate electricity, much like that of the electric eel, which Galvani believed was stored within the nerves, muscles, and, most importantly, brains of most animals, in what he described as a 'nerveo-electric fluid.' The brain, he posited, secretes nerveo-electric fluid to the rest of the body via the nervous system."

The lecturer chuckled, presumably at the quaintness of the outmoded science. The crowd didn't seem to notice, their attention remaining absorbed by the disembodied leg, which continued to absently pump, beckoning like a moist digit, like the gnarled finger of a crone, but also, with its repetitive motion, seeming to gently massage the words of the lecturer, who went on to detail the experiments of Galvani's contemporary and (friendly) rival, Alessandro Volta, whose theory of "metallic energy," the lecturer explained, named the metal object as the source of the contractions, and who, though ultimately as wrong as Galvani, had his surname immortalized (Volta being the origin of *volt*), just as Galvani did (Volta himself having coined the verb *to galvanize*), all of which came only after a rather lengthy digression regarding eels, more specifically the eel's means of reproduction, which had mystified biologists for centuries, thinkers as far back as Aristotle (wrongly) believing that perhaps the eel asexually reproduced in the mud at the bottom of the streams and rivers in which they congregated, the lowly eel essentially stumping the naturalist community from that point on, until the middle of the 18th century, in fact, when another contemporary of Galvani's, another Italian, Carlo Mondini, proved the existence of genitalia in female eels, an enormous leap forward in eel-science which, sadly, remained stalled for another century or so, until a young Sigmund

Freud proved that the male eel possessed genitalia of his own. "Freud being the first non-Italian in our brief history," the lecturer asided with a practiced chuckle, adding after a pause, "though we might note that, perhaps not coincidentally, Freud was working and experimenting *in Trieste*—at the time, the most Italianate of Austrian territories—when he made his discoveries." Galvani thought of electric eels as the most eloquent demonstration of nerveo-electro fluid in nature, was how the eel digression came about.

Bart found the eel-science of interest, having trapped and hawked eels for years, though, admittedly, he'd never before given much thought to their mating rituals. As the lecturer droned on, he made a mental list of eel sexual positions. (The Double Helix. The Slipknot. The Tangled Extension Cord.) He thought back to his eel-trapping days. (One trapped an eel by baiting a narrow-mouthed receptacle with tiny fish. No need for a trick door or walls of glue, as the eel, once inside, remained, in most circumstances, too dim to muddle its way back out.) He thought back to his eel-hawking days, to the old women who insisted upon a pre-purchase right of eel inspection, as if they were checking cantaloupes for ripeness, only in this case Bart the one in charge of the proverbial thumping, which meant rolling up a sleeve and fishing out the selected eel in question. "Like to check the teeth?" Bart would ask the *strega*, clutching the writhing eel hand over hand as if he were preparing to climb it. "Maybe you'd like to stick your finger up his—"

Balbo.

No. False alarm. A tourist in a scarf and mustache.

Bart sighed, loosened his necktie and checked the time. He decided to step outside.

It was noon, and already sweltering. Bart gazed up at the giant thermometer, despite an earlier resolution to stop checking it. Ninety degrees. Balling up a sleeve, Bart gave his forehead a quick sop. The boon of an ill-fitting suit.

He scanned the promenade running along Lake Michigan. The entire fairground was thronged with fun-seekers. Snippets of conversation floated past, in every direction.

"A good deal of Spain has not been perambulated, bu—"

"—a less preposterous display of human suffering—"

"—think he was pulling your dick, In—"

"—nocent victims? No such thing. If you've been reaping the rewards of a corrupt and evil regime, even if you choose to remain blissfully oblivious to the corruption and evil, you're still committing a crime, you're at the very least a willing accomp—"

The 1933 World's Fair was focused on the past hundred years of technological advances, meant to coincide with the centennial of Chicago herself. The title of the exposition, "A Century of Progress," also implied inevitability and momentum, a futureward thrust whose path one would be foolish to impede. Bart glanced at a map of the fairgrounds. The Midget Village butted up against a Manchu Temple, which one could reach most efficiently by proceeding along the Avenue of Flags. The exhibit on prehistory was titled "The World A Million Years Ago." The exhibit on electricity was titled "The Servant That Has Transformed the World." The exhibit on agriculture was called "The Drama of Agriculture."

The Color Organ, a centerpiece of the fair, faced a section of promenade affording the clearest view of Balbo's flying boats, docked and anchored with a carefully posed majesty on the cobalt sheen of the lake. Bart sighted Balbo, finally, standing beside the massive instrument with a small party led by the mayor. The organist, small enough to pass for a jockey or child, and in fact performing with the stiff-backed solemnity of a precocious little girl presenting a recital, played Bach, the fugue synchronized with a dozen or so glass pillars flashing a spectrum of tinted lights. Balbo wore his aviator's outfit, still. As the mayor held forth, Balbo nodded blandly, his eyes drifting to the organist and any smart-looking woman passing near.

Bart moved closer. He narrowed his eyes as Balbo gestured at his own Savoia-Marchetti and proceeded to rather melodramatically describe what must have been another, more harrowing flight, yesterday's landing having been, by all accounts, as smooth as a Tyrolean waltz. Balbo used his palms as wings, the swoops of the palm-wings coming dangerously close to the nervously laughing mayor's cigar.

Was he actually making engine noises with his cheeks?

The mayor laughed. The Fascist guards smiled and nodded. Balbo shrugged, false-modest.

In private, Bart conceded the difficulty of resisting Balbo's charms. "I am just the moron who is willing to climb into the mouth of the cannon," Balbo insisted at press conferences. "I don't ask about the length of fuse, or how they mix the gun powder, or even what materials they use to construct my helmet. I simply make sure it is properly affixed to my head, and that my goggles have been well-adjusted. And then I slide into the tube. If I die, the people will say, 'Oh, Balbo? He was a very stupid man, to risk his life in that way.' But if I *survive*? Then I am the bravest. My will, to take this gamble, that is my only skill." Even his nationalistic drum-beating regarding Italy's "aerial fate," which he claimed had been predestined since the days of da Vinci's sketches of flying machines, when delivered with such an arch smile, managed to avoid offense. Witnessing such a grotesquely caricatured embodiment of the Italian male—equal parts *braggadocio* and Lothario, garlic and irony—still, somehow, filled Bart with the sort of racial pride he despised in others, and he chided himself for being so easily seduced, issuing constant self-reminders as to his detestation, politically, personally, and symbolically, of Balbo and all he represented. And yet, in moments of honesty, Bart would be forced to admit that his Balbo-hatred had not arisen naturally—certainly not in the way, say, Nic had conjured an immediate, almost visceral dislike of the rascal in the Fascist aviator, most likely because it was a shade too close to his own. Whereas Bart possessed, he knew, an innate attraction to Balbo's (and for that matter Nic's) type, a straight man's tendency to act as complement to a more extreme personality.

Inside the Italian Exhibition, Balbo returned the salutes of the Fascist guards with an amused nod, his own sporadic half-salutes easily mistakable for mocking. The mayor attempted to point out various exhibits, but Balbo appeared disinterested. He flirted with the telegraph girl at the Marconi display. He bound his face with his scarf, pretending to be a mummy and mock-menacing a girl working a panini press. He dropped an orange from a fake Tower of Pisa. He continued dropping oranges until he hit the mayor. He sent a telegraph to Mussolini complaining about the heat in Chicago, and how he couldn't get a decent cup of coffee. He joked with the mayor about the Italian's blood-propensity toward assassination. (The mayor's predecessor had been killed just one year prior, by an Italian, Giuseppe Zangara, who had been attempting to assassinate President-elect Roosevelt.) Balbo mock-strangled the mayor with his scarf. The frog's leg continued to kick. Balbo asked, "Which way to Pompeii?" The ruins of Pompeii had been recreated in Chicago, for an exhibit meant to teach children about volcanic activity. The "recreation of the ruins of Pompeii" turned out to be a diorama. The preserved body of a little boy, curled like a sculpture beneath an ash-dusted kitchen table, was, in fact, an actual Pompeiian body shipped over by Rome. Balbo said he felt, at times, as if his entire country had been covered with a blanket of volcanic ash, freezing all progress sometime around the Renaissance. He said the Duce had been the first statesman since Garibaldi brave enough to stir the ashes. He said after a boyhood trip to Pompeii, he'd sat in his bedroom for hours, imagining how the objects surrounding him would decompose if the room were sealed for eternity. He wondered if the half-eaten sandwich on his bedside table would dissolve, or if a mold would blanket his entire mattress? And just *how* thick would the dust, eventually, become? What manner of insect would use his skull for a nest?

Balbo said his mother discouraged this line of inquiry.

Bart, tailing from a safe distance, watched as the mayor steered his charges in the direction of the University of Bologna's display on wine fermentation, which included a tasting room for VIPs. En route, Balbo paused in front of a knife grinding display, the technological focus of this particular exhibit being the new electric-powered grinding wheel. Nic stood behind the machine, sliding knives between a pair of grooved wheels, their counter-spins powered by a humming motor. Beside him, another grinder sharpened knives on an old-fashioned wheel, using a foot pedal to propel its revolutions as water leaked from a conical receptacle to maintain the stone's moisture. A third man explained the ease and superiority of the new process.

"To sharpen a knife, you must take the blade 'down to zero,' grinding away metal to create a new edge," the speaker explained. "With the electric wheel, your work capacity is easily trebled, often more. See how many knives Massimo can sharpen, compared to Nicola, over here?" The man had accidentally called Nic "Massimo" and Guido "Nicola." To demonstrate the sharpness of the knives, the speaker cut a slice of salami, then held up the slice, measeled with fat and thin nearly to the point of translucence.

Balbo watched the demonstration, rapt, eventually moving to the far side of the podium, the better to see Nic. Bart remained at the back of the small crowd. One of Balbo's handlers said something in Italian, his voice too low to hear. The second handler nodded, then turned to the mayor. "He say Minister Balbo use to sharp the knife when he was a boy." The mayor said, "Ahhh," and smiled, though he seemed thrown by the late receipt of such a key piece of intelligence.

"*Ma varda che bello,*" Balbo remarked, directly to Nic, who stole a quick glance at the aviator, handed him a nod, but never stopped grinding.

"*Posso—?*" Balbo held out his hand.

Nic looked up from the wheel again, then turned to the lecturer, who shrugged. Nic switched off the machine. Slowly, blade first, he extended the knife he'd been sharpening in the direction of Balbo. It was a boning knife. The aviator reached toward the narrow, six-inch blade, touching the point with his index finger. The point of the knife pressed into Balbo's fingertip, stopping just shy of breaking the skin. A circle of whiteness appeared on the pink of his flesh, encircling the tip of the blade and expanding like a spill as the pressure increased.

Bart closed his eyes and waited for the scream, the scramble of Fascist boots, the mayor's official gasp.

Nic, smiling, held the knife perfectly still.

The Kidnapping of the Fascist Aviator, Italo Balbo (I)

(a scene from the 1943 picture Sacco and Vanzetti Meet the Fascist Aviator, Italo Balbo*)*

The kidnapping of the Fascist aviator, Italo Balbo, went as planned.

Later, in an undisclosed location (the fourteenth-floor office of a bankrupted paper wholesaler, vacant since the crash), the pilot, blindfolded and tied to a chair, his head sagging in a posture conveying resignation, but also (perhaps) the better to gore any captors foolish enough to venture too close, remained oddly unreceptive (for someone bound to a chair) to the idea of relinquishing even a bit of his former flyboy luster. Also they couldn't get him to shut up.

"So where are we, exactly, boys, maybe you will just tell me that?

"Might I at least wash off some of this custard?

"Ballpark location is all I ask.

"How about, if we are still in greater Chicago, you stomp your foot twice?

"I could make one phone call and everyone in this room is dead. Under an hour. This is what the Americans call 'a word to the wise.' You will want to keep me away from all active lines.

"I do not require food. Do you think I need to eat? Do you think I need to sleep or shit or piss, unless I so choose? *Do you fucking know who you have here?*

"Gravity cannot contain Balbo.

"I am the wrongest decision you ever made.

"Really, though. The jacket is from Milan. You know what a stain like this will do to leather?"

He also went on, frankly to the point of tedium, about his captors' whore grandmothers, and how if only they had possessed the basest level of self-control over their own whorishness they might have avoided impregnation by the syphilitic dogs who would come to be known as "granddad," which resultant whorespawn eventually whorefully begat the present company. Though in terms coarser and more difficult to translate.

Nic fell for a feigned sleep, one afternoon. He crawled too close to the chair, having dropped a screw from the back of a dismantled hotplate (normally used to heat soup), and ended up head-scissored, Balbo only unclenching after repeated shin- and knee-whacks with the dull end of an old paper cutter, Bart telegraphing every swing with the buck-toothed, overstudied precision of an amateur lumberjack.

After that, Balbo calmed down, some. Stripped of scarf and goggles, he'd aged, been made shabby. He looked like he should be selling day-old fruit from a stand, or soaking pools of spill atop some bar, the beery rag otherwise hanging from his rear pocket like an assward parody of a gentleman's handkerchief. One of Balbo's buttons had popped loose, his shirt's wound revealing a reedy patch of chest hair and the upper-left corner of a plastic-sheathed saint's medallion. (Blue sky, golden scepter's orb, an edge of halo, or perhaps the Holy Spirit's flaming presence.) The boys had stumbled across the office during one of their window-washing gigs. The room had been extremely dusty—verdigrised with dust in the cant of late-day light pouring through the blinds at the time of their arrival— but otherwise untouched. Nic had thought of Pompeii and felt vaguely disrespectful, like a treader across the width of a grave. The quartet of file cabinets were all filled with blank sheets of paper, meticulously filed samples organized by stock, shade and more than likely a dozen or so other classifications of which the consumer could remain happily unconcerned. A wall of shelving archived bound volumes of discontinued styles that, one assumed, could still be special-ordered upon request.

They kept a radio tuned to the news. Balbo's sudden and unexplained disappearance from his hotel room received reliable and thorough coverage. As per the kidnapping note's specific instructions, no reporter breathed a mention of any organized plot or demands.

Nic had tied Balbo's scarf around his waist like the belt of a robe, using the end to fan himself, wipe minestrone from his upper lip, polish the desk.

Whenever he tired of baiting his captors, Balbo maintained a running invective with the radio announcer.

"*Minister*, not Secretary. Minister! *Imbecili*.

"I broke that record in '29. *Pazzo!*

"'The Latin Lindbergh'? Did he just refer to me as 'the Latin Lindbergh'? How much time must you spend in America before your brain rots to the degree that you find such a phrase *amusing*, I wonder?"

"Should we gag him?" Nic wondered.

"I'll gag you mothers, I'll gag your mouths with my Fascist cock, I'll—"

They gagged him. He grappled with his bindings until his chair toppled over, then pummeled the floor with his head until he lost consciousness.

They righted him and bound the chair to the radiator, eventually removing the gag.

"I'll gag your anuses with my steel-toed boo—"

They replaced the gag.

Finally, his head sagged—this time, clearly a white flag. They removed the gag again.

(a scene from the 1943 picture Sacco and Vanzetti Meet the
Fascist Aviator, Italo Balbo*)*

They took turns.

Balbo could tell Bart's from the rustle of the pages of the newspaper.

Also, there was Bart's natural reticence.

"So are you planning to kill me?" Balbo wondered.

"Would you call this an act of political terror, or more like two
guys asking for a obscene amount of money?

"Because if it's money, I have got people who can pay. I am
loved.

"If it's politics, I don't know what to tell you. I will not lie.
Fascism works. Look at Italy before Mussolini, look at her now.
There is a quantifiable difference. Killing me and mailing my head
to the offices of *Il Martello* will not win that debate.

"That's all I will say on *that*.

"I'm joking, of course, about the decapitation.

"Please don't kill me.

"Why me? I'm not a hero. I'm just the moron willing to climb
into the mouth of the cannon. I—"

"We've heard that one before," Bart interrupted.

"Right," Balbo said. "Sorry. I am under a lot of pressure." He
sat mute for a moment, the admission suffusing him with a new
equanimity. Bart stared at the pilot, examining his latest pose. The
blindfolded man seemed to have retracted any antennae that may,
once, have been tweaked to plumb his dark surroundings. His nos-
trils were slack and unflared. His mouth was not clamped or sealed
but quite simply at rest.

The blindfold was a striped necktie. Three different shades of brown, plus a gold band for sparkle.

Bart started when Balbo finally spoke.

"Bum a fag?" Balbo asked.

Bart nodded, then, recalling the blindfold and feeling absurd, cleared his throat and muttered, "Yeah." He wondered if Balbo had been listening for the pages of the newspaper to turn and, absenting that, had puzzled out the staring. He lifted a cigarette to Balbo's mouth, now slightly agap. "Here," Bart said. It was like the mouth of a child, like testing a nephew for fever. He struck a match on the edge of the chair. "Flame," Bart said. Balbo nodded and puffed. "You're good," Bart said, waving out the match. Balbo took a mean inhale, coughing out smoke through clenched lips.

"Hey, could you—?"

Bart leaned over and took the cigarette from his mouth.

"Obliged."

After a moment, Bart replaced the cigarette between Balbo's lips, this time holding on while Balbo inhaled, loosely scissoring the butt with his fore and middle fingers. Every time Balbo took a pull, the cigarette twitched to life.

"*Grazie, neh?*" Balbo muttered, using only an eighth of his normal mouth range.

Bart removed the cigarette.

Balbo said, "You're a silent one. That is your methodology? You keep silent. Eventually I will be driven to fill the void. Secrete the state secrets you covet so dearly. Is that it? You have chosen a punk road, my friend. I'm sorry. Oh, I will talk. I enjoy talking. But I have nothing of any import. Not for you. I'm a figurehead, my man. The emblem on the grill of the automobile of state. Or, in this case, flying machine. I am a handsome man. I smashed some heads in my day, as a youth, working for the cause. I was *noticed*. And now I have been rewarded. This? What you are looking at? It's skillful casting. You

201

think I would wear this costume unless it was ordered from on-high? Please. I am not the one you need to be talking to. I am not even a functionary. I am all form. You are interrogating the form."

Balbo stopped abruptly, then shrugged. "Any thoughts on the matter?"

Bart, who had been smoking the remainder of Balbo's cigarette, stubbed out the butt on the heel of his boot but offered no response.

During his shifts, Nic had trouble with the sheer amount of stillness. The room, your standardest of office spaces, from the squall-weary oak battleship of a desk to the aforementioned chair, shelves, and file cabinets, provided little in the way of inspiration. The only book containing writing, stuffed deep within one of the shelves, was a Gideon's Bible, nabbed from some Texas motel room, the flanking paper sample archives folding over it like meaty loins squeezed tight on a fast hand. Which, some comfort. Some company. Pages too thin for even rolling smokes.

The floor was littered with pistachio shells, flicked by Nic from a far corner in the direction of the wastebasket, his scatter-to-dunk ratio approximately ten-to-one in favor of missing completely.

He did a soft-shoe dance on the broken shells.

He chipped at the gold leafing of a congratulatory sales plaque (shaped as a long, unfurling strip of toilet paper and inscribed NO JOB IS FINISHED UNTIL THE PAPERWORK IS DONE), double-checking that it was leafing and not solid. (It was leafing.)

He paced the desk, corner to corner, Bible tucked beneath an arm.

"Say, could you perhaps cut out the pacing?" Balbo asked.

"Don't make me, pal," Nic said. "You know I will."

Eventually, he got bored with the pacing and stopped, sinking a thumb into the book's filling and flipping it open, making ready to declaim.

Balbo sat there like a stump. Like: *Impress me, Preacherman.* Though, really, blindfolded, he had no idea about Nic's Bible, was more likely listening for a radio report about himself.

"You fellows left a note, I'm assuming," he said.

Nic stood on one leg, the Bible held aloft like a bird of prey captured and being displayed to an audience. The other hand struck a conductor's pose.

Steady. Steady.

He held the pose. "Note?"

"A list of demands. Delirious manifesto. I'm just getting the impression from these reports that they think I defected with a farm girl from Dubuque."

Nick violently mussed his own hair with his conducting hand, also giving his face a rubdown while he was at it.

"Don't you worry. Ain't your concern."

"No worries. I'm just listening to these reports, and they're beginning to sound a tad monotone. 'Fascist aviator Balbo still missing.' So forth. Missing is a whole different animal from kidnapped."

"We left specific instructions in the note with regards to not alerting the media and/or the populace, okay, Tonto?"

"Mmm. This makes sense. This is very sensible. So, have they contacted you, yet?"

"Who's that?"

"I don't know. Whoever you left the note with. The mayor's office? The Italian consulate? The Chicago Rotary Club? How am I supposed to—"

"Nope. No word as of this morning. Bart's checking as we speak."

Blind Balbo gave a directionless nod. "Right. I just wondered. Because it seems like some time has passed and—"

"Hey, we know the amount of time that's passed, and we're making adjustments to the plan accordingly."

"Right. Of course. So, going back to your demands. They're not completely unreasonable demands, are they?"

"Say again, Chadwick?"

"The demands you're making of, I assume, the Italian government. It's a price I'm assuming to be not wholly unreasonable. A price they might reasonably pay. Not to devalue my own worth. But, for the sake of argument—"

"Oh, this ain't about money." Nic had walked to the windoward edge of the desk and leaned all the way out- and against-, chilling his nose and forehead on the glass. Bart insisted on drawn blinds, always, but Nic occasionally lifted the ban, unilaterally, at dusk.

"No money? Oh. Well. That is interesting. So you have other demands, I assume?"

"Mmm."

"Release the political prisoners. Free the press. That kind of thing?"

"Them lines."

"And if they don't accept?"

Nic tried to make a throat-slitting sound with his tongue, but ended up with more of an indecorous gargle.

"Are you okay?"

"*Hrrrm.* Yeah. Look, don't sweat it. I'm kidding. This whole thing's more about making people aware. If we wanted to assassinate you, you'd be assassinated. A king, yeah. A president or some other symbol of power who's also an actual oppressor. Then, yeah. Assassination's a valid route. But don't worry. You're not on that level."

Nic dropped from the side of the desk and crossed the room, in the direction of the hotplate.

"You hungry?"

"We just ate."

"Right. Still, it was a light dinner, wasn't it? There's some leftover sauce. I could slice up some eggplant."

"I'm fine."

Nic sighed. "You ever get lonely?"

"Pardon me?"

"Out there. Flying."

"Mmm. Sure. Well, it's not exactly *loneliness*. There's a whole group of us, so."

"Flying in formation."

"Right. We have radios."

"Still. It's a long flight. You're alone, in that little bird a yours."

"We never call them birds."

"Sorry. You should, though."

"We tell stories. That's one thing we do."

"Stories?"

"Kind of a queer game. One member of the formation will begin, then leave off at a climactic moment. Then the next man picks up. Like a serial."

"Huh."

"I told you it was queer. It's a long flight. It gets tedious up there, especially if the weather's smooth."

"What kinda stories?"

"Well, it's a group of men, so they often start off in the realm of the bawdy fable. 'Once upon a time there was a peasant in Sicily with a *huge* penis, and the Empress of Austria happened to come to town . . .' That sort of thing. From there, they often become adventure stories. Young men, having adventures. Alone against nature. Serving their country. Searching for gold. Not many women in these stories, unless the hero visits a whorehouse. Stumbles on a harem. Milanese detective stories are popular, the crimes tending toward the sexual or anti-clerical. Mountaineering stories also fare well, as do safaris. Sailors are hated in art as in life. For some reason, aviators never seem to turn up. And then certain guys in the formation have their own fortes. Zanoni is the wise guy, responsible for all of the funny lines. You can always count on Germi to work in a pirate. Buzzanca, no matter what the scene, somehow manages to incorporate anal sex. If Buzzanca takes over a scene involving the Virgin Mary's appearance in a vision, you can be fairly certain she's getting it up the ass. In the end, the stories are more like parodies. Cheers erupt when a cask of wine is discovered, and we all take a drink."

"You all—?"

"A four-course meal is described in orgiastic detail. Enter Colosanti, the flatulent eunuch. '*Sacramento!*' interrupts the actual Colosanti, the third rib of the upper-left wing of the formation, but he is drowned out by the laughter of the rest of the men. Of course, not being professional storytellers, many of my boys end up drawing from their own lives. The hero stops to visit his dying mother. He hopes to find her at peace, but instead she pulls him close and whispers curses against God, and life, and begs to be poisoned. Later, he discovers he's been cuckolded by the town butcher, and imagines, from a far-off battlefield, his Mariana splayed on a wooden block, marbled with fat, the dirty butcher slowly removing his bloody gloves, his charnel-smeared apron. Everyone in the formation knowing the truth when they hear it, understanding that, as men, these stories are their only means of discussing these personal matters, even offering advice and consolation through their own segments of story by introducing other characters to instruct the hero on how to deal with the death of a parent, or the inconstancy of a loved one. The medium creates its own feeling of distance. As acutely as I might remain aware that Fuocca, pilot of Number Seven, hovers approximately seventy meters to my right, his voice, flattened by the radio, its timbre's canvas cracked and aged by static, its volume pitching and dropping as if buffeted by winds on its long journey to my ear, all contribute to the illusion that our stories are messages from distant lands. The transmissions begin to take on a nagging, malarial buzz. As the leader, I always go last—"

Nic, as Balbo spoke, had retired to the opposite side of the room and begun making airplanes out of sample paper. Initially, he'd tried to create a Savoia-Marchetti flying boat, but he couldn't get the blunt nose right. After several attempted foldings ended in crumpled wads, he gave up, instead halving and beaking a simple V-glider and tossing it absently in the direction of the wastebasket. It arced the length of the room, the flight parabola dipping as it approached the desk. After a swoop past the dust-filled inkwell, the plane banked out toward the window, taking a sharp upturn just before impact to loop back at Nic. Spiraling in a circular eddy near the ceiling, the plane then made a sudden, precipitous drop, only pulling out of the nosedive at the last second to whiz by Balbo—the pilot's narrative taking a pause as he considered the pointed breeze cutting a slice across his cheek. Nic watched the plane's fantastic flight pattern as it continued its tour of the room, waiting for a landing that never came. Balbo's voice receded to a background drone. Nic eventually licked a finger and held it aloft, testing for an odd draft or some other explicable phenomenon. He had a vague notion that Balbo had begun asking him questions, but he ignored the chatter. Still following the plane with his eyes, he tore another sheet from the sample booklet and creased out a second plane, hastily flinging it in pursuit of the maiden flyer. The new plane immediately began coasting and looping a circuit as dizzying as the first. Nic stared on, tearing sheet after sheet from the booklet and sloppily folding plane upon plane, launching them as quickly as he could flatten out the wings, the room now a blizzard of misangled flakes. By this point, enough planes had taken flight for the occasional collision to occur, but for the most part the air remained thick, *swarmed*. Nic grew anxious for Bart to arrive, for someone else to bear witness to the extraordinary scene. With a start, he realized he'd sat against the door. As he shifted aside to allow for Bart's entrance, something in the air shifted as well. At once, the planes, every last one, dropped, as if dumped from a box in the rafters. They crashed to the floor with a sound like breaking surf.

Nic stared at the littered scene.

Balbo screamed, "*Tell me what's happening!*"

At that moment, Bart entered the room. He'd bought the afternoon newspaper and a loaf of bread.

"They met much later, in 1917, when, on the United States'
entry into the war, a group of the anarchist Luigi Galleani's
followers fled to Mexico to avoid the draft, and also to await
the wave of revolutionary activity that would, inevitably,
sweep across Europe from Russia." (p. 7)

Anarchism is often misunderstood to mean "chaos." In fact, though there were certainly nihilistic branches of the movement—Nietzschean advocates of total individual freedom at the expense of all others—most anarchists remained closer, in spirit, to eighteenth-century Utopian Socialists such as Morelly, Charles Fourier, Claude Henri de Saint-Simon and Robert Owen, placing their faith in rationality and the idea that humans, if freed from the inherent oppression of a centralized governing body, would choose, through "free agreement," to cooperate with one another on a local, communal level —though many anarchists *did* come to lose faith in so-called "propaganda of the word," turning instead to dynamite, *attentats* and other violent terrorist actions which, they argued, were merely meeting the violent, terroristic state in kind. (Galleani would become the loudest and most articulate proponent of "propoganda of the deed.")

It was a Russian, Mikhail Bakunin, who more or less sparked the Italian anarchist movement when he settled in Florence in 1864, the year of the founding of the First International in London. (He'd met Marx in Paris, twenty years earlier; they didn't hit it off.) Unlike Marx and Engels, Bakunin felt preindustrial societies—for instance, the nascent Italian state—with their masses of disadvantaged workers, were rife for revolution, that the masses, however ignorant, had the seeds of revolution bred inside them. That they were "socialist without knowing it." Countered Engels, "The Italians must still attend the school of experience a little more to learn that a backward nation of peasants such as they only make themselves ridiculous when they want to prescribe to the workers of the nations with big industry how they must conduct themselves in order to arrive at emancipation."

The Kidnapping of the Fascist Aviator, Italo Balbo (IV)

(a scene from the 1943 picture Sacco and Vanzetti Meet the Fascist Aviator, Italo Balbo*)*

They had been wondering, for some time, why no one had showed up at the appointed meeting place, or made any sort of response to their demands. When the papers reported Balbo "likely dead" and insisted that the Italian government had halted its search, their concern intensified.

A few days later, over breakfast, they realized someone had used the ransom note to wrap a pat of butter. (The Fascist Embassy, they later learned, had been mailed a crayon drawing by Paolo, the six-year-old from apartment 3-F; it hung for a month on the bulletin board of the consulate.)

"So, wait," Nic said. "You're implying that when I bought groceries, I accidentally wrapped the butter in our note? This is your implication?"

Balbo, across the room, perked up. "What did you just say?"

Bart clubbed Nic on the side of the head with the butter, leaving a greasy smear.

Balbo, piecing together what happened, began shouting.

"You morons!

"You bumblers!

"My loved ones think I'm *dead*. Come closer so I can piss on you. Tell me where you are, so I can castrate you with my teeth!"

Bart, meanwhile, was chasing Nic around the room with the butter, Nic eventually escaping via the window, onto the ledge, from which he promptly toppled, only to find himself dangling from the minute hand of the enormous clock face, one story below.

"Nic!" Bart shouted.

"I'm sorry, pal," Nic said.

The clock hand was surprisingly sharp. It was 6:15. With each downward tick, Nic winced, as if preparing for the big plunge.

"Nic!" Bart shouted.

Nic's feet scrambled across the clock's smooth surface. The buttery note blew out of Bart's hand, into Nic's face. Thanks to the butter, it stuck. With his uncovered eye, Nic saw Bart reaching down in vain. Nic could also read a couple of the letters on the note: a huge E, and the beginning of a word. "ANA?" he wondered aloud. Another minute ticked by. A pigeon fluttered dangerously close. Nic noted that even pigeons appeared graceful in the bright sunlight. He kicked at the 5. It was a raised-face numeral. He traced the shape of the 5 with his foot. Another minute's tick and he would be able to reach the bottom curve of the 5's hook.

"Nic!" Bart shouted.

He craned his neck around, glancing down, recoiling from the vertigo-shot, then peered over his left shoulder. Behind him, the city's majestic skyline had already been lit to counter the dusk.

The clouds moved in the background, slow as armies.

Chapter Eight:
The Trial (II)

*The stars discuss their legal troubles—the plaintiff speaks—
a scene from the trial*

*(from a series of interviews with Nic Sacco and Bart Vanzetti
for* Motion Picture Monthly, *conducted the week of July 14,
1963, at the Beverly Hills Hotel)*

Getting back to the trial.

Tragic, eh?

*Well, expand on that for me. What aspect of the Bonapace affair
struck you as the most "tra—*

Oh, by trial, you meant *our* trial. See, the minute I heard that
word, I thought Arbuckle's.

Now. *There* was a tragedy.

That. Yeah.

You will hear no denials from this side of the room.

One of the greats, brought low by tragedy. You know Arbuckle's
often cited by scholarly types as the first guy on film to take it in
the face?

With a pie, is what Nic means. That is true. Fatty pioneered, in
many aspects of the medium.

Speaking of, I got a theory.

Mmm. Here we go.

May I?

Simply trying to warn our friend here that perhaps double-checking the red lights and rotating spools on his recording device might
be prudent, as missing a single syllable of what's to follow would
gravely disappoint.

(*long pause*)

Please.

You sure now?

Go-head.

Obliged. Anyhow. His *name.*

I'm sorry. I think I lost the thread during the whole exchange about my tape reco—

I'm saying it's all simple as his name. Do I need to spell it out? Mr. Roscoe "*Fatty*" Arbuckle throws a party in his hotel room. One of the ripe young aspirants in attendance takes ill and then four days later this broad kicks. Her friend, who, by some strange coincidence, happens to be a notorious Hollywood procuress, cries rape, as in, "The grotesque silent film clown Roscoe '*Fatty*' Arbuckle has forced his oily girth upon this poor petite creature, rupturing her insides, and after once again sating his bestial hunger, however fleetingly, abandons her to a slow agonizing . . ." Need I say more?

Mmm.

Do I got to spell it out?

Please.

A slenderer gentleman wouldn't have been so quickly condemned.

Oh, come, now.

We going somewhere?

You're not serious.

As a PLAGUE SPREADS headline.

He jests.

His tie, every morning, in the mirror, before he travels forth to spread the serious gospel truth.

Fatty got a raw deal. You'll hear no debate from these quarters on that point. But surely you don't attribute the harsh treatment he received to some kind of irrational prejudice against—

The average citizen abhors the sight of a fat man.

In a Swedish-style buffet line, or do you refer to more generalized circumstances?

Is, matter of fact, repulsed. But does the average citizen ever pause for a sec to ask himself why?

He is about to tell us.

Because we have appetites, and appetites is another word for needs, and needs is another word for weakness. And who wants that front-and-centered? Nobody. We're appetite made visible. Weakness made flesh.

Remember our Coney Island picture? It climaxed in a hot-dog eating contest.

The world hates to be reminded that it pants and craves and sweats and shits.

We actually recruited one of the legendary hot-dog-eating champions, Witold "Outhouse Hole" Kasprzykowski, to take part in the shoot.

Oh, the fat man's allowed to be funny, 'course. *That's* just fine.

The man could eat. Though he was well past his prime, by that point. Very sad to see.

"Hey, look! A stout gentleman's tumbled backwards down a muddy incline while attempting to pull up his pants!"

I can still picture Kasprzykowski, slumped on one arm, holding a frank in the other. He always wore a safari shirt, open to the navel. The dribbled catsup made his exposed patch of chest hair appear as if it were sheltering a wounded rabbit.

"Check out Piggy, unable to fit in a normal-sized chair!"

There had been nasty rumors, early on, that Kasprzykowski had surgeons replace his stomach with an adult baboon's.

A fat guy can take a pie in the face. A fat guy can fall for the old crab gag. A—

Just for the sake of clarity, the old crab gag involves the illicit and/or accidental slipping of a crab into a coat pocket. The crab in question then proceeds to use its claws to pop balloon vendor's balloons, pinch ladies' tightly-skirted bottoms, snatch kerchiefs from purses, so forth. All of these actions take place unbeknownst to the owner of the pocket. The humor lies in the pocket-owner repeatedly being blamed for the actions of the crab, and subsequently threatened, slapped, so forth.

A fat guy can fall for the old crab gag. A fat guy can suffer any variation of indignity. But can he, can *we*, ever, just for goddamn once, get the girl? Well. You seen what happened to our pal Fatty, when he dared to express his sexual nature. Call in the justice system!

Not to sound prudish, but the girl *was* dead.

He was acquitted! The jury issued an *apology*.

Not that your rhetorical tack doesn't intrigue. You essentially imply that the obese are seen and judged as 'types' based solely on their body size. That the courts may as well be measuring the contours of their skulls and consulting a phrenology textbo—

Fatty did have a huge head. Give you that.

I'm not—

It was like a parade float. Kind of bobbing there on his neck, like it was fastened to the ground with ropes.

The point is—

Can you imagine that head of his, bearing down on you like a moon?

A moon, now?

You know one of them anthropomorphized, Méliès sort of moons? Fatty had those rouged cheeks, too. I mean, to be fair, guy was a bit of a grotesque.

Going back to your trial.

Utterly specious.

We was cleared.

Perhaps we can direct you to the settlement?

It ends with three words: "No. Admission. Of. Guilt."

Still, the verdict of history often differs from that of the court. Would you care to make any predictions as to what your ultimate verdict might be?

History delivers only one verdict, whether the man in the docket be pauper or king.

The sentimental existentialist, I call this guy.

We never stole that guinea's—

Right.

VO: And now we move to the Big Apple, to a tenement building in East Harlem.

(*Shot of unassuming building at the corner of First Avenue and 125th Street.*)

VO: Inside, residents shout, share laughs, and sing to one another in their pidgin tongue, their voices echoing from open doorways, as if amplified by Victrola funnel. Mr. Toscanini had nothing to do with *this* record! On to apartment 5-D, where we meet Clemente Bonapace, a knife-grinder by trade.

(*Shot of door labeled "5-D." Opens to reveal a diminutive Italian in his early thirties, wearing an ill-fitting shirt and tie.*)

VO: Mr. Bonapace, or "Mente," as he's known to his friends, has toiled in obscurity in America, his adopted home—until now. Though it may be difficult for some viewers to believe, this working-class immigrant, single-handedly, is poised to bring down his native country's most beloved export since the pepperoni pie.

(*Clip from the Sacco and Vanzetti picture* Chump Change.)

VO: On the big screen, Nic Sacco and Bart Vanzetti have dropped and given twenty for Army drill sergeants, dodged the nightsticks of angry London bobbies and stepped into the boxing ring with that heaviest of heavyweights, Primo Carnera. But their greatest battle yet, ironically, may be with this shabbily dressed former neighbor, who has filed a lawsuit alleging *he*, not Sacco and Vanzetti, developed the acrobatic knife tricks that have become the duo's stock-in-trade.

(*Clip from the Sacco and Vanzetti picture* Whichever Way You Slice It.)

VO: Sacco and Vanzetti have declined to comment on the cutler's charges, other than releasing a statement through their attorney dismissing the case as "baseless and, furthermore, entirely without merit." Sources close to the duo have described them as hurt and puzzled by this vicious attack from a fellow countryman.

(*Shot of Bonapace in his tiny flat, posed stiffly in front of a threadbare sofa.*)

VO: Until now, Bonapace, too, has avoided the harsh light of public scrutiny. This afternoon, for the first time, he has consented to speak to the press. Besides Bonapace and his lawyer, his wife and four children are present. Kitchen smells hang over the room. The wife, Maria, toils over a quartet of cauldrons, humming happily to herself.

(*Shot of Maria Bonapace tasting marinara sauce from wooden spoon.*)

VO: Bonapace's counsel, Hill Brewster.

(*Tight shot of Brewster, a portly lawyer with thinning hair and a flat delivery that sounds like recitation.*)

Brewster: My client comes from the north of Italy, from a village in the Dolomite mountain range where most of the men are grinders by trade. Of course, they cannot all find work in the immediate region, so there has been a mass migration over the years. My client boarded a ship bound for Ellis Isle when he was nineteen. My client has never returned to his native land, not for any lack of nostalgia, but for simple lack of means. Any money he can scrape together through his trade goes to feeding his family, or is sent back home to his ailing, elderly parents.

VO: And what does this client have to say for himself? Not much that's comprehensible to this reporter, unfortunately—Clemente Bonapace cannot speak English. His eldest daughter, Pina, translates.

(*Shot of Pina, a demure eleven-year-old, and her father, seated on couch.*)

Pina Bonapace: My papa, he says that he always did tricks with his knifes, even back in the Old Country. He says he used to get tired with spending all his days just sharpening, sharpening. So he started fooling with the knifes—juggling, things like that. For us kids, and then for the people in the neighborhood. Big crowds of people used to come and watch him do his show.

(*Clip from the Sacco and Vanzetti picture* The Daily Grind.)

Pina Bonapace (VO): Mister Bart and Mister Nic, they lived two floors down below us. My papa knew them well. Everybody knows everybody in this building. It's all Italians, here. We stick together. This was back when Mister Bart was selling eels. Mister Nic, at that time, he worked in the shoe factory.

(*Tight shot of Brewster.*)

Brewster: My client did not consider his feats an 'act.' My client was simply entertaining the downtrodden of his neighborhood, bringing some little joy to these folks the only way he knew how. My client had no aspirations to 'make it,' as they say, in vaudeville or Hollywood.

(*Shot of the Bonapace family eating dinner around an impossibly crowded table.*)

VO: Bonapace claims Sacco and Vanzetti, as a young and eager comedy team, witnessed his tricks on many occasions, even asking for lessons.

(*Tight shot of Pina Bonapace.*)

Pina Bonapace: They made jokes with my father, like, 'Oh, if we come into it big with your knife tricks, you'll get half of every one of our millions.'

(*Clip from the Sacco and Vanzetti picture* Ventriloquism and Its Discontents.)

VO: The portion of the story not in dispute comes next: Sacco and Vanzetti began to incorporate knife tricks into their own act. The public loved them, and the pair quickly left the slum behind for more upscale trappings.

(*Clip from the Sacco and Vanzetti picture* Sacco and Vanzetti Dessert the Cause.)

Brewster (VO): My client had no interest in financial gain. My client wished his friends nothing but good luck.

(*Shot of Bonapace's daughter, Teresina, wobbling across room on crutches.*)

VO: Things changed, however, after Bonapace's youngest child, Teresina, took ill with rachitis, that dread disease known in the colloquial as rickets. If the child did not receive the expensive treatment recommended by her physician, she would be left permanently bowlegged, perhaps even confined to a wheelchair. Bonapace could not raise the funds necessary to save his child. And so, he claims, he turned to the only men with means he had ever known. Swallowing his pride, he wrote to Sacco and Vanzetti, asking for a loan.

(*Clip from the matchstick girl sequence of the Sacco and Vanzetti short* Hobo Riviera.)

VO: Sacco and Vanzetti insist they never saw *any* version of the plaintiff's act. They also claim the grinder threatened a specious lawsuit if an undisclosed cash payment was not transferred into his bank account.

(*Shots of various sensational newspaper headlines detailing the lawsuit and its allegations.*)

VO: When word of the lawsuit became public, Sacco and Vanzetti suddenly found themselves cast in an unfamiliar role—that of the heavy.

(*Tight shot of Brewster.*)

Brewster: My client did not wish to involve the courts. It was only when associates of Mr. Sacco and Mr. Vanzetti began to circulate stories besmirching the good name of my client and of his family that he agreed to the lawsuit, and this only to restore the Bonapace name.

(*Shot of newly pressed bills moving along conveyer belt.*)

VO: Oddly, counsel neglects to mention the several-hundred-thousand dollars in damage Bonapace's suit also seeks. Though we assume counsel will remember to mention this segment of the lawsuit once he makes it to court!

(*Shot of Bonapace's tenement neighbors, standing in front of the building and engaged in animated discussion, rife with the sort of gesticulations common to the Italian race.*)

VO: Interviews have been conducted with men from the neighborhood who know the disputing parties. Some back the grinder's version of events, others Sacco and Vanzetti's. Lawyers for the comedy team maintain that the "eyewitnesses" produced by Bonapace—men who claim to have witnessed Sacco and Vanzetti witnessing Bonapace's knife act—have been bribed with promises of a share in any future settlement.

(*Shot of trash-heaped alley behind tenement.*)

VO: Before departing, we asked Mr. Bonapace for a demonstration.

(*Shot of Bonapace dragging grinding wheel from padlocked storage shed. His wife hands him a fagot of common kitchen knives, loosely bound with an old towel.*)

VO: As you can see, his performance was quite impressive.

(*Shot of Bonapace sharpening, tossing, juggling and barely dodging knives of various lengths and curvatures, eventually becoming entangled in a loose clothesline.*)

VO: As with Sacco and Vanzetti, the beauty of Bonapace's act is that he becomes both Knife-Thrower and Girl on the Spinning Target. Still, the key question remains unanswered. *Did* Sacco and Vanzetti steal their act from this man? Or did Bonapace *hone*, if you'll forgive a pun, *his* skills by means of careful observation, in darkened movie palaces, of "Mister Nic and Mister Bart"?

(*Shot of Bonapace, now entirely bound in clothesline. A dozen or so knives are also bound up in the line, their handles protruding from various angles. The grinder has suffered no apparent cuts.*)

VO: We conclude on an editorial note. If Bonapace is lying, this final image may become more than metaphor. The knives of justice, when turned upon one of Her Abusers, *cannot be dodged.* In this reporter's experience, they cut deep—and rarely miss. Pray to St. Sebastian, Mr. Bonapace, that your knives will not become HIS ARROWS.

Traditionally, a hot foot may be pulled with nothing more than a pair of matches, the first inserted between the shoe proper and a flap of sole, the second used for ignition. To quote a dime-store gag book from memory. To quote, more specifically, a dime-store gag book written by Nic. Well, *half*-written, in his head, and never published. Though highly quotable from memory. It had been his manager's ill conception, though Nic took a brief shine to the project. *The soles, ideally, will be loose. New shoes work less well in a hot foot, which is an unfortunate irony, as the most desirable mugs, historically speaking, tend to be of a wealthier persuasion, and thus in possession of new, intact footwear.* To quote, more specifically, the chapter entitled "The Hot Foot." Stuck in the dock—moored, so to speak—what's left to one but quoting one's own gag book from memory? "One dreams, in one's youth, of perchancely grooming into the great titular roles, the Kings and Moors and ever-pondering Danes. But then one realizes, in a powder-flash of epiphany, that the name Falstaff has been indelibly inked upon one's certificate of birth, and that placing a crown upon one's head, or blackening up, t'all merely makes one *more* what, in fact, he already 'tis." And so one works with what he's got. Nic's mind had the propensity to wander in the best of circumstances, and even more in a situation such as today's, one combining gravity with stupefaction, that along with the knowledge he should really be paying attention. *Attentat.* He took aim at the judge, with his eyes. An imaginary bullet hole flashed onto the judgely forehead like a Hindoo's teak. *During insertion and ignition, a partner, ideally, would act as a distracting element, keeping the mug occupied with clownish antics, sudden weeping, the feigned fits of an "epilep," violent self-mu-tilatory pantomime, to give but four examples.* The judge presided, in his white mustaches, his expression that of someone giving careful thought on whether he ought to sneeze. Nic leaned back in the wooden chair, collapsing his girth for maximum creakage. He should really pay attention. *His* neck, after all. It reminded him of all the wasted nights he'd spent sitting across from pretty, dull women, realizing that focusing on a single thread of inanity, just enough to make an adequate response, was all that was required, and how hard was that? And still letting the thread slip free. *Before lighting the match (or fuse), signal your partner with a prearranged hand gesture, allowing your partner time to slowly back away from the mug. (If his antics have been sufficiently clownish, a backwards soft-shoe "shimmy" is highly recommended, and is unlikely to arouse mugly suspicion.)* A judge in a wig would be funnier. Though perhaps not. A corollary to the rule of the comedic prop-costume being that, sometimes, the *too*-funny becomes just that, while the inherently *not* funny—a plaid mackintosh, say, or sensible boots—*can* be, when draped over a funny-enough player. The clown takes the stage in his civvies kind of thing, putting a natural tension into the affair, a drama in which the outrageous is suddenly forced to duke it out with the banal in order to seize the pie. Their counsel stood front and center, declaim-ing. "Gentlemen of the jury, perhaps you have heard of my famous clients? Do not let that prejudice you, please, I beg in the name of Justice." *The shoelace gag is similar to the hot foot as far as the distrac-tion techniques recommended. Once the shoelaces have been bound to-gether, signal your accomplice, who, in the case of this gag, must also be prepared to startle the mug. The recommended startling technique in-volves having said accomplice bellow something along the lines of, "Look out, he's lost control of the carriage!" or "Bats!"* Nic, in all frankness, found their counsel's tactics on the depressing side—if transparent race-baiting spiced with dubiously interpreted patent law and an assumption of rube-juror stupefaction in the face of Hollywood star-power could be described as "tactical"—even moreso in light of their likely effectiveness. It came down to the hatred of an average juror for a dirty, scheming guinea, subtly assuaged by the presence of two of the same made good—*See!* And so there is no hatred, there is only fair play, and a respect for those who played fairly by the rules and found success in the game, fury and righteous indignation reserved for the foul foreign refuse(r). To Nic's left, the wop grinder sat looking uncomfortable in his new suit. Save the receipt, Guido! Nic realized he should pay attention. The list of comics who'd come to bad ends . . . Well. That sort of ending was far more common than swelling string music and a soft fade. Fatty. Mabel. Linder. McCullough. Meanwhile Bart remained fastened to his own chair, looking rapt, puckered, quietly furious. Nic had initially agitated for representing themselves. He'd even worked out an opening statement, which involved his citing an old *commedia dell'arte* routine involving an axe-grinder. "*I'm no lawyer,* but unless one of Signor Bonapace's great-ancestors moonlit as a scriptwriter in sixteenth-century Tuscany, then you gotta concede that this particular gag has resided in what I believe is commonly known as the public domain for quite some time now, which I would argue makes this particular lawsuit a tad bit, how they say? *Superfluous.*" In the *commedia* version of the grinding routine, Mezzettino, one of the *zanni*, when handed a knife, pretends to sharpen it by miming the pedaling of a grinder's wheel and simulating the sound of steel scraping stone with his mouth. Admittedly, not a hilarious-sounding gag. But one must imagine the man-made sound effects, in particular, and also the precision of movement involved: the exactness of the wheelward slide, of the honing wrist, of the foot's pump, all calibrated to conjure a machine from the ether. Nic had never been much of an impressionist. The well-timed sound effect, though, remained a key element in any number of gags. A judge's gavel, for example, produces a rap satisfying in both resonance and authority, and so can be funny as a means of rudely interrupting a dull monologue or (say) of clubbing silly a loudly testifying Brooklyn gangland boss. Breaking glass: also funny. Hollow pipe on bone: uh-huh. Bone, snapping: never works. Industrial vacuum on face: only in extremely brief doses. Bad ends. There was Fatty, of course. His trial had been a zoo. Acquitted, exonerated, yet never forgiven by the public. Nic and Bart had been fresh meat, those days. Fatty knew how to throw a serious party. He will not be exonerated for that. Nic flashed back to his fresh-faced self, even Bart (though always old beyond his years) exhibiting some manner of youthful-ambitious twinkle. Nic, looking to use the loo at one of Fatty's wilder fetes, had burst upon Fatty bent over the tub, receiving a rum enema, as administered by Miss Clara Bow, whilst John Bunny (of the groundbreaking fat-skinny comedy team Flora and Bunny) sat on the toilet masturbating into a pornographic magazine devoted to the copulating Negro. Welcome to Hollywood. Fatty-Atty-Atty: First to take a pie in the face on film, first to crash in scandal. Bad ends. He'd worked up a theory about the last films of comics, how they tend to be far sadder than the saddest of tragedies. Yes, yes: how original. The sad clown! The secret tears of a pratfaller! Nic had once seen Fatty nearly die, he (Fatty) having been in the (unwise) habit of swigging beer from enormous steins in which he would deposit (pre-swig) (inexplicably) the detritus at the bottom of any martini glass within reach. So this one party, he'd accidentally swallowed an olive and its plastic spear. Lloyd had had to perform an emergency tracheotomy with his pocketknife, using a hollowed pen for a breathing tube. They'd had to stop Clara from putting a flower in the pen, for a joke. She'd been fairly blotto. Bonapace shifted in his seat, scratched his mustache. Fucking wop. Have some self-respect. Nic glanced back at the peanut gallery. He noted how the benches looked like church pews. The judge could pass for a Baptist preacher in those robes. *Lord! I! Know! I! Can!*

Chaaaange! He leaned over and whispered to Bart. "It was the St. Francis." Bart gave him a look. "The St. Francis," Nic repeated. "Scene of Fatty's bust." A reference to a previous discussion. Neither could remember the hotel's name, at the time. How quickly one forgets. Why was Bart so worried? He glanced in the direction of the window. No birds. He should get a pet bird, for his shoulder. What was that line of St. Francis's? Oh, yes. He leaned over, closer, and whispered, "Harm not the fire." The judge rapped his gavel and warned the defendants about speaking out of turn.

*"The list of comics who'd come to bad ends . . . Well. That
sort of ending was far more common than swelling string
music and a soft fade. Fatty. Mabel. Linder. McCullough."*
(p. 229)

"Mabel" was Mabel Normand, once known as the "female Chaplin,"
and Arbuckle's partner in numerous silents. (It was, in fact, Normand
who threw the first on-screen pie at Arbuckle.) Her own vehicles
included *The Diving Girl, Hot Stuff,* and *The Fickle Spaniard.* She
became addicted to cocaine, supposedly as a means of coping with
the pain from a head injury. Numerous stories explaining the cause
of the head injury surfaced, including Normand taking a beating
from a boyfriend, Normand cracking her skull during a failed suicide
attempt (she attempted to jump from a pier), and Normand being hit
in the head with a vase by a boyfriend's jealous girlfriend. Normand
herself joked that Fatty had sat on her. Later, she was rumored to
have shot and killed her then-boyfriend, a Hollywood film director.
Though she was cleared of the crime, a subsequent boyfriend, a bil-
lionaire oil tycoon, was shot and killed by her chauffeur. Her career
did not survive the second scandal.

"Linder" was Max Linder, the great French silent film comic of
the Twenties and Thirties. Linder's on-screen persona was that of
the dapper Frenchman, *un boulevardier.* He was never seen without
a mustache, suit and tie. Some of his most famous creations include
the sleeping statue gag (used by Chaplin in *City Lights*) and the
broken mirror gag (in which a fumbling butler accidentally breaks
a mirror and so must stand behind the empty frame, mimicking his
boss's every move in order to make his boss believe he is staring at his
own reflection). At one point in his career, Linder was turning out a
short a day. He preferred simple, declarative titles. *Max Takes a Bath.
Max in a Dilemma. Max is Afraid of Dogs. Max—Aeronaut.* He came

to Hollywood after the war, but failed to connect with American audiences, eventually returning to France in disgrace, where he fell into a deep depression. Shortly after his final film, Linder and his wife killed themselves in a suicide pact. (Poison. Slashed wrists.)

"I was just going to mention that we worked in a classical tradition. The commedia. *Speed plus incongruity equals funny."(p. 21)*

The *commedia dell'arte* was an Italian theatrical tradition that lasted approximately 400 years, though its heyday was primarily the sixteenth and seventeenth centuries, the *"arte"* referring not to any product of the Muses but rather to the idea of an artistic professional guild. The essential structure of the *commedia* —the characters, their costumes and the rough plotlines—remained standardized, though dialogue and action tended to be improvised by the actors, who needed to be quite deft at wordplay and skilled in a variety of the performing arts, from song to dance to acrobatics. The comic interruptions of the drama, often broad non sequiturs, were called *lazzi*, while the comic characters were known as *zanni*—generally valets or servants who somehow upstaged their masters or created anarchy within the scenario.

The excellent reference book *Lazzi: The Comic Routines of the Commedia Dell'Arte*, edited by Mel Gordon, collects hundreds of the old routines. Gordon gives each *lazzo* a name and a brief description, dividing them into a number of different sub-categories. For instance, a section on Acrobatic and Mimic Lazzi features the Lazzo of Spilling No Wine, which finds Arlecchino performing acrobatic feats while holding a full glass of wine. The chapter entitled Comic Violence/Sadistic Behavior includes the Lazzo of the Flogging, in which the Captain is tricked into making love to an old woman. (When he discovers what has happened, he beats her.) The chapter on Food Lazzi contains the expected gags involving pies and food-fights, as well as the much darker Lazzo of Eating Oneself (in which a starving Arlecchino, beginning with his feet and working up to his neck, slices off pieces of himself for supper) and the Lazzo of Being Brained (featuring Arlecchino again, this time receives a thrashing so savage his brains begin to leak out of his skull, at which point, nervous about "losing his mind," he begins to eat the brains.)

The section of Illogical Lazzi collects some of the book's strangest routines. For instance, there is the Lazzo of "There is No Knowledge!" In toto:

"Pantalone, confused by the strange events and tricks around him, begins to go crazy, shouting after each bizarre action, 'There is no knowledge!'"

Sexual and Scatalogical Lazzi abounded as well, including the Lazzo of the Enema, the Lazzo of Vomit, the Lazzo of the Rising Dagger and the Lazzo of Urinating on Her.

"He leaned over, closer, and whispered, 'Harm not the fire.'"
(p. 231)

One of the episodes in *The Little Flowers*, a collection of stories about St. Francis of Assisi written by an early Franciscan monk, details how St. Francis refused to extinguish candles or lamps, as he considered every element of nature as sacred and infused with Creation as his beloved birds and beasts. One day, St. Francis stood too close to a flame and his breeches caught ablaze. Even *then*, he would not douse himself, telling a fellow mendicant, "Nay, dearest brother, harm not the fire!"

The other mendicants were eventually forced to summon the head priest, who overrode St. Francis's wishes.

Chapter Nine:
Zanni

Nic Sacco's favorite gags—Paul McCullough gets a shave

(Sacco, Nic. How to Beat Cancer and Live; *the following outline is all that remains of Sacco's never-completed
gag book.)*

The Tack Gag

*Timing crucial. Selecting a proper seat. Mug, unlikely to take chair
already covered with tacks. Blind mug: too sympathetic? The offered
chair. Possibility of tack disruption. Dinner party with assigned seat-
ing. Restaurant with bribable maître d'. Tacks, number of. Single tack,
purity of. Necessary sturdiness of. Bent tack. Tipped tack. Holding tack
in place, dangers of. The trapped hand. The tacked hand. The flipped
tack. Ass-as-hammer, driving flipped tack into chair: worst possible
outcome? The scattered handful. The careful arrangement: overly fussy?
Pliers, removal of tacks from rear with.*

The Tie Snip

*Gratifying simplicity of. The approach. The stare. The grin. The re-
moval of shears. The snip. Surprise vs. speed. Senseless destruction, appeal
of. Bizarre non sequitur, appeal of. Importance of sharpened shears.
Importance of use of professional cutler. Ties, more difficult to snip than
you'd think. The partially cut tie. The jammed shears. Making the
scram. The calm return of the snipped end. (For advanced students only.)
Variations. The snipped ponytail. The snipped suspenders. The snipped
saint's medallion. (Possibly sacrilegious). The snipped monocle cord.*

The "Pick Two"

*The offering of the fingers. The wombing of the thumb. The importance
of never allowing the thumb to be chosen. Thumbs, use in poking, evo-
lutionary inefficiency of. Mugs who insist upon choosing thumb. Gags
spoilt by early bickering over which fingers are allowed to be chosen.*

Gags spoilt by attempts to poke with thumb and second finger, despite high and repeated discouragement of use of thumb. The firm poke. The authoritative poke. The quick "sting." The retractable "nip." Fingers, proper erection of. The surface bruise vs. the rupture. The quaking-within-the-socket vs. the full-dislodging. Crossing line from poke to gouge, discouragement of. Proper place of gouge. Difference between gag and alley brawl, wrestling ring. Permanent blinding, discouragement of. Pointer finger, middle finger, ideal nature of. Pinky finger, discouragement of. The inquisitive mug. Possible questions. ("What you gonna do after I pick two?" "This a magic trick?") Proper response: forceful repetition of "pick two." The mug who attempts a block, possible comic advantage of. The mug who covers eyes, pop in stomach of. The mug who covers eyes, bop on noggin of. The mug who moves hands to cover popped, bopped area, poke in eyes of. Repeat as necessary.

The Inferior Decorator

"Prep work." Tossing furniture from window. Rolling carpet without moving objects from carpet. Mug, presence of. Wallpapering mug to wall. Possible follow-ups to wallpapering to wall. The noticed lump. The flattening of the lump. Possible flattening tools. Roller. Bevel. Paint bucket. Shovel. Brick. Lamp base. Candelabra base. Own fists. Own forehead. Bust of Mozart. Battering ram fashioned from diminutive servant and empty paint bucket. When wallpapered to wall, importance of not panicking. Calm, deep breaths. Humiliation of stranger entering and seeing entirely wallpapered sitting room with raised outline of your body beneath a single panel of wall, acceptance of. Importance of perspective. Attempts to speak through wallpaper, general ineffectivity of. Possible counter-lazzos. The fist-over-fist-style "rope-climb" grapple over the paint roller shaft. The "accidental" groin-poke/eye-poke/head-crack/clothesline with paint roller shaft. The mining of floor with open glue buckets. The yanked painters' caps over eyes. The tins of glue swapped with tins of Limburger cheese.

The Perilous Ladder

Common seduction techniques. Kitten on roof. Family of baby birds
in gutter. Infant on ledge. Disguising doll in baby's nappy as infant.
The fake job posting. The paint job. The window-washing gig. The
Oktoberfest-banner-hanging assignation. Means of setting Perilous
Ladder in motion. The old "No, I'll hold it, you go on up," crudeness
of. Vexing difficulty to combat of. Rubber-mallet-like simplicity of.
Artlessness of. Vulgarity of. Similarity to pushing club-footed widower
down spiral staircase of. Setting the fumbling in motion. Importance
of props. Loosed marbles. Leaky canisters of ether. Our whiskered old
friend the banana peel. Natural response of mug to ladder-quake:
hanging on at all cost. Desired response. White-knuckled desperation of
response. Prolongation of plight, importance of. "Three-act" structure
of humiliation. Simple tumbling from ladder, unimportance of. Why
not just tip the ladder completely and shout "Timber!", if that's all
you want? Benefit of "Timber!" gag: no known defense against gravity.
The Neat Vertical Split. Rungs, surreptitiously sawed-through. The slow
and painful separation, elegance of. The increasingly schismatic ladder.
The spread-eagled mug. The drawn-and-quartered-by-gravity pose.
Groin, fully exposed to all manner of thwackery. Tossed ball. Tossed
life preserver. Model aeroplane on kamikaze mission. Mug's attempt to
reunite ladder's divided poles, as if performing a chest exercise involv-
ing weighted pulleys at a mechanized health spa, doomed to failure
nature of. Mug's attempt to reappropriate split ladder as a pair of
stilts, marching off into legend with a triumphant cackle, perhaps first
delivering a bottom-rung arse-kick to the stunned and agoggle zanni,
doomed to failure nature of. Mug's attempt to grab nearest rainspout.
Importance of pre-loosening of rainspout. Detachment of rainspout from
roof's-edge. Swinging of mug into brick wall. Swinging of mug into
clothesline. Swinging of mug into live electrical wire. Dropping of mug
into something unpleasant. Drained pool: too harsh? The trash bin, a
perennial favorite. Barrels of molasses, also popular choice. Dangling

mug, importance of avoidance of gratuitous flailing. The Chute. A full rung-collapse. A top-to-bottom, momentum-gaining collapse. Possibility of mug propelling self through first open window. Importance of pre-arranging stock tableaux. (Crowded Irish dinner table; buxom society matron dressing for evening ball; Negro dishwasher or chef.)

The Toll Call
(a.k.a., The It's-For-Me!, The Crowded Line)

Superiority of phone booth. Other options workable. Broom closet. Taxicab. Ship's sleeper cabin. Confessional. Phone booth, transparency of, adding to superiority. Comedic rule: muddled fishbowl always funnier than muddled kettle. Baiting the mug. Genuine vs. prearranged calls. Hapless mug wandering into booth to phone loved one and crushed by upwards of twelve zanni vs. hapless mug lured into booth by ringing phone. Latter scenario, preference of. Gag climax: phone booth, explosion of. Gag line, echoing from dangling receiver, post-explosion, spoken by compatriot on other end of line, if aforementioned latter option chosen. ("I'm getting some static. Can you hear me?") Zanni, order of entry into phone booth of. Examples. Morbidly obese businessman eating hot dog, squeezing in second- or third-to-last of. Small child or dwarf, final explosion-triggering entrance of. Investigating police officer, dead-center entrance of. Full opening and shutting of door of booth with every entrance, importance of. Merely cramming bodies into booth as if booth is sausage-casing, lack of artfulness and aesthetic appeal of. Weird formality of full opening and closing of door, in face of overweening absence of logic, appeal of. Incongruous body part nuzzling, recommended. Foot-ear. Elbow-small-of-back. Neck-bosom. A good tie-choke and/or face-kneading, never hurts.

Paul McCullough entered a barbershop in Medford, Massachusetts, near the sanitarium where he had been recuperating after the tour.

"Just a shave, friend," McCullough said, taking the chair, the barber replying, "Sure thing, Mr. McCullough. Call me Smitty. Big fan."

Smitty, a big fan, had never been to New York for the vaudeville show, but he'd caught the *Thumbs Up* revue when it had passed through town. A framed Clark & McCullough publicity still even hung on his shop's wall of fame. It was a three-quarter body shot of the pair hoisting an empty gurney. McCullough, with his Chaplin-style mustache and potato-faced grin, "reared up the bring," as some comic—Nic Sacco, maybe?—used to say, while the far slenderer Clark led the charge with his signature walking stick tucked beneath his right arm and his signature porkpie hat planted at a rakish cant. And, of course, his signature painted-on eyeglasses, which, sure, a corny gag, but it worked. Smitty distrusted people who thought their tastes too refined for a handful of corn now and again.

McCullough was staring at himself in the mirror, hard. Smitty wanted to ask how Clark's name had come to be the lead, the clown's name traditionally *following* the straight man's in your comedy team billings. Sacco and Vanzetti, as a matter of fact, were the only other exception coming immediately to mind. But McCullough was looking fairly intent. Smitty wondered if being so well-documented had the tendency to speed up time. He figured yes. All that photographic evidence lying around. Couldn't help but remind a fellow how young he'd once looked.

Still, if the man needed cheering, Smitty felt up to the task. He was no slouch when it came to the small talk, having barbered for going on fifteen years. "So whose idea was it to paint them glasses on, Mr. McCullough, you don't mind me asking?" Smitty asked. As he spoke, he worked McCullough's face like a pot on a wheel, loosening up that beard with fingers and lather. McCullough responded with a flurry of intent blinks, as if momentarily disorientated by bright sunlight.

Finally: "Funny, Smitty, at this late date? I cannot rightly recall."

"Fair enough, Mr. McCullough, fair enough," Smitty began. "You know, now, I read somewhere—"

"I believe," McCullough interrupted, "it was Bobby's."

Smitty said, "Oh yeah? His face, so guess it makes sense, hu—"

McCullough went on, "Yes, it was Bobby's idea. I was pushing for a blackface act."

"Whoa, darkies, huh?" Smitty said. "Would've been a different act altogether, Mr. McCullough, gotta say gotta—"

McCullough continued, "Yes, I remember, we tried blacking up, but it never looked right. On me, that is. By not right I mean too right. Black up my face and I would pass for an actual Negro. Which is not the desirable end result in a blackface act. The crowd, you see, becomes unsure of what they're laughing at. This wasn't a problem for Bobby. He has very fine features, as you know. But with me, well, we tried different combinations of polish to make my look more and more outlandish, as an overt signifier to the audience of my real racial identity. Extremely dark mixtures of polish, to the point where I looked more like a Welsh coal miner than a colored man. But people still believed I was a Negro, a Negro in blackface! I will not lie to you, Smitty, I was beginning to despair. Then, one afternoon, while I was experimenting with yet another shade of coon, Bobby, in a fit of boredom, dipped his finger in the polish and absently painted the eyeglass-frames onto his face. He'd never worn glasses in his life, so it was particularly funny to me, that first time."

"Gee, that's a great story, Mr. McCullough," Smitty said. "And the rest is history, as the great men are wont to say. So how much mustache you like today?"

"I usually say a half-thumb," McCullough said, "is my rule of thumb, Smitty."

Later, when he told the story, one of his so-called friends (Huebel) had asked if Smitty'd ever "considered doing it [him]self?" Huebel went on: "You know, guy's right there, eyes shut, neck bared. You could so easy. Say you're having a bad day. Say—" Smitty blew up. "What kind of idiot question—"

It was explained to him that the crack been just that, a joke, nothing more.

Smitty said, "Them jokes can be told outside but not in my presence."

One of his pals said, "Okay, okay. Hey, Huebel, why don't you take a walk around the block, huh?"

Smitty had read somewhere they asked Mr. Clark his favorite playwright. Clark picks Shakespeare. Fair choice, right? Well, this cheeky reporter, he says, "Why Shakespeare, then, eh?" And Clark, he says, "Because in Shakespeare the clown never dies." Ha.

Smitty had finished the shave, the toweling-off, had just made a move in the direction of the powder when his telephone rang, the wife, with a reminder to swing by the sausager's. He'd yearned to tell her who, at that moment, sat in his chair, but he played it cool. He wondered if McCullough overheard him say, *Oh, nothing much.* If he'd take offense at the implication he was just an average customer, getting an average shave. Hard to know. Smitty opted out by simply saying, "Hair still seems to be growing, so I think we'll do okay this week." He'd glanced in the mirror to see if McCullough had overheard his little joke, hoping to have made the great straight man crack one, and that was when he noticed McCullough holding the razor. His wife went on about the sausager: "Don't let him short-sausage you this time, and—"

McCullough did not exactly slash his throat, to use the papers' description, so much as he stabbed it, like an unmeditated attacker. The blood sprayed outward, obliterating his image in the mirror. Smitty dropped the phone, crying *Jesus Holy*. But McCullough had somehow already done both wrists as well. He drove Smitty back with half-bloodied fists, Smitty managing to grab the razor, at least, though he recoiled from the gore, from the soiling of his smock. Staggering back to the phone, he screamed at his wife to call an ambulance. She was also screaming by this point, not knowing what was going on. His smock truly, awfully smeared.

McCullough died two days later in a hospital in Boston.

Chapter Ten:
Mexico

Historical Interlude (IV)

*"They met much later, in 1917, when, on the United States'
entry into the war, a group of followers of the Italian anarchist
Luigi Galleani fled to Mexico to avoid the draft registration,
and also to await the wave of revolutionary activity that
would, inevitably, sweep across Europe from Russia." (p. 7)*

They took the train down.

He eyed his reflection, furtive on the glass, a sad-eyed ghost spread as thin as tea.

The others dozed, hummed old phrases across the aisles, shot dice. Complained about the coffee.

This is coffee? they asked, rhetorically, dreading the future more than ever.

Enter a tunnel and suddenly the window becomes a mirror, his reflection sharp enough to shave by.

He thinks, mock-philosophic, *Only in the darkest moments does one truly see one's self.*

Chuckles. Neighbor says what. He doesn't explain. Watches his reflection shake its head in an absent little *rien.*

They couldn't find decent bread. The designated chef, that first
night, garnishing each proffered dish with apology.

The paucity of proper Italian ingredients here.

Pio. We understand.

Hamstrung. Painting with my feet. Scratching out love sonnets in
the dirt, with a bent twig.

They understood. They insisted the designated chef not worry.
Though, in truth, everyone secretly agreed. The designated chef had
been hamstrung. No mushrooms. Unfamiliar greens. Forget about
pasta. Still, he tried his best. For a *primo*, he attempted *risotto*, though
the yellow Mexican rice, no *arborio*, failed to froth up to the requisite
level of creaminess, with the eventual result being closer in texture
and density to a wall-surfacing compound such as perhaps stucco-
work. The *secondo* faired marginally better: an improvised *insalata*
di fagioli, made with black beans he cooked to mush, shoring up a
gnarled cut of alleged beef, the latter marinated and cooked in tequila
to approximate a *marsala* sauce. When someone asked about bread,
the chef, his eyes dipping below his chin, dropped a wicker basket of
tortillas in the center of the scarred wooden table. A silence fell over
either flank of bench. One of the men tentatively tried out a riff on
cultural imperialism, the immorality of shackling indigenous popula-
tions with foreign standards of culinary "goodness," that sort of rap.

Someone else said:

Ma, questo sono pane?

Despite an aversion to ritual of any form, honed over years spent
plotting in various undergrounds, there had existed an unspoken

expectation when it came to the first meal, a general hope for some level of auspice.

Objectively speaking, we're not a bunch of Indians.

And this ain't bread.

Objectively speaking, Italian bread is superior to whatever is in this basket.

A tortilla draped over steepled fingers. A tortilla whisked off like a white handkerchief. A coinless palm, fingers flourished in an ascending arc, pointer to pinkie, a spiral staircase leading the audience to the trick's majestic focal point.

Cover. Repeat.

You baked these right you could have a little pizza.

A cracker with cheese and sauce, maybe. Far cry from a pizza.

Closest to pizza you find here.

Tortillas used to pat the sweat from overheated brows.

The wives had been left behind. A necessity, finances being tight. Still, Rosita's cooking would not have proved injurious to morale. A reactionary observation? Perhaps. On the other hand, one cannot deny biology, even in revolution, and the general feminine superiority, biologically speaking, in certain aspects of domestic living, e.g. kitchen life, could be argued as a neutral point of fact, and therefore an aspect of modern life fruitless, or at least prohibitively difficult, to revolt against. One more example of sound theory not necessarily transferable to applied theory. One more example of propaganda that should remain of the word rather than deed.

They hoisted their *cervezas* for a toast. No wine being another sad truth. None of them were used to drinking this bloating, fizzy stuff.

Here is a depressing fact: optimists live longer.

That's not a toast.

A hand on a tortilla, its outline traced with a meat knife. He predicted a descent into tortilla-handed cheek-slapping, come a few more rounds of *cerveza*.

One of them made a Last Supper joke at the next toast, nearly spoiling it by belaboring the punchline. Namely the fact that it was, technically, their first supper.

Who would be Jesus then in this scenario?

Well one hates to nominate oneself but—

They all fought for the next five minutes over Christ and Judas. No one cared about the rest, though they decided Marco would have to be St. Mark. Marco said he'd always been bothered by the story about St. Mark tearing out of his clothes and running away from the Roman guards nude, that as a boy this story had made him blush, though no one in his class had even made the connection.

None of them felt thrilled about being in a large group of men. It was no boys' night out. They were not hunters, panfrying the venison brain, before the ride home to their wives, who would cook the actual meat. They would be filing off to the bunkhouse, like prisoners on the lam.

A period of silence, except for the brittle percussion of metal on plate. They would be spending an indefinite period of time with each other. The thought settled in. Mopping a plate with tortilla, trying to fold it over several times to make it more breadlike. The tequila-marsala actually quite nice.

I feel like I'm a butler, polishing the china.

Hoisting the *cervezas* again.

One more toast.

Maybe we should all grow beards.

They paused and considered this.

They followed the war and, more importantly, the progress of the Revolution, via British news service, on a quavering transistor receiver. To stave off indolence during the lull times, they organized daily field trips to remote sections of desert, where they practiced the construction and detonation of various types of explosive.

Along with the radio, they had brought a copy of Johann Most's *The Science of Revolutionary Warfare*. They read passages aloud to one another.

"The best shape for a bomb is, and always will be, a sphere."

We standing on one.

Was that supposed to pass for pungent observation?

More like pointing out one of life's rare conveniences.

Heh.

"This is because the resisting of the casing is homogenous, and so the explosive effect will be the same in all directions."

He dug a shallow hole in the sand, with his hands. The sand slid over his fingers, resettling at the bottom of the hole, forcing him to hold the sand at bay while the others planted the bomb. When he let go, the sphere was immediately buried. They pushed the remainder of the sand down, gently, the fuse coiling out from the ground like the tail of a very clever insect. He slashed a match across his neighbor's forehead, then tapped the end of the fuse, lightly, feeling like a wand-fingered granter of wishes.

Make them scatter. Abracadabra.

They stumbled to their feet, bolted across the sand, dove for cover behind a hastily excavated trench. The dive was perhaps excessive, but one can never be too careful with homemade explosives, even when the fuse length is carefully measured out by the carefulest measurer present. Still, post-dive, they had plenty of time to flip themselves around and stare at the horizon they'd just fled, trying to pick out the exact spot where they'd sown the blast.

Isn't that that the fuse right there?

Pointing at nothing. Shrugs all around.

Nonono, it's right the—

No point in describing the explosions. Only that eventually, they too lulled. Violently, but.

They say (he noted) that it's been proven impossible to train oneself to resist certain stimuli. For example to *not* flinch in response to a loud explosion. This is true. Still, the blasts evolved in the direction of the celebratory. It cooled down at night, was the given reason for the bumping back of the detonations, though in truth the flame and light contributed to a more spectacular effect after dark. Not to mention *cerveza* could be allowably consumed, the workday at that point complete. They developed remote detonators, not remote enough for practical use in an actual attack, but, again, permitting a recline against comfortable natural rock formations, as opposed to a scramble through sand in a mad dash for cover.

Least subtly, they began to add coloring powders to Most's recipes. For this, they could proffer no excuse, merely jokes. *Bit of Chinese spice to make the German cooking less heavy, more exciting.* And so indeed, the nightly explosions began to take on the character of an Asiatic New Year's celebration.

Though to be contrary, he liked to close his eyes and just listen.

Eyes closed, the blasts like a drum corps, marching up front.

Vanguarding the Revolution, they would say. *Open your eyes, dummy, you wanna see it.*

They read aloud:

"It is also necessary to point out that nitroglycerine and dynamite can be handled with bare hands, but having your skin in contact with these materials for any length of time has an effect on the nervous system which is very unpleasant, and induces strong headaches. People who constantly work around these materials become accustomed to it over the course of time. But they usually have to avoid drinking spirits, or they will suffer the consequences."

Several coughed "Carlo" into their hands. Carlo too tipsy to notice until the fourth or fifth time, after which he muttered a semi-proud *hey, now.*

Their shadows yawned like chasms across the moonlit sand. The idea for a bonfire had been raised as soon as it became clear that the explosives would run out well before the *cervezas.* They piled timber salvaged from a rotting barn a few miles back. Teepeed it to the sky. Pointing the barrel at the source. The heavenly host.

Bang.

"Modern warfare is by no means limited to the use of explosives . . . Fire is an extremely effective weapon. Further explanations of the use of this material in social warfare are unnecessary. Anyone can discover for himself how to make the most suitable use of it. We shall make just one further point—clothing is among the things that can readily be set on fire."

They realized it was not a vacation. Still, who could resist an open-air movie night? Every second Wednesday, the villagers strung a bedsheet between the tallest yucca trees in the square. An itinerant projectionist supplied the necessary equipment (bedsheet excluded) and the week's film. Local boys, hired as ushers, collected *pesos* and led audience members, laden with blankets and picnic baskets, to a free patch of earth on the dusty square. Fifteen minutes before dusk, the projectionist tightened his reels and sketched, for the leader of the town's best-loved mariachi band, a rough map of the dramatic highs and lows of the evening's entertainment, the better for the bandleader to guide the musical accompaniment.

As most of the pictures involved crime-fighting masked wrestlers, the plot points, and thus the live scores, varied only subtly. If improvisation failed, "El Rey" always did the trick in a pinch.

Bandits attempt to hijack a train. A second-class passenger lowers his copy of *El Diario*. The passenger is wearing a wrestling mask.

A fire in an orphanage! A few blocks away, grappling with a medicine ball in a basement gym, an athlete cocks his head, seems to actually *twitch his nose* beneath his wrestling mask.

Title Card: *Smoke?!*

An obese, loutish theater critic raises his hand to slap a beautiful young actress impudent enough to refuse his moist advances. A gloved hand grabs his cocked fist. The critic whirls around to face . . . a masked wrestler, nude but for a towel!

The audience later learns that the wrestler happened to be showering in an adjoining hotel suite.

And so forth. Back at the house they found themselves loath to retire straightaway to the bunk room, despite half-hearted exhortations by Giovanni, easily the most earnest of their number, regarding the importance of allowing a horse its due rest if the morning ride is to be steady and swift. But like children called in from the play yard at naptime, they could not allow the day's excitement to pass away so easily. One night, they shoved aside the furniture, stripped to their shorts and attempted to replicate various moves exhibited in the evening's film, ostensibly as practice for hand-to-hand combat with reactionary elements sent by the State.

Greasy leg scissors. Overwrought Nelsons provoking arm-flappings that could pass for lunatic attempts at flight.

Though more likely they'd simply be shot like dogs in their sleep, Umberto noted with self-satisfied pessimism.

Winded and agloss with sweat, they shifted the party to the back courtyard, which was not much cooler but at least offered stars and the chance of a breeze.

They passed a bottle of cheap tequila, trying at first to keep the talk in the realm of shop, though it inevitably drifted into gripes and tangentials.

I can't read Proudhon.

I'm sorry. We could tutor you on the big words.

Bakunin once blamed his taste for destruction on his domineering mother.

By "can't" you mean "can't stand him"?

Hopelessly bourgeois.

His mother? Of all the limp-wristed Freudian—

I'd always heard Bakunin was impotent.

Lies disseminated by the State.

To dismiss one of our greatest theorists as "bourgeois" simply because he was in favor of educating the worker—

And so impotence inflames crazed anarchist thought, was the thinking behind this rumor?

I'm not an expert on the psychological side effects of impotence. Mario here, on the other hand . . .

Ma va fungoo.

Don't try to discredit my argument by making it sound like I'm anti-education.

Hey. Just repeating what Mario's old lady told my old lady.

Merely pointing out the fact that, like Marx, Proudhon considered education a prerequisite for revolution. Which I find elitist and unnecessarily divisive.

"Marx is ruining workers by making theorists of them." To paraphrase Comrade Bakunin.

Like all good one-liners, a bit overstated for effect. But I think more or less accurate.

Did you ever notice, in the Courbet portrait, what an unnatural pose Proudhon is striking?

Overstated and, like much of Bakunin, overly bellicose. But essentially the truth. The lumpenproletariat, having less to lose, would, it stands to reason, produce the superior revolutionary.

He does look a bit stiff.

It's meant to be contemplative, right? And yet, Proudhon looks so posed, especially surrounded by an otherwise naturalistic scene. The splayed books. Daughters playing at his feet. The scene has always, to me, at least, had the opposite effect, in that it makes him seem utterly fatuous. Like a man who spends his days cultivating the air of the philosopher rather than actually, well. Philosophizing.

Courbet was a realist. He painted what he saw. Of course, in light of the Romantic bullshit going on at the time, this could arguably be considered a political act.

What made you decide to leave the Old Country?

My mother died.

Oh. So sorry.

I held her in my arms. My father was unable to bring himself to enter the sick room. After her death, I wandered the woods bordering the nearby Maira River and contemplated suicide. I departed for America two days before my twentieth birthday.

They were old friends. Believe they grew up together in the same French village.

Do you know the story of how he found his wife?

Courbet?

Proudhon. Apparently spotted a woman on the street, made his approach not knowing a thing about her, all because he felt like she looked sufficiently "working-class."

Was she wearing a hard hat?

By all accounts, turned out to be a fairly happy marriage.

As good a method as any, I suppose.

How did you meet your Rosa?

Oh, so is romance now also a bourgeois construct?

That's not what you told me last night.

So. Why didn't you?

What's that?

Ah. What you said. Off yourself.

Not that we regret—

Nervous laughter.

Expecting him to say he'd stumbled across a perfect sunset. A fawn sniffing at the dew on a mossy stone. That sort of jive. The beauty of the natural world.

Finally: *There are more productive ways to mourn.*

They had made a pact: no discussing wives or girlfriends. It would only make things more difficult. So he did not immediately launch into his story.

The dance had been a benefit for his friend Emilio, an accordion player who had been paralyzed from the neck down in a recent accident. She had been nervous.

Aren't you Black Hand? she whispered, as they held each other awkwardly on the dance floor. *Don't you go to listen to that Galleani?* She was only seventeen, he found out later. He didn't think she looked so young.

I only ask because my father would not like me to consort with such folk.

On the stage, Emilio had been wheeled forth to sing a cappella. Emilio had been, in truth, a mediocre accordion player, but his voice, on its own, proved surprisingly beautiful. Emilio had insisted on having his accordion hung around his neck. (The accident had only increased his famously perverse sense of humor.) As they danced their first dance, Emilio began to softly sing, "*Give flowers to the rebels who failed . . .*" In Italian, of course. The old anarchist poem. Emilio, though not a true believer, had sympathy with the cause.

He had stammered a sort of denial. He felt like an apostle denying Christ, though Galleani, of course, would hate the comparison. He quickly, clumsily backtracked.

Follower? I mean, what does that mean, exactly? I've heard the man speak, sure. But the only thing I follow is my own heart.

She said she didn't care if he did or not. From that point on, he couldn't stop himself.

You should really come listen. I'll let you know about the next speech. Would you like that? It sounds dull but it's not. It's like listening to poetry. He speaks like Dante. He says, "All that is needed in this immutable task is to persist: to kindle in the minds of the proletariat the flame of the idea; to kindle in their hearts faith in liberty and in justice; to give to their anxiously stretched out arms a torch and an axe." Is that not lovely?

She said Galleani sounded like quite the speaker. He was not sure whether she was humoring him, or even gently mocking his fervency. He felt like he hadn't done the man justice. She asked what he did for a living and he said edge trimmer and she wondered what that meant, exactly, so he began to explain, clumsily, until, frustrated, he stopped their dance and reached down and pulled off his own shoe, the music and other dancers flowing around them like a stream over a jutting rock. *See right here this is the edge,* tracing it with his finger, pointing out the sloppiness of the trimming on his own cheap shoes. *I'd never let that slide. And yet still we are exploited. Can you believe the average trimmer makes—* He noticed her suppressing a smile. Later, she told him she found his passion charming. *That is a very attractive quality in a man.*

He did not tell the others any of this. Instead, he explained how, normally, he did not respond well to the pressure of the approach, when it came to women, but how with Rosita, he had steeled himself, watching as other men honked and performed head stands to get her attention. How he finally got a second glass of wine. How he walked past her. How he made eye contact, hoisting the glass, as an offering. How he had prepared a little story about how he had gotten the drink for a friend, and then the friend had disappeared, so here he was, left with an extra glass of wine, ha ha. And how, when she had just smiled sweetly and said *grazie*, he'd nodded and did not bother with his lie, and instead asked for her name, and where she was from, and, eventually, for a dance. How, after that, the rest of the evening fell into place.

Which was also true, and summed things up rather nicely.

Part
Three

Chapter Eleven:
Lazzi

Lazzi—a poem and a letter—President McKinley falls foul of an anarchist's revolver

Nic, in a dentist's robe, with gag pliers.

Nic hides in a sack.

The flea is invisible.

(There is not really a flea.)

Removal of perfectly good teeth.

Unnecessary enema administered.

Bound, back-to-back, the bowl of ricotta cheese just out of reach.

"Shhh! Can't you see I am dead!"

Nic barks like a dog.

Bart starts.

Bart, yelling into a cave.

Swaddled in hog meat. The distant sounds of a butcher working his knives upon a steel. *Oh dear!*

"Anyone there?"

Nic bends; Bart, hoisted.

Vice versa.

Both extremely hungry.

The echo, retorting: "*Up yours!*"

The ladder bends at the top, causing Nic to enter the wrong window.

Nic, upon releasing the ladder, "gravitationally abandoned."

Bart, not really a statue.

Bart receives an unnecessary enema.

Bart vomits.

Bart urinates.

Bart has an erection.

You wanna me I should precipitate?

(Meaning participate.)

Nic, asleep, receives a kick.

Bart, unconsciously slapped.

(A reflex.)

Nic tells a ridiculous parable.

Bart beats his father.

The action continues, in tandem.

An unnecessary circumcision, by Jews.

Kisses, not punches, are the fruits of love.

Still, Nic is slapped.

The ubiquitous macaroni.

Bart's head, emerging from an enormous pie.

Food snatched from their mouths.

The jailer is not amused.

"No more will I commit suicide!"

"But how can you be mute, when you have just answered my question?"

No, blind.

No, lame.

"But I am not a doctor!"

Nic hides.

There is no place to hide.

"I'm fine. *It was, after all, an extremely tiny pin.*"

Men will enter an open gate.

The movement, combined with the odd cut of the breeches, giving the appearance of Bart's genitals bulging.

"The forest beneath her house."

(Meaning her pubic hair.)

"Shut up!" shouts the Master, for the third time.

The creditor, demanding payment.

Then hits him with a shovel.

It is the fault of the doves, not Nic.

Returning to his pathetic monologue.

They smile at each other.

This continues.

Total darkness overtakes the scene.

Blind groping.

"Do what you will, you are still a cuckold!"

Nic, discovering the difficulty of self-asphyxiation.

Nic repeats the question.

"Why don't you?"

They beat him.

"There is no knowledge!"

Nic repeats the question.

The look on the moneylender's face.

Nic is promised a tart.

Bart manages to fondle her at the same time.

Nic repeats the question.

"Before we depart, gentlemen," Nic interrupts, pointing to his shoe.

Grabbing their ankles.

The guards, caught unawares, sent a-tumble.

Nic, mistook for a corpse.

Nic, frightened by their reactions, though he is the one dressed as a ghost.

The argument revolving around who should be the first to sample the macaroni.

Nic, disguised: "*That Nic, I like-a that fella.*"

"There is no knowledge!"

Nic was not really talking in his sleep.

Nic repeats the words to the girl.

Is slapped.

Nic repeats the question.

(Almost) the Joy

If I was a poet
probably
I could discribe
the red rays
of the loving sun
shining
and the bright blue sky
and the perfume of my garden and flowers,
the smell of the violet
that was comes
from the vast verdant prairie,
and the singing of the birds,
that was
almost
the joy
of deliriany.

From Nicola Sacco's letter to Mrs. Cerise Jack, February 26, 1924. Sent from Dedham Jail. Mrs. Jack, a member of the New England Civil Liberties Committee, attended the trial and gave Sacco English lessons.

"Every night when the light goes out I take a long walk and really I do not know how long I walk, because the most of the time I forget myself to go to sleep, and so I continue to walk and I count, one, two, three, four steps and turn backward and continue to count, one, two, three four and so on. But between all this time my mind it is always so full of ideas that one gos and one comes . . . I find one of my mostly beautiful remembrance while I am thinking and walking, frequently I stop to my window cell and through those sad bars I stop and look at the nature into crepuscular of night, and the stars in the beauti blue sky. So last night the stars they was moor bright and the sky it was moor blue than I did ever seen; while I was looking it appear in my mind the idea to think of something of my youth and write the idea to my good friend Mrs. Jack first thing in morning. So here where I am right with you, and always I will try to be, yes, because I am study to understand your beautiful language and I know I will love it . . .

"The flowers you send to me last week it renew in my mind the remembrance of my youth. It complete sixteen years ago this past autumn that I left my father vineyards. Every year in autumn right after the collection I usd take care my father vineyard and sometime I usd keep watch, because near our vineyard they was a few big farmer and surronder our vineyard they was vast extension of prairie and hundreds animal they used pasturage day and night on those vast prairie. So the most of night I remane there to sleep to watch the animal to not let coming near our vineyard. The little town of Torremaggiore it is not very far from our vineyard, only twenty minete of walk and I used go back and forth in morning an night and I usd bring to my dear an poor mother two big basket full of vegetables and fruits and big bounch flowers. The place where I used to sleep it was a big large hayrick that my good father and my brothers and I build. The hayrick it was set in one corner near the well in the middle of our vineyard, and surronde this sweet hayrick they was many plants and flowers except the red rose, because they was pretty hard to find the good red rose and I did love them so much that I was always hunting for find one plant of those good—red rose!

"About sixty step from our vineyard we have a large piece of land full of any quantity of vegetables that my brothers and I we used cultivate them. So every morning before the sun shining used comes up an at night after the sun goes out I used put one quart of water on every plant of flowers and vegetables and the smal fruit trees. While I was finishing my work the sun shining was just coming up and I used always jump upon well wall and look at the beauty sun shining and I do not know how long I usd remane there look at that enchanted scene of beautiful. If I was a poet probably I could discribe the red rays of the loving sun shining and the bright blue sky and the perfume of my garden and flowers, the smell of the violet that was comes from the vast verdant prairie, and the singing of the birds, that was almost the joy of deliriany. So after all this enjoyment I used come back to my work singing one of my favourite song an on way singing I used full the bascket of fruit and vegetables and bunch of flowers that I used make a lovely bouquet. And in the middle the longuest flowers I used always put one of lovely red rose and I used walk one mile a way from our place to get one of them good red rose that I always hunting and love to find the good red rose . . .

275

"P.S. How you find the day of our dear Mrs. Evans birthday? I have here very beauti bag to suprise her. If you hap to see her give my warm regard."

The President had been looking forward to the Temple of Music. "Do you suppose," he asked Ida, "there will be an Esquimaux choir?" Ida rolled her eyes. "Perhaps a Mexican violin duel? That would be something." Ida smiled, though she'd meant not to. Still, in the end, she opted to remain behind at the hotel suite, pleading the tour of Niagara Falls, earlier that afternoon, had depleted her reserves. McKinley made a crack about how she needn't worry, as she'd already visited the true Temple of Music. He was referring to the Falls, and went on to purply describe "God's melodious roar," or some such nonsense—mock-oration, in private, having become a favorite running joke of her husband's. Though Ida was no longer sure how much mock remained.

Pretending to look forward to the Temple of Music, incidentally. Another joke. "A Chilean operatic diva, mayhaps?" McKinley asked, as Ida straightened his collars. "I would settle for Seminole war-whoopers. I would be delighted by exotic animals trained to play the piano."

Among the items in the President's pockets at the time of the shooting: $1.20 in small change; three knives; a lucky nugget; nine keys (six on a ring, two loose and the ninth on its own heart-shaped ring); a pair of gloves; three handkerchiefs (the weather in Buffalo having been barbarously hot); a gold watch; a pencil.

"God's own music, played with a melodious roar unreachable by the fierceliest trained of human throats, the grandliest sized of orchestras." Ida snorted, deliberately yanking his collars crooked. "Save it," she said, "for Rochester." Though he was serious about the

Mexican violin duel. He'd witnessed one, as a boy, in Manhattan. He could still remember the dim basement arena, the pungent smell of unfamiliar food simmering and being sweated out, the trio of violin necks nearly touching, like the spokes of a wheel, as the combatants leaned into each other and attempted to win psychological advantage through facial expression and aggressive tuning. "According to the rules, the musicians are not to know what the others plan to play," McKinley's father had whispered as they awaited the wave of the kerchief which would signal the start, adding in an even lower voice, "Though many duels are fixed."

The Temple, however, turned out to be more of a church—an auditorium with vaguely Byzantine pretensions, the only musical instrument to speak of an enormous organ, its pipes pointed yearningly towards the heavens. A man in a tuxedo hunched over the keys, playing a Bach sonata. McKinley rolled his eyes, thrust a hand in a pocket, fingered one of his knives. "Couldn't we take another gondola ride?" he asked. The previous day's agenda had included a speech on reciprocal trade (well-received), a leisurely float through the majestic canals of Buffalo (the Expo having been constructed along a loose Venetian theme) and a dusk viewing of the illumination of the Temple of Light (an admittedly dazzling effect.)

Earlier today had been the trip to the Falls, pleasant enough, including a hearty picnic lunch on a scenic overlook. "I wonder if, some day in the future, man will devise a barrel capable of withstanding the ravages below?" McKinley wondered aloud. The previous day's viewing of the Expo's mechanical marvels had put the President in a speculative frame of mind, though the minutiae of science generally escaped him. No one at the picnic engaged the President's hypothetical. After an awkward silence, during which the gathered aides and officials stared dolefully at the Falls, all waiting for another to speak, McKinley finally chuckled and said, "Well, as President, it is my duty to be an optimist, so I will go on record as believing in the possibility of such a barrel. Though, if I live to see it built, I make no promises to take the inaugural ride!"

At the Temple, the President slipped on his gloves and stepped into the reception line. Contrary to what one might expect, politicians, as a species, did not all look upon the handshaking portion of their job as an unfortunate necessity. Many, McKinley included, thrived on close contact with their citizenry.

"Don't let them hurt him," legend had the President murmuring, later, as he slumped in a quickly proffered chair. The organist continued to play Bach.

At least it wasn't a marching band. One of the downsides of being President, McKinley thought, entailed not only being a captive audience to a dismaying amount of that kind of shit, but actually having to pretend to enjoy it.

After the initial cacophony, one strain usually emerges as the dominant. The crowd will perhaps begin clapping along, or even singing. "At this point," his father explained, "the others must quickly adapt to the melody and work to either undermine or overpower it."

One of the Mexicans could not keep up, eventually bungling his own melody to such a severe degree the he threw down his violin in disgust, as the crowd roared.

"And then," McKinley's father whispered, "there were two."

Legend has the gun wrapped in a handkerchief, extended in lieu of a palm to shake. This was not the case. McKinley, seconds before the shots were fired, noticed the tip of the barrel, ever-slightly a-jut. *Oh*, the President thought. Involuntarily, he clenched his stomach, as if he were about to receive a punch.

SUPPLEMENTARY MATERIAL
*"Involuntarily, he clenched his stomach, as if he were about
to receive a punch." (p. 279)*

The nation mourned, President McKinley having fallen foul of
an anarchist's revolver. This was September 6, 1901. The assassin,
Leon Czolgosz, had attended several speeches by Emma Goldman.
Czolgosz was of Polish origin, though Detroit-born. (From *Arena*
magazine, 1902: "Despite the fact that the assassin of our President
was born on our soil, he was to all intents and purposes alien; he was
of alien birth and alien stock; his whole mind was alien.") Czolgosz
was tried and executed seven weeks later, his body subsequently
destroyed with acid in lieu of a Christian burial. Thomas Edison,
an early proponent of the electric chair (a more humane means of
capital punishment, his claim went), made a three-and-a-half minute
silent film, *Execution of Czolgosz With Panorama of Auburn Prison*, a
combination of documentary footage of the prison where the execution took place and reenactment of the execution itself; Edison also
eager to deliver a jab to his arch-rival, the Russian Nikola Tesla, as
well as Tesla's commercial backer, Westinghouse, by making the
pair's "alternating current" method of electrical transmission syn-
onymous with death by electrocution. (Edison's electrical patents all
involved his own "direct current" system.) Westinghouse refused to
sell the state of New York the generators necessary to operate their
new "electric chair," the first in the nation. (They were purchased
secondhand.)

The film opens with a slow panorama shot of Auburn Prison.
The sky above the prison wall is scarred, the ageing of the film's
print having created the effect of a violent storm. (Or billowing
ash. A meteor shower.) The film then cuts to an interior shot of a

guard standing in front of a prop-brick wall. A cell door is opened and "Czolgosz" emerges. He wears dark pants, a dark jacket and a white shirt, his hair on the verge of unkempt. He is not shackled and makes no attempt at struggle. A single guard links either arm. As the guards march "Czolgosz" screen-left, the film, slightly sped, gives the entire scene a whiff of Keystone, the off-screen march at once measured and manic. (The arrhythmic velocity—speed without visible effort—making for an interesting juxtaposition.) In the next room, a pair of men stand on either side of the electric chair, eyeing it, as if it might move. "Czolgosz" is strapped into the chair, his right pant-leg lifted, as per custom.

A nod.

The attendants flanking the chair lean closer.

An arm is lifted. Signals. Drops.

"Czolgosz" seems to swell up, as if he has been ordered to take an impossibly deep breath.

The attendant on the left leans closer.

"Czolgosz" hovers for several beats. Deflates.

The attendant on the right leans closer.

"Czolgosz" swells a second time, but far less intently. Quickly sags.

The attendant on the left touches his wrist.

The attendant on the right touches his wrist.

The attendant on the left unbuttons "Czolgosz's" shirt and listens for a heartbeat with a stethoscope.

The attendant on the right listens for a heartbeat with a stethoscope.

(The attendant on the right takes longer.)

The men eventually nod at each other.

The attendant on the left turns to the camera and nods.

The nod is stagy and overemphatic, clearly for the camera.

One of the guards does the same.

Chapter Twelve:
Sacco and Vanzetti
Entertain the Troops

An excerpt from the private journals of Bart Vanzetti—Bob Hope, Ezra Pound, the Italian Futurists, a singing cowboy, and a brief contemplation of suicide—further biographical notes—the innate violence of the Italian race

May 16, 1945

Landed in Rome early this morning. Soon after, we boarded a train for Naples, where a number of troops have been stationed. The first stop in our "V for Victory" tour—or, as Nic prefers, "V for *Va fa in culo!*" Roll opening credits: *Sacco and Vanzetti Entertain the Troops!* "Over There" might be too obvious an accompanying track. "G.I. Jive," though, could work nicely. Perhaps over a montage?

My cynicism may be unfashionable in these triumphant times. Cynicism being the enemy of hope, ergo ally of the Axis. Though Hitler's no cynic. Fellow believes in something. Secret of many a success. Rightness, wrongness of the beliefs in question ultimately become a concern for pettier minds. The *truly successful* leave such questions to the academics, understanding, as they do, how the wrongheadedness of any belief becomes irrelevant in the face of said belief's intensity. See: political ideologies, world. See: religions, world. See: Sacco, Vanzetti, careers of. Though, in this particular case, my cynicism happens to be justified. See: Nic's, my own, utter absence of patriotic zeal, irrational affection for "our boys." Though Nic's antipathy for the recently departed Duce ran deep, on occasion outweighing his natural recoil from the militaristic rah-rah of the crowd. Which is not to say that I felt a lesser revulsion for Mussolini. But some of us refuse to allow rage to bend our core beliefs.

"Core" makes me sound very noble. Like there's something inside. A buried bean, worthy of protection.

Not that insights into Nic's psyche have been easy to come by, of late. Our last conversation not mandated by professional concerns was sometime around the New Year. Which made Manager Danny's interruption of our long-scheduled hiatus—a bare week after we wrapped *Horse Sense*—particularly unwelcome. But he insisted we could use the publicity—that *not* doing it, when *everybody* was doing it, would be less than *no* publicity, it would be negative publicity, which, Barnum notwithstanding, was not always preferential. Nic asked if we could do a press photo hanging upside down, side by side, in the Piazzale Loreto. Manager Danny chuckled at a volume equaling but not exceeding ten percent of a genuine chuckle. I kept to the far side of his office, studying his framed photographic evidence of at least a party-pose's cordiality with starlets of the day, shot at various premieres and awards ceremonies, arms draping shoulders, fingers squeezing tumblers, all the while expertly miming some level of deep personal connection. Manager Danny told Nic he had better behave, then promised us private train compartments a minimum of three cars apart for the duration of the tour. Day one, onboard, I ended the evening blotto with LaVerne and Maxene Andrews. Contraband gin. Patty's apparently teetotalling after a three-day drunk ended with her having to chop up and hide the body of a prize racehorse named Mexican Altar. Or so says Maxene. Who is, to be fair, a notorious bullshitter, particularly where the affairs of her sisters are concerned.

I retreated to my sleeper when they began to duet on an old Benny Goodman number, making up new lyrics involving war bonds and Churchill's cock.

May 17, 1945

Dinner tonight, in a little town a few miles from the base. This particular town's specialty is tortellini. The meal: a five-course tortellini dinner. Hope kept asking the waiter when the "meat-a-balls" were coming. "And I don't mean these guys," he said, pointing at Nic, myself, with splayed thumb and pinkie, as if he were throwing

286

some kind of hoodoo. The dinner had been arranged by the USO's public-relations fellow. A sort of pre-tour, get-acquainted meal for the talent: Hope, Dorsey, the Andrews Sisters, Madame T, couple of her girls. Oh, also, this Kelly kid, a singing cowboy, looking even more gargantuan, blonde amidst the dark complexions and stunted statures of my countrymen. "Call me Saw," he said, crushing every hand he shook like it was whatever part of the bull you hung onto for dear life. Nic asked if "Seen" wouldn't be more authentic-sounding. Kid explained it was short for where he was from. Nic said he thought they was all sissies in Sausalito, not to say that sissy-cowboys was unheard of but— "*Arkansas*," the kid interrupted, smiling now that he'd figured out Nic enjoyed yanking people's knots.

Hope still has the uncanny knack of insulting and glad-handing simultaneously. Palpable tension, incidentally, on the comedy end of the bill. Manager Danny had waited until the day prior to our scheduled departure to casually mention that, oh, good news, actually you and Nic won't have to bother with any *verbal* sort of joke-telling, as Hope's got that covered. Of course, he meant contractually. And so we must confine our act strictly to the physical—specifically, the knife routine, a send-in-the-clowns sort of thing, while the native speaker does the talking. I asked if they would supply us with pancake makeup and seltzer bottles, or if we should pack our own. Manager Danny laid out a few half-hearted come-on-now's, but he knew. Hope's *clown act*. We were not amused.

Hope seemed very amused. We sat around a long table in a garden dining area behind the restaurant. Old pillars, olive trees. A fountain with an Adonis-type cupping his spout, not in service. Flies skated across the pooled water, which was stagnant enough for a child to draw his initials with a stick. They served the savory tortellini courses first. Oily, translucent bonbons stuffed with lamb (*primo*), radicchio (*secondo*), and veal ground as fine as pepper. Meal ended with gorgonzola tortellini and, finally, a sweet *zucca* course.

First time back to the Mother Country, incidentally. So many years have passed, it's difficult to remember enough of my former self to make an adequate comparison with present company. Maybe I feel exactly the same. Maybe I've regressed. Maybe youth and ambition were not callow, but fearless. Laudable. I had intended on returning sooner. But as with other immigrants, I was too poor, early on, and later, too busy. Then the war. And Mother's death, just prior to my departure, absented what had been the most compelling reason for a return.

Hope thumped our balls. Asked if we'd order in Italian. The USO attaché, an enlisted man from the West Coast with a tan the color of bourbon, said it wouldn't be necessary, that the Army had preordered. Hope shot him a look, like, kid, do not interrupt the talent, rule number one. Which, had to side with Hope on that one. Hope asked if we'd ever met Mussolini. Nic spat, hard, in the direction of the fountain. His discharge sat on the surface for the remainder of the meal, like a decorative white pebble. I told Hope how the Duce had courted us, before the war, when he still cared about world opinion. How he'd assumed he could win our support by playing on nationalistic pride, hoping to display our achievements as part of something greater, racial. "He got Carnera, the boxing champ," I said. "Marinetti, the Futurist." Hope was not interested in those sorts of details. He wanted to know if Mussolini lisped, limped, openly whored, frothed like something rabid. "These turtle . . . whatever they're called," Hope said. "They sure slide around on your plate like something that belongs in a shell. *Garçon? Un cerveza, por favor.*" Maxene asked if we still had relatives in liberated Italy. "They strung 'em upside down in that square in Milan," Hope interjected. "Don't you read the papers, honey?" LaVerne poked him with an elbow. "Cripes," Hope said. "Spilt wine on myself. Hey, Bart, let me borrow that mustache, willya?" I mock-pointed my fork, mumbled something about the sculptor leaving a thumbprint on his nose. Hope's the type of guy who bonds over a round or two of the insult game. Nic pounded his own fork with his fist. It performed a triple-salto across the table and pierced an untouched tortellini, dead center of Hope's plate.

"Waiter?" Hope said. "Be sure you keep the sharp knives away from these boys, okay?"

May 18, 1945

Overnight train to Pisa. Opening night surprisingly free of hitches. Military efficiency rubbing off on showbiz folk? Seems unlikely. We performed on a makeshift stage in front of a few thousand GI's. Opposite of a tough crowd. They were so damn *grateful*, which everyone on the bill seemed to thrive upon. To me, it felt like cheating at a crossword puzzle. What's the point? Unconditional love neuters the game. If I don't *have* to dance to win your affection, then where's the drama? Nic felt the same way. But we've been quarrelling so long, he contraries anything I say, on principle. "They loved us," he muttered, as we exited the stage, "and this one—" A thumbed fist jerked back and forth in my direction, like he was shaking a can. "—puts on a performance so hostile. I wonder, what could this guy be thinking? Is he *uncapable* of enjoying the *occasional delicacy*?"

I snorted. "Day I accept a gimme from those squares—"

Nic held up his hand, primarily (I believe) because he did not want to hear spoken what he truly felt. We were alone at the time.

Hope slayed. Dorsey, slightly less so. The girl acts, of course, received the warmest response—particularly Madame T's Bathing Beauties, who were wheeled out in a giant aquarium, in which they swam suggestively alongside a garish collection of tropical sea creatures. The loudest howls came when a gesture from Madame T, who had been narrating the action and cajoling the audience from a sort of lifeguard's chair, tank-left, caused the bottom to drop from the aquarium, flooding the stage (and the delighted front rows) with water and soaked girls, who completed the act by performing various feats of contortion whilst stagehands in wading boots rushed out to net the flopping fish for later reuse. The feats of contortion apparently involved the spelling of appropriately patriotic messages with their contorted bodies, though if you were standing on the side of the stage (like me) the girls merely looked stretched by fun house mirrors. For an encore, they formed a human pyramid. Madame T directed its construction with a whip.

We got onstage, tossed our knives around. Narrower and narrower misses, these days, incidentally. An irony, as this, of course, makes the act more exciting. So we killed, the closer we came to literally doing so. Young "Saw" Kelly, surprisingly, might have killed most of all. To my eyes, his act looked like a bunch of State Fair lasso tricks, bantamed with some half rate yodeling. But it makes sense. So many of the draftees I've met seem to come from poor, rural backgrounds. Naturally, they'd find comfort in familiar routines.

LaVerne agreed. "Bet you if he beat the shit out of a colored guy, he'd get a standing ovation."

May 19, 1945

Arrived in Pisa this morning. Next show tomorrow. Nic, Hope, most of the others procured cars for drive to the Tuscan countryside. An all-day feast at the allegedly untouched villa of a wealthy acquaintance of Dorsey's. I hung back, pleading train fatigue. Actually, though, got word the Army was holding Ezra Pound at a disciplinary center in Metato, a village just north of town. Our attaché secured an audience, though swore me to keep the entire affair on the QT. (Pound had been ordered held with absolutely no outside contact.) The attaché also made sure to express as much disdain for my curiosity re the treasonous poet as he could manage without betraying his charge to keep all talent content. "Deliberately undermining American troops," he noted gravely, "remains a hangable offense."

They kept Pound in an open-air cage about six foot square. Not a cell. Literally a *cage*. More befitting of a reptile or one of the lesser mammals. Concrete floor. No bedding save for thin patches of strewn hay. Guard stood at attention a few feet away. Enormous spotlights hung from the cage's uppermost bars, presumably to keep the prisoner illumined after the sun had set. Pound himself sat cross-legged, center-cage. A book lay propped open in front of him, its pages crowded with Chinese lettering. He squinted at a worn Chinese-English dictionary, seeking out a specific word or letter with his finger. The disciplinary center liaison banged roughly on the cage's bars with his helmet. "Hey there, Mr. Moto," he shouted. "You got a visitor."

Pound glanced up and smiled faintly, as if our meetings were routine, pleasant, and in no way unexpected. His eyes darted back to the page he'd been reading, stealing an end mark to whatever phrase or thought had been interrupted. Then he sandwiched the books together, using each to bookmark the other. Rising to approach me, he looked gaunt and ravished by age. As we shook hands through the bars, he leaned forward and stage-whispered, *"Avete portato la torta?"* Then he mimed a woman filing her nails.

We'd only met once before, in fact, at a Futurist dinner-banquet thrown in London, a number of years back, by Marinetti. "More Apician, myself," Pound said. *"Ad omne luxus ingenium natus,* or so dixit Pliny. Give me pigs fatted on figs and honeyed wine, or a nightingale's tongue, over Filippo's zang tumb tumb. Though, linguistically, a terrific menu. 'Immortal Trout.' 'Fisticuff Stuff.' 'Manandwomanatmightnight.' Hee. The 'Bombardment of Adrianopolis' sent Miss Moos running to the toilet. 'Phlegethon! Phlegethon!' she cried. Meaning the river's flow from a.h. *Cum grano salis,* these stories, save a dash for *mon pot-au-feu.* Signore Marinetti, in hindsight, appears a bit the huckster, no? Scribbler of manifestos. Professional barker. Stand him outside the ten-in-one. 'She was once a beautiful woman! She was known as the Peacock of the Air!'

Brilliance notwithstanding. But that said: stunt dinners? ΟΥ̓ ΤΙΣ. ΟΥ̓ m.f. ΤΙΣ. Enjoys that shit." He shrugged, then continued, "You still making pictures? I quite enjoyed your last one."

Safari Don't Really Seem to Be Enjoying Your Company? I wondered.

"Nope. You played a hobo." Pound shrugged. "*I filmi americani sono rari, questi giorni.* War and all."

Pound asked for a cigarette and went on about the current state of the motion picture industry, pausing to pointedly complain about the "moneymen" in Hollywood, with their "obvious ties" to the usurers in America and abroad. Otherwise steered clear of controversial topics. He favors musicals, comedies, "anything with Marlene Dietrich"; abhors Westerns, gangster pictures, "that fellow with the stammer who speaks as if his mouth is filled with porridge."

Kept waiting for Pound to ask why I'd come. Not sure myself. Certainly not a lover of the poetry. Bit willfully obtuse, for my taste. Too elaborate a joke.

Perhaps it's merely fascination with the notion of genius gone awry. Here is a man who has spent his life as cloistered in esoterica as a Carthusian, a Cabalist. Poring over sacred texts. Attempting to reach a place where few others will ever breathe the air. "A Mt. Erebus of the mind," to parody the old man.

Perhaps a mind preoccupied with matters wholly incomprehensible to the world at large leaves itself *more* susceptible to infestation by poisonous or alarmingly wrongheaded notions. Imagine mother never understanding what you are thinking. Nor the butcher who sells you bacon in the morning. Nor the lovely young girl whose every word fascinates if she happens to be wearing that special dandelion frock. Would not a moral arrogance naturally follow? A conviction that one understands far more than the yawning majority?

How easy, then, to reject the din of conventional opinion—Fascism "corrupt," anti-Semitism "paranoid," Mussolini "a thug"—when convention so often proves the fool's path.

Pound made no mention of his arrest by the *partigiani*, his pending trial in America, the broadcasts on Radio Rome. I tried to examine his face for signs of mania. But he seemed fine, all things considered. Weary, certainly. But alert. Pound noticed my appraisal, nodded. "I need a shave, I know, I know," he said. *"Ils ont peur que je finirai comme le grand gastronome romain, quand il a manqué d'argent pour se régaler."* He pinched his jugular vein with his thumb and forefinger. It kept slipping free, like a worm trying to escape the hook. He eventually secured it, mimed a razor's slash with his other hand. "This, though," he said, flicking the bars of his cage with his finger. "Understated as K., eh?" He clutched his breast theatrically. *"I would stop starving myself, if only I could find something I wanted to eat."*

I cleared my throat and said, "I think you backed the wrong man, Ez. But this—" Gesturing at the cage. "Seems a bit harsh." I shrugged.

Pound nodded. *"Caro Bartolomeo. Uomo di poche parole.* Something I respect. Did you learn to ride for the new picture?" In hindsight, an odd question. I had not mentioned *Horse Sense*, and it seemed unlikely that the Army'd provided him with a subscription to *Variety*.

At that moment, a guard appeared, informing me it was time to leave. I stepped away from the cage, grateful for the reprieve.

"Est con summatum, Ite," Pound said, winking broadly.

The attaché snorted. Turned out he'd been a classics major at UCLA. Spent the entire ride back to the hotel complaining about Pound's "Sunday school Latin."

May 20, 1945

Maybe I just enjoy the notion of all genius as corruptible. Meaning: everything proven by geniuses past is potentially *wrong*. What, after all, can be "known," if the most knowledgeable amongst us know so little?

In which case, maybe there is hope that something exciting will turn up, in the future. Something unexpected.

You cannot trust their minds. You cannot trust your own. You cannot trust the world. So. Who knows?

May 21, 1945

Night train, Pisa to Lake Maggiore. Exhausting show, but find it impossible to sleep. Adrenalin, most likely. (Our misses getting nearer by the day.) And the coffin-bunks no help. Definitely not built for two.

Though LaVerne sleeps like a man. Eventually, my shifting created enough mattress fallout to cause a stir. "Girl needs her beauty sleep," she mumbled. "You, too. Another gig tomorrow. Wind up nine-fingered." Before I could respond, her breathing had shifted back down to a deep wheeze. I slipped free of her arm, lowered myself to the carpeted floor. Stole along a series of darkened compartments, until I came to the smoking car. Inside, found Hope on the floor, face down, wearing a pair of blue silk pajamas and in the process of being hog-tied by Saw Kelly.

"Not how it looks, pal," Hope said, crooking his neck in my direction.

"Mr. Hope requested a demonstration," Kelly explained, hardly glancing up from his work.

I nodded and stepped behind the bar. We had the compartment to ourselves.

`"Hey, what you getting up to, back there?" Hope wanted to know.

"A Negroni," I said. "Quite refreshing."

"Make that *uno duo*," Hope said. "And I'll take mine with a *come se dice* straw?"

I placed the drink on the carpet, directly in front of Hope's face, bending the cocktail stirrer to reach his puckered lips. Kelly, meanwhile, no slouch with a rope. I told him so. "We worked with cowboys on our last picture," I said. "Not real ones. Based out of Bakersfield, I believe."

"Well, to be square, I'm from Michigan, originally, not Arkansas," Kelly said. He held up a hand and jabbed at the center-left of his thumb, traced its outline. "Thumb of the state. Water on three sides."

"Please," Hope said, "don't let me interrupt."

"Okay, so when you're tying?" Kelly told him. "You've got to be quick, or the little fuckers will reward you with a shot to the head."

"Calves kick?" Hope asked. He grunted as the kid yanked one of the knots tight. After letting out an exaggerated huff of air, he added, "How bad could that be?"

"Bad," Kelly said. "Okay. Try and get loose."

"Oooh, mama," Hope gasped. Tried squirming. "Last time anybody had me in a position like this, I was in Vegas, on Zukor's expense account." He began a painful-looking full-body wriggle. "Is this the part of the act where the French dame comes out with the baby thermometer?" Another grunt. "So you're from Michigan, huh? What's with the cornpone shtick?"

Kelly took a seat at the bar. "Well," he said, "I always loved rodeos when I was a kid. Whenever they came to a city nearby—Saginaw, or Flint—I'd have a ticket. Guess it seemed romantic, somehow, these guys rolling from town to town. Then, after my wife passed away—"

"Wife?" Hope exclaimed. "Jesus, kid. How old're you?"

"I celebrated my twenty-fourth birthday about a week prior to our shipping out. Young face. High school sweetheart." He paused, took a sip of his own Negroni. "Cancer got her."

We were all silent. Then Kelly slid off his stool and said, "You know what? I forgot the most important part of the hog-tie. This might help you out a bit, Mr. Hope. Focus the mind, as they say."

Hope said, "Well, yeah, of course, I knew there must be some mistake on your part, some good reason I couldn't—" At which point Kelly briskly gagged him with his checked bandana. Hope went fuchsia, began thrashing wildly. He smashed into a table, which would have toppled over had it not been bolted to the floor. He threw himself against the bar, causing a row of glasses and a bottle of Montalcino to crash to the floor. Kelly grinned, easily side-stepping the commotion.

"So, yeah. Michigan," he said. "And then I headed out West. Old story. Needed to forget. Wanted to make myself over. So my question is, why would anybody choose to leave this beautiful country?"

I told him that, actually, a death had prefigured my own departure, that I took my mother's quite badly, at one point even contemplating suicide.

Hope, his voice muffled by the gag, bayed something like, "You will fucking wish you had, you wop fuck!" Though it sounded more like, "WRSH! WRPP! FRKKK!!!"

"How would you have done it?" Kelly wondered. "I mean, did you get that far?"

I told him about the woods of nearby Maira, how I'd simply wandered, desolate, hoping to lose myself, with no clear plan. Had no rope, no knife. (Kelly laughed, here.) Only my belt. There was no moment of epiphany. I napped beneath a tree. Then it was morning, and cold. I had to piss. My thoughts returned to suicide, but I decided there would be time enough for it later, that I would be able to do a better job of it back home, with the proper equipment.

I shrugged. "I suppose I was never serious."

Hope, with a bestial gurgle, hurled his body across the train compartment. Kelly easily made the dodge. Hope collided with another table. There was a cacophonous crash, followed by a low moaning.

Kelly said, "Yeah, I reckon that was a good call. And I mean, like you say, you can off yourself later, at your convenience. You always retain that option." As he spoke, his fingers nervously worked one of the cocktail straws into a miniature lasso, dizzyingly knotted. "This, by the way," he mentioned, "is another nice trick to know. I don't mean this way, with a straw. An actual full-sized rope. It's not as hard as it looks. Thing is, I teach you this one, you have got to teach me the one with the pizza knife and the unpeeled banana. Deal?"

Made a note to myself to use the kid in our next picture.

May 22, 1945

Midway through an obligatory base tour, in a mishap so lame one of our scriptwriters might have come up with it, Nic and I are accidentally locked in a warehouse of contraband goods. Suspiciously, the rest of group failed to notice our absence for hours. During the course of the lock-in, we blamed each other. Bickered about the lack of professionalism on the set of *Horse Sense*. Accused one another of intentional mistosses during live performances. Floated, and rejected, a series of escape plans too numerous to list. (The most plausible, sadly, involved a crate of Howitzer shells and Nic's cigarette lighter.) Shouted our throats raw. Pounded our fists purple. Briefly grappled. Finally, stared each other down, panting.

Nic: "Your. Mustache's. Crooked."

Then: "Ha. Madeya. Check."

Shortly thereafter, Nic stumbled across an old Futurist noisemaker. One of Russolo's *intonarumori*. An awkward, organlike thing. Exposed pumps and gears, looking mainly for show. Probably meant to accentuate the notion of "future." An engraving on the side read: "Created by Luigi Russolo, in order to advance the Art of the Noise, the mighty Howler." (In Italian, of course.) Sure enough, each key produced a different pitch of howl. (An animal with its leg in a trap. A man being nailed to a crossbeam. A roomful of schoolchildren being denied cake. A woman mourning the news of her son's death in battle.) Nic pounded out an all-howl rag. I grudgingly laughed, wondered how it worked. He said, Magic, dummy.

Their execution (by electrocution, Vanzetti a few minutes after Sacco) took place shortly after midnight, all appeals having been exhausted. Over one hundred poems were written about the case in the days just before and after the execution.

The Sacco and Vanzetti Anthology of Verse, contemporaneously published, included Mary Carolyn Davis's "I Am the Chair," written from the point of view of an electric chair. (In the second stanza, the anthropomorphized chair expresses shock at the approach of two men who "have not won me fairly": "They are not lovers of mine . . . / What have they done that they / Should think to know my embrace?")

The trial also inspired novels (Upton Sinclair's *Boston*, John Dos Passos's *The Big Money*, Howard Fast's *The Passion of Sacco and Vanzetti: A New England Legend*), paintings (a series of works by Ben Shahn, also titled *The Passion of Sacco and Vanzetti*), and popular song (Woody Guthrie's *Ballads of Sacco and Vanzetti*).

"Ever since I could remember I'd wished that I'd been lucky enough to be alive at a great time—when something big was going on, like the Crucifixion. And suddenly I realized I was!" (Shahn, 1944 interview.)

Fast's *The Passion of Sacco and Vanzetti*, like the film version of his most famous novel, *Spartacus*, features a vaguely erotic bathing scene. (In the Sacco and Vanzetti book, the bather, unfortunately, is Mussolini.)

As the execution date neared, they were allowed more privileges, e.g. an hour together, daily, in the jail's courtyard, where Sacco enjoyed challenging Vanzetti to games of bocce.

"(Italians are) especially qualified by training and predilection for the dark deeds of the conspirators." (*The New Review.*) "Another reason which makes the Italian a recruit of Anarchy is his hereditary leaning toward secret societies." (*The Independent.*) "No matter where one hears of the life of some ruler or royal personage being attempted, one may always be sure to find that the assassin bears an Italian name." (*The New York Evening Journal.*)

(Santo Caserio: French president, an eleven-inch poignard, 1894. Michele Angiolillo: Spanish prime minister, gun, 1897. Luigi Luccheni: Austrian empress, homemade dagger, 1898. Gaetano Bresci: King of Italy, gun, 1900.)

The criminal phrenologist Cesare Lombroso never posits the propensity toward anti-State violence as an attribute that is distinctly Italian, though he does note, in *L'Uomo Deliquente*, "Dark hair prevails especially in murderers."

"Oh, da greata poet, da greata man. You reada heem, you know Italia, you lova da people! He was frienda da people . . . I no read heem till I come America. I younga man, worka by cloobba New York—great reecha cloobba, I washa da deesh." (Vanzetti, on Dante, in Sinclair's *Boston*.)

"Swindlers," on the other hand, tend to have "curly and woolly hair."

Dos Passos, at a protest in Boston, fled from police officers, despite earlier plans to force mass arrests. The young novelist suffered from poor vision, and so ran directly into the arms of another officer.

Later told *The New York Times* that he'd only been running to make a deadline for *The Daily Worker*. This is during the trial.

One scene in the Fast novel depicts a conversation between Mussolini, who is referred to only as "the Dictator," and "a well-known Viennese psychiatrist." (Presumably Carl Jung.) The pair speak of immortality. The Dictator confesses his affinity for the Roman emperors and their own aspirations to godhood. The Viennese says, "We know so little about the body . . . Consider the ductless glands—what secrets they might reveal . . . Who is to say that man is dust?—out of dust and into dust again? Why do men die? We can only guess." The Dictator points out that all men do, in fact, die. The Viennese, raising an eyebrow, asks, "Do they? How do we know?"

"Have we a record of the births and deaths of all men?"

"The blast," according to *The New York Times*, "strewed the street in its vicinity with the bodies of its dead and injured victims . . . From the excited, oft-times incoherent, stories of eyewitnesses and the first rescuers to arrive there developed a composite picture of frightfulness . . . First a blinding flash of bluish-white light that illuminated the whole of Wall Street; then the deafening, bewildering roar of the explosion . . . It seemed, the eyewitnesses said, as if there was just the slightest lull after that through which was heard the tinkle and smash of glass as hundreds of windows showered down over the stone fronts of buildings, or were blown back through rooms where busy men and women bent over desks. Those who went through those dread moments heard the glass before they saw it. A great cloud of smoke surrounded the immediate seat of the explosion, a great cloud of dust blotted out the whole of the street."

Sacco and Vanzetti had been indicted six days earlier, on September 11, 1920. The bomber, Mario Buda, a comrade and fellow Mexican expatriate, parked a horse-drawn wagon laden with dynamite near the New York Stock Exchange, in lower Manhattan.

Buda's nickname: "Nasone."

("Big Nose.")

Thirty-three dead, over two hundred seriously injured.

Sacco wears a bowtie. Vanzetti, all mustache, assumes the more severe pose. Woolen trenchcoats. Fedoras in laps. It remains the most iconic photograph from the trial. They are handcuffed together, seated on a bench.

"The thought of getting married has never crossed my mind. I have never had a girlfriend, and if I have ever been in love, it has been an impossible love, the kind that had to be stifled in my breast." (Vanzetti, writing to his aunt in 1914, as quoted by Avrich.)

"Immigrants to America were the beaver types that built up America, whereas the newer immigrants were ratmen trying to tear it down; and obviously ratmen could never become beavers." (President Coolidge, during the Sacco and Vanzetti trial.)

Asked, on the night of his arrest, why he was carrying a gun, Sacco told police, "It seems to be a habit of Italian people."

A rumor, cited by Sinclair in *Boston*, has Vanzetti personally constructing the pipe bomb that destroyed much of the home of Judge Albert F. Hayden, who had delivered harsh sentences to a group of Mayday demonstrators a month earlier.

"In the photograph of Luccheni being led away by a pair of Swiss police after stabbing the Empress, it is the young anarchist who appears perversely heroic—or anti-heroic, if you prefer. A grinning Billy the Kid, his brimmed hat cockily a-cant. Luccheni is the photograph's only modern-looking character, the singular figure who might stride from the portrait, leaving his captors, with their ludicrous epaulets and waxed mustaches, behind in their grainy scene." (Source unknown.)

"Oddly, because Sacco and Vanzetti were never directly linked to any bombings or violent acts, they have become a symbol of martyrdom more than of violent strikeback, and thus in certain ways less romantic, or rather, romantic in a different way, romantic as *victims*, displays of stoicism, bravery, eloquence, in the face of hopelessness being a very different sort of romance." (Source unknown.)

The same night, Sacco, when asked if he was an anarchist, replied, "Some things I like different."

Chapter Thirteen:
Sacco and Vanzetti
Find the Real Killers

The boys take the case—a missing heiress, shoe thievery, the Verdi underground, anarchist sweethearts, and "a Little Italy of the mind"

EXCERPT

(Dougherty, Malcolm, ed. The Comedy Film Encyclopedia.
Detroit: Gale, 1988.)

A Couple of Wops in a Jam (1944) One of the more successful of the **Sacco and Vanzetti** knife-grinding vehicles, the film is a meticulous parody of the popular **Charlie Chan** detective pictures, substituting broad Italian stereotypes for the similar portrayals of the Chinese in the Chan series. The boys play crime-solving cutlers in the Little Italy of an unnamed city. (Many critics assuming Detroit, due to the automobile industry subplot.). The neighborhood, an audaciously designed fantasia, serves as a character all its own—a "Little Italy of the mind," as the critic Pauline Kael wrote—with Sacco and Vanzetti's knife shop part of a teeming warren of neon-signed trattorias, garish storefront chapels and shadowy espresso bars. (At one point, Bart and Nic make a grand escape from a trio of gangsters by commandeering a gondola in a replicated Venetian canal.) The plot hinges on the disappearance of a beautiful young heiress (**Audrey Jacobs**, in her first screen role); she has, her family suspects, run off with Joey "Frank" Morelli, Jr. (**Tom Bennett**), of the notorious Morelli shoe-thief gang. As amateur detectives able to move with ease throughout the Italian underworld, Sacco and Vanzetti are hired to recover the girl, and soon find themselves enmeshed in an impossibly convoluted web of genre complications. After infiltrating a subterranean opera bar, the boys are blamed for the murder of young Morelli and engage in extended chase sequences with both cops and mobsters. In the process, they disguise themselves as topiary gardeners, infiltrate an anarchist bomb factory, and destroy the home of the heiress's father (**Robert Bailey**), an eccentric automobile baron rather indiscreetly modeled after Henry Ford. (The car mogul was reportedly enraged by the caricature—in particular, a scene mocking an idea hatched by Ford, an avid birdwatcher, to pipe steam heat into birdhouses on his Michigan estate in order to thwart winter migratory patterns.) Through an unlikely set of coincidences, the film's denouement, which unfolds in a hangar-like warehouse, comes in the form of a massive shoe fight, with all of the major players eventually knocked unconscious, arrested and/or dynamited soot-black. Bart and Nic slip away scot-free, a pair of shoes—mismatched!—their only reward.

PHYSICAL WORK EMBRUTES NOT ENNOBLES MAN

(scenes from the 1937 picture A Couple of Wops in a Jam*)*

So in walks this dame. Daughter's run off with a wop of ill-repute. One of Morelli's boys. Notorious shoe thieves. Always struck Nic as an odd specialization, but hey, could say the same thing about knives. So this dame, her missing daughter, a hundred bucks for photographic evidence of the happy couple. Q: *Why us?* She pulled up in a sight-gag limo. Meaning one sees the front end of the limo coming round the bend and expects the back end to follow reasonably and thusly, but the thing just keeps coming and coming and coming. Get it? From the doorway of the knife shop, Nic catches the limo's endless arrival, reacts with comic excess, popping his eyeballs like a colored porter spooked by a white sheet. Her chauffeur turns out to be an actual colored guy, name of Brownford, whether that name's given or sur- is unclear. A: *If my daughter had run off with a Chinaman, I'd have gone to Charlie Chan.* Nic mouthing: "*Brown*ford?" Colored guy makes a rude, potentially threatening gesture. Bart, meanwhile, keeping his nose just about literally to the you-know-what, his entire demeanor remaining as serious as competitive chess. (Only sign of the back-forth of the knife a ripple in his shoulders as he slides the blade across the spinning wheel.) Whole time the dame is laying out her story. *This is my daughter, who seems to have gone missing.* Nic whistles. The gag of the photograph being the girl is on her back and nearly nude (a slip of a slip the only thing veiling God's intentions), her legs veeing a victory of unspecified sorts, her half-smile no less inviting for being upside down. *A shot*, mother explains, *from her school play.* The gag of the knife shop being the place is like a walk-in iron maiden. Meaning knives everywhere, scattered like matches, stuck into walls to double as coat hooks, piled precariously in wooden boxes, protruding from cubbyholes at eye-, chin-, chest-, and groin-level. *Take a seat, ma'am, please please please.* Nic gesturing with a boning knife at a wobbly stool. (A couple of curved blades, missing handles, stacked flat under the short leg for balance's sake.) Later on, Nic's pretty sure she calls the chauffeur "Brownevelt." This particular dame, incidentally, would be a *femme fatale* in the Gorgonian sense of the word. As in one peep and you're marble. Get it? Dames making appearances in this genre traditionally of the knockout variety. Bart's always claiming he'd rather pass on the dicking jobs. Though Nic's convinced he secretly digs the thrills. They bump heads checking out the picture of the girl. Nic notes (to himself) that if they'd literally drooled, it (their salivation) would've commingled on the glossy surface of the photograph, moistening her open thighs. *I think we ca—*

Nic, peering into a barrel of roiling eel. Looks like an ink cloud in there. Squid-produced. Bart flashes the eel monger the glossy of the missing girl. Looks like a prop-room pile of fake beards in there. Earlier, they rolled their grinding wheel along the main drag, where dull knives were snatched, sharpened, returned with aplomb. *Allora, chief?* Playful fake-stab at the balloon man's swollen gut. *You dirty so-and-so. Stay away from them underage dogs.* Funny how Bart's initial reluctance, once overcome, switches to insane perfectionism. Collaring pigeons, flashing glossies like a professional gumshoe. Whereas Nic pulled the opposite, now as restless and unprofessional as when he'd been cooped in the shop. The gag of questioning the eel monger being, while he and Bart study the glossy, Nic, in the near-background, peers into the barrel and gets flicked with a tail. Why youses the thing. Gets squirted in the eye. Furiously attempts a grab. Gets soaked by the increasing roil. Makes a full bob. Emerges with an eel clamped to his nose. Howls. Thrashes. Tugs. Is python-choked. Get it? Across the street, an old woman ladles out *putanesca* sauce from a ramshackle stall. In the alleyway behind her, a crowd of soccer fans jostles for a better view of a pickup match. A gondolier wolf whistles through funneled fists as his taxi coasts along a replicated canal. *Hey!* the monger cries. *What the hell are you doing to my eels you sona—*

The club, La Scala, entered via unmarked alley door. Looks like a real dive, though actually quite exclusive, the majority of the clientele being local mob-types, their ilk, come to sip rare imported *amaretti* and hear favorite arias as performed by the opera stars of the day. Tiny stage at the front of the house, no costumes or sets, the stars cabbed direct from their marquee gigs uptown. *Da rich bastard up-a there? I give them three-quarter. For you, my friends, I save the whole.* And then (say) "*E Lucevan le Stelle*," Cavaradossi's sob louder and more devastating than the crowd has ever heard, recorded or otherwise. And more *real*, somehow. Is it the tenor's tight-in-the-waist gabardine slacks, the open-collar silk shirt, the trace amounts of eyeliner? In the kitchen, Nic distracting the help with ludicrous demonstrations involving a sharpening steel, while Bart keeps an eye on the porthole of the swinging door, scanning for the happy couple's arrival. Later, the girl douses Morelli with her Campari and grapefruit, dashes for the exit with Morelli on her tail, his sauce-stained napkin still dangling, cravat-like, from his throat. By the time Bart and Nic make it outside, there's nothing to see but a parked car. Morelli in the driver's seat, appearing asleep. One of their own knives juts from his neck like a tiller. (His beaked face rather rudderlike, maybe explaining the tiller bit coming to mind.) Of course, Nic's got his grip around the handle of the knife going *Yep, s'definitely one of ours*, when the goons emerge. It looks bad. No denying. Nic: *So, we realize this looks bad.* Inside, earlier, wild applause, the tenor responding with an arrogant little half-bow. To be fair, the paucity of the bow could be the result of his stomach getting in the way. Men throw their hats, women violently patterned scarves. A knockout in low-cut finery darts around the packed tables and tosses a basketful of rose petals. The tenor tilts his head back and accepts the shower. He tells a story about the crude and buffoonish *Americanos* who pay twenty dollars a ticket to watch him sing, how midway through the second solo they're mining their noses for *canipi*. He says he once substituted the nursery rhyme *I scampa la pipi* for the lyrics of *La donne e mobile*, and the *Americanos* not only failed to notice, they gave him a standing ovation. He sings *I scampa la pipi* after G. Verdi. Morelli leads the cheers. Bart peeping all of this via porthole, champagne buckets and tossed scarves all floating past like undersea fauna. Bart peeping at the girl more intently than he'd have appreciated Nic noticing, though Nic wasn't one to judge, especially in the case of *this* particular girl. Gag involving Nic, Bart, sporting ill-fitting waitstaff costumes, having locked actual waitstaff in supply closet. Gag involving Nic, Bart, performing waiterly duties with extreme incompetence (e.g. pasta excessively cheesed, peppermilled) while attempting to get close enough to Morelli and date to obtain the desired photographic evidence. Gag involving tenor dedicating heartwrenching aria to happy couple, who have already begun to loudly bicker, and who continue to do so throughout said aria, despite actual tears pouring from tenor's eyes. Get it? Get it? Get it? *L'ora e fuggita e muoio disperato! E non ho amato mai tanto la vita . . .*

Translation: *I die hopeless, despairing, and never before have I loved life like this . . .*

Gag involving Irish cop (face like a gloveless fist in winter), nearly slapping the mustache off Bart in the interrogation room. (The primary concern of the police department being the big shoe heist the Morellis allegedly have in the works.) The minute the cop leaves the room, Nic whispers, *Don't worry, this happens to be a technique they call the Nice Cop and the Unpleasant Cop . . . this brute is clearly the latter, but the next one he'll treat us with kid glo—*

Cop #2 enters, punches Nic dead in jaw, knocking him out cold.

Gags involving ludicrous excess of Wade Estate, Harland Wade's heated bird feeders, his arms and armor collection, his fanatical anti-Semitism, his orders to *find the real killers*. (Subtext: *Not my daughter.*)

Mrs. Wade's clumsy attempt at dual-seduction in back of limousine.

The disguise. (Topiary gardeners!) A disastrous topiary seal.

The Italian tailor shop fronts a grappa bootlegger's that in turn fronts an anarchist bomb factory. You make grappa with the byproducts of wine, all the bits you'd normally throw away, peel and stem and seed. Bart and Nic, then, covered in grape detritus when the heating duct gives way, making their clamorous crash landing that much more awkward—though their fall is broken (somewhat) by a pile of sugar sacks. Earlier, the stout Italian seamstress peered into the darkened tailor's. *Who deh?* she wanted to know, in Italian, then English, then English again. Speaking required her to remove the pins from her mouth. She proceeded to stick said pins into the nearest dress dummy. (Nic in disguise.) (Sugar plus potassium chlorate plus sulfuric acid equals a fire, or for anarchist bomb builders a simple and inexpensive means of dynamite detonation.) Earlier still, Roberto, the Wades' gardener, returned with intelligence. *The girl run around with a Red, name of Caesare. She doing two-time on Morelli. That why they fight, the night he die.* Now, a dozen or so anarchists, guns drawn and pointed. This is after the crash. *Well, hey, looks like you don't got any knives to be sharpened. We must be in the wrong place.* The Caesar kid's a hothead, an idealist. The Wade girl has turned Red. *My father is a monster. There's blood on his hands. He's part of the problem. Property is theft.* That kind of jive. *Propaganda of the idea is a chimera. Wherever Carthage is fought, Rome is defended.* Sort of thing. She claims she had nothing to do with the offing of Tony M., but that, pre-offing, Tony let slip regarding the big shoe heist, which involved hitting what's known in the biz as the Fort Knox of shoe warehouses, and so the anarchists have counter-planned to get there first and heist the heist, so to speak, only for them it's not crude robbery but revolutionary expropriation, for a *cause*. Caesar studies the interlopers. *They seem too dumb to be Fascists or cops. I think I believe their story.* Nic winks at Bart. *Still, we'd best keep them close. You two are coming wi—*

The shoe-fight commences the moment Mrs. Wade (who shows up after the anarchists, the Morellis and her husband, but just before the cop-cavalry) accidentally tips a shelf of ladies' pumps, creating a domino effect of toppling shelving unit around the perimeter of the shelf-lined warehouse. When the cops burst in, the commanding officer immediately takes a work boot to the back of the head, causing his hat to slide over his eyes, the ensuant blindness resulting in his nightstick, already in full swing, realigning the nose and dentures of his second- and fourth-in-command, respectively. As in a pie fight, a direct hit to the kisser the most desirous of outcomes. (Limbs are worthless. Chests can have resonance, but only if the payload is delivered with a terrible force. While a nondirect hit can still be considered worthy if the projectile is primarily composed of custard, a shoe-graze merely confuses, and is tantamount to a full miss. A shoe to the groin or posterior, however, works terrifically, while a pie to the same body parts falls flat. Sitting on a pie being the major exception to this rule.) The Fort Knox of shoe warehouses: maybe an exaggeration. Not to minimize the gross quantity of the stockpile. The air thick with shoes. Nic thought about how his pal Guido's ex-wife had remarried and Nic had referred to the new guy as Guido's husband-in-law, which Guido had not found funny enough for Nic's taste. The arrival of Harland Wade had for some reason reminded him of the husband-in-law joke. And there was Morelli Senior, bizarrely invigorated by the close combat. How many years had it been since the old man had personally beaten a cop? He had a handful of one rookie's shirt, a thick-soled boot slipped over his pounding fist. Nic was pretty sure the old man was humming the pop hit "They Needed a Songbird in Heaven (So God Took Caruso Away)." Nic at this moment deciding to yank his shirt open. Buttons popping like corn in oil. A group of the Black Hands cowering behind a makeshift shoe-fortification. Another difference between a piefight and a shoefight is the level of mania. (Shoefights end up far more frenzied, as the stakes involve real pain.) (Ever been clocked in the head with a shoe? It ain't custard.) One of Morelli's goons takes a shot in the balls, courtesy of a wind-up finger-slip by Bart, the clog Bart had been clutching sailing back and goon-groinward. Mrs. Wade swings an Oxford by its laces, wildly, clubbing men out of her path. Nic says, *I got a bomb*. Bart glances up first, the only one to hear. There is something terrible about a roomful of abandoned shoes, is there not? Perhaps because shoes are only abandoned in the most dire of circumstances. Or because the shoes themselves resemble dead things, with all those tongues (aflap) and eyes (hollow) and mouths (gaping) and even the laces, though lacking a corresponding human body part, dangling limply as if once they hefted and coiled with the force of limbs. Nic had considered going with the classic black sphere with a ridiculous birthday-cake fuse. (Most writes: "The best shape for a bomb is, and always will be, a sphere. This is because the resisting of the casing is homogenous, and so the explosive effect will be the same in all directions. Where can you obtain these hollow spheres? The best ones are made of iron, and you could have them cast at a foundry. However, apart from the matter of finding the necessary funds, there is also the question of security. If the people at the foundry are not loyal comrades, there is the possibility of betrayal.") The Wade girl is on her knees, a trickle of blood clotted just below her left nostril. (Not Nic's doing. She was hit in the face with a shoe—tossed, ironically, by one of the more bookish of the anarchists, who'd never had much practice in sports involving throwing things.) Note the inherent unfunniness in exposing Fatty's belly. It is a padding rife with visible stretchmarks, a pasty and distended gut, patchily hirsute, one perfectly free of moisture and yet somehow managing to appear not exactly *dry*, calling to mind certain types of cheese. All of this lacks humor, as does the targetlike nature of the exposed stomach, rudely thrust forward and seeming to invite not only a punch but perhaps even stabbing, evisceration. *I mean*, Nic said, *what's a guy gotta do to get some attention around here? Blow himself up? Oh, wait.* To be fair, part of the unfunniness may have to do with the four red sticks of dynamite that have been taped to Nic's chest, their curlicue wires wending off to a little detonator of the silent film villain's variety. His other hand twists the girl's hair whenever she makes a move. Harland Wade steps forward, seeming ready to deliver something along the lines of *Take me—I'm the one you're after, you Red bastard, she's innocent!* That old chestnut. Besides which, *Il n'y a pas d'innocents*, cocksucker. But especially this brat. Come on. Q: Why not kill the father? And well, yes, they were *his* sins. But the children are the ones who have callously benefited, and if they fail to consider the source of their inheritance, if they ignore the blood buoying their yachts, well, willful ignorance is not the same as innocence. Get it? Nic makes eye contact with Bart, gives him a wink. You can see the eel bites on his bare chest, still. Also taking away from the humor. Q: Has Bart been seduced by the girl's beauty to the extent that he will oppose that which he knows is not only just but necessary, considering the warlike situation in which they find themselves? He won't have been the first. Bart: *Nic. What are you doing?* Nic: *Expropriating this Revolution, I would say.* Bart: *This isn't funny.* Nic: *You know what's funny? I feel like I've been thinking about funny for so long, I have no idea what is. Funny, I mean. I'm just shooting in the dark at this point.* Bart: *Nic you—* Nic: *Hey, Bart, what if, when the smoke clears, we're all sooty, and, I don't know, my collar's all turned up? That'd be funny, right?* Bart: *Nic.* Nic: *And don't give me that look, man. You're always giving me that look. It's too late. You want it too. You know you do.* Q: So where exactly you going with this? Well, just remember two things: the old men, the fathers, they're *already* old, so what's the point there, right? And *secondo*, everyone, *always*, wants to save the children, so, Bart: *Nic.* Nic: *Stay back.* Bart: *Nic.* Nic: *Stay.* Bart: *Nic.* Nic: *Try me.* A:

Chapter Fourteen:
Bocce on Mars

The boys behind bars—lawn bowling, a planet of women,
and dreams of escape—Bart Vanzetti meets his accuser

Vanzetti, the Doomed Philosopher, Gives Views on Life, Death, Love

(a scene from the 1958 picture Mars Needs Sacco and Vanzetti!*)*

Bart cocked his head at the guard's approach. He'd been jolted awake by the echoes of her march, rebounding up the narrow stone corridor that led to his cell door. (Against which they piled, awaiting the real boots.) Still, Bart forced himself to remain on the bunk, feigning nonchalance. *Oh—here to fetch me already? I lose the time.* Where, he wondered, as she stepped aside, holding the door—not, of course, in a reverse nod to chivalry, but as one holds a potential weapon close to one's chest, as preventative of potential violent pivots and/or slammings—said cell door, of necessity, a heavy fucker—*where*, though, did he learn that the worst thing in the world, even worse than the pain itself, was the admitting to it? Someone had once described him as a pathological stoic. Which he'd found extreme, this judgment. And yet, here he was, being marched along a cell block and yet not allowing himself to act or feel marched. Just out for a stroll. And for whose sake? The guard's?

Q. Why pretend your cell is the Senator's suite?

A. To not give the satisfaction.

Q. Does the guard truly care, either way?

A. To "keep a stiff upper lip," in the words of the Englishman.

Q. Does not the guard's satisfaction actually *increase* when her job's difficulty is lessened?

Q. Does not the pretending by the prisoner that it's all poppyfields significantly lessen said job difficulty?

Q. Not to mention, is there any way the guard could not help but see *right through* your prisoner's walk, your *faux*-stroll, through-beneath to the specter-Vanzetti on his specter's knees, the momentum of his marching self dragging his spectral-supplicant-self backwards by the ankles, his spectral-fingernails digging into the stone floor of the corridor, leaving behind eight faint and shaky tire treads of dust . . . ?

A. That was a question?

Nic, in the meantime, already in the yard, gathering stones. They'd found the rocks unnaturally round, here. From which point, it had been a short leap to the idea of a game.

Why not?

Bart watched Nic's gathering. He considered strolling over to help. Instead, he stuck out his tongue and tasted the afternoon air. He guessed afternoon. Time, here, a different animal. The air tasted the same. Like nothing. A dry heat, but perforated with the odd little chill. Gauzy, in that way.

"Hey, you ever wonder why they leave us these rocks? We could easily chunk 'em in the guards' direction."

"They wear helmets. Armor."

"Form-fitting bikini-armor. Plenty of exposed flesh, which, hey, no complaints from this guy. Though, you know, pleasing to the viewer can be impractical for combat. Not to mention poor defense against prisoner rock-chunking."

"They carry guns."

"And how exactly are they gonna figure who chunked the rock, Dad? Ball-breaking as they be, our lady friends don't strike me as types for the indiscriminate trigger-squeeze."

"We're the only two people out here."

"Fifty-fifty odds, for us. Better than baccarat, tell you that much."

"Could we—"

"Care to make it interesting?"

"Just not?"

"Loser dies first."

"Please?"

"Know what your problem's always been? You think the way the warden wants you to think."

The miniature ball is known, in the parlance of the game, as a *pallino*. You threw the *pallino* first, after which it became the fixed target for the other, larger balls, the planets, for once, orbiting a moon.

Nic fixed Bart with a hard stare and then held up the *pallino*. Bart nodded, and Nic tossed him the stone. Bart crouched and squinted out across the yard.

"What, you counting periscopes?"

The ground, here, the color of questionable cooking, a labial shade of ruddy gray.

They didn't look like astronauts. They looked like old men who had reached the point in their lives where playing children's games had become a welcome distraction.

Bart, crouching, squinting. Then, finally, he stood and released a perfect little *puntata*-style roll, the ball (in this case, rock) skimming across the surface of the court.

(In this case, prison yard.)

He'd been depressed, he assumed for the obvious reasons. But of late had come to wonder if it had more to do with the lack of birds. There were no birds here. For that matter, no insects, no rodents, no . . . Well. That was all he could attest to, having not ventured beyond the prison's walls since the crash. Still, it seemed unfair, he and Nic being robbed of that staple of sentimental prison literature—the chance to train the normally untrainable beast, and to learn in the process that all creatures, no matter how small, remain God's, and therefore not only befriendable, but of use.

He dreamt a pet mouse in a diaper. He dreamt flies from Nic's cell, dragging tiny banner signs.

MARRY ME ? ?

THAT WHICH DOESN'T KILL YOU MAKES YOU
STRONGER: DRINK MOXIE ! !

He dreamt the prison yard a playground filled with children, the sky a normal sky of birds, and then a sudden flash, the birds all falling like fruit, hitting the ground likewise—that is, ripely—the children, now hysterical, jumping swings on the fro, taking cover under the giant slide.

So, sure. Maybe the blues worked in ways so simple you didn't even notice. Maybe you assumed the drag to be the weight of the inevitable, when really it just came down to missing some singing.

Of course, if it wasn't the birds, it would be something else.

"Can we breathe the air here? I mean, obviously, we *are* breathing it, yeah. By 'can' I mean you think it's good for us? Like what if it's coating the inner linings of our lungs with cancer? If it's one of those counterintuitives, like drinking saltwater. As in, something we should be able to do, in a just world, but the cruel reality being that we cannot. How about that?"

Speaking of obvious: Nic's distraction techniques.

"Or, hey, how about the gravity? You think it's different, here? I gotta say, I'm feeling a little heavy."

They had not seen any other prisoners.

"You're not even gonna bite at that one? Come on. I set you up. What's a guy gotta do?"

Bart tossed his first stone at the *pallino*. It hit the earth. "Earth." Well. It hit *the ground* with a muffled plangency. As if, with the thump, you actually heard a give, a glove hitting a stuffed bag.

The stone landed and rolled, resting approximately seven o'clock and sixteen paces from its target.

"Not bad. Not good, either. I guess more bad than good, you want to get technical. All right. I'm up, huh?"

Nic soft-shoed his way to the line, hefting a stone in either hand, his manner suggesting weight, inspection, and the possibility of return to the produce man. He began to juggle the stones from hand to hand, eventually snatching one from its flight, allowing the other to career out of its orbit and crash roughly to earth.

"Earth."

Nic hefted his chosen stone with satisfaction, admiring it like something he'd made himself. He glared up at one of the turreted guards.

"Hey, sweetheart, how ya doin'?"

Turning to Bart, in a lower voice, he said, "That one there's a real four-fingered *putana*. That was an old saying of my *zio*. You know, it means she's such a whore you can stick four fingers up her—"

"I get it."

Bart squinted into the birdless sky. Their situations had been getting increasingly ridiculous as the years progressed, true. But a *planet of women*? That beat all. You could argue a certain symbolic merit in the upending of feminine nurture, a certain appealing frisson in the stereotypical Mother Earth ("Earth") gentility of the less-foul sex turned oppressive. Gaea tossing thunderbolts like Zeus. The old *vagina dentata*. The Cleopatra grip. As in, a worshipful approach to nature, creation, is a futility. A fool's wish.

So fucking obvious. And death row? *Death row?*

Perhaps the governor would grant them an eleventh-hour pardon.

Maybe somebody would sneak them a chisel, they could dig their way out. File would be fine. (As grandpa's red wine.)

Nic was more of a tosser, the toss known in the game as a *raffa*, an underhand lob that Nic pulled off with surprising grace, his body and spread legs collapsing into a squat in perfect symmetry with his arm's rise and release.

Even without birds, without clouds, still so much to look at. Bart stared at the sky, listening for the throw, waiting for the stone to break the frame of his stare, for the stone to sail through, up, over and back out again. He knew his eyes would be tempted to follow the stone, would naturally drift with the movement. But he would hold them steady. He did not know why. This just seemed like an important meditative gesture. Then the stone would pass, and he would listen, listen, listen, and then finally he would hear the dull thud as it hit the ground.

The collision of Nic's stone with another made a sharp crack.

Nic complained that his stone was not perfectly round. Nic noted a regulation ball would have traveled further and with more accuracy. Nic yelled, animatedly, as if a referee were present. Nic waved his arms and kicked up dust. The guards, in their turret, either failed to notice or did not care.

Bart stepped up for his turn, spotting for the first time how Nic's stone had hit his own and in the process knocked it closer to the *pallino*.

"Much obliged."

"Oh, now you look, you prick moth—"

Bart crouched, squinted.

"Don't throw too hard. Too hard, you overshoot. Too soft, though, you look like a pussy. Keep that one in mind. Nobody wants a weak wrist. Strong and decisive is what the ladies are after. It's better to go too far than not far enough. Doesn't even matter if it's in the wrong direction. The ladies do not care. Believe that? Still, it's true. Better to sail past the mark than fall way short. Eh?"

Bart tossed. His ball rolled to a stop just short of the *pallino*.

Nic drew an outsized penis in the dust with his toe.

"I talked a handjob out of that guard with the red hair. Know the one I'm talking about? Ponytail. Jewel-encrusted kind of ankle-dagger."

"I feel like I should feel more distracted."

"Not a bad throw, incidentally. Not bad in the least."

"Isn't that the point of this? Distraction from the inevitable?"

"Only inevitable I know about is my kicking your ass at bocce."

Bart fell silent.

Nic turned and offered a lopsided grin. He looked as if he were about to attempt some queer sort of juggle, or stick the rock down his pants. Instead, he grinned farther, to the point of looking pained. Then he said,

"You can't fight them every second of the day. What do you want to do?"

Nic turned to face the guard turret, holding his stone like a shot put, now.

"Should I do it?"

Bart did not answer.

"Should I?"

Bart stared up at the suns.

"Say the word."

Where the hell *were* they?

"Oh, by trial, you meant our *trial. See, the minute I heard
that word, I thought Arbuckle's . . ." (p. 217)*

From the Aldino Felicani Sacco-Vanzetti Collection at the Boston
Public Library, one of Bartolomeo Vanzetti's handwritten notes on
various miscarriages of justice, written in Dedham Jail, 1922:

*"Nel caso di Fatty Arbuckle la giuria delibero 40 ore di sequito, no-
nostante che de primo ballottaggio vi furono voti d'assoluzione. Vogliano
non solo dargli la liberta ma riabilitarlo con un verdetto assolutorio. Il
giura che non si corruppe era una donna e disse e chi l'andró a prendere
per accompagnarla a casa.* Bring me out of here as soon as possible."

The trial ended abruptly, with an out-of-court settlement for an undisclosed sum. Clemente Bonapace's counsel, Hill Brewster, had been resolutely opposed to any manner of settlement, but the pressures of the trial—particularly the endless public scrutiny that comes with participation in such high-profile scandal—had eroded the Bonapace family's will to see the thing through, and so they accepted the cash with eagerness.

In fact, the notoriety stirred by the trial so rattled Bonapace that he used the settlement to repatriate, moving his family back to his tiny home village in the mountains. Bonapace and his wife divorced shortly thereafter, with Bonapace quickly remarrying a childhood sweetheart and using his portion of the family's gains to purchase a dilapidated chalet-style pensione. A year later, a state-of-the-art ski lift was built along the mountainside, and the entire valley experienced an unprecedented tourist boom. Bonapace bought several more hotels and became one of the wealthiest men in the valley. He never discussed the trial, only referring to it obliquely as "our unfortunate past." On occasion, a child would ask the former grinder to perform a knife trick. Bonapace always responded with a chuckle and an insistence that he was a simple innkeeper, now, and that his only tricks, these days, involved convincing German tourists to pay double-room rates for a single. As Sacco and Vanzetti fell out of the public eye, such requests from children grew rarer, and the origins of the Bonapace fortune were either forgotten or politely ignored by most adults.

After the trial, Bonapace never laid eyes on Nic Sacco again, though he did run into Bart Vanzetti once in Los Angeles, about seven months after Sacco's death. Vanzetti, in his late seventies, still lived alone in his rather modest home in the Hollywood hills, dining nightly, also by himself, at his favorite Italian restaurant, Silvano's, a once-glamorous destination that had long passed its prime. Vanzetti always arrived at the same time, promptly at seven, after which he would be seated at his regular table, tucked in a corner, and brought his standard meal, the pasta of the day, followed by, depending on his mood, the veal or the fish, a salad and the chef's choice of dessert. This would be accompanied by two glasses of red wine (fish or no) and an espresso with dessert. Vanzetti never read with his meal, nor did he seem to have the need, found in many solitary diners, to feign some level of distraction that might imply important business. Instead, Vanzetti receded into the background, with all of his body language focused with unhurried purpose upon his food. Bobby Silvano, the owner, played selections from the operas that Vanzetti loved during these hours, as a subtle tribute to his most famous regular. (Later in the evening, Silvano favored jauntier Italian-American fare by the likes of Dean Martin and Frank Sinatra.)

Bonapace and his second wife had semi-retired, leaving their children to run the hotels, and had decided to spend their autumn years taking long trips around the world. While on a visit to the western United States, they spent two days in Los Angeles; the concierge at their hotel, taking note of their age and assuming they would appreciate a restaurant of the "old school," mentioned Silvano's when they asked for a dining recommendation. The possibility of running into Vanzetti had, of course, briefly crossed Bonapace's mind when they arrived in Los Angeles, but he'd just as quickly dismissed the thought as absurd, never truly believing a pair of simple tourists could cross paths with a legendary film star in such an enormous city. When he spotted Vanzetti in his corner table, hunched over his veal marsala, Bonapace thought it was a trick of his mind, that he'd projected Vanzetti onto an old man with similar features.

Still, he had to be sure. And so, after ordering, he informed his wife he needed to use the facilities and then surreptitiously made his way to the restaurant's front room. Sure enough, it was Vanzetti seated at the corner table. He looked much older, and frail—but frail in a wholly sustainable manner, like an ascetic who has trained himself to shed all that is unnecessary and so could survive for months, with little effort, on crusts and rainwater.

Vanzetti noticed the man approaching his table and assumed that he was an autograph-seeker. He felt a twinge of satisfaction, almost immediately thereafter wondering at what a pathetic old man he'd become. He'd started to explain he had no pen when he realized the man was Bonapace. The cutler looked tan and comfortable, his clothes expensive and European.

Vanzetti apologized for not recognizing him, complimented his appearance and invited him to sit. Bonapace put his hand to his chest and said he would not think of interrupting. Vanzetti insisted. Bonapace gave in, explaining his wife waited in the back room and so he could only sit for a moment. Vanzetti did not, oddly enough, feel the slightest animosity towards the cutler. He wondered at this fact, and supposed that, in part, it had to do with the general fading that comes with the passage of enough time. The money, then, had seemed like quite a sum, but he still had plenty, and what they'd always considered the far more grievous aftereffect of the suit, the besmirchment of their names, their career, their (ha!) "art" also seemed less dire, now, considering they had, in recent years, been forgotten by all but a handful of septuagenarians and rather sad film aficionados.

Bonapace was calling him an old hound dog for still living alone. At precisely this moment, Arturo, the waiter, brought Vanzetti his dessert, a slice of spumoni ice cream. Though Bonapace insisted he eat, Vanzetti always felt slightly childish when eating dessert as a grown man, so he held up his hand. Bonapace had already told Vanzetti about his new life and was now offering his condolences regarding Nic. Vanzetti said it had been quick. Bonapace remembered reading that Nic died of stomach cancer, which was probably *not* quick, and thought how Vanzetti's manner had always been to placate. Bonapace asked if he was making any pictures. Vanzetti said it was funny, that after the Mars picture flopped, they'd stopped asking. He said that Nic had badly wanted to keep working, but that it had become impossible to find money, and that Nic had even been talking, before he got sick, about financing another picture themselves. He said he'd told Nic that people's tastes change, that one has to accept the fact that one will not always be on top, but Nic didn't want to listen, insisted quality is quality. And then he got sick, and so the question became moot. And then he died and, here's the funny part, suddenly, after all of the tributes had appeared in the newspapers and movie magazines, suddenly the studios became interested again. Vanzetti had a handful of offers, including playing comic relief in a Western picture with Duke Wayne, but he had, thus far, committed to nothing.

Bonapace said it's funny, this is like the plot of a movie. Vanzetti said, Oh? Bonapace said, Well, you are more expert than I, of course, but this meeting of ours strikes me as something written for the cinema, coming as it does after so many years under the bridge. Vanzetti said he could see that. Bonapace leaned forward conspiratorially and asked, "So who do you think they believed, in the end?" Vanzetti said, "Who's who?" Bonapace said, "This is starting to sound like one of your old routines." Vanzetti said, "You remember the knife bit?" He picked up his steak knife, greasy and speckled with bits of veal, and feinted a toss. (If you didn't know better, you might think a stab.) Bonapace said, "Who is you and Nic and me. They is the people. The public. What is did they think you were guilty." Vanzetti dropped the knife, exhaled deeply and said he hadn't considered the question in years. He said, "It doesn't seem so important anymore, does it?" He said, in fact, nowadays, he would be happy if people thought of him period, guilty or innocent. Bonapace nodded, holding up his hands in a gesture of agreement. "But still and all," he continued, "I think they believed you. That's what breaks my heart, to this day. How people must assume I did it for the money." Bonapace looked genuinely pained as he spoke these words. "Cold comfort, knowing the truth!" After this puzzling outburst, he abruptly changed the subject, asking Vanzetti for a taste of dessert. "My wife would never allow it," he confessed. Soon after, he excused himself, and made Vanzetti promise to look him up if he ever visited Italy.

The entire conversation, of course, took place in Italian.

Other than this brief interruption, Vanzetti's evening proceeded like any other. He returned home, built a fire, listened to the news on the radio, followed by a quiz program, followed by a recording of the London Symphony. In bed, he thumbed open the mystery novel he'd been reading, though by this point he was far too drunk to concentrate. His thoughts kept drifting back to Bonapace. Vanzetti had never before questioned the idea that the lawsuit had been mo-tivated by anything other than money. But tonight's little speech had been convincing. "Breaks my heart!" His eyes had been honest, undeniably so.

But if not money, why, then? For the rest of his days, whenever his thoughts turned to the trial, it never made sense to Vanzetti. What had they done?

Chapter Fifteen:
Sacco and Vanzetti
On the Run

Fat, Skinny, in ascent. They'd been lamming for days. Cuffed at the wrists. Breathing through straws. The dogs sniffing around the edge of the marsh. The railroad dick rousting a couple of tramps with his lantern. *Relax, I'm looking for a pair of escaped felons—dangerous killers—and there will be a reward. Don't think the breaking of your tramp oath wouldn't be duly rewarded.* The boys had leapt from the moving boxcar moments earlier, hands held so as not to dislocate one another's shoulders upon landing, rolling, the chain linking the cuffs liable to jerk one or another of the cuffees if allowed its natural play. Before that, the boys had submerged themselves, not hearing the barks of their pursuers fording the swamp, hearing only the pressure of the viscous marshwater, wadding their submerged ears. Bart considered how a songbird landing on his straw, or better yet Nic's, would make an amusing opening tableau: placid swamp, reeds swaying in the warm breeze, a songbird at rest, gently warbling, and then suddenly an uproarious depth-charged expulsion, ka-BOOM! Before grasping one another's hands, they exchanged meaningful glances, which implied—no, insisted—this should not be read improperly, meaning as succor of a womanly variety in a time of crisis, because, of course, they were merely succumbing to the practical, taking preventative steps. Who, however manly, wants a dislocated shoulder?

They managed to climb several notches farther up the nearest tree than a reasonable guess might hazard. As handcuffs were involved, they proceeded incrementally. A right hand. The other's left. (The old mirror gag reduxed.) Same back-forth with the same side's feet. Next, the cuffed arms. (Together, of course.) And finally the uncuffed feet below. All of the proceedings as incremental as the legs of a longish insect.

The leaves had just started to turn. In the distance, you could still hear the dogs.

"Plus side," Nic said, breathing with some difficulty, "we haven't come across a fork in the road."

There was no reply from the other side of the tree.

"Forked signage," he continued. "One arrow marked TOWN, the other ANNUAL SHERRIF'S PICNIC WEEKEND. The signs all turned around, course, so the paths and arrows don't line up right." He paused, got nothing, added, "Least not *that.*"

Breathing through straws, their necks tilted back like a couple of servants' wrists, awaiting plates. Bart opened his eyes, risking swamp-water-induced blindness, in a vain attempt to see up through the underside of the surface. May as well have been the foggy panes of a greenhouse.

Before that, using the cuffs to clothesline the chain gang foreman with the square-bottomed beard.

Later, at an abandoned mine, a stray stick of dynamite wedged into the center link of the cuffs. Fuse, lit. Links, pulled taut. Nic, Bart, turned cowering from the blast-to-come, using their non-linked hands to plug (Nic) or cup (Bart) the ears closest to the boom, this move forcing them to stretch arms over heads in a ballerina's pose.

A dud stick, turned out.

At least not *that.*

Nic at one point quoting Grimaldi's farewell, his hand to his heart.

"*Sickness and infirmity have come upon me, and I can no longer wear the motley! I filched my last custard!*"

Before the final plummet, their cuffs, hooked over a jutting branch, gave pause. The pause lasting approximately seven seconds.

Longer and they might have bickered, maybe even slapped each other while dangling by their wrists. As it was, Nic only had time to stare up at his cuffed hand, which was already beginning to turn maroon, and mutter (in part) *Sacramento*. (Meaning "sacrament," a common Italian profanity and personal favorite of Nic's. His cursing had offended a pious ex-girlfriend, and so he had taken to adding a quick "California" whenever the word slipped out, which, such deft transubstantiation from blasphemy to geography made the oath doubly pleasing, so much so that even after the girl left him for a failed divinity student he continued to rage at the 31st capitol whenever a straight razor slipped or a nutcracker went awry or—in this case—a painful fall seemed more likely than not. The branch snapped on the "for" in "California," as if jumping the gun on a brief countdown.)

Three.

Two.

"This isn't working."

"No."

"I'm thinking maybe how about a rock."

"A rock?"

"A big enough rock, brought down upon the links with proper force, might shatter 'em."

"It's not impossible."

"That's all I'm saying. We're out in nature. Rocks are indigenous to nature."

"However."

"You hate to reject my ideas out of hand but."

"However, I am right-handed."

"Give my right hand to be ambidextrous."

"I believe you are left-handed."

" 'The genius' disease.' Or, wait. Is that epilepsy?"

"So, because of a cruel whim of the fates, or perhaps an intentional precautionary measure on the part of the guards, who can say, my right hand is chained to your left. Which means, whichever of us wields your rock will be wielding at a distinct disadvantage."

"Your point?"

"We try this stunt, someone's getting hit in the groin with a rock."

"I see what you're saying. Well. Okay. So, I'm stronger, I'll do the rock part."

"I think perhaps we should come up with an alternative plan."

"You're such a pussy."

"As amusing to an audience as a rock to the groin can be."

"You love being twinned to me."

"A timeless gag, no one would argue, and yet—"

"Why are you so terrified of being alone?"

"Perhaps if we could procure some kind of oil—"

"You would rather die Siamesed than live by yourself."

"That may be true."

In the awkward silence that ensued, they noticed the barking had stopped.

"I was *kidding*."

"Of course."

Nic, in attempting to swat a mosquito with his left hand, jerks Bart's right, the mosquito's escape making the inadvertent slapping of Bart's face with Bart's own hand that much more of an indignity. This is followed by apologies and glares. Nic, shrugging, reflexively turns up and lifts both of his hands in a friendly gesture of *What can you do?*, which causes Bart's right (balled into a fist, he's still so furious about that mosquito) to catapult and strike.

"Oh, my. Your nose. That looked painful."

Further glaring. Nic folds his hands across his stomach in a gesture of piety. Bart's hand settles upon an awkward spot. They both stare.

Drawn-out fight sequence. Spent collapse. Panting all around.

"This isn't working. We need a new plan."

"Before we fell out of the tree? Believe I saw a town. In the distance."

"You're telling me now?"

"There've been distractions."

"But so, a town?"

"A town!"

"Well. I suppose we could walk there. Steal clothes from a clothesline. Find a smithy's."

"Freedom! You ever think we'd make it this far?"

"We haven't, yet."

"Will you at least admit things are looking up?"

"I suppose, in the loosest sense of up."

"We shook them dogs."

"Point conceded."

"There's this possible town."

"Possible will not buy us a steak dinner."

"*Might.*"

" 'The optimist may be right and I, wrong.' "

"Who said that?"

"A letter I wrote from jail, once."

"And look how far you've gotten. See? There are towns on the horizon. Every once in awhile. There might be magic in this world."

"Townward, then."

"Off to town!"

"When you thrust your finger triumphantly in the air like that? Maybe use your other hand."

"Sorry. Eye?"

"Ear, actually."

"Sorry. Anyway, uh, town. It's over this way, I think."

The town turned out to be a movie set. A studio had bought several hundred acres of undeveloped land in the area to use for shoots that demanded a natural setting. The logging town set had been built for a new "Big" Jack Chester lumberjack picture. Bart and Nic kept to the fringes, peering through the window of a sawmill's facade as Chester and his rival for the leading lady's affection traded axe blows on a pair of enormous stumps. This was in the "town square," a contest of sorts, cameras filming not only the stump-chops but the cheering-on of a rough-looking crowd. When a prop boy wheeled a cart of sandbags down the trick-side of the street, passing Bart and Nic at their window, they assumed they'd been caught. But the boy merely gave an absent nod and rolled on, whistling a military march. They stared dumbly at each other. When a second assistant passed, he offered a few words, at which point Bart and Nic grasped that they'd been taken for extras from an escaped convict picture being filmed elsewhere on the lot. Upon this realization, they began to stroll freely. They stood behind the director and watched Chester play take after take; the moment the cameras stopped rolling, a team of grips, standing at the ready, would dash into the frame to sweep away wood chippings and harness the actors to fresh stumps. They sat in the bleachers of a dog track while an animal trainer wrangled a pack of greyhounds, after which they strolled to a mock-up of an African village, where an oversized black kettle presumably awaited white men on a safari gone awry and a pair of elephants (chained to railroad spikes hammered into the earth) drowsily lifted soiled hay to their gaping maws. A small group of Zulu savages milled in front of a thatched hut, smoking cigarettes and sipping coffee from thermoses. Though clad only in facepaint and loincloths, they spoke in the urban argot of American blacks, mainly praising certain attributes of an apparently infamous local girl named Paulette. One, leaning on his spear, advised Bart and Nic to make high-tail in the direction of the commissary if they hoped to nab any of the decent sandwiches. En route, Bart recognized Woody Guthrie, the Okie singer, sitting in a folding chair (the back labeled MISS TURNER) and teaching a rudimentary guitar chord to a little boy dressed as a street urchin. The boy, Nic whispered, was a member of a comedy troupe called the Tiny Tramps, archrivals to the better-known Little Rascals. Bart, meantime, had been agitating in favor of a more aggressive search for a tool shed or prop room in which they might find an instrument capable of snapping their chains. Nic remained unhurried, joking that the longer they remained "in costume," the higher the likelihood of collecting a paycheck come quitting time. And indeed, since their arrival at the camp, things had proceeded so smoothly that Bart felt like a bit of a scold bringing up the possibility of capture at all. Even the police officer who shouted at them as they gazed upon a field of garishly painted plastic flowers (Clara Bow's comeback picture, set on a Holland tulip farm) turned out to be a movieland Kop, and his cry a friendly one: he only wanted to make sure they weren't left out of the big publicity photograph being taken over on the Zulu battlefield. The photo, he explained, would be a two-page spread in one of the trade newspapers. "You guys must be new. Largest gathering of extras since Griffith, or so I am told. First-off they'd planned to photograph Zulus only. Thought it would be more impressive. But last minute, higher-ups decided the general public might get kinda spooked at the sight of so many spooks. Now everybody's invited to join the shot. Talent, crew, the works. Lighten up the chiaroscuro, so to speak." They shrugged and followed the Kop, weaving their way through the flawless rows of *faux* tulips, then scaling a rise and passing through a line of scrub trees, which hid a fence, on the other side of which lay a vista that had not been overstated: several thousand African warriors (any spears, shields or other signs of militancy replaced by decidedly nonthreatening tom-toms, feathered staves and, in the case of one savage, a gag placard, designed not by the extra in question, an orphaned teenager who had never known his parents, but rather by a rogue element in the prop department, reading HIYA MOM) arrayed upon a clear-cut field with a slight incline. As per the Kop's explanation, white men had been invited to join the pose, and they had apparently been instructed to stand in the front rows, where they goosed and mugged or else beamed proudly in the direction of the camera—which had the effect of all the more juxtaposing their pale, clothed figures with the mass of neutered warriors (dark and nearly nude) forming their backdrop, the Africans having been ordered to stand still, stare meekly and make no gestures that could be interpreted as menacing, or in any way disrupt the desired air of festivity—the crew of the S.S. *Venture* posing, triumphant, in front of the felled Kong. There was a man with a handlebar mustache dressed as a gold prospector, his arms around a couple of horn players from the studio orchestra. There was Primo Carnera, the Italian heavyweight champion, help-ing Buster Keaton to unwrap a mummy. Surrounding a chair-bound accordionist, a line of dancers from *The Girls of the Moulin Rouge* displayed various unclad limbs, each of their bodies like a finger in a pair of spread palms. There was Woody Guthrie, the Okie singer. There were the Tiny Tramps, rivals of the Rascals. It was a deliriously motley scene, though controlled, its director—the pho-tographer—standing on a ladder barking orders at the participants while peering into a box camera the size of an orange crate. Bart recognized the camera as an old Kodak Cirkut, a panoramic. They'd been the rage some thirty years prior, when he was a boy, and, in fact, a man who lived in his village in Italy had been a photographer specializing in panoramic shots, and had used a similar Cirkut camera, which was mounted on a tripod and would pan from left to right, a slow and methodical rotation that would produce prints between five and six feet long. The photographer, Signore Aldo—Bart, for his life, could not recollect a surname—hung a number of his prints in the window of his store. Shots of the mountains at sunset. Shots of the *mare*, taken during a trip to Naples. A group shot of drunken American sailors on shore leave, the men lining a ridge with the harbor providing a fuzzy backdrop, each holding a single letter of a message to their newly engaged cook: CONGRATULATIONS FRENCHIE DUROSIER FOR HES A JOLLY GOOD FELLOW FOR HES A HORSES ASS! Another group shot, this taken from above: a group of schoolboys, arranged across the length of a soccer field into the shape of an Italian flag.

One afternoon, Signore Aldo decided to shoot a group of children from the neighborhood. He rounded up Bart and six of his friends and brought them to a vacant lot behind a row of houses. There were not enough children to make for a full panoramic treatment, so Signore Aldo tried an experiment. He instructed the boys to remain frozen as the Cirkut rotated past the spot where they stood, after which the posers were instructed to run in the opposite direction, making a loop around the backside of the camera and then reinserting themselves into the shot further along the lens's path. The camera moved slowly, taking about two minutes to complete a full turn, so with enough speed on the part of the runners, this process could, conceivably, be repeated several times during the course of a single exposure, with the end result being a shot in which the same bodies reappeared at different points throughout, like ghosts. Bart could still recall the *actual* end result, though, which had so disappointed Signore Aldo that he hadn't hung the print in his window, or even inside his store, but rather piled it on a table next to the darkroom door, sandwiched between various over- or underexposed prints and other failed experiments, a pile that Bart and the other boys would rifle through with regularity to get a glimpse of their moment of glory. Starting off on the far left of the frame, where the camera began its leisurely swivel, the boys appeared composed, attempting the tough poses of city youth, lazily straddling homemade scooters or else standing spread-legged, one of them raising a clenched fist in a half-hearted gesture of rebellion, their faces either bored or defiant. About a fifth of the way into the revolution everything began to fall apart. Some of the boys had begun to dash off to their next poses. The boys left behind became too excited to wait for the camera to completely pass them by, so they bolted as well, leaving blurry half-selves in their wake. Eventually, to speed up the process, and in spite of the near-apoplectic rantings of Signore Aldo, some of the boys began running *with* the camera, overtaking the lens, stopping for a beat, then moving on, their poses likewise becoming more creative. They attempted handstands, they leered freakishly, they flashed rude finger gestures picked up from older siblings. Eventually, they ditched their scooters so as to move even faster, and by the middle of the frame, chaos reigned, the shot having degenerated into what could only be described as a roiling mob. The original gang of seven had multiplied to dozens. Boys goofed around a few boys down from themselves, linked only by a smudge of warped air. A worn boot might be the only thing visible in the haze, or else a half-face—an ear, an eyeball, a partial grin. One of Bart's friends, a boy named Leonardo, had tied a handkerchief across his face in the manner of a bandito from an American western, and he nabbed the most exposures, looking like a squad of guerillas inexplicably assigned to menace a playground. The shape of the print itself (stretched-out and narrow) naturally drew the eyes from left to right, as if following the panels of a comic strip; naturally implied some sort of movement, so that one's eyes ended up following the actual movement of the boys, the entropy of the entire scene, a pose and its glorious dissolution.

Now approaching the battlefield, they realized the camera was already in motion.

"Uh-oh," the Kop said. "We're late."

They ran, coming to a full stop towards the front of the line, between Marlene Dietrich and the youngest of the Tramps. Bart had crashed into Nic at the sudden stop, nearly toppling over backwards. It was the handcuffs, in the end, that stopped him from falling, that and Nic's sheer anchorlike bulk. The Tramp scowled at Bart and said, "You're late." Nic had hardly noticed the collision, having already swiveled to pantomime a hat-tip in Ms. Dietrich's direction, Bart meanwhile poised in a stance at once off-balance and suggestive of an ornamental swan. At which point he glanced up and met the eye of the Cirkut. Inwardly he cursed and outwardly he froze, not wanting to spoil the shot. Seconds later, somewhere off to his right, he heard Nic whisper, "We doin' all right, Joe." Though Bart did not move or look in the direction of his partner, the line made him smile. "Hey, fool, are you *grinning?*" Nic whispered. "You grinning motherfucker. This is not permitted. This is an obscene dereliction of your duties. Wipe that silly grin off your face." Bart stared straight ahead at the camera. It moved so slowly it was difficult to determine where, exactly, the lens was pointing. Could be at him. Could be on the Chinese fellow with the beard of bees a few bodies down. To be safe, he remained still as a statue. Nic whispered, "In all these years. Man. I'd have figured I'd have needed to topple the cameraman. Give them Zulus a collective hot-foot. At least hit old Carnera with a pie. But not a thing. Look at you."

The most harmless grin can, in fact, appear lunatic on a straight man.

Nic whispered, "You know they say there are only seven original jokes in the world. That it's how you sell 'em gets the laughs. That without somebody to bounce off, funniest guy in the world's all at sea. You's putting us at sea, boy. You crackin' up."

He whispered, "Are you just feeling giddy because we managed this distance without some manner of disaster? Did running like a little boy take you back, somehow? Or is it just the barking's stopped?"

He whispered, "Or do you believe, for the first time in all these years, we might actually pull this thing off?"

Bart remained frozen.

Nic whispered, "'Common sense may be enough to condemn our world.' And I *agree* with you, man. Always have. Why I left it behind a long time ago. Sense. And now here you are, joining me. That's the only thing throwing me off."

The camera continued its slow turn.

"So what, exactly," Nic asked, "are you so fucking happy about?"

Bart did not move or reply until long after the lens had passed, though his heart continued beating loud enough and fast enough to make him feel like he was still on the run.

*"Nic at one point quoting Grimaldi's farewell, his hand
to his heart." (p. 340)*

Giuseppe Grimaldi, perhaps the most famous Italian clown, performed in London in the late eighteenth and early nineteenth centuries. A specialist in pantomime, he won an enormous following, though was forced to retire at the age of forty-five, all the flips and pratfalls having taken their toll. In his final years, he could barely walk; the landlord of the tavern where he spent his retirement carried him home each night on his back. His memoirs were edited by Charles Dickens.

ACKNOWLEDGMENTS

The following resources were indispensable in the writing of this book: Paul Avrich, *Sacco and Vanzetti: The Anarchist Background*; John E. DiMeglio, *Vaudeville, U.S.A.*; the Aldino Felicani Sacco-Vanzetti Collection (Boston Public Library); Mel Gordon, editor, *Lazzi: The Comic Routines of the Commedia dell'Arte*; Brian Jackson, *The Black Flag: A Look Back at the Strange Case of Nicola Sacco and Bartolomeo Vanzetti*; James Joll, *The Anarchists*; Roderick Kedward, *The Anarchists: The Men Who Shocked an Era*; the Labadie Collection (University of Michigan); J.C. Longoni, *Four Patients of Dr. Deibler: A Study in Anarchy*; Chris Mead, *Champion Joe Louis: A Biography*; Max Nomad, *Political Heretics*; T.R. Ravindranathan, *Bakunin and the Italians*; Nicola Sacco and Bartolomeo Vanzetti, *The Letters of Sacco & Vanzetti*; Richard Schweid, *Consider the Eel: A Natural and Gastronomic History*; Claudio G. Segre, *Italo Balbo: A Fascist Life*; Anthony Slide, *The Encyclopedia of Vaudeville*; Bernard Sobel, *A Pictorial History of Vaudeville*; *The Sacco-Vanzetti Case: Transcript of the Record of the Trial of Nicola Sacco and Bartolomeo Vanzetti in the Courts of Massachusetts and Subsequent Proceedings, 1920-7.*

Much of the information about panoramic painting comes from Jonathan Crary's "Origins of Modern Visual Culture" lecture at Columbia University. The paralyzed accordion player's song comes from the compilation *Italian Treasury: Folk Music & Song of Italy*, produced by Alan Lomax. The author would also like to acknowledge the documentary films *The Kings of the Ring* (which features a segment on Primo Carnera), *The Man in the Silk Hat* (about Max Linder), and *Buster Keaton: A Hard Act to Follow*.

ABOUT THE AUTHOR

Mark Binelli grew up near Detroit. He attended the University of
Michigan and later studied at Columbia University. He is currently
a contributing editor at *Rolling Stone* and lives in New York. *Sacco
and Vanzetti Must Die!* is his first novel.

LANNAN SELECTIONS

The Lannan Foundation, located in Santa Fe, New Mexico, is a family foundation whose funding focuses on special cultural projects and ideas which promote and protect cultural freedom, diversity, and creativity.

The literary aspect of Lannan's cultural program supports the creation and presentation of exceptional English-language literature and develops a wider audience for poetry, fiction, and nonfiction.

Since 1990, the Lannan Foundation has supported Dalkey Archive Press projects in a variety of ways, including monetary support for authors, audience development programs, and direct funding for the publication of the Press's books.

In the year 2000, the Lannan Selections Series was established to promote both organizations' commitment to the highest expressions of literary creativity. The Foundation supports the publication of this series of books each year, and works closely with the Press to ensure that these books will reach as many readers as possible and achieve a permanent place in literature. Authors whose works have been published as Lannan Selections include Ishmael Reed, Stanley Elkin, Rikki Ducornet, Gilbert Sorrentino, William Eastlake, Svetlana Alexievich, and Carlos Fuentes, among others.

SELECTED DALKEY ARCHIVE PAPERBACKS

FOR A FULL LIST OF PUBLICATIONS, VISIT:
www.dalkeyarchive.com

SELECTED DALKEY ARCHIVE PAPERBACKS